THE SILENCE OF

Volume Five of the Jayson Wolfe Story

THE SILENCE OF Snow

Volume Five of the Jayson Wolfe Story

A Novel

Anita Stansfield

Covenant Communications, Inc.

Covenant
Communications, Inc.

Cover image *Couple Embracing in Snowy Mountains* by Thomas Barwick © 2009 Getty Images.

Cover design copyrighted 2009 by Covenant Communications, Inc.

Published by Covenant Communications, Inc.
American Fork, Utah

Printed in The United States of America
First Printing: August 2009

16 15 14 13 12 11 10 09   10 9 8 7 6 5 4

ISBN-13: 978-1-59811-846-9
ISBN-10: 1-59811-846-3

TO THE READER

This is part five of a five-part story. If you've been following the story of Jayson Wolfe, you will know that originally it was only a three-part story, and then I realized there was a fourth volume. But the fourth volume grew too large, and it had to be divided to make a fifth volume. Therefore, a review of volume four would be in order, just in case you missed it, or it's been a while since you read it.

Part four of the Jayson Wolfe story begins with Jayson acknowledging how good his life has become. He's survived a great deal of heartache, and now he's come to a place where he's truly happy. A gifted and brilliant musician, Jayson has devoted his life to succeeding in an industry that will allow him to use his talents to contribute something positive to the world. Long before he found the gospel of Jesus Christ and became a baptized member of The Church of Jesus Christ of Latter-day Saints, he had strong convictions about creating quality music with moral values.

Jayson and his wife, Elizabeth, have known each other since high school. Their lives have been challenging and complicated, but the happiness they've found in sharing a family and living the gospel is something that neither of them take for granted.

Jayson's daughter Macy is happily married to Aaron, and they are currently living with Aaron's single mother, Layla, and her other children. Macy is helping care for the family since Layla is suffering with a serious health issue that hasn't yet been diagnosed. Macy is also struggling to deal with a traumatic miscarriage and her ongoing desire to have a baby.

While the recording of Jayson's new album slowly comes together with the help of his brother, Drew, and many other musicians, Jayson discovers that Trevin, his teenaged stepson, has clearly inherited his uncle Derek's gift of being able to play the bass guitar magnificently. The connection brings back tender memories for him, Elizabeth, and Elizabeth's father, Will. Jayson counts it as one more piece of evidence that his life is richly blessed, and he's able to move forward on his project and in his life with hope and faith, in spite of other pressing challenges that test his faith.

CHAPTER 1

Highland, Utah

Jayson Wolfe rose from the dinner table after sharing pizza with his family and wandered into his studio, which was attached to the home. For a long moment he just stood there, taking in the instruments and equipment that represented his life's work and his career—the most meaningful aspect of his world beyond the gospel and his family. His life had been a roller coaster of incredible highs and horrifying lows. And today had covered that gamut. He'd gone from feeling rock-bottom earlier today, all the way to being overcome with positive feelings and proper perspective regarding the goodness of life this afternoon. But here, alone with his instruments and his fragile emotions, he felt himself slipping back down as the reality of his present challenges came rushing back over him.

Jayson sat at his beloved piano and placed his hands on the keys. But no music came through him. Instead his thoughts roiled with recent events that weighed him down. He thought of the joy he'd felt during the time he'd served in the Young Men program, and his devastation when he'd been released. He felt certain the release was mostly due to the complaints of Sister Freedman, a woman who felt certain the influence of Jayson's career on her only son was nothing short of evil. Sister Freedman had said things to him that were so hurtful he could hardly breathe even now as he recalled them. And then she'd clinched it by saying some of them in front of several people in the ward following church last Sunday. Jayson knew where he stood with the Lord, and he knew he had the love and support of many good and reasonable people. He'd discussed it with his counselor, Maren, just this morning, and he'd been feeling pretty good about the whole thing. But now it was all coming back to him, and he realized it wasn't going to be easy to apply what Maren had taught him hour to hour, day to day. He thought of the fact that he had to speak in sacrament meeting on Sunday and groaned. His breathing became more strained, and he pressed a hand over his chest. The bishop's request had come with full knowledge of the situation, and the bishop was a good man. Jayson knew he could call the bishop and bail out, but he believed in doing what his leaders asked of him, and he knew he just had to do it. In that moment, however, the thought of standing at the pulpit in front of people who had likely heard in one way or another a variety of vicious accusations against him felt tantamount to jumping into a volcano.

Jayson glanced at the clock and realized that the brass musicians he'd hired would soon be coming to the studio to record the final track of his song, "Good, Clean Fun." He'd been looking forward to taking this step, but even that prospect provided him no joy at the moment. He hated the way his own musical gift had become a paradox. He groaned again and turned around on the bench in order to lower his head to his knees, feeling suddenly light-headed.

"Please help me, Father," he muttered. "I can't do this." He thought about that a moment and clarified, "I can't do this alone." Still aware of his own labored breathing, and conscious of a tightness in his chest, Jayson continued to pray aloud. As he verbally recounted the steps he'd taken to understand his painful situation and have faith in dealing with it, he began to feel calmer. He prayed for strength and the ability to trust in the Lord, and to shift these fears and concerns—and even the hurt— to his Savior's shoulders. He muttered a heartfelt "Amen" but remained with his head down, breathing slowly in and out, focusing on breathing peace and strength into himself and breathing out his anxiety. He was going to record this album, and he was going to make it great. He was going on tour, and he was going to use his gifts to the best of his ability to have a positive impact on the people who would be exposed to his music. He was going to continue to fulfill his Church calling, live the gospel, and care for his family. And he was going to get through this. He imagined a day on the other end of this trial when it would all come into perspective and not seem so bad. He didn't know what the outcome would be, but he believed all would be well.

"Are you okay?" Elizabeth asked, and he shot his head up, startled. He hadn't even heard her come in.

"Yeah," he said, but she looked dubious. "I am now. I confess I'm still having a hard time with all of this . . . but I've been having a little chat with the Man upstairs."

"And you're better now?"

"I am," he said. "One hour at a time, I guess."

"Yeah," she said and sat beside him. "It's going to be okay, Jayson."

"Let's talk about that again after we're done speaking in sacrament meeting."

"You're going to do just fine," she said with confidence and a smile, then she kissed him.

"If I don't, you're going to be at least as embarrassed as I will be."

"I'm not worried," she said and kissed him again. "But we're going to have to worry about that later. The guys will be here in a few minutes."

"Oh, my gosh." Jayson glanced at the clock and hurried toward the door. "Hold them off for just a few minutes while I get cleaned up a little."

"No problem," she said.

While Jayson was splashing water on his face and blotting it dry, he acknowledged that he did feel more calm about having to speak on Sunday. He just felt completely blank on what exactly he was going to talk about. But he'd have to stew about that later. The recording session would soon be under way, and suddenly he almost felt giddy with excitement at the prospect of hearing the song come fully together tonight. His anxiety over that was completely gone. He thought of Trevin's eagerness and smiled. His son *loved* this song, and Jayson was thrilled that he did. He hoped that Trevin's idea for the music video to go along with it would come to fruition. It could be great fun, and one more thing they could work on together.

The recording session went so smoothly that they were done much earlier than expected. The evening turned into somewhat of a jam session with the horn players joining in. Jayson messed around with the piano while Trevin experimented with both guitars. Roger, who had come to help manage the recording equipment in the sound booth, just watched and listened and appeared to enjoy every minute. Jayson and Trevin both said more than once that they wished Drew was there. Nothing was ever quite right without the drums.

They were losing steam when Trevin said, "Hey, Dad. Can't we just play the drum track for the song we just recorded? I've heard it so many times I think I could do the bass—tolerably, at least—and you do what you do, and . . ." he motioned dramatically to the brass players, "we have live horns."

"Oh, do it!" Roger said. His enthusiasm for Jayson's music had never added awkwardness to their friendship. Quite the opposite, in fact. Roger treated Jayson like a normal human being, but he also helped Jayson keep perspective on his gift.

Jayson set it up in the sound booth, telling Roger which switch he needed to flip on the right cue. "After you flip it, you can take a seat on the front row," he said, motioning to where he'd been sitting most of the evening. They were nearly ready to begin when Elizabeth came in, saying, "The bishop is here."

Jayson was pleased that he felt nothing negative at the announcement. He lightly said, "Trevin, are you in trouble?"

"Yes," he said, "I have to speak in church on Sunday."

"So do I," Jayson said.

"You do?" Trevin asked.

"Nobody's in trouble," the bishop said, coming into the room right behind Elizabeth, who just smiled and waved, closing the door behind her when she left. "Roger mentioned that he was helping you record this evening. Truthfully, I just wanted to join the party. There *is* a party, isn't there?"

"I guess you could call it that," Jayson said. "We got done early, so we're just having some fun. Have a seat." He pointed at Trevin and said playfully, "If the bishop doesn't like what he hears, maybe we won't have to talk in church on Sunday."

"You're not getting out of it that easily," the bishop said with a smile.

Jayson pointed at the college boys who had momentarily set their horns aside and were lounging comfortably. "Bishop Bingham, that's Corbin, Spencer, Bryan, and Jared. I don't know their last names because I have a terrible memory, but they're practically family by now."

"We'll just go by the Wolfe boys, then," Corbin said, and the others agreed enthusiastically. Jayson was liking these guys more every time they worked together. The prospect of touring with them was appealing.

"You go for it," Jayson said. "Okay, I think we're ready." The "Wolfe boys" picked up their horns and got into position. Jayson pointed at the bishop with the hand holding his guitar pick. "This is what my wife fondly calls screaming guitars. It's going to be loud. You want some earplugs?"

"No, I'm fine," he chuckled.

"The drums were recorded by my brother. The rest is live, as you can see. Okay, let's do it." Jayson jumped right into it with the guitar intro. He played three bars then pointed at Roger, who flipped the switch, and the drums came in. Then the bass, right on cue, which prompted Jayson to smile at his son. Then the horns. And Jayson started to sing, *"The designated driver has had one too many drinks. The hero on TV takes a puff and blows his smoke. The pretty lady drinks a shot to calm her rattled nerves, while boys and girls wonder if this is some kind of joke."* They went smoothly into the chorus, with Trevin doing backing vocals as if he'd been cued. On the official recording it was Jayson's voice twice, but he liked this better. *"Whatever happened to good, clean fun? The kind that doesn't take a pill or booze to loosen up. Laughter's free and doesn't leave a hangover. Come on, boys and girls, let's get addicted to good, clean fun!"*

He laughed spontaneously and moved into the second verse. *"Are the A A meetings just a hoax for losers who are bored? Is the surgeon general lying when he says this stuff can kill you? Do the rehab centers fill their rooms just for fun and games? Does big brother simply push this stuff so he can later bill you?"*

Jayson then went into the lengthy, intricate guitar solo that made up the bridge, playing along with the drum recording as if Drew were in the room. Trevin kept the bass up perfectly and again they played side by side, the way he'd done with Derek. It was eerie and wonderful, and he loved it. And then the chorus again: *"Whatever happened to good, clean fun? The kind that doesn't take a pill or booze to loosen up. Laughter's free and doesn't leave a hangover. Come on, boys and girls, let's get addicted to good, clean fun!"*

When the song ended, the bishop and Roger were clapping and cheering ridiculously loudly. Jayson felt relieved beyond expression to see that the bishop was genuinely pleased. Nobody could act that excited for the sake of diplomacy. Roger then talked Jayson into doing the Mozart number. He was in such a good mood that he agreed with no argument. Since he'd set up a recording earlier that had everything except the piano for him to practice with, he was able to do it and make it sound the way it was supposed to.

After the lengthy song was over, the bishop laughed and said, "That was incredible!"

"That's what I keep telling him," Roger said.

"I really can't take all the credit," Jayson said. "Things like that don't happen without a lot of divine intervention."

"Yeah," Trevin said, "but my dad's the guy who sits in front of the piano sixty hours a week until he gets it right."

"Sixty?" Roger said.

"You've been keeping track?" Jayson asked.

"Six days a week, ten hours a day, I know where to find him. The rest of the time he's helping with the dishes, changing diapers, stuff like that."

"Okay, that's enough of that," Jayson said. "I'd like to maintain a little bit of a macho reputation with these people."

Jayson was relieved when Elizabeth came into the studio with warm cookies. While everyone was chatting and laughing, she said quietly to Jayson, "Did the bishop like your music?"

"It would seem so."

"It's too bad Sister Freedman couldn't have been here to feel the true spirit of the music."

"I think it takes an open heart—and an open mind—to feel such things," Jayson said.

"Then we can both be grateful that our bishop's heart and mind are open."

"Yes, we can be grateful for that," he said and gave her a quick kiss. "Thanks for the cookies."

"I heard once that you like cookies . . . warm."

"Where did you hear that?" He feigned innocence.

"You told me, in high school."

"And you told me you couldn't marry a musician. You wanted a stable life where you could bake cookies."

"I was wrong . . . about marrying a musician, that is."

"You're baking cookies."

"And I have a stable life."

"Just wait until the summer tour."

"Oh, that's just . . . vacation," she said and laughed.

Before the bishop left, he shook Jayson's hand and told him it had been a pleasure, then he teased him about speaking in church on Sunday. Jayson noticed that on his way out the door, Elizabeth handed him Jayson's solo CD, the one he'd made after they'd been married. He was clearly pleased and appreciative, and Jayson thought of how far they'd come in so short a time. He was grateful for a good wife and the guidance of the gospel that kept him on track, but he still wished he was serving with the Young Men. He missed them. He liked accompanying the choir, but he would like to do *both*. In his head he could almost hear his mother saying, *We don't always get what we want, but we usually get what we need.* The memory made him smile. He recalled her saying that many times, and he suspected she'd been loosely quoting the Rolling Stones. She did things like that. He missed her.

With the recording session behind him, Jayson focused on trying to write a talk for sacrament meeting. When the talk felt bogged down, he worked on the musical number he'd been asked to do. He couldn't decide between "How Great Thou Art," and "I Stand All Amazed." He loved them both, and they both expressed the message he wanted to convey. Then it came to him that a medley of both, using selected verses from each, would be lovely. If he came up with the core of what he was doing, Elizabeth would be able to fill in the violin and extra vocals without much trouble, and they'd only have to run through it a few times.

On Saturday evening, Elizabeth and Trevin both had their talks ready to go, and Jayson still didn't have a single word. But the song sounded really great after he and Elizabeth had practiced for only half an hour. After the kids had gone to bed, except for Trevin who was out with his friends until eleven, Jayson said to Elizabeth. "I don't know what the problem is. I am completely stuck. I have studied, read, looked for quotes and scriptures, and nothing gels. Why is it that I can get up and talk at a fireside for more than an hour, no problem, but this is messing with my head?"

Elizabeth smiled. "The first time you were asked to speak at a fireside, you were pretty nervous. Now you do it so naturally." She then chuckled as if she'd gotten an epiphany.

"What?" he demanded.

"If you want my opinion . . . Do you?"

"Yes!"

"You're not getting inspiration for your talk, because you already have it. A portion of your fireside address is about the healing power of the Atonement. You just need to get up and share that. There. Easy."

Jayson thought about that for a minute and felt certain she was right. "Okay, I can do that. But I feel nervous to think of doing that."

"Why?"

"That includes talking about drug abuse and being suicidal. And I can't make that point without admitting how many people in my life died or left me."

"So? You've talked about it a lot."

"But . . . it was usually to people I would never see again. I have to go to church with these people every week."

"And maybe they should know. The healing power of the Atonement is more profound for someone like you who has had so much that needed healing. Maybe that's what needs to be said. And maybe, just maybe, Sister Freedman will hear something that will make a difference."

Jayson made a scoffing noise. "*If* Sister Freedman comes to church, I'll bet you the royalties off a gold album that she gets up and leaves as soon as she realizes I'm on the program."

"I can't afford that bet. I lost the last time you bet me that. But since all the money's in a joint account, I don't suppose it matters very much."

"No, it doesn't. And it shouldn't matter what Sister Freedman thinks about me. I just wish she'd keep her opinions to herself."

"I don't think the bishop asked you to do this for Sister Freedman's benefit."

"It's mostly for mine, I'm sure," Jayson said.

"Yes, I agree. But I think he believes that the rest of the ward—the people who might have heard any gossip, or who might yet—will see this side of you and be more likely to think that they can't believe everything they hear." She touched his face. "How can anyone listen to you bear your testimony of what you know and question the kind of man that you are?"

"I'm trying to figure that out," he said and kissed her. "But I have to admit I'm handling this better than I thought I would. I've been thinking about that, and I think that's part of the healing power we're talking about. It's healed me over and over, Elizabeth. I'm trying very hard to have no ill feelings toward Sister Freedman, although I admit that's challenging at moments. But I'm trying to give it to the Lord. And it's working. He's guided many people—you included—to say the things I needed to hear. I've learned a lot about myself through this, and my testimony has not been weakened; more the opposite."

Elizabeth smiled. "I knew you had it in you. I knew you wouldn't stay away from church over something like this."

They prayed together as they did every night before bed, then they sat in bed and read from the scriptures until Trevin came in. He reported that he'd had a good time, and that Clayton Freedman had been among the group of friends he'd been with. He jokingly said that there hadn't been any gossip about the local rock star, and Jayson bit his tongue to keep from retorting with a sassy remark.

The following morning was more crazy than usual in getting everyone ready for church. Fortunately Will and Marilyn came to watch the children and take them so that Jayson and Elizabeth could go early and practice the musical number in the chapel before people started arriving. Trevin rode with them. Jayson took one of his own microphones and set it up at the piano with Trevin's help, plugging it into the jack for the chapel sound system. Their practice went smoothly, and he felt equally confident about what he wanted to say in his talk. But he still felt nervous. Ridiculously nervous. Before the meeting started he had to go outside for a few minutes and talk himself out of some serious anxiety. With some prayer and deep breathing he went back in and sat on the stand next to Elizabeth and Trevin. He'd barely sat down when Derek hollered, "Hi, Daddy," loud enough to be heard over the organ prelude music. He waved at Jayson from where he was sitting on Will's lap on the second row. Jayson chuckled and discreetly waved back.

"Sister Freedman is here," Elizabeth whispered to him.

"Are you calling my bet?"

"No, I'm just telling you."

"Give her a few minutes," Jayson whispered back.

During the sacrament portion of the meeting, Jayson felt a gratitude that was deeper than normal for having the gospel in his life, and for being able to renew his covenants this way. He silently asked forgiveness for the struggles he might have handled better, but he was glad to be able to assess his life and know that he really was alright with his Maker. While the bishop was making his way to the pulpit following the sacrament, Jayson saw Sister Freedman stand up and leave the chapel, dragging Clayton by the arm. He exchanged a discreet glance with Elizabeth, then tried not to think about it.

When the bishop introduced the program for the rest of the meeting, he didn't say anything about callings or releases, criticism or gossip, careers or musical gifts. Not that Jayson had expected him to, but he still felt grateful to simply be introduced as part of the Wolfe-Aragon family, all of whom made a great contribution to the ward.

Trevin's talk was great, and Jayson felt proud of him. Elizabeth's too was as remarkable as he'd expected. She did everything remarkably. He didn't feel at all nervous when he moved to the piano to do the musical number. He was in his most natural element at the piano, and being able to sing words that so perfectly expressed his deepest feelings felt as natural as breathing. He played two bars of piano music before Elizabeth came in on the violin, and then he softly sang the first verse and chorus of "How Great Thou Art."

Elizabeth played a beautiful bridge on the violin that merged the melody into that of the other hymn, and Jayson sang a verse and chorus from "I Stand All Amazed." He took his voice up an octave and sang the chorus again, along with Elizabeth, who had moved a step closer to the microphone so it would pick up her voice, as well; then the violin took the melody back to the first hymn, and he sang the final verse before he and Elizabeth sang the chorus together. Following another beautiful bridge where the piano and violin reached a lovely crescendo, they finished together with one final chorus.

As Jayson left the piano, grabbed his scriptures, and stepped up to the pulpit, he couldn't help noticing some sniffles in the room. He was okay with that. He liked knowing he could bring the Spirit closer with his music. That's why God had given him this gift. And it was nice to have someone besides himself crying for a change. If his rendition of the hymns had softened their spirits and opened their hearts, he had a better chance of riding out the storms of inevitable gossip and judgment that were in the air.

Taking hold of the sides of the pulpit with his hands, he felt himself slip into the comfortable routine of speaking at firesides, and he felt more relaxed. "First of all," he began, "I would like to say that I'm grateful for this opportunity. At first I wasn't, I admit, but I hope I get points for being obedient when the bishop asked me, even though I wanted to tell him no." This got a chuckle. "But now I am receiving the blessings of that obedience, because I can think of no greater privilege than to publicly express my feelings about the healing power of the Atonement. It has changed my life. It has given me peace over and over and over. And I appreciate the opportunity to share my testimony through music, because it's a big part of my life.

"I had trouble preparing this talk. I just couldn't get any ideas to mesh together; then my wife reminded me that my own experience with this topic was probably all the Lord would want me to share. I have prayerfully come to agree with that, and so I hope you'll bear with me while I get somewhat personal. And I'll warn you, I cry more freely than the average five women, so I'm glad there's a box of tissues up here."

Jayson took a deep breath and dove in with an abbreviated version of the trials in his life. "I woke up one day and realized that I had lost practically everything that meant anything at all to me. I'll just give you a brief summary. I grew up in a home where my mother, my brother, and I were trying to avoid my drunk father. My best friend had been killed in a car accident near the end of our senior year in high school, and I'd never found anyone to replace him in my life. I'd been forced to divorce my wife when she surprised me with her boyfriend, and then my teenage daughter had run away from home; I'd not heard from her in years and had no reason to believe she was even alive. I had been working closely with my brother and two other guys in the music business. Our project had been very successful, but at that point it had completely fallen apart. My brother was now working elsewhere. The other two guys were both dead—one from AIDS, the other from a drug overdose. Then my mother died of cancer. There were only two people in the world besides my brother that I had any positive connection to at all, and they lived very far away. The only thing I had that gave me any peace was my ability to play music, and then a freak accident injured my hand severely, necessitating a surgery. One of the results of all these events was my becoming addicted to the many drugs the doctors had prescribed for sleep, anxiety, depression, and pain. I learned later that I'd inherited my father's alcoholic tendencies, and even though I'd never taken a swallow of liquor, my body had latched onto the prescription drugs. I was taking more than forty pills a day. That's where I was at when I made the decision to end my own life."

Jayson blew out a slow breath. As many times as he'd said it publicly, it still took him back to that moment. "I hope that's not too depressing for sacrament meeting, but in order for you to understand how the Atonement has healed me, I think you need to understand the depth of pain and loss in my life. I only had two things in my favor at the time. I *did* believe in God, and there was someone out there who cared whether I lived or died. Between the two of them, I was saved. I remember praying out loud. I told God that this was it. If He couldn't show me a reason to go on living, this was it. The pills that would kill me were all lined up and ready for me to take. And that's when the phone rang. It was the middle of the night, but the Spirit had apparently awakened a dear friend of mine with strict instructions to call me. I was on a plane to Utah the next day. I went through drug rehab, and the woman who saved my life eventually agreed to marry me." He glanced toward Elizabeth and was surprised to see that she was crying. She'd heard this story a hundred times. Why would she cry now? "It's okay, honey," he said into the microphone. "The story has a happy ending." His comment lightened the mood, and both the congregation and Elizabeth chuckled.

Jayson glanced at his family sitting on the second row and added, "Elizabeth's father also had a lot to do with getting me through that. He's here today, and I never want to pass up an opportunity to thank him for everything he's done for me. While I was in rehab, I came to know with absolute certainty that for all of the counseling I'd gone through, it was only what Jesus Christ did for me that could free me of my deepest pain. And it did. My daughter came back, and I got rid of the drugs *and* the pain. While I was staying with Elizabeth and her father and children, following the tragic deaths of her husband and son—some of you may remember that—a very special missionary came into my life." He turned to look at Trevin, who was watching him serenely. "This fine young man that I gladly claim as my own son is the one who put a Book of Mormon under my pillow after he'd previously shared his convictions with me. I believed in Christ, but I wasn't so sure about Joseph Smith, living prophets, and scriptures coming from gold plates. But Trevin challenged me to read it and get my own answers. I was expecting to tell him that I'd tried, but it didn't work for me. Well, as you can see, it *did* work for me." Emotion broke into his voice. "Brothers and sisters, I stand before you today to tell you that I know . . ." His tears increased. "I *know* that Jesus is the Christ. He has healed my every pain and taken my every sorrow. I have been blessed beyond my wildest imagination since the gospel has come into my life."

He regained his composure and went on. "I also want to tell you that I fell in love with Elizabeth the first time I saw her. That was back in high school, by the way. She was my best friend's sister. After her brother was killed, our lives didn't take the paths we'd expected, but we remained friends and eventually ended up together. And as I said, she saved my life. We are now all one family—forever. At home we have a family portrait taken on the steps of the Salt Lake Temple the day we were all sealed together as a family. We're all dressed in white, and it's one of the most beautiful things in our home because it represents our greatest blessings. This picture hangs in our front room, across from a picture of the Savior. The two reflect off of each other when there's sunlight in the room.

"When Elizabeth and I were sealed, a year after my baptism, my daughter and Elizabeth's children were sealed to us. We'd just had Derek—named after his uncle—and he was there too. We've had another baby together since then. This family picture we have represents what . . ." He became so emotional that he couldn't speak for an excruciating length of time, during which many sniffles could be heard. "This is what . . ." he began again, "I would have missed if I had gone through with it and ended my life before my time. I am living proof that God is merciful and the Atonement is real."

Jayson finished by expressing appreciation for a good ward family, a wonderful bishop, and his beautiful family. He said that he wanted all of the young men to know that he knew the gospel was true, and that being faithful and true to those beliefs was far better than where any other path would take them. He once again bore his testimony of the healing power of the Atonement, then closed in the name of Jesus Christ and sat down—right on time.

After the meeting ended and everyone stood up, the bishop shook Trevin's hand, since he was standing closest. He complimented Trevin on his talk, then said something about how impressed he'd been with his ability on the guitar during his visit to the studio earlier in the week. The bishop then complimented Elizabeth on her talk *and* the song, and he shook her hand as well, while Jayson unplugged his microphone and started rolling up the cord. He stopped when the bishop extended his hand. Jayson took the firm handshake but was surprised when the bishop gave him a quick hug. "That was wonderful, Jayson. It was perfect."

"Thank you," Jayson said.

"There are a lot of people here today who needed to hear what you have to say." Jayson's thoughts went to the possible gossip in relation to himself, and he was surprised when the bishop clarified, "There are many who are struggling with difficult issues and need to rely more on the Atonement. Your message was very powerful."

Jayson removed the microphone from the stand. "I'm always glad when my experiences can make a positive difference in someone's life."

"And your music," the bishop said.

"And my music," he repeated and disassembled the stand while the bishop remained there. Elizabeth and Trevin had already left for their classes.

"I guess I can tell you now that I've had a few people call to ask me if I was sure you were worthy to be serving in the Church."

Jayson stopped what he was doing and swallowed carefully. "I don't even want to know who."

"Good, because I would never tell you. It doesn't matter. I assured them that I was well aware of every facet of your life, and that I had no question as to your worthiness to be a member in good standing. Every single one of them took the answer in good faith and simply told me they were glad to hear it and that as long as I knew everything was okay, there was nothing they needed to be concerned about—or words to that effect."

"Thank you," Jayson said.

"There's nothing to thank me for, Jayson. I just told them the truth. I have a request to make, however."

"What's that?" Jayson asked, perhaps expecting him to suggest that Jayson cut his hair, or dress more conservatively, or tone the guitars down a bit.

He only said, "I realize that you're in the limelight, and you've told me that things can often not be what they appear. Just keep me abreast of anything you think might cause any problems. If I know about such things before anyone else, I won't be caught off guard. Since I have to approve your firesides, as well as handle this crowd, I think that would be best."

"I would be more than happy to do that," Jayson said, especially if it could prevent any further gossip or misconception.

Again the bishop offered his hand. "Thank you once more. Good luck with the big project. I'll see you next Sunday?"

"I'll be here to play for the choir."

"I'm glad to hear it," the bishop said with a facetious smile just as Will approached and said to Jayson, "Can I help you with that? Everyone else has abandoned you."

"You can get the mike stand," Jayson said, then to the bishop. "Bishop Bingham, this is my father-in-law, William Greer."

"A pleasure to meet you," Will said as the two men shared a firm handshake.

"You're Elizabeth's father, then?"

"That's right," Will said and put a hand on Jayson's shoulder, "and this kid has been as good as my son since he was sixteen." More to Jayson he said, "You did great. You never stop making me proud."

Will walked out to the car with Jayson to put the microphone there. Will told him that Elizabeth had taken Derek to nursery and Marilyn had Harmony and would meet him in a few minutes. After the car was locked again, Will said, "That was remarkable, son . . . especially because I know things haven't been easy for you lately."

"Your daughter tells you everything about me, doesn't she."

"Only the stuff you don't tell me yourself," Will said with a chuckle. "But we both know that just saves you the trouble. You've never had anything to hide from me."

"No," Jayson drawled and chuckled. "You always knew everything there was to know."

"She tells me you're doing better. But I would have known that for myself after hearing that talk you just gave."

"If I think about it too much, I can work myself into a fit," Jayson said. "And I'm sure it's not over yet. But . . . I *do* feel better. I guess I've just got to learn to not let such things upset me."

"Well," Will chuckled, "I think what's happened would upset anybody who was the target—for whatever reason. In some ways, this woman's behavior is easier to contend with than some situations would be."

"How is that?" Jayson asked, stunned.

"The fact that she wasn't subtle makes it easy to see her behavior as out of line. If she were more passive-aggressive or manipulative, it might be harder for people to distinguish between the truth and the rumors."

"Okay, you got me there. I must admit that I'm grateful people can easily see that her behavior is extreme. Truthfully, I worry about her—and I worry about her son."

"How very Christian of you!" Will said with a smile.

Jayson gave him a comical scowl. "You sounded just like your daughter."

"Or maybe it's the other way around," Will said. "There's not really anything you can do, is there? About her or her son?"

"I'm praying for them. I don't know that I can do anything else. Speaking of people you can't help beyond praying for them, Macy told me her mother's having some real problems. I worry about her, too. I worry about how it might affect Macy. But how can her choices not catch up to her? I just don't know what I could do to help her, either."

"Probably nothing. I'm certain if there *is* something you can do, you'll know. Does Macy have much contact with her?"

"They talk on the phone once or twice a week, I think. And you know she and Aaron have been to Los Angeles a couple of times to visit her. I think they consider her a project. Macy loves her, of course, and I think Aaron would like to save her. I just hope they both don't end up sorely disappointed."

"I hope for that, too. Maybe Debbie will surprise us."

"That's what scares me," Jayson said. "Debbie has sprung many surprises on me, but they've never been good. Hey, are you going to Sunday School with me?"

"Marilyn should be saving us seats. We're invited to dinner at your house; bribery for watching the kids through the meeting."

"Sounds fair," Jayson said, "for us, at least."

Will chuckled. "They're great kids."

They walked back into the building, and just inside the door, Jayson said, "Have I told you lately how glad I am that you're my dad?"

"I haven't been keeping track, but I'll never get tired of hearing that."

"Good," Jayson said. "I'm really glad that you're my dad."

CHAPTER 2

Life went smoothly over the following weeks. The final rehearsal and recording for all the little extras with the orchestra musicians were completed before the fine group of college students all went home for Christmas break. Jayson was thrilled to have the album all but completed, and during the holidays he set his work aside completely, wanting to be involved with all of the preparations and celebrations as much as possible. Macy and Aaron were involved in many of those activities as well, although they remained very busy with their other family. Aaron had a break from school through the holidays, but he would be back at it in January, and he was still working full-time. He was a great kid, and Jayson loved him. He worked hard and he took good care of Macy, as well as the rest of his family.

Just before New Year's, Drew came from Los Angeles with his family to celebrate part of the holidays with Jayson's family. They always kept the Christmas tree up until Drew's family came and gifts were exchanged, then they had a great time together on New Year's Eve. It had become a tradition during the past few years, and they all loved it. The timing was also good in the respect that Drew could help Jayson go carefully through all the recordings and make certain everything was the best it could be. Once the kids went back to school with the new year, the men went to work in the studio, listening, discussing, tweaking, rerecording little bits and pieces. Occasionally Elizabeth came in to help with her parts or in the sound booth. The other musicians were brought in for one more Saturday to make a few corrections and polish up some things. Before the middle of January, Jayson officially declared that the album was finished. The family had a big celebration before Drew and his family returned to Los Angeles, and Jayson prepared to move into the next phase of the project. He'd been in close touch with Rick at the record company for many weeks now, formulating some plans, and Rick had heard enough samples of the music to feel confident in putting certain things in motion so that they could be ready for the optimum release date of the album prior to a summer tour. Rick was a great advocate, and Jayson was grateful for the cooperation of the record company, when he knew from prior experience that it could be very much the opposite. He considered this and many other little facets of the situation as great evidence that God's hand was indeed in the project. As it was, things were going fairly smoothly, and he prayed that it would last.

With the album completed, Jayson had to go to Los Angeles to meet with the record company and take care of many details for upcoming promotions and the summer tour. He would also be auditioning some musicians, since he needed a bass player and someone who could alternate guitars and piano with him. He always did the complicated stuff himself, but he liked to go back and forth between his instruments, and he needed someone who could cover for him with skill and ease. Drew had already been asking around and had some auditions lined up. Drew would help him with the process, and since Jayson would be staying with his brother, they would get to spend some time together. They could never have too much of that.

Elizabeth drove Jayson to the airport early Monday morning, while her father stayed with the kids. They kissed good-bye at the curb where she dropped him off with his one piece of carry-on luggage. The flight wasn't very long, but Jayson hated air travel, and he hated going to Los Angeles. This was the part of doing an album that he would not miss when he was finally able to retire. But it had to be done. He believed in being *in the world but not of the world.* Well, he couldn't provide something good that was not of the world if he didn't step into the world. Missionaries couldn't do what they did without being in the world. The tour itself wouldn't be so bad, because he had enough clout to be in complete control. But hobnobbing with record-company executives was distasteful, and he dreaded it. He wasn't worried about them liking the music. If they didn't, he'd just take it somewhere else, or he'd save it for a better time. He had no expectations; or perhaps he was comfortable in his expectations and therefore felt no anxiety. He marveled that there had been a time when he couldn't get a record company to give him the time of day. It had been a long, hard road. But the payoffs weren't bad—most of the time.

Drew picked him up at the airport. Even though it hadn't been that long since Drew had been to Utah, just seeing his brother made the trip worth it for Jayson. He called Elizabeth to let her know that he'd arrived safely. She had a busy day planned, and they agreed to talk again in the morning. Jayson and Drew went out to lunch together, then to the house, where Valerie hugged him tightly and he played with his little niece, Leslie, for a while. They visited most of the afternoon, and were just discussing what to do for the evening, since he didn't have to be at the record company until tomorrow, when Macy called Jayson on his cell phone.

"Are you in LA?" she asked, sounding panicked.

"Yes, why?"

"Where are you?"

"I'm at Drew's house."

"Oh, good!" she said. "I need you to check on Debbie."

"What? Why?"

"I can't get hold of her, Dad. I'm really worried about her."

"She's probably just left town and didn't tell you, or she's turned off her phone for a day at the spa, or something."

"Dad!" She started to cry. "I just . . . have this feeling. Please . . . go check on her."

"If she's not answering the phone, she's not going to answer the door. What do you want me to do? Break in?"

"I can tell you where she keeps the key."

Jayson sighed, torn between his daughter's tears and distress, and the loathing he felt at the very idea of finding Debbie's key and going into the house he'd once shared with her. Fortunately it wasn't very far away, since he and Drew had purchased their homes in the same area many years earlier. Debbie had gotten the house in the divorce, and Jayson had moved in with Drew until he'd gone to Utah.

"Okay," he said, thinking he could have this over in half an hour. "I'll check on her. I'll call you back."

"Oh, thank you, Dad. I think your being there is a miracle."

"We'll see," he said and hung up. He gave a quick explanation to Drew and Valerie, then borrowed one of Drew's cars to drive the short distance to Debbie's house. Pulling into the driveway, memories assaulted him—mostly of the day he'd come home in the middle of a tour to surprise her, and he'd found another man in his shower. He'd long ago gotten over *that,* but the memory was ugly, nevertheless.

"Let's get this over with," he said to no one and went up the steps of the high-end condo. He knocked and rang the bell, and repeated the process four times. He grumbled under his breath before he discreetly looked behind a flowery bush and under a rock where he found the key, right where Macy had said it would be. He opened the door and called, "Debbie! Are you here?" Nothing. He closed the door, hoping he wouldn't find something unexpectedly shocking. His memories made the thought especially distasteful.

He was surprised at how the house smelled like stale food and . . . what? Dirty laundry? Something like that. Obviously she wasn't paying a housekeeper to come and clean it anymore, and *she'd* stopped cleaning a long time ago. Jayson quickly and quietly peeked into all the rooms on the main floor, relieved to find nothing. He wanted to find an empty house and call Macy to tell her that he'd checked. He took the stairs three at a time, glad to be wearing tennis shoes that were silent and easy to move in. The door to the master bedroom was open. The memories made him sick. He knocked on the door and called out her name again. Then he saw her, and his sickness deepened.

Macy's prompting suddenly made him feel guilty for protesting. He rushed to the bed where his ex-wife was laying with a sheet over part of her, the rest of her barely covered by black lingerie. She looked dead. He almost expected her to be. He found she was breathing and pulled the sheet up higher for the sake of modesty, but he couldn't get her to respond. He shouted at her and shook her, but she barely made some groaning noises and no other response. He glanced around, wondering what to do, looking for the phone. That's when he saw the needles and other drug paraphernalia. And he cursed. He hadn't cursed aloud for a long time, but he felt so sick and scared that the words just jumped out of his mouth. He grabbed the phone and dialed 911. He reported the problem, told them the address, then answered their questions, including his own name and the name of the patient. As soon as he'd said it, he knew this was going to backfire on him. But how could he be thinking about gossip magazines at a time like this? Then again, how could he *not* when he knew that paparazzi used emergency dispatch radios to seek out fodder for their sleazy news? In an area like this, full of musicians and actors, it was common practice.

The EMTs arrived quickly, relieving him of his ongoing vigil to try to get Debbie to come around. Once they had strapped her to a gurney and taken her away, he slumped into a chair and didn't know whether to cry or throw something. If she wasn't in such bad shape, he'd feel tempted to slap some sense into her. He couldn't believe it! How could she be so stupid? He thought of the days when they had been happily married, struggling with low-paying jobs and taking turns looking after Macy in their dumpy apartment, while he'd clawed his way into the music industry. How had it come to this? He'd brought Debbie into the world of all the horrible things that were often associated with the music business. He had shied away from the worldly things, and she had gravitated toward them. The separation had been inevitable from that point on. But how could it have come to this? He'd once loved her more than life. She was the mother of his child.

Reminding himself that he didn't want to be found in Debbie's house by *anyone,* he left the house and locked it, returning the key to its hiding place. In the car he called Macy and gave her a report that made her cry. Then he had to say, "I'm proud of you for acting on that prompting, baby. I'm sorry I was stubborn about going. You probably saved her life."

"Do you think she'll be okay?"

"I don't know," he said. "I hope so. I'm on my way to the hospital now. I'll keep you posted."

"Thank you, Dad," she said, and he hung up to call Drew and give him the same report. Drew cursed, as well.

"I guess I'd better be at the hospital," Jayson said, angry over having his time with his brother cut short, even though he was sincerely worried about Debbie. Maybe he'd just had too many experiences where Debbie's bad choices had made his own life miserable. "Someone who cares needs to be with her until her family can get there," he told Drew, "and they're a few hours away. I'll be in touch."

At the hospital he had to wait, but he did give them most of the information they needed. He told them he was just the ex-husband who had happened to find her. He didn't have contact information for her parents, but he knew their names. A while later they told him that they'd contacted her parents, and they were on their way. They had also contacted a sister who lived closer and would get there more quickly. Jayson was considering calling Elizabeth, but he knew she was busy, and it could wait. He was wondering what he was doing there, when he was really wanting to be with his brother. Just then, Drew walked into the ER waiting room and found him.

"Hey, let's go get some supper," he said. "If you're just sitting here, you can go get something to eat."

Jayson asked at the desk how long it might be until he could see Debbie, and they said it could be a while. She was still unconscious and being monitored closely. But apparently they'd assessed that she was going to be okay. Jayson gave them his cell phone number and asked that they call if anything changed. He was grateful for Drew coming to get him, but the dinner conversation ended up being mostly about memories with Debbie, for both of them—some good but most bad. He hated having their time together dampened by this, but he was grateful to have someone to talk to who knew his history with Debbie, and who had once been close to her as well. They finally changed the subject, enjoyed the rest of their meal, then Drew took Jayson back to the hospital and dropped him off. Jayson sat and waited again, wondering if Debbie's family had shown up yet. But the nurse said no one had. He was finally allowed to see her and was shown to a room next to the nurses' station. The nurse told him she was going to be okay, but she wouldn't have been if she hadn't been brought to the hospital when she was. His relief when he saw Debbie conscious was indescribable. He almost started to cry but managed to hold back the tears.

Jayson entered the room and scooted a chair close to the bed, but Debbie looked groggy and unaware of him until he said, "How are you feeling?"

She turned toward him, and her eyes widened with surprise, then embarrassment. "Jayson? What are you doing here?"

"I just happened to be in the neighborhood when you were trying to die from an overdose."

"I don't understand."

"I was in town on business, staying at Drew's. Macy had a bad feeling and couldn't get hold of you. She talked me into checking on you; she told me where you hid the key."

"You're the one who found me? You called 911?"

"That's right," he said, and she started to cry.

"Oh, Jayson," she said, "my life is such a mess."

"You want me to argue with you?"

"No. It's obvious, isn't it? I'm sure Macy's told you how bad it is."

"She's said very little. I'm not sure she knows how bad it is. But she does not bad-mouth her mother."

"I wouldn't expect her to. She's a good girl—no thanks to me."

"I'm not going to argue about that either, Debbie. If there's one thing you can count on from me, it's that I'll be completely forthright."

"You always were," she said. "And I was so awful to you."

"Yes, Debbie, you were. What do you want me to say?"

"So, why are you here?"

"Because your life is a mess and you need somebody to care. I thought I should at least stick around until somebody else got here. I can't fix your life, but I can give you some suggestions. If you're not interested, fine."

"I'm listening," she said, turning her head more toward him.

"You need to get into a good rehab program," he said. "There is *no way* you will *ever* kick this on your own. Trust me. I've been there."

"You've been *where?*"

"Rehab."

"For drugs?"

"Prescription drugs. I never touched the hard stuff."

"Why did I never know?"

"I have no idea. I thought it was in the tabloids. Or maybe it's just on the Internet. I don't know. It doesn't matter. The world knows. I don't care. I'm happy now. It's in the past." He leaned closer toward her. "Do you have any idea how close you came to dying? Is that what you want? To die . . . like that . . . now? I know you were hanging out with the druggies, but I can't figure what made you stupid enough to start shooting up with them. What were you thinking?"

"I don't know," she cried. "I really don't know. I just . . ." She got so emotional she couldn't speak. He took her hand and prayed for guidance. He knew he couldn't get too involved in this; no matter what course it took, he wasn't the person to help her through this. But he wanted to say something that might help her get on the right path.

"Hey, listen to me. I can't stay long. Your parents and your sister are coming. They'll take care of you. But I just want to give you a word of advice; take it or leave it."

"Okay," she said, sniffling loudly.

"Sell the house. It's prime real estate, and it was yours, free and clear, in the divorce. You haven't mortgaged it, have you?"

"No. I've thought about it, but I never did it."

"Good. Sell it and get out of this place, Debbie. Use the money to get into rehab and start a new life. If you're careful it will give you enough to get by on for a long time. You can do this, Debbie. You don't have to live this way. It's never too late to choose a different path."

"You really mean it," she said. "You really do care what happens to me."

"I really do," he said, "but I'm not going to be the one to help you get there. I can't. You have to understand that."

"I do," she said.

At that point, Debbie's sister came into the room, being overly dramatic about the situation, which was exactly how Jayson remembered her.

"I'm going now," Jayson said, interrupting the drama enough to squeeze Debbie's hand one more time.

"Oh, hi, Jayson!" the sister said brightly. He honestly couldn't remember her name.

"Hi," he said, certain her enthusiasm was more for his being famous than for his being her sister's ex-husband. To Debbie he added, "You let Macy know what's going on, and she'll keep me posted. Okay?"

"Okay," Debbie said. "Thank you."

Jayson hurried out of the room, glad to have that over with. On his way out he realized that the blinds on the large glass windows of the room were wide open. Anyone could have seen him sitting there holding his ex-wife's hand. His gut told him this was going to get into the tabloids. He just *knew* it.

Once outside the hospital, he called Elizabeth on his cell phone. She sounded sleepy but not asleep when she answered. It was an hour later there. "Sorry to call so late," he said, "but we need to talk."

"It's okay," she said. "What's wrong?"

"You are never going to believe what just happened. I thought you'd better know about it before it hits the tabloids."

"Are you being serious, Jayson, or—"

"Oh, I'm quite serious. Show me a paparazzi who doesn't have a connection with an emergency dispatch radio, and I'll show you a zebra without stripes."

"Emergency dispatch?" she said, sounding fully alert now.

"I'm fine. Everybody's fine . . . in a manner of speaking. It was Debbie."

"Debbie?" she asked skeptically. "Is she okay?"

"She's going to be fine . . . as long as she gets herself out of the gutter."

"You'd better start at the beginning."

"I intend to," he said. "It's not complicated. Macy called me. She couldn't get hold of Debbie and felt panicked. She asked me to check on her, and she told me where Debbie keeps the key. She didn't answer the door. I thought she probably wasn't home, but I needed go in and take a quick look around so I could assure Macy that I had checked. Well, she was there. Stoned out of her mind, unconscious, needles and other drug stuff all over the place."

"Oh, my gosh!" Elizabeth said. "Is she really doing that stuff?"

"She really is. So, I called 911. And guess where the EMTs found Jayson Wolfe when they arrived?"

"Oh, no," she said, but then she chuckled. "Oh, no." She laughed louder. "I'm sorry. This is not funny. I mean . . . it's not funny about Debbie, but . . . the other is kind of funny. Okay, tell me. I'm ready."

"I'm sure glad you trust me, or this would be a nosedive for our marriage. I will be extremely surprised if one of those EMTs didn't get a couple of good shots with a cell phone camera. Such pictures are worth a lot of money."

"Okay, I'm waiting."

"She was in her bed when I found her, and I left her there. But when they came in the room I was leaning over her, still trying to get her to come around. Drug stuff everywhere."

"Oh, my gosh," Elizabeth said again.

"And then I was with her at the hospital. I gave them information so they could call her parents. I talked to her after she came around. She was more humble and sweet than I've seen her since . . . well . . . the last time I was in her bedroom, when I found her boyfriend there."

"That's good, then . . . that she's humble and sweet."

"I hope so. I hope she gets into rehab and changes her life. I told her to sell the house and move and start over, and I told her I couldn't be the one to help her. I left when her sister got there. But the blinds were open in her room. Anyone could have seen me in there holding her hand. And if they run a *new* story, they'll pull up old pictures too; something really great from when we were married and she'd wear those horrible dresses to every PR function." He groaned, then sighed. "So, I'm coming clean. You're not going to throw me out when you see the tabloids, are you?"

"Well, let me think about that," she said with sarcasm. "It is what it is. We've survived tabloids before."

"Not like this, and not with Sister Freedman just waiting like a hawk for some piece of disparaging evidence to persecute me with. Can't you just see her in the grocery checkout line and getting a glimpse of . . ." he raised his voice to mimic her, "'those trashy magazines with that *man* all over them. It's scandalous and unseemly. A decent man wouldn't have tried to save his ex-wife's life.'"

"That was unkind, Jayson," she said, but she was giggling while she did.

"This is not funny!" he insisted.

"I'm sorry. I think it is." More seriously she said, "Jayson, it's gossip. *Real* people do not believe what's in those magazines."

"We can hope," he said. "Okay, I've got to get some sleep, and so do you. I'll call you tomorrow."

"I love you, Jayson Wolfe."

"I love you too, Elizabeth Wolfe." He laughed softly. "I love sharing the same last name with you."

"Only because you love the way giving me your name means we get to share everything else. Same address, same dirty dishes, same potty training."

"Same kids."

"Same religion."

"Same bed," he said. "I miss you. I hate it when we don't wake up in the same bed."

"I hate it, too. But hey . . . I'm going on tour with you this summer. I'll never be far away."

"How glorious!" he said. "I'll talk to you tomorrow."

"Good night," she said and hung up.

Jayson called Macy to give her a quick update, then he went home to Drew's house, a place where he'd once lived with his brother and mother. This was where his mother had died. More memories.

The following morning, Jayson had to get up without having gotten nearly enough sleep and go to the record company offices to meet with Rick. He endured three days of meetings that started with sitting together and listening to the entire album in a room with a number of people who represented different departments of the company. They all made notes and comments, and he was relieved to see that the overall response to the album was positive. They were all in easy agreement about the songs that should hit the radio as singles and have accompanying music videos.

They complimented Jayson for knowing the formula well enough that it was easy for them to hear the obvious. They discussed promotions and public relations, the tour and the CD cover, photo shoots and the bottom-line deal. He endured a fair amount of bad language and crude comments that were common among these people, and he was offered coffee or liquor enough times that he lost count. But when all was said and done, Jayson signed some papers that guaranteed him a great deal of money. More important to him was the guarantee that this company would put a great deal of effort into promoting his product, and that meant it would get out into the world and give people a positive option for entertainment. In the scope of the world's media market, he might only be making a tiny splash in a large lake, but it was a splash, nevertheless. And he could put the money to good use. He figured it was better that someone like him get such money, as opposed to the rockers who would waste it away on riotous living. Jayson would be making donations to missionary and humanitarian funds with the bulk of it.

Jayson spent Friday auditioning musicians for his tour. He was glad for the work Drew had done to get the process down to a few possibilities, and he'd already had background checks done on them. Part of Jayson's method was to actually play *with* them, because he needed to get a feel for how well they could mesh musically without much preparation. The circumstances surrounding the rehearsal and tour schedule were laid out very plainly, including Jayson's declaration that since they would be rehearsing in his home, and his family would be on the tour, he would not tolerate even a little bit of foul language, and they would be required to put that in writing. He also informed the candidates that he was a religious man, and prayer would be common prior to each event. The final question of the interview was always, "Do you have a problem with that?" And as long as the answer was no, the rest came down to their musical abilities. One guy actually said that he was a family man himself, and active in a Christian religion. He told Jayson he respected the attitude, and he turned out to be a great bass player.

The choices ended up being easy, and Drew would take care of the paperwork the following week. They finished up by the middle of the afternoon, which meant that Jayson had about twenty-four hours to just spend some time together with Drew and his family before he flew back to Utah. Jayson enjoyed their time together thoroughly, but he was also very glad to get home. He was standing at the airport curb with his bag on his shoulder when Elizabeth pulled up. She got out and ran around the car to hug him tightly. He dropped the bag in order to make the most of it.

"Oh, it's good to see you!" he said and kissed her, not caring who might see. He wished somebody would take a picture of *that* and put it out for the world to see.

"I missed you so much!" she said and laughed. "And those kids of yours; I don't think I'm cut out to be a single mother."

"I'm glad to hear that."

"We're all driving each other crazy without you there."

"I'm glad to know I was missed," he said and opened the passenger door for her. He tossed his bag in the back and got in to drive home. Oh, it was good to be back!

Jayson had fun just hanging out with his wife and kids that evening, even though Trevin was only there part of the time since he went out with friends, as he usually did on weekends.

The following morning Jayson played for the choir without a glitch, and he didn't feel the least bit awkward at church. He did, however, feel the need to speak with the bishop and pulled him aside after sacrament meeting to ask when might be a good time.

"Right now is fine," he said, and they went into his office. Jayson told him what had happened in Los Angeles with his ex-wife, and his belief that it might get into the gossip magazines. He made it clear that he was not worried about such a thing affecting any of his personal relationships. He was only concerned what conclusions people might jump to when they didn't know him well enough to know if there could be truth in the headlines.

"So, if anyone calls you," Jayson said, "you'll have the right answers . . . I hope. I don't want this to cause problems with my doing firesides."

"It will blow over," the bishop said with confidence.

"Or maybe I'm flattering myself and it won't even hit the news. Maybe I'm a has-been and no one even noticed."

The bishop chuckled. "I guess we'll see. Either way, I don't think you're a has-been. Maybe no one around here would ever make the connection even if they saw it."

It was only four days later when Macy came to the house in the middle of the day and found Jayson and Elizabeth having a quiet lunch while Derek and Harmony were napping.

"To what do we owe this surprise?" Jayson asked, standing up to hug her.

As he sat back down she said grimly, "Drew called me. He begged me to be the bearer of bad tidings. He thought you should know what you were dealing with. So I took a quick trip to the grocery store in American Fork."

Jayson groaned when she pulled tabloids out of her bag and tossed them on the table. Elizabeth handed him his glasses. There was no laughter, not even a word spoken as the headlines came into view. One of them said boldly, *Drugs, Sex, Rock and Roll,* and underneath it, *Jayson Wolfe doing drugs with ex-wife?* He doubted most people would notice the question mark. *Overdose nearly kills her!* There was a large picture of Jayson with one knee on Debbie's bed, and her passed out, the needles on the bedside table very clear. An inset picture was of them many years ago, when they had loved each other. But she was wearing a dress that had embarrassed him then, and it mortified him now.

The other paper had the headline, *Jayson and Debbie back together!* There was nothing but presumption with that exclamation point. This paper had a picture of him sitting at her bedside in the hospital, which must have been taken with a great telephoto lens. He was holding her hand. Beneath the picture it said, *Is the Wolfe supplying the drugs? Details of Jayson Wolfe's rehab revealed.* There was an inset picture of him in the bedroom with the words next to it, *What's he doing in her bedroom while his wife is at home in Utah?*

"So, what's the verdict?" Macy asked.

"The verdict?" Jayson countered. "Am I supposed to do something about this?"

"No, but . . . I need to know how you feel."

"I should think it's obvious," he said. "I . . ." He just threw his hands in the air when not a single word could get from his brain to his lips.

Macy started to cry. "This is my fault."

"How is this *possibly* your fault?"

"I told you to go over there. I—"

"You saved her life, Macy!" he said with anger, but it was not directed at his daughter. Her felt angry with Debbie for being so stupid with her life, and for the people of the world who took part in such malicious evil. "Clearly," he added, "Debbie's life is more important than this." He slapped the papers on the table.

"I can't believe it," Elizabeth said.

"Not so funny now, is it," he said to her.

"No, it's not funny. I had no idea it would be this bad."

"Neither did I," Jayson said. "I thought it would be bad, but not this bad."

"It's unbelievable," Elizabeth said. "It's like Satan himself set this up to persecute you."

Jayson stood up so abruptly that his chair fell over. He left it and hurried to the studio. He felt so angry that he wanted to be alone before he said something he would regret saying in front of his wife and daughter. The studio felt like a sanctuary, but as he leaned against the door and surveyed its contents, the reality of the blessing-slash-curse in his life overcame him with too much emotion to handle. Logically, he could tell himself that it was only gossip. It would blow over. The way he lived his life was between him and the Lord. The people who knew and loved him were well aware of the truth. But it was also logical that some people would forever associate his name with the words and phrases they would see if only in passing the magazine stands. Logic aside, it pierced his heart with so much hurt and anger that he felt nauseous. It only took him a minute's thought to realize that his emotions had a lot more to them than the assault of gossip magazines. He wondered what weed with deep roots in his psyche had just been tapped into. He wasn't sure he even wanted to know.

CHAPTER 3

Elizabeth tried to open the door to the studio, but Jayson was leaning against it. He moved away and pulled it open. "Is Macy okay?" he asked.

"No, but she will be. I reassured her that it wasn't her fault, and thanked her for bringing the papers, because we *do* need to know what's going on. I told her you would be fine when you'd had some time, and I sent her home."

"You're very good at smoothing over the fallout of my life," he said. "No wonder I married you. But I have trouble believing a woman like you enjoys putting up with the garbage that comes with being married to me."

"Excuse me?" she said. "The garbage that comes with being married to you? The garbage is one-tenth of one percent of what I get in this marriage, Jayson Wolfe, so don't start making the tabloids a marriage issue. I'm not here to tell you all the things you already know. I just want to know why you're so upset. I mean . . . I'm upset, too. It's awful, but . . . you seem . . . more upset than I expected."

Jayson crossed the room and sat on the piano bench, his back to the piano. He leaned his forearms on his thighs. Elizabeth took a chair and leaned back, indicating that she would sit there until he said something to reasonably answer her question. He had to think about it a few minutes, inwardly asking himself what Maren, his trusted shrink, had taught him to ask. *What's the weed? What deeply rooted issue had been triggered?*

"All I ever wanted," he said, "was to make good music and give it to the world; music that would help people get through the tough times. My mother always talked about music that got her through the tough times. That's what I wanted. The fame never mattered to me. Its only appeal was . . ."

He hesitated and she said, "The indicator it would be for how many people were listening to your music."

He looked at her. "You've spent way too many years with me."

"Not nearly enough," she said. "Go on."

"I never asked for this. I never wanted this to be a part of the deal."

"But it is," she said. "You can't get one without the other."

"Why?" he demanded, erupting to his feet. "Why can't I just do what I came to this world to do and not suffer for it?"

"Because that's not part of the plan," she said so quickly that it got his attention. "Sit down, Jayson. You already know this, just like I know how to finish your sentences. But I'm going to tell you, anyway."

He sat down and faced her directly. "I'm listening," he said, sincerely hoping that she could say something to ease this ache and anger that was consuming him.

"It's basic doctrine, Jayson; bottom-line, plan of salvation stuff." She leaned a little closer and quoted scripture. "'For it must needs be that there is an opposition in all things . . . if these things are not there is no God.'" She waited, as if that was all she had to say.

"I know about opposition, Elizabeth, but I don't understand what you're saying."

"For every darkness there is light, and for every light there is darkness. It doesn't say that there *might* be opposition, or it *sometimes* happens. It says that there *must needs be.*" Elizabeth moved to the piano bench to sit beside him, taking his hand into hers. "Don't you see, Jayson? You have been given an incredible amount of light. How can such remarkable light be met with anything but opposing forces of darkness? If you weren't bringing about good things, Satan would have little interest in persecuting you. The fact that he's doing such a good job of it makes me think that it's very important for you to do this album, and this tour. And you have to be your strongest, most righteous, most faithful self to rise above the persecution and shine, so that people can feel the strength of your spirit and seek to understand its source. You're entitled to be upset, and riding out the storms won't always be easy. This is a tough one; I won't dispute it. But we need to keep perspective here. Think of the light and miracles in Joseph Smith's life. Was he not assaulted with equivalent persecution and darkness? Surely we can learn from that."

Jayson digested Elizabeth's wisdom and felt remarkably calm. "How do you do it?" he asked.

"Do what?"

"You always say the right thing at the right time."

"That's what marriage is all about, Jayson," she said and kissed him.

* * * * *

Jayson called the bishop as soon as he knew he'd be home from work. "I thought you should be the first to know that it *did* hit the tabloids, and it's bad."

"Okay," Bishop Bingham said. "How are you?"

"I'm trying to have faith and accept that opposition is a part of this world—and my work. But it's not easy. I feel slandered and betrayed. I feel violated."

"It's that bad, eh?"

"Did you want me to read the headlines to you?"

There was a moment of silence. "Why don't I just come over and take a look and we can chat . . . if that's okay?"

"Come on over," Jayson said. "We're all just sitting here reading the gossip."

Elizabeth answered the door when the bishop arrived. She brought him to the dining room where Jayson was sitting at the table. Bishop Bingham shook Jayson's hand, then sat across from him. Jayson turned the tabloids around so he could see the topic for tonight's discussion. He watched the bishop's eyes widen. "Wow!" he said, taking in all of the headlines. "You really do attract opposition." He said it almost as if it were a good thing. "And what do the articles actually say?" the bishop asked.

"They're very brief," Jayson said, "which means that they don't really have much to go on. It's all very carefully worded speculations and implications. The content of the articles is not what's important here, because there are only certain people who will actually pick up the magazine and read it. The impact of this is the impression the photos and headlines give to people who just take a long glance at them while they're buying groceries." He sighed and got to one of the most difficult points. "Do you have any idea what could happen when Sister Freedman sees this?" Jayson asked. "And she will see it; I'm absolutely certain of it. Satan wouldn't go to so much trouble to do this and not be certain that Sister Freedman would be guided to find it."

"You're probably right," the bishop said. "But you know what? There is absolutely nothing you can do about that. We'll just do our best to deal with the fallout as it happens. How are the kids doing with this?"

"The ones who are old enough to care are having a hard time with it. But I think they're more upset on my behalf than feeling much concern over how it will affect them. I guess we'll see. I'm very grateful that Trevin doesn't have to go to high school with the same last name as me. Apparently very few people really know we're connected. I hope that doesn't change, under the circumstances."

"So, how are you *really?*" the bishop asked.

"I'm better than I was earlier. I can thank my good wife for helping me keep perspective. She had some wonderful insights on opposition. It crossed my mind that maybe this was happening because I was being punished, somehow. But I've searched my soul and prayed very hard, and I can't come up with anything I've done wrong that hasn't been put in order with the Lord. I'm not perfect, by any means, Bishop. But I did nothing to warrant this. I suppose the principle of opposition explains everything. If I'm going to do what I do for the reasons I do it, I guess I just have to expect such things in my life."

Jayson felt suddenly emotional without understanding why. He leaned his elbows on the table and put a hand over his eyes. An enormous rush of information came into his mind with clarity and perfect understanding. And tears came with it, as if to verify the truth of what he'd just learned.

"What is it, Jayson?"

He coughed and wiped the tears from his face. "It just occurred to me that . . . maybe that's what's been happening my whole life." He put a hand to his chest as just saying the words seemed to verify their truth again. He tried to articulate the idea that had occurred in his thoughts so naturally. He looked straight at the bishop, as if doing so might help him process what he'd just learned. The intensity of his thoughts reminded him of when a song would come to him, suddenly and with purity. No, it was not a reminder; it was exactly the same. He'd acknowledged for a long time that his gift was a spiritual gift, but he'd never realized until that moment how the ability to hear music in his head was so obviously mechanized by the gift of the Holy Ghost. They were exactly the same! And now he knew things about his life and his gift that he'd never known before. Here, in the middle of a conversation with this good man, a completely separate conversation was taking place inside his mind. Questions he'd never thought to ask were being answered in ways that answered the questions that had always haunted him. Now he knew. He knew! He heard himself laugh softly as the joy of such an experience washed away the fear and trepidation he'd been struggling with for weeks.

"That's it, Bishop," he said. "I came to this world with my gift already inside of me. God had a plan for me to be able to hone it and have it grow. He provided the means and the motivation to find my way. He sent me to the right family at the right time. And he allowed the opposition to serve its purpose to teach me and strengthen me and humble me, and . . ." Emotion overtook him again. "He gave me a good woman who was there for me all along, and . . . through her . . . He led me to the gospel."

Jayson blinked fresh tears out of his eyes and realized the bishop was crying, too. With quiet confidence, he said, "All of that just came to you, didn't it—just now."

"Yes," Jayson squeaked, then he laughed again and wiped more tears.

"So, what are you going to do now?"

"I'm going to do everything in my power to live close to the Spirit so that I can be everything my Heavenly Father wants me to be. I'm going to do my best to do it the way He wants me to do it. He's brought me this far, and He's not going to let me down now. Even if I had made choices that had brought this stuff on, He would forgive me and help me through. But I didn't. I need to remember who I am and what I'm doing here. I need to—"

Elizabeth came into the room and stopped abruptly the same moment Jayson stopped talking. He saw her taking notice of the way they were both crying before she said, "I'm sorry. I obviously interrupted something, and . . ."

"Come and sit down," Jayson said, taking her hand.

She sat beside him and asked, "What's wrong, honey? Are you—"

"Nothing's wrong, babe," he said. "I'm doing great, actually." He laughed again. "The most amazing thing just happened." He repeated the experience in detail, which helped cement it in his mind, and again the Spirit verified the truth of what he was saying, not just to him, but to Elizabeth and the bishop, as well. The bishop explained to them the principle of pure intelligence, and how Joseph Smith taught that the

Spirit could teach something to the human mind instantly that would otherwise take long periods of time to learn. Jayson appreciated the wisdom and knowledge of this good man, especially when he and Elizabeth were both converts to the Church and there were still many things they didn't have practical experience with, or the deep understanding that comes from a lifetime of learning.

Long after the bishop left, Jayson marveled over what he'd felt and learned—about the gospel plan and about himself. He slept peacefully that night, when only hours earlier, he'd believed that he would be a sleepless wreck. During the following days he enjoyed being more laid back, now that the recording was done and there would be a little time before promotions and tour preparations began. He liked spending more time helping with the kids, and he and Elizabeth went to the temple twice that week. He began to wonder if all of his anxiety over the opinions of others and the presence of tabloids had been blown out of proportion in his mind. And then Bishop Bingham called and asked if he could come over.

"Of course," Jayson said. "Is something wrong?"

"We'll talk when I get there," the bishop said.

Jayson found Elizabeth and told her how the phone call had gone. She put Trevin in charge of the children so that she could be with Jayson and hear what the bishop had to say without interruptions. When Jayson answered the door, the bishop's solemn countenance did not help his anxiety. Elizabeth took his hand and squeezed it tightly once greetings had been exchanged and they were all seated in the front room.

"I'll get straight to the point," he said. "I know you're expecting me to. Last night Sister Freedman called me. I'd expected her to, and I was prepared. I assured her that I was well aware of the situation, and that the accusations and implications were completely false."

"And how did she take *that?*" Jayson asked.

"It's not my place to repeat the conversation that followed. Suffice it to say I told her that it would be best if she kept her opinions to herself, and that as her bishop, I had done all that I could do. I encouraged her not to let this affect her own standing in the Church, or her personal testimony. Enough said. That's not the bad news."

Jayson tightened his hold on Elizabeth's hand and straightened his shoulders, as if that might help him better receive *the bad news*. The bishop took a deep breath, as if his needing to give the news was equally difficult. "The stake president of the stake where you have a fireside scheduled this coming Sunday called to talk to me about the situation. Members of the stake have seen the tabloids and have expressed concern." Jayson's heart was pounding long before he finished. "Even though I explained to him what I know, he said that he needed to cancel the meeting."

"What?" Jayson spouted spontaneously. He felt so hurt and angry and upset that he was almost dizzy.

"He asked me to relay the message that there was no need for you to show up. I told him what I knew about you, about your testimony, your experiences. I told him that I really believed the message you had to share should not be quieted because of opposition, that the youth especially could surely benefit from your testimony. I suggested that canceling it would give more of a wrong impression to a great many people if they believed that there was something out of order in your life that would keep you from giving the fireside."

"Exactly," Jayson said, the very idea making him nauseous *and* dizzy.

"He was very kind, Jayson. He's sincerely trying to do the right thing. But he was firm about his decision. He said that he was glad to know you were a member in good standing, but whether the rumors were true or not, he did not feel comfortable endorsing you as an example to his youth when there was that kind of scandal associated with your name." The bishop sucked in a shallow breath. "There, I said it. That's it."

"I can't believe it," Elizabeth said.

Jayson shook his head, trying to take it in. He searched for all of the principles and theories that had helped him cope with these problems so far. But his brain was such a muddle that he couldn't find a single one. He let out a noise of disbelief. "If one fireside gets cancelled, then more will be," he said, his voice rough. "I think I have five or six more on the calendar."

"Jayson, I . . ." the bishop began, but then he had to compose himself. "I . . . don't know what to say. It breaks my heart, but . . . there is nothing that any of us can do to change it, any more than we already have. You can only do the best you can do. In the end, the Lord's work will carry on, and good will triumph. But getting through the effects of opposition can be a horrible thing." He sighed deeply, as if he literally carried Jayson's burden. "When times get tough, for me or for people I care about, I often think of the Saints at Far West, while the Prophet was in the jail at Liberty. Those were horrible times for our people. The persecution and depravities taking place are beyond my ability to understand or comprehend. And Joseph's anguish over the situation is the same. You know, of course, that this was the time that Joseph received some of his greatest revelation. Maybe you should read those sections of the Doctrine and Covenants, especially section 122, I think."

"I have read them," Jayson said, "but I hadn't thought about that section for a long time. I'll read it."

Bishop Bingham asked if Jayson or Elizabeth had anything they wanted to say or needed to talk about. They were both too stunned to talk. The bishop stood up to leave, saying that he was available if they needed anything. Elizabeth stood up to escort him to the door. Jayson couldn't find the strength to stand. When Elizabeth returned, she had the scriptures in her hand. She sat close beside him, and he knew she was looking up the section the bishop had suggested.

"Is it okay if I read this out loud?" she asked.

"Go for it," he said, and listened as she read the Lord's words to Joseph Smith that had come to him in the midst of unspeakable persecution and suffering, not only for himself, but for all of the Saints. At the end of a long list of examples of possible trials, the intensity of the message began to settle in. "'. . . *If thou be cast into the deep; if the billowing surge conspire against thee; if fierce winds become thine enemy; if the heavens gather blackness, and all the elements combine to hedge up the way; and above all, if the very jaws of hell shall gape open the mouth wide after thee, know thou, my son, that all these things shall give thee experience, and shall be for thy good.'"*

Elizabeth paused to collect her tender emotions, and Jayson felt petty and selfish as he considered what he was up against as opposed to what those before him had gone through. In the next thought it occurred to him that the purpose of these scriptures was to have a point of reference to apply to the reader's individual circumstances. Trials were relative, and right now this one felt very heavy. Then Elizabeth cleared her throat and added the next verse. "'*The Son of Man hath descended below them all. Art thou greater than he?'"*

Jayson squeezed his eyes closed; that's when his tears finally broke through the barrier of shock. The statement offered him perfect perspective in humbly taking on this trial and doing his best to face it with faith and dignity. But more than that, it was a stark reminder that because the Savior had done what He'd done, Jayson *could* get through this.

* * * * *

Two more firesides were cancelled, but the others went on as scheduled, and Jayson felt a deepening of gratitude that he'd never felt before. Even though he didn't handle the presentation any differently than he'd done in the past, he felt a deeper sense of responsibility in being a good example of living the gospel to anyone within the sound of his voice. Doing his best to focus on all that was good in his life, instead of the opposite, Jayson found an inner calm that counteracted the difficult feelings and concerns when they came up. He came to see that he had the power to encourage negative thoughts and worries, or to consciously replace them with a trust in the Lord to help take care of the problems that might arise. He discussed the theory with Elizabeth, and they talked about the difference between this theory and being in denial about a problem. She believed that when a person could honestly acknowledge a problem he was facing—rather than ignoring it—and then do all that was in his power, the Lord *would* make up the difference according to His will. With that theory in place, Jayson daily counted his blessings and prayed for Sister Freedman and her son. He prayed for Debbie, that the rehab program she'd begun would be effective and make a significant difference in her life. And he prayed that he could press forward and do the good he'd come to this world to do and not be thwarted by Satan's fiery darts, whatever form they might take.

Jayson came awake on a snowy morning with the thought that he needed to check on Macy. It didn't feel like an emergency, but it did feel like it needed to be his highest priority for the day once he'd cleared the snow around their home and the homes of several of their neighbors. He'd talked to Macy nearly every day, but their calls had been brief because she was so busy. He knew that nothing had changed with Layla, and that Macy was worried. But she'd assured him repeatedly that they were all praying and hoping for answers and doing the best that they could. Jayson was praying for them too. In fact, every prayer uttered in their household included a request for Layla to return to good health, and for all of her family to be blessed and strengthened through this trial. Jayson told Macy every time he talked to her that she was in his prayers, but his repeatedly asking what he might do to help was always answered with an insistence that they had everything they needed. Now, Jayson wondered what she might not be telling him.

Jayson went out early to clear snow and finished quickly since it wasn't very deep. While he was helping Elizabeth prepare breakfast for the babies, he shared his feelings with her, and she wholeheartedly agreed that he should go see his daughter that morning. She suggested that a surprise visit might be better in giving Jayson a more accurate picture of what the situation was *really* like. As soon as the morning routine was over and the household under control, Jayson made a quick stop, then drove to Macy's home. Approaching the door, he wished he had done this sooner. He shouldn't have just taken at face value her brief assurances that everything was alright. Now he wondered if she'd just been putting up a brave front, not wanting to burden him. That was like her, and he should have seen through it. On the other hand, maybe it wasn't all that serious and the prompting he'd gotten had been simply to help lift her spirits. Either way, he was glad for the nudge he'd been given, and his prayer was that he could make a positive difference in his daughter's life today.

He rang the doorbell and waited, then he rang it again. He was about to call Macy from his cell phone to see if she was there when she pulled the door open.

"What are you doing here?" she asked, looking pleasantly startled— and also frazzled, tired, and like she hadn't put a brush to her hair yet today. He stepped inside, and she closed the door.

"I came to see you," he said. Handing her one of the large bouquets of flowers he was holding, he added, "These are for you." He handed her the other bouquet. "And these are for Layla. Or the other way around. You choose which one you like best, and . . ."

Macy threw her arms around him, holding the flowers in each hand. While he was reciprocating her tight hug, he realized she was crying.

"What is it, baby?" he asked softly. "Talk to me."

She eased back, and he wiped her tears since her hands were full of flowers. "I'm so glad you came," she said. "And the flowers are beautiful." She laughed softly. "Here," she handed him one of the bouquets, "take these to Layla. You know where to find her. I know she's awake. I'll find some vases. After you visit with her for a few minutes we'll talk."

"Okay," he said.

He followed her a few steps, then she stopped and said in a softer voice, "It's been a while since you've seen her."

"Yeah," he said.

"Try not to act too startled," she said and went toward the kitchen, leaving him to continue down the hall. He hesitated, wondering what he should expect, and whether he *was* prepared for whatever he might encounter. He tried to recount everything Macy had told him since he *had* seen Layla last, but all he'd heard was reports of her not doing any better, and that the doctors still couldn't figure out the problem. He moved on down the hall and stepped quietly into the open doorway. Again he hesitated. Since the TV was on and she was resting with her eyes closed, she hadn't heard him. He was glad for a moment to become accustomed to what he was seeing, but he still couldn't believe it. She'd lost a great deal of weight since he'd seen her last, and she had been thin then. She looked sickly pale, almost dead. Was that the reality?

He was just thinking he should talk to Macy before he talked to Layla, but Macy moved past him into the room, saying, "You've got company, Layla. Look who came to see you!"

Layla opened her eyes and turned her head weakly on the pillow, catapulting Jayson into a series of difficult memories. "Oh, Jayson," she said, holding out her hand. "It's so good to see you!"

"It's good to see you too," he said, giving her the flowers.

"Oh, they're lovely!"

"He brought me some too," Macy bragged. She allowed Layla to admire them and breathe in their fragrance for a minute before she took them, saying, "I'll put them in a vase and place them right where you can see them."

"Thank you, dear," Layla said and turned her attention to Jayson again as he sat in a chair close to the bed. "You're so good to me," she said to Jayson. "I've been listening to your CDs. They keep my spirits up."

"I'm glad to hear it. I'll come back with my guitar sometime soon and play anything you want."

"That would be wonderful," she said and smiled. "I told Macy that I want you and Elizabeth to do all of the music at my funeral."

Jayson swallowed to keep from choking and tried not to appear as alarmed as he felt. He was grateful for Macy saying, "We're not talking about funerals today. You've had way too many blessings telling you that you're going to get better." She went on about that for a few minutes while Jayson noticed his daughter bustling around the room, and in and out of the attached bathroom, putting things in order and apparently tidying up from having helped her mother-in-law get cleaned up. "We've still got to believe in miracles," Macy concluded, sitting on the edge of the bed, opposite where Jayson was sitting.

"Your daughter is very good to me," Layla said to Jayson. "I can't even imagine what I would be doing without her."

"She's a one-in-a-million," Jayson said. He asked Layla about all of the kids, and enjoyed hearing her talk about something that was a distraction from her health. She asked him about his family, and they went through each of them, as well.

She started to look sleepy, and Macy said, "I think you'd better rest. He'll come back again soon, I promise."

"Yes, I will," Jayson said, "and I'll bring Elizabeth."

"I'll look forward to it," Layla said. She thanked him again for the visit and the flowers, then Macy told him she'd meet him in the front room after she'd helped Layla get to the bathroom and back to bed.

Jayson felt sick to his stomach as he sat on the couch and waited. He looked around and noticed that the house was tidy. He could see the kitchen from where he sat, and it too looked in order. Macy had obviously been very busy. Aaron worked all day every weekday, and he was also gone a number of evenings for school.

When Macy appeared, he could tell she'd brushed her hair, but she still looked frazzled and tired. He patted the couch beside him and she sat down. "Why didn't you tell us it was this bad?" he asked.

"I told you she wasn't getting better. She's always telling me that she doesn't want people to know she's sick; she doesn't want them feeling sorry for her."

"Well, that's just pride."

"Maybe. Maybe it's a desire for privacy."

"How long has it been since she's worked?"

"I don't know. Months."

"How is the family managing? On Aaron's income?"

"The family is getting some help from the government, and some from the Church. We're getting by."

"Getting by? Why didn't you say something?"

"We're getting by!"

"You should come to family for help first," he said. "I thought Layla was still working part-time. I had no idea it was this bad. What about medical bills?"

"She's qualified for government help with that; they're all covered."

He hurried on to the most important issue. "She looks half dead, Macy. Is that accurate? She's talking about her funeral. Is she dying?"

Macy started to cry. "I don't know. How could that many priesthood blessings be wrong? I understand that sometimes God's will isn't what people want. But she's been promised over and over that she would get well and her life would be long."

"I don't know, Macy. What's being done? In order for those blessings to work, we have to do everything we can."

"She's had so many doctors tell her they don't know what's wrong that I think she's given up. She's tired of the tests."

"Okay, but . . . how long has she been like *this?*" He motioned his hand absently toward the room where Layla was wasting away. "Has a doctor actually seen her looking like *this?*"

"No, I suppose not," Macy said.

"She looks like my mother did when the cancer had withered her down to almost nothing."

His comment encouraged her tears to increase. "Aaron and I have both suggested dozens of times in the last few weeks that we take her to the hospital, but like I said . . . I think she's given up. Aaron is so busy he can't think straight. He's horribly worried, but he doesn't know what to do."

"Well, *we* are not giving up that easily," Jayson said and stood up, walking down the hall.

"What are you going to do?" she demanded as if she feared he might do something extreme.

"We're taking her to the hospital. Get whatever you need; do what you've got to do. I'm not taking no for an answer."

Jayson sensed Macy's relief as she nudged Layla awake and said gently, "We're going to take you to the hospital. My dad insists." She looked at Macy, then at Jayson, but said nothing. He couldn't tell if she was too ill or too sleepy to protest, or whether she was relieved.

Jayson called Elizabeth and explained the situation while Macy helped Layla put a bathrobe over her pajamas. Macy took Jayson's car keys and he picked Layla up, following Macy out the front door, which she locked. Then they proceeded to the car. Jayson was stunned at how little Layla weighed, which increased his fear *and* his determination to see something done about it. At the hospital he carried Layla right into the ambulance entrance and made a few kind but firm requests, which immediately got Layla to a bed with the help of a sympathetic nurse. Within minutes they had an IV in her arm and someone taking a detailed medical history. Jayson was amazed at how much Macy knew about Layla's condition. She was spouting off the names of the tests and the diseases that had been eliminated, and the medications that had been tried. And she knew everything that had been done in an attempt to solve the problem. She held Layla's hand in hers while she helped her communicate with the nurses, tears of concern and compassion glistening in her eyes. Jayson felt scared for Layla *and* for Macy. But he also felt proud of her. His daughter was truly one-in-a-million.

CHAPTER 4

While Macy was still talking with the nurse, Jayson went to the nurses' station and started asking questions. He was kind and patient, but also firm on the fact that he wanted a diagnostic specialist who could figure out what was wrong with this woman before she died of whatever it was. They were helpful and courteous, but it didn't take him long to realize that this was not going to move nearly as quickly as he would have liked. Still, Layla was now under medical supervision. Members of the emergency-room staff had acknowledged how seriously ill she was, and she had been officially admitted while they were looking for a doctor who might be able to help her.

Soon after Layla had been moved from the ER into a regular room, Jayson turned around in the hall to find Elizabeth there. He hugged her tightly. "What did you do with the kids?"

"I called my father, of course. How is she?"

"I don't think it's good," he said and told her everything he knew.

They went into the room where Layla was sleeping, and Elizabeth put a hand over her mouth to hold back her emotion when she saw Layla looking so skeletal. "Good heavens," she whispered. "She looks like she's dying of malnutrition."

"Yes, she does, doesn't she? What would do that?"

"If only we knew . . ."

Jayson and Elizabeth stayed there until Aaron came. He tearfully expressed his gratitude to Jayson for taking some action, admitting that he'd been scared but just hadn't known what to do. Together Jayson and Aaron gave Layla a blessing, and once again she was told that answers would be found and she would recover. Jayson admitted to Elizabeth on the way home that he believed it truly would take a miracle to make that possible.

Jayson had just climbed into bed when Macy called to give him an update. She'd gone back to the hospital to take Layla some of her things, and she'd taken the flowers Jayson had brought. She'd spoken to the Relief Society president, and arrangements had been made for some meals to be brought in so that Macy could spend more time at the hospital. Jayson suggested that she also take some time to rest so that she didn't make herself sick, which would make her useless to anyone. Macy thanked Jayson for his intervention; he just assured her that he'd only been listening to that still, small voice and trying to do what it told him to do.

"Can we talk?" she asked when he'd thought she would say good night so she could get some sleep.

"Of course, baby," he said. "What's on your mind?" He kissed Elizabeth and left the room with the phone so that Elizabeth could get some sleep.

"I guess now that the situation isn't right in my face, I've been able to acknowledge something I've been thinking a lot about but I haven't really wanted to look at too closely."

"What's that?" he asked, noting that she'd become very emotional.

"What you said today about . . . Layla looking the way Grandma did . . . with her cancer."

"Yes?"

"I've been thinking about Grandma a lot while I've been helping Layla. And I've realized that I missed all of that. I should have been there when she was dying." She sobbed, and Jayson started to cry himself. "I should have been there for her . . . for you . . ." It took her a minute to calm down enough to speak. "I didn't know until she was already gone."

"I know," Jayson said.

"I remember crying when I found out, but I was living with that . . . *creep* who would yell at me if I cried, and . . . I don't think I ever really grieved over losing her. Now . . . with all this, I think it's just hitting me, and . . ." Again she sobbed. "I miss her so much, Dad. She was so good to me. She took such good care of me when Debbie was being a complete idiot."

"I know," Jayson said. "I miss her too. You go ahead and grieve all you need to, baby. I'm here as much as you need. But I don't want you feeling any guilt or regret over what happened. What's done is done. Your reasons for being away were complicated, and we've both dealt with all of that. Don't confuse that with needing to mourn the death of your grandmother."

"Okay," she said, sounding more calm.

They talked for nearly two hours about memories of Leslie Wolfe. Macy wanted to know more details of what the cancer and death had been like from Jayson's perspective. Macy finally needed to get some sleep, utterly exhausted for a number of reasons. Jayson suggested that she take a good, long nap tomorrow and that she call him if she needed anything.

A week later, there were still no answers concerning Layla. She was doing better under hospital care, the most significant improvement a result of the IVs that were sustaining her better than actual food. She'd seen two specialists who were baffled with the variety of symptoms, and she'd received three more priesthood blessings. Layla's bishop had arranged for a ward fast on her behalf, and Elizabeth had spread the word to many people in their ward as well who were more than willing to participate, even though they didn't personally know this woman.

The day after the fast, Macy called to say that Layla seemed worse, and they were all afraid that an answer wasn't going to be found. She asked if Jayson and Elizabeth could come to the hospital and if he could bring his guitar. He gladly agreed, feeling sick at the thought of actually having to do music for Layla's funeral. He thought of how traumatized he'd been by his mother's death. But he'd been a grown man. What would the children do? How would Macy and Aaron handle it? He couldn't even imagine!

Jayson and Elizabeth sat in Layla's hospital room, along with Aaron and Macy, and did several quiet songs that wouldn't disturb other patients. Layla was utterly pleased, and Macy and Aaron both commented on how encouraging it was to see her in such good spirits. When they were getting ready to leave, Layla took Jayson's hand and said, "Would you help Aaron give me a blessing?"

"I'd be happy to," Jayson said, at the same time feeling discouraged at the prospect of saying the same things she'd heard over and over.

"I just felt like I should ask," Layla said. "I keep thinking about the Lord's timing. I know it's said that we need to trust the Lord's will, but also His timing. I've been praying to accept both. I don't think I'm supposed to die yet." She started to cry. "I'm praying that perhaps something might change, and the answers will come. It feels to *me* like maybe something has shifted, but maybe that's just my imagination. Anyway, I'd like another blessing, if that's okay."

"I'm honored," Jayson said.

Aaron asked Jayson if he would speak the majority of the blessing. He reluctantly agreed and uttered a silent prayer that his words would be guided, and he felt prompted to ask Elizabeth to offer a prayer before the blessing. She prayed that the fasting and prayers of many people would be heard on Layla's behalf, and that they would be guided to the answers. She asked that the Spirit would guide the words of the blessing and that Layla and her family would be comforted and strengthened through this ongoing trial.

When Jayson began the blessing, he heard himself saying that the staff of life, which was beneficial to the health of most people, was toxic to Layla, and her health would return when that toxin was removed from her body. And then he said little else; the blessing was very brief. When it was over, Macy was the first to ask, "What does that mean?"

"I don't know," Jayson insisted. "I just said what I felt like I was supposed to say."

"Could this be a food allergy?" Elizabeth asked. "That's what it sounded like to me. Has that ever come up?"

"No," Layla said. "Could it really be as simple as that?"

"I'd say it's a good question to ask your doctor."

Layla looked thoughtful, then said, "The staff of life. Isn't that what they call wheat?"

"Yes," Macy and Elizabeth said at the same time.

"But it could be metaphorical," Jayson said.

"It gives us something to think about," Macy said, "which is more than we've had for a long time."

On the way home, Elizabeth said, "Could that be it? Could that really be it?"

"I have no idea. If that *is* the problem, I wonder why no doctor has thought of it before now. It seems so simple."

"Maybe they've been talking to the wrong kind of doctor."

"Maybe."

The evening became swallowed up with more than the average challenges with the kids, and Jayson didn't talk to Macy again before they went to bed. The phone rang a few minutes after seven the following morning, and he heard Macy say with excitement in her voice, "I think we may have found it."

"What?"

"Aaron and I were up a long time looking on the Internet. We actually found it late last night, but we didn't want to wake you. Listen to this."

"Wait a second. Let me put you on speaker phone so your mother can hear." He pushed the button. "Okay, go ahead."

"You know what gluten is?" Macy asked.

"It's in wheat," Elizabeth said, sharing an amazed glance with Jayson.

"It's in wheat, rye, and barley," Macy said. "Now listen to this. It's from a website about this disease. 'Celiac disease, also known as gluten intolerance, is a genetic disorder that affects one in 133 Americans. Symptoms of Celiac Disease can range from the classic features, such as diarrhea, weight loss, and malnutrition, to latent symptoms such as isolated nutrient deficiencies but no gastrointestinal symptoms . . . Because of the broad range of symptoms Celiac Disease presents, it can be difficult to diagnose. The symptoms can range from mild weakness and bone pain, to chronic diarrhea, abdominal bloating, and progressive weight loss.'"

"Good heavens," Elizabeth said.

"Yeah," Macy actually laughed. "Now, get this. I called a nurse on the night shift, and she talked to a gastroenterologist that was on call; basically a stomach doctor. He said the symptoms fit, and she's scheduled for a test later this morning where they scope the stomach and upper intestines and take a biopsy. There's some blood tests that determine if you have the genetic marker, but only the biopsy can tell them for sure if she's got the disease."

"And if this is it," Elizabeth asked, "what can be done?"

"She just has to stop eating gluten. That's it."

"That's it?" Jayson asked.

"Yeah," Macy went on, "but from what I'm reading, that's not so easy. It's in *everything*, and you have to be really strict. It will be a big lifestyle change, but if this is the answer, it will save her life."

"That's incredible," Jayson said.

"It is," Macy said and then got emotional. "If this is it, we're so grateful, but . . ."

"What is it?" Elizabeth asked.

"I just think of the stuff she's been eating. She hasn't had much appetite, but the things she's been eating a lot of are like . . . Cream of

Wheat, and toast, and crackers. We've been doing easy meals like pizza and spaghetti, and . . . it's like we've been poisoning her while we've been praying that she'd get better."

"Who would have known?" Elizabeth asked. "You can't blame yourself."

"I know, and I'm not. It just makes me kind of sick to think of it now. Anyway, I'll keep you up to date. I should go. Thanks for everything. I love you both."

"We love you too," Jayson said, and they ended the call.

A few days later, Layla finally had an official diagnosis. The results of the tests were absolutely clear. She *did* have Celiac Disease. It was an autoimmune disease triggered by the presence of even a molecule of gluten in her body—which meant she had to entirely eliminate anything from her diet derived from wheat, barley, or rye—or anything that had come in contact with them. The diet restrictions were rigorous, and it was going to be a tough adjustment. But Layla was thrilled to have some answers, and the hope of getting better. Macy was helping her study all that she needed to learn, and had made a plan to reorganize the kitchen. The doctor had said it could take months, or even years, to get back to normal, but not having to worry and wonder any longer was a great blessing. Layla had come home from the hospital, and was voraciously reading and studying to learn everything she could about what she had and what to do about it. When it became evident that all of the gluten-free foods, cookbooks, and other materials were going to be expensive, Macy graciously accepted Jayson and Elizabeth's help in getting Layla started with what she would need. Jayson had also made an anonymous contribution through Layla's bishop to help meet the family's needs. He didn't want even Macy to know the source, and the bishop agreed.

Each time Jayson talked to Macy, she was freshly astonished over what she and Layla were learning together, and she was keeping very busy. But he was glad to hear that Macy was in good spirits over the matter, and especially glad to hear that a solution had been found.

* * * * *

Another story hit the tabloids, but it was mostly repetitive of the last one, focusing on the fact that Debbie was in rehab and implying that Jayson was visiting her and sneaking drugs in. There was a picture that was several years old on the cover. It was of Jayson going through the door of the clinic in Los Angeles where he'd gone to see his personal physician when he lived there. The headline implied that it was him going to see Debbie in rehab. He was able to let this one roll off a little easier than last time, but it still bugged him.

When Jayson and Elizabeth needed to make a trip to Los Angeles, and he knew they would be spending some time in the limelight, he feared that the tabloids would find a way to mix it into the problem. But he tried not to think about it, and was glad to know he would have Elizabeth at his side whenever he would be in view of a camera. The purpose for their visit was the annual Grammy Awards. Jayson wasn't nominated for any awards, since he hadn't released anything for a few years. But he'd been asked to present an award, and the record company wanted him to take the opportunity since it was good PR. On the brink of releasing a new album, they wanted the music community and the television audience to remember him and his music. They'd originally asked him to present along with a young female artist who was known for her foul mouth and immodest manner of dress. The last thing Jayson wanted was to walk out onstage in front of America with this woman on his arm. He didn't complain about the situation; he just asked if he could have his brother present with him. Since Drew was known as a great drummer—and Jayson's brother—they agreed. Elizabeth and Valerie would be going, as well. Jayson was grateful for an opportunity to be seen in public with his wife.

Jayson and Elizabeth left the children in the care of Will and Marilyn and flew to LAX, where Drew picked them up at the airport. They had a few hours to spend visiting with Drew and Valerie before they needed to get ready for the big event. Jayson and Drew wore classic tuxedos, and the ladies wore glamorous dresses that they would probably never wear again. Valerie's was lavender and covered with sequins. Elizabeth's was dark blue, with sequins and beads on the jacket that was worn over a long, silky skirt. A limo provided by the record company picked them up, all for the sake of appearances. Once in the elaborate vehicle, Jayson said to his brother, "We haven't done *this* for a long time."

"Just like the good old days," Drew said with mild sarcasm. When they'd been with Gray Wolfe, trying to get their career to soar and both living in Los Angeles, they had taken every possible PR opportunity, and this kind of thing had been more common. The majority of Jayson's memories of that time weren't good, and he preferred to focus on the present.

As the car pulled up in front of the red carpet, Jayson said, "Here we go, babe. Act like you love me."

"Do I have to act?" Elizabeth asked, sounding a little nervous. "Do I look okay?"

"You look fantastic!" he said, and the driver opened the door.

When Jayson got out of the car the crowds lining the red carpet went crazy. He felt a little taken aback, since he hadn't faced such a crowd in a while. He just smiled and waved and helped Elizabeth out of the car. He put his arm around her and started up the red carpet, hearing another cheer, which he knew was due to Drew getting out of the car.

The ceremony went well, even though Jayson felt relatively bored through a lot of it. He'd never been able to enjoy other people's music all that much when his own was in his head all the time. Even when he wasn't creating new music, strange montages of the old stuff just seemed to roll around in there. When he and Drew walked onstage to present an award, a portion of one of their top hits was being played, and the audience responded with a great deal of applause. They read from the teleprompter, presented the award, and returned to the audience to sit with their wives. Once they were back at Drew's house, it was great to get out of the formal wear and get a good night's sleep. The next day they just had some fun together before Jayson and Elizabeth flew home the following day.

"Maybe next year you'll be nominated for something," Elizabeth told him, "and we'll have to go again. I could wear the same dress, and it would get in the tabloids that I was tacky enough to wear it in public twice."

"How delightful!" he said and chuckled. "It is a nice dress," he added. "I think you and Leslie were the only ones wearing dresses that weren't embarrassing to look at. I could hardly make eye contact with any woman there."

"And I bet my dress cost a great deal less than most of them that had much less fabric."

"You are frugal *and* beautiful," he said and laughed. Sharing the music business with Elizabeth was just so much more fun than being in it without her.

A picture of him and Elizabeth *did* show up in the tabloids, but it wasn't on any covers, and it was accompanied with speculations over their public appearance as opposed to their private marriage problems while he was doing drugs and supplying them to his ex-wife, with whom he hadn't managed to sever his relationship. The whole thing made him angry, but he forced it away and focused on much more important things—like tickling his kids and kissing his wife as frequently as possible.

* * * * *

The following Sunday Jayson was getting ready for church when he realized that his hair was long enough to pull back into an elastic, which made him look a little more respectable. While he was doing so, Elizabeth commented on how good she thought it looked.

"I keep wondering if I should cut it," he said.

"But you don't."

"I don't know why I don't. Just lazy, I guess. Or maybe it's some subconscious defiance." He chuckled. "Maybe I'm just waiting for Sister Freedman to complain to the bishop about my hair."

"Well, I like it," Elizabeth said and kissed his cheek before she finished putting on her makeup.

After sacrament meeting it was nice to take both Derek and Harmony to the nursery, since Harmony had now passed the age of eighteen months. Jayson liked being able to sit all the way through Sunday School without having to take her out to the hall, but he had barely sat down in his class when he felt a tap on the shoulder. "Excuse me, Brother Wolfe," a sister said; he couldn't remember her name. "Our pianist in Primary was just called away due to an emergency with her mother. Do you think you could fill in?"

"I'd be happy to," he said and stood up to follow her.

In the hallway she said, "Sister Perkins told me I should find you; she seemed confident that you would be willing. Most pianists I've known couldn't do it without being able to practice the specific songs ahead of time."

"I might stumble a little," Jayson said with a smile, "but I can probably manage."

"Oh, that's very kind of you," she said, and they entered the Primary room where the leaders were just trying to get the children settled down. Jayson eased onto the bench where the Primary songbook was already opened to "I Am A Child of God." As he started to play, the children quickly quieted, and a mood of reverence prevailed. He enjoyed playing through both junior and senior Primary, and he managed with very few mistakes. The furthest thing from his mind was Sister Freedman, until later that day when she called Elizabeth to express her disdain about his playing the piano in Primary, and his poor example to the children—especially when he so badly needed a haircut.

"I knew it," Jayson said to Elizabeth when she repeated the conversation.

"Are you going to cut your hair?"

"No," he said. "Does that make me defiant?"

"Have your church leaders asked you to cut your hair?"

"No."

"Would you if they did?"

"Yes."

"Then that doesn't make you defiant. But I think Sister Freedman could use more than one lesson in being judgmental. I noticed that Clayton's hair is getting a little long."

"Yeah, she probably blames that on me," Jayson said.

"We need to just let it roll off," Elizabeth reminded him.

"I'm trying," he said with a forced smile, and he changed the subject. But the next day while he was running through each number he would perform on the tour, he found his thoughts continually intruded on by Sister Freedman's criticism and judgment. He stopped more than once to pray, but still felt assaulted by her fiery darts catapulting around in his mind. He finally put the music aside and went to find Elizabeth. The children had just gone down for naps, and he found Elizabeth lying down in the bedroom. If Elizabeth was nothing else, she was strict about the children's nap time. She'd declared that she didn't really care if they slept or not, but they had to stay in their beds during this time of the afternoon. They usually *did* sleep, because their mother had made it clear that she wasn't going to come and get them. She knew they were safe, and she knew she could be a better mother if she had a couple of uninterrupted hours in the afternoon. Jayson had noticed that this was often the time of day when problems got solved and necessary conversations took place, which made him very grateful for Elizabeth's rules on nap time. Occasionally she just did what she needed most, and today that was to get some rest herself. Snuggling up next to her, Jayson talked it all through—again—and she offered the same compassion and gentle advice that she'd offered many times before.

When he was all talked out, Elizabeth kissed him, and it had a calming effect. He urged her to kiss him again and passion crept into it. "Oh, Lady," he murmured and took her face into his hands. As their eyes met, he felt a hundred memories come to his mind in an instant, and the breadth and depth of the lifetime they'd shared struck him, filling him with awe and gratitude, overflowing in the words that came through his lips with no premeditation. "I imagined this moment the moment I saw you, but I never could have truly imagined it." He saw tears in Elizabeth's eyes and asked, "What kind of tears are these?"

"It's just . . . sometimes when you talk like that, it's so . . ." Elizabeth wondered how to explain that it wasn't just the eloquent way such beautiful words came together so naturally for him, but combined with the way they flowed off his tongue with a subtle rhythm, there was an underlying nuance of music even in the way he spoke. She had to settle for her standard, "You're talking like a songwriter. I love it when you do."

"I can't help it."

"I know. That's why I love it."

He kissed her again, a warm and lengthy kiss that deepened his gratitude for having her in his life, a kiss that further soothed his aching spirit. He whispered close to her ear, "Your love is my breath and your life is the beat of my heart." He kissed her again. "It fills me completely and spills so repletely into every moment of the life and the love that we share."

"Wow!" she laughed softly. "Are you writing this down?"

He laughed as well. "I'd better, huh." He kissed her. "Don't . . . move." He turned away and reached for the pad and pencil he always kept on the bedside table for just such moments. He quickly scribbled the words down while he repeated them aloud, and Elizabeth helped him remember exactly how he'd said it.

"Did you really?" she asked.

"What?"

"Imagine such a moment the moment you saw me?"

"Yes. I think I imagined a lifetime," he said thoughtfully. "Ooh," he added and wrote that down, too. Once that was done, he commenced kissing her again, so glad to know that she was his forever, and he didn't have to stop with a kiss.

* * * * *

Jayson held Elizabeth close to him, counting his blessings and feeling certain that he could take on whatever life might dish out. The contrast to his emotions an hour ago was remarkable. He glanced at the clock and asked, "How long do you think the children will sleep?"

"Hard to say."

He pressed a kiss into her hair and chuckled. "I love nap time."

"Me too." They heard the front door open and close, and Elizabeth added, "But Trevin's home."

"Do you think he'll notice that we're missing?"

"He'll probably just hurry to his room to play that silly guitar; that's what he usually does. He probably won't even . . ."

A knock at the bedroom door stopped her. "Dad, are you in there?" Trevin asked.

"Yeah?" Jayson hollered. "What do you need?"

Apparently Trevin took that as an invitation to enter the room when they could hear him trying the doorknob to find it locked.

"I'll be out in a few minutes," Jayson called.

"Okay," Trevin said, sounding confused.

Jayson got dressed and left Elizabeth to rest a while longer while the babies miraculously continued their nap. He found Trevin in the kitchen, pouring himself a glass of juice and looking mildly distressed.

"What's up?" Jayson asked.

He realized how well Trevin had been taught to be straightforward when he asked, "Why was the door locked?"

Jayson almost felt like they'd reversed roles and he'd been caught doing something inappropriate. His response was simply, "Excuse me?"

"I'm just wondering why the door was locked. I mean . . . if the door is shut, I always knock before I come in. You know that. So why would you lock it?"

"Because we needed complete privacy," he said without apology. "You've never found our bedroom door locked before?"

"I don't know. I don't remember."

"But today it's an issue?"

"I'm just wondering."

"Your mother and I are married, Trevin. It's not unreasonable to think that there are times when we would need complete privacy. It's a fact of life."

"Fact of life?" Trevin echoed, almost sounding alarmed. "Are you talking about . . ." He couldn't finish.

Jayson considered the implication and the way he felt about appropriate communication between parents and teens—especially with the sensitive topics. He hurried to say, "What do you think I'm talking about, Trev? I know you know what I'm talking about because we've discussed it before. What did you think I meant when I said that what two people share in a marriage is one of the greatest experiences in this life? Did you not suspect that such things were going on in *this* marriage when Derek and Harmony are a part of our family?"

"Well, yeah . . . but . . ."

"But what? Why do you seem distressed, Trevin? Talk to me."

"I don't know. It just seems . . . weird. The middle of the afternoon? My own parents?"

"You make it sound like we're doing something wrong, something that's disappointing to you."

"I guess I just . . . never thought about it like that before. I had no idea that . . ."

"That what?" Jayson saved him from having to say whatever he didn't want to say and offered a simple clarification. "It's private and sacred, Trevin, so obviously we are discreet. It's between your mother and me. There are many reasons we might lock the bedroom door. Sometimes we just need to talk privately without interruptions. Sometimes one of us just needs to rest . . . or have a good cry, or something. The point is that it doesn't really matter why the door's locked because your mother and I are married, and any time we spend together privately is just between us."

"Sorry," Trevin said. "It's just . . . weird."

"Why is it weird?" Jayson asked with a chuckle that lightened the mood. When Trevin didn't answer, Jayson went on with what he strongly suspected was the problem. "Listen, Trev. Remember when we talked about this, and I told you that because sex is talked about so casually and crudely in the world today, it can distort our perceptions of the fact that in its proper time and place, it is one of the most wonderful gifts that God has given to us. I think it can be confusing when you're assaulted with that kind of talk everywhere you turn, no matter how hard you try to avoid situations where that happens. It's important to make a clear differentiation in your brain between what is inappropriate and unholy, and what is sacred and righteous—even though the topic at the heart of the issue is the same. Does that make sense?"

"Yes," Trevin said, and Jayson could see by the look in his eyes that this conversation was helping him more comfortably assess his own feelings.

"But it's still weird?"

"A little, I guess."

"Well, you're just going to have to trust me when I tell you that someday when you're married, it won't seem weird. In the meantime, stick to what you know is right and remember the things we've talked about and you'll be just fine. Now, what did you need?"

"What?"

"Why did you want to talk to me the minute you got home from school?"

"Oh, it's about Clayton."

"What about him?"

"I'm worried about him, but I don't know what to do."

"Why are you worried?" Jayson asked, already feeling a little sick. At such moments he realized how much energy he put into his concern for Clayton Freedman.

"He's just . . . hanging around more and more with kids that aren't a good influence. They're not the really obvious defiants, the ones who want everyone to know they're into creepy stuff. These kids look like good kids, and when they're home with their parents, or at church, they probably act like good kids, and they probably take pride in faking everybody out. But they cuss a lot, and around their friends they brag about all the bad stuff they're doing."

"And that's Clayton's new crowd?"

"Apparently," Trevin said, his voice heavy. "I wish I knew what to do."

"There probably isn't anything you *can* do beyond what you're already doing. You can pray for him, and you can be open to any opportunity to let him know that you care. The Spirit will let you know if there's anything else to be done."

"I guess I knew that," Trevin said. "I just needed to hear it." His vehemence over the situation became evident with the way he added, "It just ticks me off. I don't want him to do something really stupid and mess up his life."

"We can keep praying that doesn't happen," Jayson said and impulsively gave Trevin a tight hug. "I'm sure grateful that you're who you are, that you're such a good kid. Stay that way."

"I promise," he said and chuckled. "But don't be hugging me like that in front of the guys."

Jayson knew he was teasing, and that he probably wouldn't protest even if Jayson *did* try to hug him in front of the guys. But he said, "No, we wouldn't want anyone to know that you're related to a scandalous rock star."

"Or maybe we do," Trevin said, but he left the room without further comment.

The following day, Jayson did something that he had put off too long. He took Trevin to buy a new bass guitar, honoring the deal that they would each pay half. Obviously Jayson could afford to buy his son a guitar, but he knew it was good for Trevin to earn what he got, and he would likely respect the instrument more because he had personally worked for it. They picked out one that they both agreed was the best choice for the money, then they had a good time visiting with the salesman, who had recognized Jayson after he saw the name on the debit card.

As soon as they got home, Jayson and Trevin went to the studio to try out the newest addition. After doing a couple of songs together, they both agreed that it was a fine instrument and that Trevin was getting better all the time.

A couple of days later, Jayson was in the sound booth pondering more than doing any work. Trevin found him there and sat in one of the other chairs. "What're ya doing?" he asked.

"Imagining," Jayson said with drama, then added, "what it's going to look like on stage. They want my input on the special effects."

"Cool," Trevin said and asked Jayson about his ideas. They talked for nearly half an hour before Trevin changed his tone and mood completely. "Can I ask you something?"

"Sure, anything."

"You don't have to answer if you don't want to; I'll understand."

Jayson felt suspicious but said, "I don't believe I have anything to hide, but if I don't want to answer, I'll tell you."

"Okay," Trevin said and became visibly nervous. "The thing is . . . it's about the tabloids."

Jayson steeled himself and stretched his neck in anticipation of a certain blow. "Okay," he drawled. "What about the tabloids?"

"I've heard some kids talking about it."

"Are these kids that know you're—"

"No, they don't know we're connected. It's weird; I feel like some kind of spy or something when I just happen to hear people start talking about you. Of course, there *are* kids at school who know you're my dad, so I guess the rest of them'll figure it out eventually. In the meantime, I'll just keep spying."

"Okay," Jayson said again.

"I'm sure it wouldn't surprise you to hear that sometimes the way kids talk at school is pretty disgusting."

"No, that wouldn't surprise me," Jayson said, but he wasn't liking the mention of it in context with him and the tabloids.

"I just try to avoid the kids that talk like that, but some of it's . . ."

"Unavoidable, I know."

"The things is . . . today I heard a couple of guys talking about you. One of them said, 'He's a Mormon, right?' And the other one said, 'Yeah, but if this is what he's doing now, I wonder what he was doing *before* he was a Mormon.'"

Jayson swallowed and looked away, hoping Trevin wouldn't see how upset he felt to think of people—kids who went to school with his son—talking about him like that. But Trevin said, "Sorry. Maybe I shouldn't have brought it up. I guess you didn't need to know that."

"Or maybe I do," Jayson said, and annoying tears sprang to the surface. "Wow," he said. "That bites."

"Yeah, I felt a little sick myself," he said. "I wanted to defend you, but . . . these guys don't even know me, and . . ."

"It's okay," Jayson said. "Sometimes it's best to just stay silent and know what we know."

"I guess that's what I want to ask you."

"What?"

"I know what you're like now, but I *don't* know what you were like before you joined the Church . . . or I should say before you came to live with us when Grandpa was here. I know your music was always good, but I know you didn't have the gospel in your life, and I know what a lot of the people are like who work in the business, and . . . well . . ." His nervousness increased. "There's a certain reputation that goes with being in a famous rock band, and . . ."

"And you're just wondering if I lived up to that reputation back when I didn't know any better? The whole 'drugs, sex, and rock and roll' thing."

Trevin fidgeted in his seat a little. "I guess that's it. But it's not that I would think any less of you, and like I said, if you don't want to tell me, you don't have to. Once you were baptized none of that stuff matters anyway. I just don't want to ever get in a situation where I *do* try to defend you, and say something that's not true. I don't have a problem with telling someone that your life before you joined the Church may not have been so great, but it's great now, and . . . I'm sorry if this is sounding lame, or—"

"It's not lame, Trevin. And I would far rather have you talking to me about it . . . asking me up front . . . as opposed to wondering. The last thing I want is to put you in any more of an awkward situation than you're already in. And it could get worse before it gets better. I wouldn't want you to say something to somebody and then have them find proof that it wasn't true. That *would* be awkward." He let out a long, slow sigh. "First let me say that I made some mistakes when I was younger; I wasn't perfect. But there is only one in particular that I truly regret. It's not the kind of thing that would have ever hit the tabloids, because it was private and personal, and . . . well . . ." he chuckled, "I wasn't famous at the time."

"So, what great wisdom did you learn from your one greatest regret?" Trevin asked, slightly facetious. "What words of caution can you pass on to your son so that he can avoid the same pitfalls?"

Jayson simply said, "Don't mess around with sex outside of marriage even a little bit. It can get out of hand so fast that you hardly know what hit you. I got carried away *once,* and even though we didn't go all the way, I've regretted it and struggled because of it more than I could ever put into words."

Trevin looked a little taken aback but said, "Okay. I already knew that rule, but . . . when you put it that way . . . I'll be extra careful on that count."

"You do that," Jayson said with a smile.

"And that's your only regret?"

"That's the only one that isn't all over the Internet." He sighed again. "I am glad to be able to tell you that I never lived up to that rock star reputation. So, let's keep it in simple terms. I know you've probably heard a lot of this, but I just want to make it clear." Trevin nodded, seeming pleased. "I always believed in God, and I believed that if I wanted His blessings, I needed to try to be a good person. The only drug problem I ever had was with the prescription drugs. That's what the rehab was about. I never touched street drugs. I never smoked. I never touched any liquor; never, not once. My father was an alcoholic, and I considered the stuff evil. Now for the other part of that reputation, I am very glad to be able to tell you that there have only been two women in my life. My ex-wife and my wife." He chuckled. "I have to say . . . once I *did* become famous, the opportunities were everywhere. Some of those girls out there are crazy! But I had good security and good morals. There isn't any more to tell."

Trevin smiled. "That's what I thought. But I'm glad to know."

"Okay," Jayson said, gratified with the conversation, and deeply grateful for the choices of his life that made it possible to look his son in the eye and be able to truthfully say all he'd just said. He tried not to think about what other people were saying and thinking of him. As long as his loved ones knew the truth, he had to be content with that.

CHAPTER 5

The conversation shifted to more comfortable topics until Trevin left to go to the mall with some friends. That evening when all was quiet, Jayson shared the conversation with Elizabeth. She shared his sentiments on every point, but she did say, "I can't believe you told him about us . . . and our big mistake."

"I didn't tell him it was *us*. But maybe I shouldn't have said it. It felt right at the time, but maybe I shouldn't admit such things to your son."

"Our son," she said.

"Yes, he's our son. But he started out yours and you turned him over to me with the trust that I would do a good job of being a father to him."

"And you are."

"Am I?"

"Yes, Jayson. I'm not questioning your ability to be a good father. And I'm not questioning what you told him. If it felt right at the time, then it probably was. Maybe the conviction he heard in what you said will help him one day when temptation hits him—which is probably inevitable for most kids, right?"

"I would think so."

"So, it's done. It's in the past. We made a mistake and we learned from it. We are living proof that repentance is possible."

"Yes, we are," he said. After a long moment's thought, he added, "I hate to think of what Trevin—or the other kids as they get older—might have to face because of my questionable career."

"Your career is not questionable. It just comes with . . . fringe bene-fits." Her sarcasm was followed by a little chuckle. "Worrying about something like that isn't going to make it any better. Trevin's a good kid, and he's strong. He'll handle whatever comes up just fine. You think he's the only kid in town who gets flack over a parent's career? It's a part of growing up. The unique nature of our situation doesn't mean that dealing with it is that much different than what other kids face."

"Okay, you're probably right," he said, and the conversation was dropped.

A few days later, Roger stopped by on Saturday morning to bring some warm cinnamon rolls his wife had baked. Jayson was just coming in from clearing away a fresh snowfall when he arrived, and everyone fussed over the rolls. Addie ate one quickly and ran off to play. Once Jayson had shed his boots, coat, and gloves, he sat at the dining room table to visit with Roger. He supervised Harmony with her breakfast while Elizabeth was cleaning up the kitchen. Trevin was sitting at the table helping Derek put on his snow clothes so they could go out and take advantage of the new snow and build a snowman.

In the middle of the conversation, Roger said to Elizabeth, "You two have known each other a long time, haven't you?"

"Forever," Elizabeth said as if it had been a great burden.

Jayson chuckled. "She deserves some kind of award for putting up with me all these years."

"How many years?" Roger asked.

"Since we were sixteen," Jayson said. "We were high-school sweethearts."

"So, if I admit how many years, then you'll know how old I am," Elizabeth said.

"I don't need to know that," Roger said with a chuckle. "You're both the same age, then?"

"No," Jayson said as if he were offended, "Elizabeth is much older than I am."

She laughed. "Yes, I'm so much older that we were both in the same grade in school."

"Wow, that's weird," Roger said. "I didn't meet Elaine until after my mission. I can't imagine what it would have been like to know her in high school."

Jayson said, "Right after I moved to Oregon, I saw Elizabeth in a school play. She was amazing. It was love at first sight."

While Roger talked about falling in love with his wife, Jayson noticed that Trevin seemed uneasy, and he wondered if something had been said in the conversation to make him feel that way. Trevin stood up and took Derek outside, but Jayson knew he needed to find an opportunity to talk to his son. After Roger left, Jayson told Elizabeth that he sensed something was bugging Trevin. They both agreed that they needed to try to find out what it was and not let it go, and they would watch for the right moment.

Jayson got bundled up again and went out to help make the snowman and to take some pictures. It wasn't until after lunch that Trevin found Jayson lying on the couch in the living room with a magazine open over his chest. He'd been reading and had gotten tired, but he wasn't asleep when Trevin asked quietly if he was.

"Just resting my eyes," he said without opening them. "What's up?"

"Can we talk?" he asked. He'd likely noticed that the babies were down for naps and that Addie had gone to play at a friend's house.

Jayson opened his eyes and turned to see Trevin sitting on the other couch, his legs stretched out. "Of course," he said and sat up, grateful that Trevin had come to him, as opposed to Jayson needing to seek out a conversation. "What's on your mind?"

"I just have a question for you," Trevin said.

"Okay, shoot," Jayson said.

"You and Mom were high-school sweethearts."

"That's right," Jayson said, ready to pause the conversation and go find Elizabeth. "That's never been a secret around here, *or* in the tabloids."

"So . . . like you told Roger earlier . . . the two of you have been close a long time."

"Closer at some times than others," Jayson said, wondering why Trevin would seem so agitated. Feeling a strong need to have Elizabeth there, he stood up and walked toward the kitchen.

"Where are you going?"

"To get your mother," he said. "This conversation obviously involves her, so I think she should be here, as opposed to our talking about her behind her back and—"

"I don't *want* to talk to Mom about this," Trevin protested, sounding more like a typical teenager than he had in a long time.

"That's too bad," Elizabeth said, coming into the room from the hall where she had obviously been listening. Jayson went back to the couch, and Elizabeth sat beside him. "What's on your mind, Trev? Whatever it is, we're your parents, and we need to talk about it together."

Trevin hesitated, looking both angry and afraid. Jayson and Elizabeth exchanged a discreet glance of concern, wondering what could be so difficult.

Jayson took a turn at trying to urge him to open up. "If something's bothering you, we need to know what it is and talk about it, because we're not going to have unspoken feelings that cause tension around here. So, say what you have to say and let's get it over with. We all ought to be mature enough to handle whatever you need to say, but we need to know why you're apparently so angry."

"Did I say I was angry?" Trevin asked, sounding snotty.

"You don't have to," Elizabeth said gently.

"Okay, fine," Trevin said. "Did my father know?"

"Know what?" Elizabeth asked. Whatever the problem might be, Jayson wondered why *he'd* suddenly lost *father* status in this conversation. Of course, there was no other way for Trevin to refer to Robert Aragon, because the man *was* Trevin's father. But there were moments when it felt like twisting the knife.

Trevin's nervousness increased so dramatically that Jayson felt panicked. He thought of how he'd admitted to Trevin about his one regret, and he wondered if this had to do with that. Either way, it was in the past, and it was none of Trevin's business—or anyone else's.

Following a stretch of excruciating silence, Trevin finally said, "There's just something I need to know." He looked less angry and more like he was trying not to cry as he said, "I have to know . . . and please don't lie to me."

"We would never lie to you," Elizabeth said.

"Okay, but . . ." the boy's chin quivered, "I can understand why you might think that some things would be better left unsaid, or if it might be better that I didn't know."

"What are you getting at, Trevin?" Jayson asked. "It's obviously very upsetting for you, and you need to tell us what's wrong. Has someone said something about me . . . or us . . . that's got you . . ." He stopped when Trevin looked alarmed. Jayson blew out a slow breath and counted to ten. "Someone *did* say something? Is this about gossip?"

"Let's just say somebody said something that wasn't a big deal. I didn't think anything of it at first, but . . . I've just been . . . thinking . . . putting pieces together, and . . . I just have to know . . ." He cleared his throat and blurted it out very quickly, as if that was the only way to get it in the open. "Did you two have an affair? Are you my real father? Is that why I'm so much like you?"

Jayson was so stunned he could hardly breathe. He felt Elizabeth take his hand in a nearly painful grip and was relieved when she said firmly, "No, Trevin. No! Why would you think such a thing?" Trevin was apparently struggling with his composure too much to speak, and Jayson wondered how heavily this had been weighing on him. "Listen to me, Trevin. *Nothing* inappropriate *ever* happened between Jayson and me while I was married to your father. *Nothing! Ever!* Do you understand?" Trevin nodded. "Our relationship was unusual, but throughout those years we truly were just friends . . . like a brother and sister. We both respected our marriage relationships. Always! Do you understand?" Trevin nodded again, seeming more calm. Again Elizabeth asked, "Why would you think something like that?"

"I . . . don't know," he said.

"When you were a kid and Jayson came to visit, or you heard me talking to him on the phone, or . . . anything . . . did you ever hear or see anything that would make you think that something strange was going on? That made you uncomfortable?"

"No, never," Trevin said.

"Then . . . what?"

"I don't know," Trevin said and leaned forward, pressing his head into his hands, and it was evident he'd started to cry. "I just . . . I don't know. When it occurred to me that it was possible, I just . . . felt so surprised, but then . . . I felt angry. I'm not even sure why. And one thought led to another, and . . . I'm sorry."

"Okay," Jayson said, "I really need to know what somebody said that got you thinking things that led to this conclusion."

Trevin looked nervous. "I was hoping we could avoid that."

Jayson felt nervous too. After what Trevin had just said, what would he be hoping to avoid? "Just say it," Jayson said, already betting that it had something to do with Sister Freedman.

His suspicions were confirmed immediately when Trevin said, "Clayton told me that his mother said . . ."

When he hesitated, Jayson said, "Do the two of you ever talk about anything besides what his mother says about me?"

"Yes, but . . . it almost always comes up. She's really got it in for you."

"You think?" Jayson said. "Go on. *What* did she say this time?"

"Apparently she's been reading all about you on the Internet, and she knows more about you than anyone—at least according to what's on the Internet."

"This is insane!" Elizabeth said, wondering if Sister Freeman recognized her own hypocrisy in being obsessed with a person that she considered evil. "What did she say?" she pressed.

"She told Clayton that with as long as the two of you had known each other, she seriously doubted that you had *only* been friends while you'd been married to other people."

"I'm gonna kill her," Elizabeth said, sounding more angry than Jayson had heard in a long time.

He put a hand on her arm, surprised at his own ability to remain calm. "You're not going to kill her." He said to Trevin, "Your mother is not capable of murder; honest."

"It's a figure of speech!" Elizabeth growled.

"We know, babe. But let me offer some of your own advice. We need to let it roll off." He felt like a hypocrite saying it when he was fuming below the surface. The fact that this woman's idle gossip was causing so much grief for his own son made him *really* angry. But he was handling it better than Elizabeth at the moment, and one of them had to remain calm—especially with Trevin in the room.

Both their attentions turned to the boy when they realized he was really upset. "I'm so sorry," he said. "I shouldn't have believed it. I shouldn't have let it get to me. I can see now how stupid it is, but . . ."

Jayson and Elizabeth both stood at the same time and crossed the room to sit on either side of Trevin. They each put a hand on his back and Elizabeth said, "It's okay, son. We're just glad that you talked to us about it instead of letting it eat at you."

"Yeah, me too," he said with a chuckle and wiped his hand over his face to dry his tears. He turned toward Elizabeth and gave her a hug while they remained sitting. "I'm sorry, Mom . . . for jumping to conclusions like that."

"It's okay," she said.

He turned to Jayson and hugged him too. "I'm so sorry, Dad." Jayson drew that last word into himself and silently thanked God for helping them resolve this so quickly.

"It's really okay, Trev. I don't want you to ever stop coming to talk to me."

"I won't," he said and sniffled, easing out of the hug to wipe his face on his sleeve. "I don't look anything like my father, you know."

"No, you look like your mother's brother, more than anyone," Jayson said.

Trevin turned to Elizabeth, "Bradley looked like him; like our father."

"Yes, he did," she said. "But that's not so unusual for siblings to look dramatically different. Jayson and Drew don't look alike."

"No, I guess they don't."

The conversation lightened, and Trevin left to go down to his room. He said he needed some time alone. He apologized once more before he left. After he was gone, neither Jayson nor Elizabeth said a word for a couple of minutes.

"I cannot believe that woman," Elizabeth said. "It's like she just . . . throws a match on a gasoline spill, planting ideas of infidelity in people's minds. I can't even imagine how that would feel for Trevin to think that our relationship had been that way." She shuddered visibly. "Oh, my gosh!"

"I'm glad we were able to tell him the right answers," Jayson said. "If anything inappropriate *had* occurred during your marriage, that could have been hard to face up to. I suspect it wouldn't have gotten resolved in one conversation. A year of family counseling, maybe."

"It's just so weird," she said. "It's like Satan just . . ." She hesitated and turned to look at him.

"What?"

"Is that what this is?"

"What?" he asked more loudly.

"Satan can't get to you from the outside, so he's going to try to get to you in your own family. And Sister Freedman is helping plant the seeds. A little confusion, some anger, strange thoughts, questions."

Jayson took it in and felt a little sick. "You're the one who told me there would be opposition."

"Well, we can be grateful that, if nothing else, we have good communication and respect in this house. Maybe we prevented a mole-hill from turning into a mountain."

"I'd like to think so. Maybe we're being blessed a lot more than we realize."

"I'm sure that's true," she said.

That night Elizabeth had trouble sleeping as memories of the conversation with Trevin leaked into memories of too many other things. But her mind stuck specifically on a few that would always sting. No matter how much time had passed, or how much peace she'd found, some memories would always be difficult. Her mind just couldn't get away from Trevin's comment about his brother. *Bradley looked like him.* Bradley *had* looked very much like his father, and they had been very much alike. The memories associated with losing them both at the same time still haunted her if she chose to let it. She'd had the gospel in her life by then, and she'd known their deaths had been a part of God's plan. But it had still been one of the hardest things she'd ever faced.

Elizabeth thought of her oldest son and wondered what it might be like if he were still alive today. He would have been preparing to go on a mission. He'd talked of his desire to serve a mission right from the time he'd been baptized. She felt sure he was serving some kind of mission where he was, but she couldn't help wondering how it would be if he were here. Of course, Robert had been killed trying to save Bradley's life. If Bradley was still here, Robert probably would be too. Elizabeth would have never wished to lose either one of them, but neither would she trade away the life she had now. In her heart, she believed that she and Jayson had been meant to live this life, that God had known their paths, and he'd known that Robert's life would be cut short. She often thought of Robert with fondness. He was a good man in spite of his faults, and she was grateful for all he'd given her. But it was Bradley she truly missed. A day didn't go by when she didn't think of him. She was glad to know that in eternity they would be together again. Robert had wanted nothing to do with the Church prior to his death, but Bradley had been eager to be baptized. It seemed only natural then, that when Jayson and Elizabeth were sealed, Bradley had been sealed to them. The comfort she found from that knowledge was indescribable. Still, she missed him.

Elizabeth's thoughts strayed into more uncomfortable memories as she recalled the challenges in her first marriage. In most ways Robert had been the perfect husband and father, but his one big struggle had caused Elizabeth a great deal of grief. She didn't like to compare her first marriage to her second one, because her husbands were both so different, with differing strengths and weaknesses. But how could she not recognize the contrast, and acknowledge how much happier she was now than she had ever been with Robert? Jayson was passionate about everything. Robert had been passionate about nothing. And she was at the top of the list in both cases. Robert had tried to overcome his lack of interest in physical affection in order to keep Elizabeth happy, but there was something wonderful in the way that Jayson didn't have to try. It wasn't uncommon for him to just look at her a certain way that would make her feel loved and beautiful. And the intimacy and passion they shared, while part of a normal marriage, was not something she took for granted, perhaps because it hadn't been a part of her previous one. She loved the way that what they shared was so sacred and so glorious at the same time. She thought of the attraction they'd felt for each other when they'd first met, and she knew more than ever that it had been spiritual as well as physical. And musical. They had been drawn to each other in every possible way. Now the reality of all those attractions was a part of their everyday lives.

Silently thanking God for giving her such a good life, even if it had taken a lot of years and some tough experiences to get here, she snuggled close to Jayson, who was sleeping beside her, and finally drifted off herself, grateful beyond measure for this good man in her life.

* * * * *

That night Jayson had a horrible dream where long-ago memories blended into more recent issues that had been difficult for him. He woke up in a cold sweat with a montage of chaotic thoughts that he couldn't put together. He hated the way that a sleepless night could magnify every negative thought that was stored in every tiny crevice of his mind. He prayed for peace and calm, and he gradually felt it come, but he couldn't get back to sleep. It was a few hours before he drifted off again, then he came awake abruptly, aware that the little ones were awake. His next thought focused on a horrible pain over his left eye. He recognized it as a version of migraine that he'd dealt with more than once in the past; he knew it wasn't a good sign. He'd struggled with an occasional migraine for many years. They happened sometimes with the adrenaline letdown after an intense creative period, or at other times when he'd been working very hard. And sometimes they just randomly happened. But the pain was generally more spread over his forehead, radiating out to his temples. The pain over the left eye always felt more intense for some reason, more localized and disturbingly intense, and it was bad enough that he had to really talk himself into getting his head off the pillow in order to get to the bathroom and find the medication that he always had on hand for the onset of a migraine. Since Elizabeth was already up with the babies, he didn't have much choice. He found the pill and took it and went back to bed, taking with him a damp, cold cloth to put over his eyes. Lying there for a while, he was stunned by how much it hurt and found it difficult to keep from writhing and groaning. Then he realized that he *was* writhing and groaning. And praying for relief. He couldn't recall *ever* having a migraine this intense.

"What's wrong?" he heard Elizabeth ask. He hadn't heard her come into the room. "Migraine?" she asked before he could tell her.

"Yeah," he said. "But it's bad."

"I can see that," she said, her concern evident. "What can I do?"

"Nothing," he said. "I've taken the pill; I just need to wait."

"Okay," she said, seeming hesitant to leave. He heard her doing something, then she said, "Your cell phone is on the bedside table. If you need something, call the house phone."

"Okay, thank you," he said in a whisper, since the sound of his own voice amplified the pain.

Elizabeth left and closed the door. Minutes ticked by while Jayson was amazed at how the pain *didn't* ease up. He knew that if the pill didn't work after two hours, he could take a second one, but that was the maximum that he could take in twenty-four hours. Only once in all his years of experience with migraines had he needed to take a second pill. But even that episode had not been like this!

Elizabeth checked on him again, the concern in her voice growing deeper when his distress had only worsened. He assured her he just needed time, and kept praying that the pain would let up. After two of the longest hours of his life, he called Elizabeth and asked her to get him a second pill. He took it with so much hope for relief that he was reminded of the time when he'd been a drug addict, and swallowing a pill had been a deeply sick kind of comfort. While he continued to pray for relief, he continued to be amazed that it didn't come. He started to get scared that something was really wrong with him, and his praying became more intense, although he found it difficult to focus on prayer when the pain was so consuming.

He was about to call Elizabeth again when she came to check on him. "It's no better?"

"No," he said through clenched teeth. "I don't know what's wrong. It's never been like this."

"Okay," she said with subdued panic, "I'm calling my father. One of us can tend the kids while the other takes you to the hospital." Jayson hated hospitals, but he didn't protest. He was scared out of his mind and utterly desperate. It took Will fewer than ten minutes to get there, which was barely enough time for Elizabeth to help Jayson get dressed enough to leave the house in cold weather.

Elizabeth found it difficult to keep from crying as she observed the ongoing evidence of Jayson's misery. She'd never seen him like this. She'd seen him sick and weak during his drug detox, and she'd seen him stay in bed due to a migraine a number of times. But she'd never seen him in so much pain. She was helping him into his coat while he sat on the edge of bed when she boldly declared, "I'm taking you myself. Dad can stay with the kids." She didn't want to wait and wonder. She wanted to be with him every second. She hated the way thoughts of brain tumors and horrible diseases started marching through her head.

Jayson made no comment. He just came unsteadily to his feet with her help, and asked in a quiet voice for her to get his sunglasses. Even the light coming through the closed blinds was hurting his eyes now that he wasn't holding a cloth over his face. She had Jayson in the fully reclined passenger seat of the car just half a minute before her father arrived. She gave him two sentences of instructions about the kids, and he assured her not to worry about a thing.

Jayson groaned and put his arm over his eyes when the car backed out of the garage and he was exposed to sunlight reflecting off of snow. "I'm scared, Lady," he admitted.

She took hold of his other hand and muttered, "Me too, but it's going to be okay. It's going to be okay."

"You keep telling us both that," he said and groaned again. He resisted cursing aloud and hoped God would forgive him for the expletives that kept bursting through his mind in response to the pain.

At the hospital Elizabeth pulled up next to the emergency entrance and ran in. She was grateful to live near a hospital, and to have it be adequate to handle almost anything, but not so big that they couldn't get the attention they needed quickly. She gave a two-sentence explanation, and a male nurse with a wheelchair came out to the car with her. Once Jayson was in his care, Elizabeth parked the car and hurried inside to be with her husband. She was taken to a room in the ER where Jayson's shirt had already been replaced with a hospital gown, and an IV was being put into his hand. While they seemed eager to help ease Jayson's pain, it still took what felt like forever before a doctor saw him and ordered medication. Once the drug was put into the IV, Elizabeth saw Jayson visibly relax within minutes.

"Oh, thank you, God," she heard him mutter, and he absently reached for her hand. The doctor came in again and gave them some samples of a couple of different migraine drugs that might work better than what Jayson had taken. He stressed that he would need to wait at least twenty-four hours between trying different ones, which made Elizabeth wonder what they would do if trying one didn't work. They would probably end up here again.

She took the opportunity to ask, "Do you think this is just simply a migraine, or could it be something else?"

"It certainly appears to be a migraine. People *do* get that much pain, sometimes more. I would suggest seeing your primary doctor and discussing the problem with him. He might have some other recommendations."

"Thank you, Doctor," Elizabeth said.

"Yes, thank you," Jayson added somewhat groggily.

"You take care now," the doctor said before leaving the room.

Elizabeth sat with Jayson until the contents of the IV bag had emptied into him, then the same male nurse helped him back into a wheelchair and out to the curb where Elizabeth met them with the car. Jayson was groggy but awake enough to get into the car with just a little help.

"How you doing?" Elizabeth asked, pulling onto the highway.

"I am free of pain," he muttered with a little slur, "which means I'm great." He rolled his head the other direction to look at her. "Thank you . . . for taking such good care of me. I'll just add this to my list of at least a thousand reasons I'm grateful to be married to you . . . as opposed to being alone."

"The feeling is mutual," she said, then called her father at the house to give him an update and to tell him they would be home soon.

Back at the house, Will walked out to the garage when they pulled in. He opened the passenger door and helped Jayson out. "Thanks, Dad," Jayson muttered and leaned heavily on Will as he guided him into the house and to the bedroom, while Elizabeth took over with the kids.

Will helped Jayson out of his shoes and coat and tucked him into bed like a child. "Doing better?"

"Much, thank you," Jayson said.

"Get some rest, kid."

Jayson sank deeper into his pillow and again thanked God for the absence of pain. He smiled to think of Will calling him "kid." He was in his forties, and Will still thought of him as a kid.

CHAPTER 6

Elizabeth hugged her father and thanked him before he left, then she fed the babies their lunch and put them down for their naps before she peeked in on Jayson to find him sleeping soundly. Now that the trauma of the morning had settled and she had time to actually think, she felt even more scared than she had earlier. The medication had eased Jayson's pain, but she wasn't sure she could feel confident with the doctor's assurance that this was simply a migraine. Was she just being paranoid? Or was it possible that something serious was wrong with her husband?

Prayerfully considering what she might do to help ease her own concerns, she quickly did a few things that needed to be done for the sake of keeping the household running, then she put everything else on hold and took advantage of the quiet afternoon to get on the Internet and start researching everything she could find about migraines. She *did* feel a little better to realize that they really could cause that much pain, and that sometimes they could be that difficult to get rid of without medical intervention. Considering the possibility that other such headaches might occur in the future, she looked for tips on handling migraine pain and the different types of medication available.

Elizabeth also called the office of their family doctor. She explained the situation and asked for a nurse to call her back. She was surprised when the doctor himself called, saying he'd been notified by the ER that Jayson had been there and he'd wanted to check on him, anyway. In two sentences he basically told her what she'd already learned, and he said if the headaches continued to give Jayson grief that he should come in for an office visit so they could more thoroughly discuss options. Elizabeth thanked him and didn't have time to think about it anymore when Harmony woke up and Derek soon followed.

Through the remainder of the afternoon, she occasionally peeked in on Jayson to find him still sleeping, no doubt aided by the medication they'd given him. She also suspected that the intensity of his earlier pain had surely left his body drained and exhausted. She left him to sleep and explained to Trevin, and then Addie, what had happened when they came in from school. It wasn't until Elizabeth was cleaning up supper that she looked up to see Jayson enter the kitchen, looking horrible.

"Hi," she said.

He wrapped her in his arms, but she felt a lack of strength in contrast to his usual embrace. "Hi," he whispered close to her ear. "Thanks for taking care of me."

"I didn't do anything you wouldn't do for me," she said, and he moved carefully to a chair. "You okay?"

"I have a mild headache and I feel like I've been hit by a dump truck. Beyond that, I'm great. Compared to this morning, I'm really great. I think I need to eat something."

"I was just going to suggest it. We had lasagna for dinner. Do you—"

"Ooh," he said with a visible wave of nausea, "I don't think I can handle that. Do we have a can of chicken soup, or something?"

"We do," she said. "I can have it ready in five minutes. You want crackers? Juice?"

"That sounds divine," he said and put his head down on the table.

"Do you want me to bring it to the bedroom?"

"No," he said, "this is fine. Thank you." He stayed with his head down until she put a hot bowl of soup in front of him. He took her hand and squeezed it. "I was just thinking . . . when I lived in LA . . . after I hurt my hand. It was just me and Drew, and he was working, gone most of the time. Before he left for work, he'd always try to anticipate everything I'd need. But I remember being in so much pain and trying to do things I couldn't do with one hand, and . . . I'm just trying to say that I'm so glad to be here with you. I'm so glad I'm not alone."

"You and me both," she said and gently kissed his forehead.

"Oh, that's what I need," he said and pointed to the spot where it had felt like a spike had been in his head earlier. "Kiss it right there." She did, and he made an exaggerated noise of relief that made her laugh. "Now it's all better."

"We could have saved the trip to the hospital if we'd have thought of this earlier."

"Exactly," he said.

Elizabeth sat down with him while he blessed his food and started eating. He thanked her again before she went to check on the children. After he'd eaten, Jayson laid on the couch in the living room so that he could spend some time with the kids. He watched the little ones playing and smiled at their antics, and Trevin showed up for a few minutes. When Addie found him there she snuggled up next to him and stayed there for longer than she could usually hold still. She asked him more than once if he was okay and if she could get anything for him. With her maternal nature, she obviously wanted to help him feel better. He assured her that he was fine and that her hugs were the best thing he could get. But he finally had to insist at her mother's urging that she go do her homework and put away her clean clothes.

When the noise of the children began to get to his lingering headache, he kissed them good night and went back to bed. His sleep was sporadic and filled with strange dreams, probably due to the drugs. When he woke to daylight to find that Elizabeth had already left the bedroom, his head was pounding. Thankfully, there was no spike over his left eye, but the full width of his forehead was throbbing, more like his typical migraines. He took something for it and prayed fervently that it would actually work. An hour later he was thrilled to realize that it had. The intensity of the pain was gone, but he felt a mild aching through his whole body that he knew was a side effect of the drug, and the kind of weakness that made him feel like he was recovering from the flu. Even though he hadn't been ill with more than a minor cold in years, he was accustomed to the post-migraine symptoms, and had read that they were often comparable to what the body endures with a bad virus.

When Elizabeth came to check on him, he told her the adventures he'd already had this morning while she'd been caring for the children. She expressed her concern, but he assured her he was fine. He got up and took a shower. He got dressed and made the bed. He ate some breakfast and stayed on the couch in the living room for most of the morning, grateful to be free of pain. The exhaustion and weakness felt like minor inconveniences in contrast.

Jayson heard the phone ring, but it was nearly ten minutes later when Elizabeth brought him the cordless handset. "It's your daughter," she said. "I already gave her the medical history."

"Thanks," Jayson said, and then spoke into the phone, "Hey, baby. What's up?"

"Why didn't you call and tell me you were in pain?"

"I was in pain," he said. "Besides, you don't call and tell me when life is falling down around you. Touché."

"Okay, you got me there. So, how are you?"

"I'm much better, thank you. Just wiped out."

"Are you okay to talk on the phone?"

"I'm fine. It's good to talk to you. How are you?"

"I'm exhausted, but doing okay."

"And how's Layla?"

"She's feeling a little better and I think she's gained a few pounds, but it's going to be a long and slow process getting her back to normal."

"Even a little progress is a good sign though, right?"

"Absolutely, and we're grateful. But the reality of living with this is a nightmare."

"What do you mean?" Jayson asked, and Macy went on to explain all that she had been learning about making a person's world gluten-free. When even a molecule could cause damage, the food that Layla ate had to be protected from coming in contact with even a crumb of something containing gluten. In a houseful of children who were continually eating crackers and cereal and bread, Macy had come to regard the kitchen as being infested with poison as she'd tried to help her mother-in-law—and the entire family—adjust. She and Layla had discussed how they didn't want the rest of the family to feel like they couldn't be comfortable in their own kitchen. They should be able to eat the way they always had. But when it came to preparing Layla's food, special precautions had to be taken. Her food couldn't even be cooked in a pan where something with gluten in it had been cooked unless it was thoroughly cleaned first. Any minute possibility of cross-contamination from microscopic bits of gluten that could be hidden in any crack, crevice, or porous surface had to be eliminated. Layla needed her own jar of peanut butter and her own butter tub, clearly marked, so that they wouldn't get contaminated with bread crumbs from others using them. They had to use squeeze bottles of ketchup and mayonnaise and other such things for the same reasons, and in all cases they had to make sure the products were gluten-free. Jayson felt stunned and over-whelmed to hear Macy's explanation. All he could say was, "I cannot even imagine. No wonder you're exhausted. How would Layla possibly manage without your help?"

"I'm just glad I'm here to help. With her being as sick as she is, she'd be stuck with nasty gluten-free crackers. Of course, she can eat fruits and vegetables and most dairy products. Although, some yogurt and sour cream has gluten added to it."

"You're kidding."

"No, it's in so many things that you wouldn't believe. But it can be disguised under a variety of ingredients listed on labels so that you often don't know if he food contains gluten or not. We have to rely on published lists of products, or be *hugely* grateful for the companies that actually have the courtesy to declare that a product is gluten-free."

"Isn't there some law that makes it a requirement to declare such things?"

"Gluten apparently doesn't fall under the law to declare certain allergens in a product. And yet it's more insidious than many other things that people can't tolerate. Grocery shopping is a nightmare. And I'm not even the person who can't eat the stuff. If I was Layla and actually *felt* good enough to go the store, I think I'd have a hysterical breakdown every time."

Jayson listened to her complain about more of the details, doing his best to offer compassion and a listening ear while he marveled at the challenges of the disease. When Macy wound down a bit, he said, "I'm proud of you, baby."

"For what?"

"Have you been listening to yourself?"

"Yeah, I'm complaining and whining like a—"

"You've been taking on an amazing amount of responsibility, and you're doing it with genuine concern and diligence. You are an amazing, charitable woman, Macy, and I'm proud of you." When she didn't answer, he realized she was crying. "You okay?"

"Yeah," she said. "I just . . . well . . . thank you. I hadn't really looked at it that way. I've just been doing what I felt like I should do, because . . . well . . . who else is going to do it? Obviously I was put here to be the one to help her, and I need to know that I'm doing everything for her that I can do."

"Exactly," he said. "You just keep doing what you're doing, but be careful not to burn out."

"Oh, I'm okay," she said. "We've been watching movies together in between all the dreadful studying and coping. The kids are doing better with their chores and taking care of themselves. I think they're all so glad to know their mother isn't going to die that they're willing to do just about anything."

"Except clean up their crumbs in the kitchen?"

Macy chuckled. "We're working on that. It's hard to retrain old habits. The good news is that there are a lot of gluten-free products once you know where to find them, and we're trying to embark on actually baking with alternate flours. Layla sits in the kitchen while I do most of the work so that we can learn together."

"Wow," Jayson said. "When you were wondering why you weren't supposed to move out of her house, I bet you never imagined something like this."

"I sure didn't," she said. "But . . ." she sounded mildly emotional again, "I really am glad to be here, Dad. I really do love Layla; she's a wonderful woman and she's been so good to me. And I love the kids . . . even though they drive me crazy sometimes. I think . . . well . . . you know I had a pretty weird childhood."

"Yeah, I knew about that."

"I've always wondered what it would be like to be part of a family, to have a real mother, and brothers and sisters. Of course, since Mom took us in . . ." he knew she meant Elizabeth, "we got some of that, but . . . this has been different. I'm glad to have this experience. And someday when I have a houseful of my own children, I'll be really good at it, right?"

"Right," he said and laughed softly. "That's a great thing to imagine."

"What?"

"You with a houseful of kids—my grandkids."

"I think it'll happen when the time is right."

"I do too, baby," he said. "You hang in there, and if you need something, you know where to find me."

"I know, Dad. Thank you."

They ended the call, and Jayson set the phone aside but stayed on the couch until it was time for lunch. He helped Elizabeth feed the babies, then had something to eat as well before he went to the studio to run through each number he would be performing on the tour. He went through each one twice, which took more than three hours, then he laid down on the carpeted floor and went to sleep. He came awake to the sound of the door opening, then Elizabeth's voice asking him if he was okay.

"Just tired," he said.

"That doesn't look very comfortable," she said, and he opened his eyes to see her standing above him.

"All depends on how tired you are," he said and held up his hand for her to help him to his feet.

"How's the music?"

"The music is amazing," he said. "It's all a miracle. I still feel astonished when I think of where it came from."

"The music makes you feel better."

"Yes, it does," he said and put his arm around her. "And so do you."

The remainder of the day was fairly normal. He even took Mozie for a walk. The exercise felt good, and the dog enjoyed it, but the cold brought on a mild headache. Roger stopped by after work since Elizabeth had called him earlier to explain why Jayson hadn't met him to go running that morning.

"I'd forgotten all about it," Jayson said to his friend. "Sorry."

"Understandable," Roger said as they sat in the front room. He asked some questions about the headaches and sounded concerned when Jayson admitted he'd never had the pain get that bad before, never had the medication not work before, and he'd never had migraine pain for more than one day. Jayson assured him it was probably just a delayed reaction to too much work and too much stress.

Later that evening, as soon as supper was over, Jayson apologized to Elizabeth for not feeling up to helping get the kids to bed. He was just so tired he could hardly stay upright. She assured him that she could manage fine and he should rest. The next morning Jayson didn't wake up with a headache, but an hour after breakfast while he was working in the studio, it hit him like a brick. He hurried to find the pill he needed to take. Since it had been more than twenty-four hours after taking the last one, he decided to try one of the samples the ER doctor had given him to see if it worked any better or—he hoped—might have less noticeable side effects. He took the pill and laid down. Within twenty minutes the headache was easing off slightly, but he was also having heart palpitations. He called Elizabeth from his cell phone, and she called the ER. After speaking to a friendly and helpful nurse, they concluded that it was not an emergency as long as it didn't get any worse. A couple of hours later the headache was gone and his heart had settled. He said to Elizabeth, "I guess we know *that one* isn't good for me. You can throw the rest of *those* away."

"I'm worried about you, Jayson."

"Yes, I can see that. You've only left the room long enough to make certain our children aren't destroying the house or each other. I'm fine."

"The pain's all gone?"

"Most of it. Now it's just your average run-of-the-mill Excedrin kind of headache."

"I'm still worried about you. This is all just a little too weird. I think you should go talk to the doctor."

Jayson didn't *want* to talk to the doctor. But he couldn't dismiss Elizabeth's concerns, and he had to admit that he was a little worried himself. "Okay," he said. "You make an appointment, but get Grandpa to babysit if he's available. I'd prefer that you go with me."

Elizabeth left to make the call and came back to say, "He'll see you in forty-five minutes."

"Today?"

"That would be in forty-five minutes. Dad's on his way over. We need to hurry and eat some lunch."

"I was thinking it would be like . . . in a few days."

"Well, it's not. Get ready to go."

"Does this mean he thinks something is wrong with me?" Jayson asked.

"I don't know," was all she said.

They ended up in the waiting room for a long while, and then waited in the examination room another long while. Jayson's mind started running with possible things that could be wrong with him, but he kept giving himself the strongest argument—it was just a migraine and he needed to chill out. He was glad when the doctor agreed, noting that his blood pressure was fine, his heart sounded good, and he appeared to be healthy. But then he said that he wanted to be certain there wasn't some hidden cause, and therefore he was ordering a slew of blood work and an MRI, just to be certain there wasn't anything strange going on.

When Jayson was given additional samples of migraine drugs and a written prescription for more, he said to the doctor, "Listen, I . . . uh . . ." He felt as he often did lately, that his brain function was slower due to the medication—or the headache—or both. He turned to Elizabeth, hoping she could read his mind. She looked blank. "In the past," he said, "I had a problem with . . ." He saw Elizabeth's enlightenment and was grateful when she took over.

"Jayson had a bout with prescription drug addiction following a surgery some years ago. We just don't want to have him taking something that will—"

"These particular drugs that you're taking for the migraines are not pain killers," the doctor said. He went on to explain something Jayson barely understood about the way a migraine was characterized by the expanding and contracting of blood vessels, and this drug was to help that. He assured Jayson they were not in the same category as the things Jayson had become addicted to, and there was no reason for concern. Jayson crossed that off his worry list, and worried about getting an MRI instead.

Since the MRI wasn't scheduled for another week, Jayson felt sure that by then he would be feeling great and would just cancel it. But he had a migraine every single day. The medication he took got rid of the worst of the headache pain, and he managed to help with the kids, appear to be a somewhat normal father, and run through his concert numbers a couple of times every day. But he could feel an accumulating weakness settling into him, as well as an intense tightness in the muscles of his jaw, neck, shoulders, and upper back.

Sunday was no exception to the daily headache, but he took the pill and tried to pull himself together to get to church. The choir was counting on him to play for the musical number that day, and no one could take his place on such short notice. If he cancelled, the number would be postponed. He was glad to be there to partake of the sacrament, and the musical number went well. But ten minutes later he whispered to Elizabeth that he needed her to take him home. They left Trevin in charge of the kids while she did. She left him with everything he needed and a look of concern that was becoming permanently etched into her expression. He assured her that with some rest he would be fine.

An hour later the headache was still there, but since it had been more than two hours since he'd taken the pill, he took another one. Recalling one of the suggestions that Elizabeth had found on the Internet, he filled the large bathtub in the master bathroom with water hot enough that he could barely tolerate it. He immersed himself up to his neck with a folded towel behind his head and a washcloth over his forehead and eyes. Both were wet with cold water, the idea being that the heat would draw the blood from his head and the cold would encourage it. After soaking for a long while, the pain eased to a mild headache and he felt relaxed. He didn't know if it was the water or the medication—or both—but he was grateful. He realized then that his hours had become measured by the level of pain or absence of it. He felt discouraged and scared and was surprised when he started to cry.

When Elizabeth got home, she found him there, but he'd managed to stop the tears by then. He gave her a report, then said, "I guess I should get out. I'm turning into a prune."

Elizabeth had an idea related to some things she'd read. "Let me wash your hair first and give you a little gentle scalp massage. I bet it's tight."

"Like a drum," he muttered and sat up. "That sounds wonderful."

Jayson immediately enjoyed Elizabeth's gently massaging fingertips all over his scalp, but had to admit, "I can't believe how sore that is."

"Am I hurting you?"

"No, it feels good. I just can't believe it." He dropped his head forward and made a pleasurable noise.

When she moved her fingers down to the base of his skull, just above his neck, he flinched and she drew back. "It hurts that bad?" she asked.

"It does right there," he said. "It feels like I got hit with a baseball bat. Rub it anyway. Obviously it needs it. Just . . . be gentle."

"Okay," she said and repeated the whole process again before she helped him rinse his hair. He got out of the tub and went straight to bed to rest. In the distance he could hear the typical sounds of Sunday dinner being prepared, and he wanted to be in the middle of it, helping Elizabeth, teasing the children, feeling like a normal human being. He cried again, then drifted off to sleep.

His next awareness was Elizabeth nudging him. "Sorry to bother you, babe," she said, "but Roger and my dad are coming over to give you a blessing. They'll be here in about half an hour. Do you want something to eat first or—"

"Yeah," he said. "Thank you."

"Soup? Toast?"

"What was for dinner?"

"Roast beef, carrots, mashed potatoes, and gravy."

"Sounds heavenly. I want some of that, but not too much."

"I'll bring it in just a few—"

"No, I'll come to the kitchen." He reached out and grabbed her hand before she could move away. "Thank you, Elizabeth. I'm sorry I'm not more help. And on top of that, I'm just giving you more work to do."

"You have nothing to apologize for," she said, sitting on the edge of the bed. "Do you know how many times you've taken care of me when I've been sick? And what about those pregnancies?"

"Thank you anyway," he said.

"You're welcome." She leaned over to hug him.

He held to her tightly and started to cry again. "Why do you suppose I cry so easily?"

"Normally it's because you're a tender-hearted songwriter, combined with genetically overactive tear ducts." She eased back, and he saw tears in *her* eyes, as well. "Today I think it's because you're miserable and scared. I'm not miserable. I'm just scared."

He nodded and realized he was really going to start crying if he wasn't careful, and that would just make his head hurt more. "I'm glad you called Roger and Dad. Thank you. I'll come and eat in just a few minutes."

"Okay," she said and kissed him before she left the room.

Jayson made himself reasonably presentable before he went to the dining room and enjoyed the meal Elizabeth had made. He reminded her that the very first Sunday dinner he'd eaten in her home before he'd gone into drug rehab had been this same menu. "I think for that reason, and because it just tastes so good, I would call this comfort food."

"I'm glad it hits the spot," she said. "How's the head?"

"It's fine. I just feel like . . ."

"You can't find a word to describe it?"

"I can, but it's against my religion to use the word in that context."

"So, you can't think of an appropriate word to describe it?"

"I feel like . . . Jell-O. Purple Jell-O. Purple Jell-O that got left out of the fridge and it's kind of . . . melting in the bowl."

"Wow," she said. "That's a pretty good description, but I don't think I'd hold on to that one for any future lyrics."

"No, I don't think so."

He thanked Elizabeth again for the meal and went to the living room to lie on the couch until the priesthood holders arrived. Will showed up a few minutes before Roger and sat to talk with Jayson, expressing his concern. When Roger arrived, Elizabeth turned off the phone and put Trevin in charge of the kids so they could have some uninterrupted time for the blessing.

Elizabeth sat nearby and silently prayed while she waited for the blessing to begin. She realized that she was barely holding it together and feared she would burst into tears unless she exerted excessive self-control. She was more worried than she had even been able to admit to herself. She'd been calm with Jayson, and had even presented a calm façade when she'd spoken to Roger and her father on the phone. But she felt her calm dissolving with the fervent prayer that this blessing would offer some guidance, some assurance that Jayson would be alright. She cried silent tears while she heard Jayson being told of the love his Heavenly Father had for him, and how pleased He was with the work that Jayson was doing that would take good music out into the world. He was told that opposition was a necessary part of this life's experience, and that there were seasons of life when it had to be allowed in order for God's children to grow and be strengthened. He was told to rely on and trust in the Lord, and that with time this would pass and he would return to health. He was promised firmly that he would be able to do all that was required of him as a husband and father, and also in his profession; that the Lord would be his strength and compensate for any weakness that might be present. When the blessing was finished, Elizabeth had to hurry out of the room before anyone realized how much she was crying. She rushed into the bathroom where she could vent her emotion. When she came back out, Roger had left, and Jayson and Will were sitting on the couch in the front room.

"You okay?" Jayson asked.

"I'm better now," she said and sat between the two men. Jayson put his arm around her and Will took her hand. "I've just been . . . worried."

"Understandably so," Will said. "But it's going to be okay."

Elizabeth believed him, but lying in bed that night, she wondered what *okay* meant exactly. If Jayson had cancer and needed brain surgery and chemotherapy, as long as he survived, everything would be *okay*. If they had to cancel the tour, it would be *okay*. And if they had to spend the rest of their lives dealing with some dreadful disease, it might be *okay*. But it surely wouldn't be easy. She reminded herself that the blessing had promised Jayson the ability to do all that was required of him, both at home and with his profession. She took hold of that promise, and also reminded herself to do as Jayson had been instructed—to rely on and trust in the Lord. And her worrying would never help that happen.

The following morning Will and Marilyn came over to watch the children while Elizabeth did some errands and took care of some household matters that needed her attention. Jayson was in bed but couldn't sleep. He could hear his children playing down the hall but couldn't work up the motivation to go that far in order to be with them. And the noise of their playing nearby wasn't easy on his head. He heard a light knock on the open door and looked up to see Marilyn.

"You're not asleep, are you?" she asked.

"No, come in."

He moved to sit up, and she said, "Please don't. Just keep your head where it's most comfortable. I've had a few migraines in my life. I understand. Do you need anything?"

"No, thank you. I'm as good as I can be at the moment. How's my family?"

"They're doing fine," Marilyn said, and as if she'd read his mind, she added, "and you'll have plenty of time to make it up to them when you're feeling better. I was just wondering if you could use some company, but if you're not up to it and now's not a good time, then—"

"No, I'd appreciate some company, actually. Being alone in this room is getting old."

"I have some empathy for that, too," she said, sitting in a chair near the bed. "I had some problems with my pregnancies and had to stay down for weeks at a time more than once."

"How dreadful," Jayson said and meant it. "How *are* your kids?"

"They're all doing fairly well," she said. "Usual ups and downs, but nothing too serious."

"I'm glad to hear it."

They talked for a few minutes about his present concerns in regard to his headaches, and about his music. The conversation began to feel eerily familiar, then he pinpointed the reason and wanted to cry.

"Are you okay?" she asked.

"I was just . . . missing my mother. You remind me of her sometimes. Mostly because . . . you're so motherly. You take good care of us."

Marilyn smiled. "I would have loved to have known your mother. Will has talked about her a great deal."

"Really?" Jayson asked, unable to bridle his curiosity. Will and his mother had been very close at one time. They'd both been divorced and had connected strongly through their children at a time when all four of them had been in a band together. Will had asked Leslie to marry him, but she'd turned him down, claiming that the effects of abuse in her life would not make her a good wife. Will had been devastated, but he and Leslie had remained close as friends until her death. In fact, Will had been there when Leslie died. That relationship had strengthened Jayson's bonds with Will, but he'd often wondered what it might have been like if they *had* married. Or if Leslie was still alive. He'd imagined her living here with them, and the joy she would have gotten from being a part of his beautiful family.

"Oh, yes," Marilyn said. "He loved her very much; she had a big impact on his life."

Jayson felt deeply comforted to hear this woman talk about his mother, and he was amazed at how well she *did* know Leslie from Will's descriptions alone. She said right out that she didn't feel at all jealous of Will's feelings for Leslie; that had been another time and place. In fact, Marilyn shared Will's wish that Leslie would have married him. Since she'd long ago passed away, Marilyn would have still had Will in her life now.

They also talked about Meredith, Will's first wife—Elizabeth's mother. Since Marilyn had spent some time with Meredith when she'd been in their home during the days preceding her death, the two women had gotten to know each other. Jayson was amazed at this woman's charitable nature and how she could talk with kindness and appreciation about the other women that had been a part of her husband's life. Marilyn had only known Meredith at the end, when her bad behavior of the preceding years had vanished. But she'd known about all the horrible things Meredith had done, and her forgiveness on behalf of Will was touching.

Jayson thanked Marilyn for the conversation, and was again reminded of his mother when she leaned over the bed and kissed him on the forehead, saying, "You rest now. Everything's going to be alright."

As Marilyn slipped out of the room, Jayson could have sworn that his mother's spirit was close by. He took hold of the feeling and allowed it to bathe him with the comfort Leslie would have given if she were there. And with that feeling he went to sleep.

* * * * *

When the day arrived for the MRI, Jayson wasn't glad to wake up with a migraine, but he was glad to be awake early enough that he could take the medication to ease the bulk of the pain before they had to go to the hospital. In the machine, he resisted the urge to scream with the way the noise of it offended his sensitive head—even though he was wearing earplugs. He fought to hold still as he'd been instructed, not wanting to mess it up and have the experience dragged out any longer than necessary. He knew it would take a day or two to get the results back, but he really didn't believe they were going to find anything. He wasn't worried about having cancer or a tumor. He was simply worried about getting from one day to the next.

The following morning the migraine came with a new adventure—nausea. The perpetual vomiting took him back to the days of detoxing from prescription drugs when he'd never been so sick in his life. Now, even though his stomach was long emptied, he couldn't go very many minutes without retching, and the bedroom was just too far away, so he grabbed a couple of towels and put one under his head and the other over him, right there on the bathroom floor. When Elizabeth found him there she panicked. He assured her he was fine and just wanted to stay where he was, but she informed him twenty minutes later that she was going to the doctor's office to pick up some samples of a drug that would help his nausea, and her father would be there to watch the kids. "And he's going to keep an eye on you," she added, almost sounding angry before she left the room.

A minute later Jayson was retching again, even though there was nothing to come up. But the heaving made him feel like his head would crack wide open. He was on the floor again, trying to catch his breath, when Will found him there.

"Apparently you're getting worse, not better," Will said.

"Thank you for pointing that out."

"I'm just concerned."

"You and me both. But I think your daughter's angry with me."

"She's not angry with you. She's just upset and scared."

"And probably exhausted from having to take care of me and everything else, too."

"Maybe." Will sat on the floor and leaned back against the bathtub. "But Marilyn and I are going to see if we can help with that. I'm afraid we're going to start hanging around more, if you think you can live with it."

"Anything to help Elizabeth."

"And what can I do to help you?"

"I appreciate the offer . . . Dad, but I can't think of a thing." A minute later he lifted his head enough to realize Will was still there. "You really don't have to sit on the bathroom floor with me. Don't you have grandkids to tend or something?"

"Marilyn's watching them. I think I'll just stay here with you."

"If you sit there much longer, it could get real ugly. I'm puking in five-minute intervals."

"I think I can handle it," Will said. "I sat with Derek on the bathroom floor once for almost twenty-four hours. He was about thirteen, and got some nasty flu thing. We just camped out in the bathroom."

"That sounds like you," Jayson said with a stilted chuckle. "I don't think there's a better father in the world than you."

"I don't know about that." Will chuckled. "I just love my kids." He put a hand on Jayson's shoulder when he said it, and Jayson felt like crying, but he knew it would be too painful.

"I sure do miss Derek," Jayson said, imagining him on the bathroom floor with Will.

"I do too," Will said. "I'm so glad I have you."

In the span of a few seconds, Jayson considered their history. They'd shared so much, and were closer than many blood relatives. Together they'd gone through the deaths of people they both loved. And they had much in common. The bonds they shared were beyond words, so Jayson just said, "The feeling is mutual." Then he wondered if it was possible to die of a migraine.

CHAPTER 7

Jayson was pleased when the nausea medication helped, and more pleased when the headache *and* the nausea both let up. He was even *more* pleased with the phone call that reported the MRI had been completely normal, as well as all of his blood work. It was the doctor's firm conclusion that all of his symptoms fell into the category of migraine-related, and he just needed to ride it out. The doctor told them that sometimes a migraine could last days or weeks, and maybe that was the case with this one. The theory gave Jayson a little bit of comfort, but he wondered what he would do if such a thing occurred in the middle of a tour.

The bishop came to visit Jayson that evening. Jayson wasn't feeling too bad when he came, and they sat in the living room and had a nice, friendly chat, which had nothing to do with anything in particular. He did say before he left that he would keep Jayson in his prayers, and that he hoped the problem would soon solve itself.

By the time Sunday came again, Jayson was still having a migraine every single day. It came on at different times of the day, but its daily visit had become inevitable. The medication would reduce the headache to a tolerable level, and he could manage to get through the requirements of daily living. But he was always exhausted and weak, and it seemed he had some level of headache all day every day. He managed to appear fairly normal to the children, and their daily interaction remained normal. He kept going through his performance practice rituals nearly every day, but he was beginning to hate it—mostly because the music hurt his head. He told Elizabeth it was a sick irony that his own music was causing him pain. He didn't know if he could live with it; it was almost as sick as when he'd severely injured his hand in a freakish accident that still didn't make any sense in Jayson's memory.

Jayson didn't go to church, and Elizabeth came home to tell him that his ailment had been mentioned in Relief Society with a request for prayers on his behalf. That afternoon Elizabeth went to choir practice to fill in for Jayson. She came back to report that it had gone well, but she knew that for all of her own skill, she could never pull it off with the finesse that he had with the piano. He assured her that she was an excellent pianist and the choir was lucky to have her. He knew it was true, but he could hardly admit to himself how much he missed being able to simply do his Church calling. He was tired of seeing his life through a cloud of pain. He wanted this to end. That evening the home teachers came to visit, and Elizabeth asked them if they could give Jayson a blessing. He would have preferred not to talk about his health, but Elizabeth told them straight out what was going on. Then he remembered that it had been announced in Relief Society, so it certainly wasn't going to be a great secret.

The blessing Jayson was given was almost exactly the same as the last one he'd had, which he considered fairly remarkable since these were two different men who hadn't been present at the last one, and they didn't know nearly as much about the situation as Will and Roger. He figured that he shouldn't consider it remarkable, because he knew the source of the blessing. But it was still extraordinary. With this evidence that these words had come from his Heavenly Father, and they were full of love, comfort, and hope, he did feel a little better—emotionally, at least.

The next day Macy dropped by after doing some errands and found Jayson laying on the living room floor while the kids played nearby.

"Hi," he said, looking up at her. "I'm not getting up, but it's sure good to see you."

"You doing any better?" She sat on the floor and started playing with Harmony.

"My head is currently at a dull roar, as opposed to a loud scream. How are you?"

"I'm okay, now that I've actually restrained myself from punching out the guy at the pharmacy."

"You're having violent episodes with a pharmacist?"

"No, I *didn't* have a violent episode. In fact, he's about the fifth person who works in a pharmacy that I've *avoided* having violent episodes with. You should be proud of me for that."

"I am," Jayson said. "I assume you're going to explain this, as opposed to my losing sleep over it until you do."

"I'll give you the nutshell version. I told you that Layla has a bad cold."

"Yes."

"And I told you that because her disease is autoimmune, she can be more vulnerable to germs."

"Yes."

"So, the last few days I've been trying to get her what she needs to feel better. Many drugs, both prescription and over-the-counter, have gluten in them as a filler or carrier. But the labels don't actually state *what* kind of starch they use. It *could* be wheat starch, or it could be corn, or tapioca, or something else. But nobody knows! The Internet carries lists of safe drugs, but they're not always complete. We've had to instruct the family doctor on Celiac Disease, because the stomach doctor gets it, but the others do not. And apparently most pharmacists and pharmacy technicians don't know that gluten is an issue with some people. It's like they're trying to poison Layla and they don't really seem to care that much. I'm on to my third pharmacy now. They say, "Oh, you could call the manufacturer and find out if it's safe." This is at 8:00 P.M. and they're asking me to do their job for them, when we both know the manufacturer wouldn't be open that late, and Layla needs the prescription. They've apparently ignored the doctor's personal request—because I talked to *him* on the phone three times—to make sure it's a gluten-free drug. By that time the doctor's not available, and no one actually knows from the list of ingredients if it's safe, because if you look up those ingredients on the Internet, it says, 'Usually made from corn starch, but sometimes from wheat.' Aaahh!"

"Wow," Jayson said, stunned once again with the enormity of dealing with this disease. Then he stated the obvious. "You're really stressed—with good reason. That's insane! Pharmacists are really that lax—or ignorant about it—or both?"

"All the ones I've talked to have been. And get this: nurses, doctors, pharmacists . . . they all ask, 'Is she allergic to any medications?' And we say, 'Gluten.' And they say, 'No, we mean medications.' And we say, 'Gluten is in a lot of medications, and if she gets a molecule of it, she will be very ill and die of cancer eventually.' And they say, 'Oh, I didn't know that.' And on it goes. And I *want* to say, 'If the medical profession in the United States of American doesn't figure this out soon, I'm going to sue somebody!' But I don't, because I'm trying to be a nice person and

I realize that I'm only *one* person, and I do not have the time or the energy to take on the U.S. government, specifically the Food and Drug Administration, to make them declare gluten on food and drug labels."

"I'm stunned," Jayson said.

"Yeah, me too." She took a deep breath. "Okay, I'm done griping. What's wrong with your neck?"

"What do you mean?"

"You keep . . . stretching it . . . and rubbing it."

"I didn't even realize I was," Jayson said. "It's just stiff and sore. All the headaches have tightened everything that's remotely connected to my head."

"Turn over," she said. "Let me rub it for you."

"Oh, that's divine," he said as soon as she started. For more than half an hour, she massaged his neck and shoulders, and also his scalp and jaw muscles, all of which were so tight and sore that Jayson felt certain the tightness alone could bring on a headache. It was all such a ridiculous, vicious cycle.

When she finally finished, Jayson felt so relaxed he didn't want to move. "Oh, you are good at that, baby. You're gifted. You can come and do that any time you want."

"I'd be happy to," she said. Then Derek jumped on Jayson's back, which startled him and then made him laugh. He got even by tickling his son, then Harmony jumped into the middle of it and he tickled them both at the same time, creating a flurry of giggles. And Macy laughed just because watching it was so funny. The laughter brought Elizabeth into the room, luring her away from balancing the checkbook.

"Hey," Jayson said to Macy when the laughter settled down, "it's my turn to cook dinner, so I'm ordering pizza. How about if I pay for pizza for your family too, then you don't have to cook?" He heard what he'd said and immediately added, "Oh, I guess that's pretty insensitive of me, since Layla can't eat it. Man, how does she live without pizza?"

"It's not easy," Macy said. "But actually . . . I accept your offer. Most of the time the rest of the family eats something different from what she eats anyway, and she just eats in her room so she doesn't have to watch people eat what she can't. We're trying to figure out meals that everyone can eat, but that's going to take time and practice, and right now we're adjusting to more important things. So," she held out her hand and wiggled her fingers, "I'll take the pizza money. I'm not proud. The kids will love it."

"Deal," Jayson said, "but my wallet is on my dresser. Take what you need. You know I trust you."

"Yes, I know that you know."

They all had lunch together before Macy left, then Jayson repeated to Elizabeth the latest Celiac Disease drama. Elizabeth got so worked up that he felt sure she would be willing to single-handedly fly to Washington, DC, to solve the problem. But since she had a family to take care of, she had to concede that God needed to choose someone else to solve that problem.

The conversation ended when Jayson's head went from a dull roar to loud screaming almost instantaneously. He took a pill and went to bed, wondering if he would ever get his life back.

The headaches continued, some days worse than others. They ended up paying exorbitant prices for the migraine drugs when the insurance company would only allow a person to buy so many in a given period of time. They could certainly afford it, but Jayson wondered how people managed who *couldn't* afford it. The limitation seemed a bit ridiculous.

As the problem continued, there were days when Jayson couldn't even talk himself into the studio to play anything at all. He felt empty on such days, but he just didn't have the strength or motivation to do it.

Feeling relatively desperate, Jayson started trying every alternative method of easing a headache. Between him and Elizabeth, they had searched the Internet and explored every medical, holistic, and homeopathic remedy for a headache. He'd done everything from putting olive oil under his tongue to putting lemon rinds on his forehead—and several embarrassing and ridiculous things in between. He'd analyzed his eating habits, his other habits, and every other possible thing that could be a headache trigger. Considering all such options prayerfully, he could only feel stupor of thought in considering any of those things as contributing to the problem. It seemed they were just migraines with no apparent cause that made any sense, and his only method of coping was to take the medication, rest, and try to cope hour to hour, day to day.

Elizabeth had covered for Jayson with choir practices and a performance, and he desperately missed being able to do it. But not as much as he missed just being in church. Each Sunday morning he'd been determined to go, but it just hadn't been possible.

After twenty-seven straight days of migraine pain, in which he'd had four doctor's office visits, three appointments with alternative healers, an

MRI, five priesthood blessings, and spent a fortune on medications and several other hokey attempts to cure a headache, Jayson finally got to the end of a day and announced his epiphany to his wife. "I didn't have to take the big drug today."

"Really?"

"I had a headache, but it was in the normal range. I just took Excedrin."

She laughed with delight and hugged him. "I do believe that's a triumph."

"I do believe it is." He laughed with her. "Now let's just hope it lasts. I've got work to do."

"Yes, you do," she said and hugged him again.

That night when they knelt together by their bed to pray, it was Elizabeth's turn. She thanked their Heavenly Father profusely for giving Jayson a day without pain, and pleaded for the pain to be a thing of the past. Jayson added his fervent amen and slept well that night, waking up grateful to not feel any sign of pain. He prayed that it would stay that way through the day and called Roger early to say that he'd like to go running with him, as long as they could take it slow. Roger was thrilled, and Mozie was too.

Jayson ended up walking more than running, but Roger was glad to keep pace with him, and they had a good visit. It felt good to be out again, getting some exercise and fresh air. But about an hour after he returned home, he was so utterly exhausted that he had to lie down. He fell asleep and woke up with a headache, but Excedrin settled it down and he managed to get through the rest of the day.

That afternoon Elizabeth came to the studio and found him practicing. She said, "It's nice to have you back at it for more than a little while here and there."

"It's nice to *be* back at it," he said. "I just pray this lasts. I've become paranoid."

She sat beside him. "That's understandable after what you've been through."

"I suppose if I knew what had brought it on, I'd feel more like I could avoid having it happen again. But I'm stumped."

"So am I. If it's just one of those things that happens, we'll just have to pray that it doesn't happen again."

"Or at least not very often—or in the middle of a tour."

"Yes, we'll pray for that."

Contending with a lower-grade headache that had become common if not constant, Jayson reached for the bottle of Excedrin and took one along with a long swig from the bottle of water he had on the piano.

"You're still taking a lot of those," she said.

"It's the only thing that will keep the nagging headache from nagging."

"They have a lot of caffeine in them."

"I know, Elizabeth. I've read the ingredients. Caffeine is one of *the* best drugs for headaches. You heard the doctor say that."

"I know that. I respect its medicinal purposes. I also know you can get rebound headaches from taking too much of it."

"I know that too, Elizabeth. I just have to take it one day at a time and cope the best I can. Are we having an argument here?"

"No! Why?"

"You sound . . . agitated."

"I'm just worried."

"I'm worried too, but maybe you should clarify what you're worried about. You think I'm going to get *addicted* to caffeine? Or that I'm going to *abuse* it?" She didn't comment, but he knew that look, and he had to remind himself not to get defensive. They'd been through counseling together in drug rehab, and it was a well-established rule that *any* concern over drugs had to be addressed straight out. "Okay," he said, "let me make something perfectly clear. I am not taking more than the maximum dosage directed on the label; usually not even that much. My drug problem came from taking *too many.* I recognize that caffeine is not good for me, but neither are all of those other drugs I've been taking. Chemotherapy isn't good for people, but it's better than the cancer. I can only deal with this one step at a time. I'm being prayerful *and* careful. I promise. I'm counting on not needing them at all—very soon, I hope."

"I hope so, too," she said and put her arms around him. "I did read yesterday that for some people, taking a couple of aspirin along with drinking a Coke will help the headache without the buzz that sometimes comes with caffeine medications."

"You're still studying on my behalf?"

"I still am."

"Okay, well . . . maybe I'll try that. One more thing to help my good Mormon boy image." He sighed and added a thought that had been uppermost in his mind. "I'm still trying to figure out what I was supposed to learn from a twenty-seven-day migraine—and the ongoing hangover."

"Maybe you weren't supposed to learn anything. Maybe it was just . . . a migraine."

"Maybe," he said, "but it *feels* like I'm supposed to learn something. It's like I have this . . . little nagging feeling that seems to say, 'Pay attention, Jayson. You're supposed to learn something from this.'"

"Then I guess you'd better pay attention, and as long as you keep asking and living close to the Spirit—which you do—you'll get the answer when the Lord wants you to get it."

"Okay, I can live with that. I just hope getting the answer doesn't involve more pain. I know some people suffer with chronic pain for months, years, their whole life. How do they do it?"

"I don't know," Elizabeth said. "I've wondered the same. I guess we've both gained some empathy in that regard. We can be grateful for all we have in our lives that's good. And we do have a lot to be grateful for."

"Yes, we do!" he said with enthusiasm. "I'll try to remember that, instead of feeling angry over losing so many days of my life. I need to keep perspective." He chuckled. "Maybe I need to write a song about perspective. Or maybe," his voice took on a dramatic lilt, "I should practice the songs I already wrote so that I can do it like—"

"Breathing."

"Yeah, like breathing."

Elizabeth laughed softly and kissed him. "I should leave you to practice."

"Okay, but just . . . one more kiss first," he said, and she gave it to him.

* * * * *

Jayson was deeply thrilled and grateful to return to church. He loved just being there, and managed to keep his mild headache under control with a new prescription the doctor had given him to replace the Excedrin. It worked better and had less caffeine, and he was glad on both counts. He felt renewed on a deeper level to be able to take the sacrament, and he took in the talks and lessons with extra appreciation. Many people had noticed he'd been gone and had heard he'd been ill. He was met with lots of hugs and many expressions of friendship and concern from people who were glad to see him. He got a glimpse of Sister Freedman, but she scurried quickly away from his view as if just having him in her sight was painful for her. It was painful for him too, but probably not for the same reasons. He focused instead on the love and kindness of so many other people, and silently thanked God at least a dozen times during the day for allowing him to be there, to feel tolerably well, and to be part of such a great ward.

That afternoon, following choir practice—for which Jayson was able to play—the entire family was invited to have dinner at Layla's home. Macy would be doing most of the cooking, with Aaron and the kids enlisted to help. And Layla would also be helping with the preparations as she sat nearby on a bar stool. When Macy had invited them, Jayson had asked, "Are you sure? We're a lot of extra mouths to feed."

"No, we really want to have you over. It's our first complete gluten-free unveiling. Layla's always telling me how good you've been to us, and she wants to do this, so we're doing it together."

"Okay, what can we bring?" Elizabeth had asked.

Macy told her a green salad would be great. She just had to be certain in preparing it that the fresh vegetables didn't come in contact with any surface or utensils where gluten might have been, and she told Elizabeth what brand of salad dressing was okay. Macy wanted this meal to be completely safe for Layla, which was a new step for the family. They were eating separately most days, but it had been decided that from now on, Sunday dinner would be completely gluten-free, and they would work up from there.

When they arrived for dinner Sunday afternoon, the children were quickly integrated with Layla's children, the older ones watching out for the little ones and having a marvelous time while the final dinner preparations were underway. Layla looked so much better that Elizabeth actually got teary when she saw her, and Jayson felt close to tears as well. She still looked too thin, but she had more color to her face, her eyes were brighter, and she was up and about, helping a little here and there, even though she became tired very easily.

It took two tables set up end-to-end in the large front room to seat both families, but it was delightful to all sit down together and share a meal. For dinner they had chicken Parmesan that Macy had made, and instead of rolls they had some very good cornbread that Aaron's sister had learned to make. Along with Elizabeth's green salad, there was also a Jell-O salad and steamed vegetables. For dessert there was cheesecake made from scratch with a crust made from gluten-free cookies, and a raspberry sauce. Many things that were canned or made from mixes couldn't be used for Layla anymore, but the meal was wonderful, and it was obvious they were making progress on learning some things. Jayson sat back and watched his daughter, considering her hand in all that was being put out on the table, and all she'd had to learn and do that went behind such a meal's preparation—especially in making it completely safe for Layla. And he felt so thoroughly proud of her. Recalling the sweet little girl she'd been before her difficult teenage years, he wasn't surprised that she'd turned out this way. Even so, he never could have imagined what a wonderful woman she would become. While they cleaned up after dinner, he hugged her tightly and told her that. She returned the hug and smiled up at him. Not only was she doing great things for this family, but she was very happy.

After everyone pitched in to put the kitchen in order while Layla just supervised, the children went back to what they'd been playing. Even Derek and Harmony were in tolerably good moods considering that it was their typical nap time. Trevin preferred remaining with the adults, listening more than contributing to the conversation. Layla talked candidly about the slow progress she was making. She felt discouraged at times realizing how long it could take to return to her normal health, but at the same time she was inexpressibly grateful to be alive, knowing that if the condition hadn't been diagnosed when it was, she probably wouldn't have been here. She tearfully expressed her gratitude for having Aaron and Macy in her home, and especially for Macy's love and care. She said they had become the best of friends, which made Macy beam and agree fervently. Then she mentioned that eventually all of the children would need to be tested for the disease.

"It's hereditary?" Jayson asked, wondering if he'd missed that before, or if it had never come up when he'd been around.

"It is genetic," Layla said. "There's no other way to get it. You either have the gene, or you don't. But then the gene can either get triggered or not. Some people have it triggered when they are very young; others when they're much older. As long as there's no sign of illness with the children, we assume that it's either not present or hasn't been triggered, but if anything comes up, we'll know that's the first place to look."

"Which means," Macy said, "that it's a good thing I'm learning all of this, because it's possible my children could have it."

Jayson felt sobered by the possibility of *his* grandchildren having to deal with this. He wondered how a kid would handle growing up without pizza and cookies and hamburgers. Then he concluded, "I'm sure there are a lot of things that could be worse for a kid to deal with, but it certainly would be tough."

"That's exactly what I've thought," Aaron said, taking Macy's hand. "We'll have to take it on the best we can." He smiled at his wife. "We'll just be glad when we get a baby."

"We'll all be glad for that," Elizabeth said, taking Macy's other hand. "It will happen."

Macy smiled at her mother, and Jayson saw a mixture of hope and sadness in her eyes. He understood both feelings well. It had been months since she'd lost the baby, and she wasn't pregnant again. He prayed every day that his daughter would be blessed with a baby, and he hoped it would happen soon.

Harmony got very grumpy, but Jayson wrapped her in her blanket and held her until she fell asleep in his arms. The other children continued to play and have a good time, while the adults had great conversation and a lot of laughs.

* * * * *

Winter was showing hints of coming to an end when Jayson embarked on the first stage of pre-tour rehearsals. Drew came to stay in the spare rooms in the basement, as he had done before. His family remained in Los Angeles this time, since Valerie was involved in some projects. Brandon and Dalton, the musicians from Los Angeles that Jayson had hired, would be put up in a nearby hotel, with rooms that had kitchenettes so they could live there while they would be working six days a week, twelve hours a day. The college kids that comprised the orchestra attended specified rehearsals, mostly on Saturdays. They'd had the schedule for weeks so that they all had ample time to make arrangements to be there. Jayson had Elizabeth to thank for making certain that such details came together smoothly. During every hour of rehearsal when Trevin wasn't in school or doing homework, he was in the studio, just watching, listening, and soaking it all in with such eagerness that Jayson couldn't help but feel the bond between them growing.

Jayson continued to struggle with some level of chronic headaches, but had only an occasional need to take a migraine drug, which always worked quickly and made it possible for him to do the work he needed to do. He also felt blessed to realize as they were rehearsing that in spite of the time he *hadn't* spent practicing due to his long-term bout with pain, he was managing just fine.

He was enjoying the work and was glad to see how well it was coming together, but he was also glad when evenings came and he could be with his family. One Friday evening after the kids were in bed and Drew had gone out with Dalton and Brandon, Jayson and Elizabeth sat down together to watch a movie. It was nearly eleven o'clock when the phone rang, and Jayson reached to answer it while Elizabeth paused the video they were watching.

"Dad?" Trevin said, sounding panicked.

"What's wrong?" Jayson asked, sitting forward.

"I'm fine. It's Clayton. I don't know what to do."

"Just tell me what's going on," Jayson said and whispered to Elizabeth, "He's fine. It's something to do with Clayton."

"He was at the party with the rest of us, but he was there with some of the kids he hangs out with at school. I noticed them being sneaky, and I think they're doing drugs. He just left with them to go to somebody else's house, but he already looked stoned. I'm afraid he's gonna do something really stupid."

"Do you know where he went?"

"Yes."

"Okay, you tell me where. I'll take care of it. You come home."

"Okay, Dad. Thanks."

Jayson called Roger's number while he ran up the stairs, with Elizabeth right behind him. He managed to explain most of it to her before Roger answered, then Jayson explained it to him again, saying he would be picking him up in less than five minutes.

On their way to the address that Trevin had given to Jayson, Roger used his cell phone to call the police and tell them they suspected drug use. He explained the situation, what little they knew, and why they were going there. At the appointed house, they could hear very loud music when they approached the door.

"Parents not home, apparently," Roger said wryly and lifted his hand to knock, but Jayson just opened the door and went in.

"Like they'd ever hear a knock at the door," Jayson said.

"I feel like the FBI."

"I think it's more DEA," Jayson said. They found the room where the party was taking place, just off the entry hall of a beautiful home. Jayson couldn't believe his eyes. There were pictures of the temple and the prophet on the wall, and there were five teenagers sitting around the coffee table, snorting cocaine. Clayton was one of them. Roger was apparently too stunned to move, but Jayson had once had a band member with this nasty habit. He knew it well, and he was quick to just take Clayton by the arm and drag him to his feet, ignoring the protests of the others. He and Roger efficiently led Clayton out of the house and into the car, knowing the police were on their way to handle the rest. The police pulled up just as Jayson drove away.

"What are you doing?" Clayton demanded for the fifth time, his voice slurred.

"Saving you from jail time, apparently," Jayson said.

"Oh, man," Clayton said. "My mom is gonna kill me."

"No," Jayson said, "she's gonna kill *me!* She'll blame me for this, you know. If I didn't give you the coke, she'll be sure it was my music that drove you to it."

"I don't think he'll remember this conversation in the morning," Roger said. Jayson groaned and hit the steering wheel with his fist. Roger added, "Why don't I just keep him at my house tonight? I can keep an eye on him."

Jayson could hardly sleep that night. He felt sick to his stomach. Seeing Clayton in a situation that reminded him too much of ugly things he'd witnessed in his life just made him nauseous. He was still certain he got more sleep than Roger, who called just after eight in the morning, asking Jayson to come over. "He's coherent now," Roger said. "But I think you're the one who needs to talk to him."

"Me?"

"Tell him what you've seen, Jayson. Tell him how stupid he's being. I can't do it."

Jayson arrived at Roger's house to find Clayton half-reclined on a couch in the basement family room, and Roger looking horrible.

"Bad night?" Jayson asked.

"You could say that."

When Clayton saw Jayson come into the room, he said, "Oh, man. I don't know which is worse: my mother finding out I did drugs, or finding out that I was in the same room with you."

Roger said, "She won't find out about either if you promise both of us that you'll never do something that stupid again. We're not into keeping secrets, so you'd better really appreciate this one. If it wasn't for us, you'd have spent the night in jail, and your mother would be bailing you out about now."

Clayton groaned, but it was hard to tell if it was from the idea or the hangover. Jayson sat down on the coffee table so that he could face him directly. "What were you thinking?" he asked. "I mean, seriously. I never took you for somebody that *stupid*. Let me tell you something about stupid." He went on to tell Clayton about his band members, one who had died of AIDS, the other from a drug overdose. He repeated incidents he had witnessed that illustrated the horror and depravity of what their lifestyles had done to them. He talked about his own experience with prescription drug addiction, and the horror of detox. Roger joined the conversation and expressed to Clayton the knowledge that his Heavenly Father loved him, and there wasn't anything that couldn't be solved if he could rely on that love and keep his life straight. Roger offered a commitment of help and support as long as Clayton did his best to stick to the right choices. Clayton didn't say much, but Jayson sensed that the lecture was settling in. He hoped so. He left just before Roger was going to take Clayton home, and they joked about how it wasn't a good idea for Jayson to do it. He returned home knowing that he had no more control concerning what would happen with Clayton than he did with many other things in his life. He could only pray and hope that it turned out okay.

CHAPTER 8

Just when Jayson thought the tabloid issue had become a bad memory, a new story hit the stands, focusing on the fact that Debbie was still in rehab. But the magazine was apparently more intent on grossly exaggerating and distorting details of Jayson's past drug issues. Jayson wisely realized that the only people whose opinions mattered to him were his family members and the people he went to church with. Of course, there was always the general public—people who might not bother to look at his religious values due to such reputed allegations. And there were those who might know he was a Mormon and feel disgusted. But he couldn't do anything about that. He prayed every day over the matter, asking to be guided to know what he *could* do. He told his Heavenly Father over and over that he would do anything that was asked of him if it would just stop this madness. But the madness only grew. When the Associated Press carried the news that Jayson Wolfe was releasing a new album, it was as if the tabloids went on a feeding frenzy, dredging up old stuff and mostly fabricating new stuff to go with it.

Jayson was venting about the entire situation to Roger one morning while they were running, and Roger said, "So, let's sue them. I'm a lawyer, remember?"

"I remember that. I don't want to sue them. I don't think that's in my nature. I just want it to stop."

"There's a big difference in suing someone just to be spiteful or cause trouble for them, and reasonably attempting to get justice or solve a problem. So, we threaten a lawsuit and then make it clear how nice we're being when we back down on expecting any punitive damages, specifically that you'll settle without asking them for money. Instead you want retractions and an agreement for no more stories."

Jayson thought about that for a minute. He'd once had an agent *and* an attorney, but they'd all gone away when his career with *Gray Wolf* had ended. And with his solo career, he'd not had anything come up that he couldn't handle on his own. The record company had been good about taking care of many things, but this had nothing to do with them.

"Can you do that?" Jayson asked.

Roger chuckled. "My dear friend. Can you play the piano? This is what I do. And I'm very good at being charitable, having integrity, and still making the bad guys get the justice they deserve."

"Wow," Jayson chuckled. "I think it's time we started talking about *your* career. You told me it was boring. That doesn't sound boring."

They talked for an hour after they'd finished running, and Jayson agreed that he wanted Roger to help him do something about the tabloid problem. When Jayson read the letters that Roger was sending to the corporate level of these sleazy magazines, he actually laughed out loud. Even if nothing ever came of it, the letters felt thoroughly vindicating. But he was surprised at how quickly action occurred. He'd wanted retractions, and he'd wanted it to stop. He got both—sort of. The retractions were laced with the implication that Jayson Wolfe was hotheaded and threatening. But then it *did* stop. He just hoped it stayed that way.

Trevin was excited—as was the entire family—when the record company approved the idea for the video of "Good, Clean Fun" to be filmed at the high school. It would be done just before the band members flew back to Los Angeles at the completion of this stretch of rehearsals. Arrangements were quickly made, and a couple of days before the event, Jayson walked into the bedroom and found a large wrapped box on the bed. "What is this?" he asked Elizabeth, who was sitting in the chair, reading.

"A present."

"For . . ."

"You, of course."

"Now, why would you get me a present?"

"Because it was perfect and you need it," she said, setting her book aside. "It's almost time to start promoting the new album, and you're doing that video this weekend. Trust me. This is perfect."

"You're making me nervous," he said.

"Just open it."

Jayson did so and was pleasantly surprised to find a long, black coat. He lifted it up to see that the fabric was lightweight but high quality. The cut was classic and simple.

"Wow," he said.

"It's wrinkle resistant, and the fabric breathes so that you can wear it without getting too hot. It will flow with you when you move."

"Ooh," he said, pressing his fingers over it. "And how do you know that?"

"Because I tried it on in the store and imitated you in the mirror."

He laughed. "I would have liked to have seen that."

"Try it on and do some of that Jayson Wolfe rock star stuff for me." He put it on and admired it in the long mirror, saying sincerely, "I really like it. Thank you. You *do* have good taste."

"I married you, didn't I?"

"True."

"And if you remember, I was the one who gave you that really great leather coat that you wore in a hundred photo shoots, although you never actually wore it onstage. But you wore it out and I thought this would be a practical replacement. It's kind of your trademark."

"So it is," he said, then did a spin and some fancy footwork that he would do onstage, which made Elizabeth laugh.

On Friday evening, Jayson and Elizabeth went to a stake youth dance, since Elizabeth had signed them up weeks earlier to be chaperones. Jayson was feeling better than he had in a long time, and actually had enough energy to dance with Elizabeth a few times. They mostly wandered around and chatted with people there. They didn't know any of the other chaperones, but they knew the youth in their own ward, and a few kids that Trevin knew from high school. The music for the dance was being played by a DJ on the stage, and it covered a broad range of rock and popular music that was appropriate for such an event. Jayson commented to Elizabeth that Sister Freedman might be outside with a picket sign. She smiled but told him he needed to be nicer. More seriously, he said, "Of course, Clayton isn't here. Not only did they choose someone like me to be a chaperone, but the music is generally evil."

"Where do you suppose Clayton is if he's not here?" Elizabeth asked, knowing it was a rhetorical question.

Jayson answered it anyway. "Probably out doing something much more uplifting." His own sarcasm brought to mind Clayton's bout with drugs, and Jayson wondered if he was still messing around with such things. He hoped not.

A few minutes later, a big hit by Gray Wolf was played. Jayson gave Elizabeth a dubious smirk, then said, "See. What did I tell you? The music is just garbage."

Trevin found his parents before the song was over and playfully said to Jayson, "You really should be more open-minded about music, Dad. If you'd just give this kind of stuff a chance, you might grow to like it."

"Funny," Jayson said. "Very funny." Then his attempt to be serious failed, and he laughed. It *was* pretty funny.

The following day was scheduled for the video shoot, and the weather was sunny and pleasant. When Jayson, Drew, and Elizabeth arrived at the stadium, everything was set up, and the bleachers on the west side of the field were full of noisy teenagers. They'd all been told to wear dark pants and white shirts. The effect was great. Jayson was wearing a white T-shirt, white jeans, white lace-up shoes, and dark glasses. Elizabeth was carrying the new black coat. The football field was consumed with music equipment, lights, and cameras. And in front of the bleachers were some officers hired from a local security company. It was a liability requirement when doing any such endeavor, just to make sure that nothing got out of hand.

When the kids had apparently figured out that Jayson had arrived, a huge cheer went up. He waved, and they cheered louder, making Jayson laugh. He knew the kids had been promised pizza for lunch, and they had also been reminded that the day would be boring and long. But they'd also been promised a CD, a T-shirt, and concert tickets for the opening show that would be in Salt Lake City. They'd been warned that any unruly or unseemly behavior that inhibited the process would warrant them being escorted out—no second chances. Their incentive to be good stemmed from wanting to be able to see themselves in the video on YouTube. Jayson knew the day would entail doing the song over and over and over, while the cameras did different angles and effects. Filming videos had never been a favorable aspect of the business for him, but it was part of the business and he just did it. At least the enthusiastic kids in the bleachers were a new twist that would liven up the experience. Jayson talked with the director and suggested that they get good shots of the kids as much as possible this morning while they were fresh and excited, and before they got bored. The director agreed.

Over the next half hour, the rest of the musicians showed up, all wearing different varieties of black jeans and white shirts. The four brass players came wearing white T-shirts with a black wolf face printed on the front.

"Very clever," Jayson said. "The Wolfe Boys. I get it."

"It was your wife's idea," Spencer said. Jayson turned to look at her, and she shrugged.

Jayson did a mike check, then said into it, "Okay, here we go. Thanks for coming." The kids all cheered. He knew they'd been coached through the few lines of lyrics they would be singing, and how to go about it. "We're gonna run through the song a couple of times to get warmed up, then you guys can come in and we'll start filming."

The kids cheered when he started in with the guitar. Dalton came in with the bass, and Brandon was doing another layer of guitar for this particular song. The crowd cheered again when the drums hit, then again with the brass. Since they were just rehearsing, the noise was fine, and it got them all pumped up with adrenaline. The first three times they had the kids chant the chorus lyrics, it was close to disastrous, but then it started to click with the music and they got some good footage. The kids really started to get into it, and the chorus they were singing sounded great. *"Whatever happened to good, clean fun? The kind that doesn't take a pill or booze to loosen up. Laughter's free and doesn't leave a hangover. Come on, boys and girls, let's get addicted to good, clean fun!"*

Elizabeth hovered at the sidelines, out of camera range, observing the unfolding of one of Jayson's creations in a way that warmed her heart. No one else could fully appreciate what a day such as this meant in the process of taking a song to the world. She'd seen its germination, its evolution, and now it was coming to fruition. And no one else could see Jayson Wolfe the way she saw him. The way he moved as he played and sang was practically an art form. She could see him physically become a part of the song, in a subtle, unassuming kind of way. Once his guitar pick hit those strings and his voice struck that first brilliant note, he was one with his music. His ongoing practice was readily evident in the way he could move around so casually between his lines at the microphone. Somehow he seemed to be unconsciously pulled back to the mike at the very moment he needed to sing again. She watched him giving instructions to other band members, and suggestions to the cameramen and the director even while he was playing, as if the guitar were nothing and he could multitask his intricate playing with anything else that needed his attention. With a cordless guitar adaptor hooked to the back of his belt, he could move freely, dance, jump, spin, and tease the other musicians—and he did.

Between takes, Elizabeth helped make certain his clothes and hair looked the way they should. And he often gave her a quick kiss after she did. From the front, Jayson appeared to have a normal haircut, although it was waxed for the sake of volume. From the side or behind, his pony-tail had become the perfect length; the length she'd become accustomed to when she'd first met him, and during most of the years they'd known each other. She noted the cameras doing extreme close-ups of his hands on the guitar, and she loved the fact that his wedding ring was so visible. While she hovered near the director, she could see what the cameras were seeing on a monitor. They also did great close-ups of the other musicians playing, and she especially liked the angles they got on the drums when Drew was really going at it; the sticks were a blur. Seeing close-ups of Jayson singing, she smiled to recall how he'd needed all of his metal fill-ings replaced at the time he'd gotten his first record deal. He couldn't sing with a camera in his face without having every tooth visible, so they all had to be perfectly white.

Jayson found he was enjoying the day, even with the tedious repeti-tion. He did the song with the guitar, without the guitar, with the coat, without the coat; he sang it and he lip-synched his own recording. He had cameras all around him, sometimes right in his face, and the kids all stayed pretty orderly and positive. The pizza was a big hit and kept them going. For a break in the middle of the afternoon, Jayson had the band join him in playing a couple of radio hits from his last album that they'd been rehearsing for the concert. This renewed the crowd and kept them enthused. Jayson was filmed running up and down the aisles of the bleachers and along the front, giving high-fives to some of the kids and sitting among them, singing along with their chant. Recalling debilitating days of headache pain, he was grateful to be feeling well and pain-free. He hadn't even taken a single pill of any kind that day. He knew the director would take the enormous amount of footage from several cameras and different types of film to edit the whole thing together, and he believed it was going to be one of his favorite videos, if only for the memories. He was aware of Trevin in the stands, blending in with the rest of the kids. But he ignored him, knowing Trevin preferred it that way.

Back on the field to run through it two final times, Jayson noticed Elizabeth answering her cell phone, which he knew had been on vibrate to keep it silent. She looked concerned, and he wondered if the kids were okay. He held up a hand toward the other band members to indicate they should hold on a minute. She glanced toward him while she was talking, but she didn't look upset. Still, he waited, wanting to be certain everything was alright. After she hung up, she approached him and said quietly, "You need to get Trevin past security. He's coming down."

"Okay," Jayson drawled. "That was a change of heart. Why?"

"Well, I think it went something like this." She altered her voice each time she mimicked the dialogue of Trevin's peers. "'Hey, isn't that your mom down there?' 'No, way.' 'That can't be his mom because that would mean his dad was the famous guy, and if his dad was famous, he would have been bragging about that a long time ago.' 'His last name's not the same. It's impossible.' And then Clayton said—"

"Clayton's up there?"

"Apparently."

"His mom's gonna wage a new barrage."

"Maybe. But he's the one who said to the hecklers, 'He *is* Trevin's dad; his stepdad anyway. And if I were Trevin, I'd be proud to have him be my dad, not because he's famous, but because he's a great guy.'"

"Clayton said that?"

"That's what Trevin told me," Elizabeth said and looked up at the bleachers, motioning with her hand. Trevin started down the steps while she added, "Then apparently the hecklers started saying they'd made it up and there was no way you were his dad, blah, blah, blah. I think it's time these kids knew how cool Trevin really is."

"Amen," Jayson said and motioned toward the security guard who got the silent message to let the kid through.

"Can't you just hear it up there?" Elizabeth said and raised her voice again to mimic the kids. "'Oh, my gosh. I can't believe it.'"

"Then we'd better make it good," Jayson said and picked up the extra bass guitar they had with the equipment as Trevin approached. They always had extras of everything.

"What do you want me to do with this?" Trevin asked.

"Play it. We're just synching now, anyway. I'm sure you can make it look good."

Dalton, the bass player, was standing within earshot and said, winking at Jayson, "I'm gonna sit this one out, kid. You go for it." He put down his guitar and walked away to sit on the grass.

"But . . . I blew it up there," Trevin said quietly to his father and almost looked near tears. "I shouldn't need you to rescue me from—"

"Hey, you didn't blow anything," Jayson said. "Now play. You know the song well enough to pull it off. You're going to need the practice if you're going on tour with me this summer."

"Am I?" Trevin asked.

"You did last time."

"Yeah, but I just . . ."

"Hung around with the band and jammed after the show. I know. This time you're going to be onstage—at least for one number. Now play it," Jayson smirked, "or you'll be grounded."

"Yes, Dad," Trevin said and laughed.

"Okay," Jayson said into the microphone. "We're going through it two more times, and then you can all go bowling, or something. Don't forget to pick up your coupon packets on the way out so you can get all the cool stuff." The kids cheered. "You guys have been great. Thank you!" They cheered again. "To wrap it up, we're going to have Trevin Aragon on bass guitar. He's a blossoming musician and a great kid. I'm proud to be his dad."

A murmur went through the crowd, then Jayson motioned for the band to begin, and Trevin was right on cue. The crowd *really* cheered after they finished, and Jayson wondered if it was for their classmate. Jayson gave Trevin a high-five, then Drew jumped off his drum stool, ran toward Trevin, and did the same thing before he returned to sit back down. The director approached Jayson and said it was all good, and he didn't see a need to go through it again. Jayson said comically into the microphone, "Our fantastic director has something to say."

He tilted the mike toward the director, who said, "That's a wrap."

Everyone cheered, then Jayson said, "Since we're finished early, and you guys have been so great, we're going to do a song just for fun. You want to hear a different song?" They cheered. "You sick o' that other one?" He laughed. "I am." Jayson turned around to give instructions to the band, then said to Trevin, "We're doing 'Predator.' You good with that?"

Trevin nodded and smiled. How could it be this easy to make a kid so happy? If he was a computer geek who hated rock music, they might have had a generation gap.

"Okay," Jayson said into the mike, "we're all good here. How are you?" The kids cheered. "You may or may not have heard this song on the radio. If you did, it was me. But it's getting kind of old now . . . like me. Pretend you like it anyway."

He hit the first notes on the guitar, and a cheer went up. Apparently they recognized it, even if it was from hearing their older siblings or parents listening to it. The drums and bass came in on cue and the song sailed along impressively, with Dalton still sitting on the grass, watching Trevin with a certain amount of pride. They'd become pretty good buddies through all of the rehearsals.

Before Jayson played the final note, he said into the mike, "That's it. We're done. Get out of here. And thank you."

While the kids were filing out, Jayson said good-bye to Drew, Dalton, and Brandon, since they were all on their way to the airport to catch evening flights back to Los Angeles. They would be back in a few weeks to embark on more intense rehearsals just prior to the official release of the album and the beginning of public promotions.

Jayson hovered on the field and pitched in with the takedown. He wanted the kids to leave before he tried to do the same; he was well experienced at avoiding close contact with a crowd after a concert. When the stands had cleared out and most of the kids were gone, Jayson noticed a small group hovering at the far end of the field. He said to Trevin, who was rolling up a microphone cord, "Friends of yours?"

Trevin glanced. "Yeah, I think so."

"What does that mean?" Jayson chuckled. "Were they not your friends yesterday?"

"Some of them . . . I think."

"Well, you'd better go give them your autograph, or something," Jayson said. "They look pretty determined to hang around until you do."

While Trevin was walking toward the groupies, Elizabeth came up beside Jayson and said, "We're going to have to spray him with essence of skunk to keep the girls away, especially since he'll have his driver's license soon."

"Nah," Jayson said, "he likes guitars more than girls. He's a true musician."

"You liked *me*," she said. "Are you saying you liked your guitar more?"

"It was a toss-up," he said, and she playfully slugged him. Then she kissed him. "On second thought," he said, "you're definitely better looking than my guitar."

* * * * *

The following morning, Jayson woke up with a migraine. He took something, and it eased up enough that he was able to go to sacrament meeting and play for the choir, but he skipped out early from the other meetings and had to go to bed. He felt discouraged over being confronted with the pain again, and with its severity. He felt angry over missing meetings and missing out on participating in life with his family the way he wanted to. And he felt afraid of how the possibility of future headaches would fit into the rehearsals, promotions, and tour that were on the calendar. He focused his mind on prayer, and tried to be positive. He hoped that his trust in the Lord could outweigh his fear, but he was having a hard time finding the balance with that while he was actually feeling the side effects of migraine medication and the unnatural exhaustion and weakness that always followed the worst of the pain.

He did manage to get up and eat dinner with the family, but he went right back to bed. He couldn't relax enough to sleep, but he felt too awful to be up doing anything else. He was grateful when Elizabeth came and laid down beside him, snuggling close to him, talking of trivial family things and memories that helped distract him from the negative emotions that came so commonly with the pain and illness.

"Do you remember the first time we kissed?" she asked while they lay with their heads on the same pillow, looking at each other.

"How could I ever forget?" he said and kissed her. "It was raining. But I think you're more beautiful now than you were then."

"I think you need your glasses."

He chuckled. "I think you get more beautiful every year, and I can see you just fine."

"I'm a few sizes bigger."

"You were too skinny back then."

"You're just saying that to make me feel better."

"I'm saying it because it's true. I mean . . . I thought you were pretty hot. But now I'm a middle-aged man who has come to appreciate *true* beauty. And you are so beautiful."

"We were so young."

"Yes, we were."

"Not much older than Trevin is now."

"Ooh, you're scaring me." Jayson chuckled. "I think back and I know I felt so mature, but now I know I was an idiot."

Elizabeth chuckled. "Not really. You were actually pretty sharp and mature—in most ways. I'm glad Trevin has the gospel."

"You and me both. I wonder what it might have been like if we'd had it."

"I don't know." Elizabeth said. "I wonder if I would have made better choices if I'd known how to listen to the Holy Ghost."

"We probably both would have."

"Sometimes I think we should have gotten married the first time you asked me. Everything would have been so different."

"Yes, it certainly would have been different, but I thought we'd agreed a long time ago that we had needed those years apart, that it needed to be that way. Either way, it's in the past and we can't change it. So, there's little point in wondering."

"I know, but I still wonder. What would it have been like if I'd married the great Jayson Wolfe when we were both eighteen?"

"For starters, I wasn't the great Jayson Wolfe back then. I went through horrible years before anything great happened, and you were spared all of that."

"You were always great to me."

"And yet you told me you wouldn't marry me."

"Stupidest thing I ever did. We would have gotten married in the back yard of Dad's house. It would have been simple, but beautiful. Macy would be *my* daughter, and Trevin would be *your* son."

"Except they wouldn't really be who they are if they didn't have the parents they were born with. If Trevin had my genes, he probably would have been a snotty little rebel."

"Maybe." Elizabeth chuckled. "And maybe Macy would have been OCD, or something."

"It doesn't matter, because eternally they are *our* children. We have a beautiful family."

"Yes, I know." She kissed him. "I love you, Jayson Wolfe."

"I love you too," he said, his voice cracking.

"What's wrong?"

"I'm just sick of this; the pain, hiding in a dark room while life goes on around me."

"It's not going to last forever, Jayson. We'll get through this. At least it's getting better, less frequent. We'll just have to take it on the best we can."

"With the way you take such good care of me, I believe we *will* get through it. I just know that it's hard on you, as well."

"We're married. You know what they say about in sickness and in health; all that stuff."

"I've heard that, yes."

"And it's forever."

"Yes." He kissed her again. "It's forever."

* * * * *

Jayson woke up in the middle of the night, immediately overcome with a horrible feeling. It only took a long moment to realize that his entire body was consumed with an ache that felt debilitating, and he was freezing. He took some Tylenol, found an extra blanket, and went back to bed, but he never did go back to sleep. He was just too miserable. He waited until Elizabeth was awake before he said, "Don't get too close. I'm sick; I'm really sick."

"What's wrong?" she asked and rolled over to put her hand to his forehead. "Good heavens! You're so hot."

"Yeah, and that's with Tylenol in me."

"I can't believe this is happening," she said.

"You and me both," he muttered through chattering teeth.

"How did you get sick? The kids haven't been sick. Where would you have gotten it?"

"I don't know. I'm just really ticked off."

"Okay, well . . . we'll get through this. At least it's not last week when the guys were here from Los Angeles."

"Yeah, I'll count my blessings," he said, but his words held a tiny hint of sarcasm. More seriously he said, "I don't want you or the kids to get sick."

"I know how to do germ control, but you could have been contagious before you got symptoms."

He groaned at the thought of any member of his family feeling the way he felt now. "We'll just pray that it stays with me and doesn't spread," he said.

Throughout the day, Elizabeth did her best to take care of Jayson, and she used every tactic she knew of to keep germs from spreading. Observing his misery, she thought it prudent to call the doctor's office and find out what was going around and what they might expect. The nurses were busy but one called her back about an hour later. She told Elizabeth, "There are two major viral infections we're seeing a lot of. The first is a flu that hangs on for about seven to ten days, and its only real symptoms are fever and body aches; some people have had pretty bad headaches with it."

"Great," Elizabeth said with sarcasm. The symptoms sounded right; the time span and the headaches were both things that she knew would really thrill Jayson.

"The other," the nurse went on, "is a viral respiratory infection. Is he coughing?"

"No," she said.

"Well, if he starts coughing, it could be that. Hopefully it's not, because that's a doozy. It has the aches and fever *along with* a nasty cough, and sometimes breathing becomes difficult. If he gets those symptoms, he needs to come in and we can give him an inhaler—like they use for asthma—to get him through. And we can give him something for the cough. The worst of the symptoms are over in one to two weeks, but the cough and the laryngitis can hang on for a long time after that; many weeks in most cases."

"Laryngitis?" Elizabeth practically choked on the word. *Many weeks?* she added silently.

"Yeah," the nurse said as if it were only a minor inconvenience; in her world, it probably was. "If he gets that, the more he tries to use his voice, the worse it will be, so you should get him a notebook or something until it lets up."

Elizabeth knew she wasn't angry with the nurse, and that she was actually more scared than angry. Therefore, she kept her voice steady as she took the opportunity to point out that in some people's lives laryngitis was a *really* big deal. She cleared her throat and said, "My husband is a professional singer, and he's starting rehearsals for a tour in a few weeks."

"Oh dear," the nurse said, more alarmed than Elizabeth had expected. "Then he'd better take *very* good care of his voice. If he gets those symptoms, get him in right away. The doctor will do everything he can to help him. The bottom line is that a virus is a virus and it has to run its course; we just don't want it to turn into a secondary infection."

"Right," Elizabeth said, overcome with a sinking feeling.

"Or it may not be that at all. Those are the two big ones going around, but it could be something else entirely." She briefly went over symptoms to watch for that would warrant medical attention, along with suggestions for keeping the fever and aches under control. Elizabeth thanked the nurse for her time, hung up the phone, and cried. She pulled herself together by saying a prayer that whatever Jayson had, it would stay out of his throat. She prayed for the strength to be positive for him. She knew that being sick at all was going to leave him discouraged. After that bout of headaches, he was already tired of being in bed and missing his life, and worn out from being in pain. Perhaps that's why he'd been vulnerable to getting an infection; the headaches had lowered his resistance. Whatever the reasons, he was ill, and she had to keep the household running, take good care of him, and try to keep his spirits up.

Elizabeth took a deep breath and headed to the bedroom, deciding not to say a word about the possible cough and laryngitis. Ten steps down the hall she had herself convinced that her husband had the *other* infection, and he was going to feel better in plenty of time before rehearsals began again. A few more steps brought her to the closed bedroom door, and through it she could hear Jayson coughing. She sat on the floor in the hallway and cried again, then she went back to the kitchen and called her father, needing to vent to someone who would listen, someone who would share her burden. She considered it a huge blessing in her life that her father and his wife were retired and lived a few minutes away. But there were moments, such as this, when she wondered what she would ever do without him.

When Will answered the phone, he immediately said, "I was just going to call you, actually. We have some good news."

"What?" Elizabeth asked, trying to hold off her inevitable bursting dam of emotion.

"Marilyn and I are going on a mission. We're submitting the papers this week."

In a matter of seconds Elizabeth felt herself go through a case study on faith. There was nothing better that a healthy, retired couple could do with their time and resources than go on a mission. They were wonderful people and they could do so much good. She knew that she should be happy for them; it was something they had mentioned occasionally, but she'd always thought of it as sometime in the future. The timing of the news felt overwhelming, and she wondered what she would ever do without him. Logically, she knew that the Lord would bless their family as He had always done, and she needed to trust the Lord in being able to let her father go. But how?

"You're not saying anything," Will said, sounding disappointed.

"I'm sorry," she said, swallowing her tears enough to present a steady voice. "It's wonderful. It just took me off guard; that's all. How could I not be happy about that? You're amazing, Dad. You both are. I'm proud of you."

"Well, thank you. We're really excited . . . and a little nervous. But I'm sure everything will be fine."

"I'm sure it will," Elizabeth said, trying to convince herself.

"Is something wrong?" Will asked, and the question provoked her emotion too close to the surface, making it impossible to answer without giving herself away. "Elizabeth?"

"Sorry," she said, her voice strained.

"Honey, what's wrong?" he asked. She could only sob. Then as if he'd just remembered, he said, "Why did you call me?"

"Jayson is sick," she said and went on to explain his symptoms and her conversation with the nurse.

Will's overt concern was somewhat validating; it also made her realize that the situation was not good. But the strength and perspective she'd needed came through loud and clear when he said, "Now, listen to me. If Jayson is supposed to do that tour, God will make him equal to it. If he has what it sounds like he has, then getting through it isn't going to be easy, but we *will* get through it. I gave him more than one priesthood blessing while he suffered through those headaches, and I'm telling you that when the impression came to my mind that he would be able to do all that was required of him—for his family and professionally—there was no subtlety about it. I know the promise given to him was real. And I really don't think it had a time limit on it. We'll get him through this, Elizabeth. We will! I know this feels daunting for you, but you just plan on our being there for a few hours every day for as long as you need us so that you can do whatever you need to do to take care of Jayson—and yourself. We don't want you getting sick too."

"Oh, good heavens," she muttered at the thought. She'd slept in the same bed with Jayson, had kissed him good night.

"We'll pray that doesn't happen, but if it does, we'll take care of you and everybody else. Do you hear me?"

"Yes," she cried. "Thank you, Dad. We're so blessed to have you here. But . . . your going on a mission is great, Dad; really. Sorry if I didn't react very well."

"It's okay. I certainly understand. I guess the timing of my announcement was bad."

"I know it's a good thing," she said. "I wouldn't want you *not* to do it. I'm just feeling selfish. I'll miss you so much; we all will. And what will I do without you?"

"I'm certain the Lord will bless you, Elizabeth. You have a good husband, a fine son, and you live in a good ward and neighborhood. You're going to be just fine. But we haven't even submitted the papers. You don't have to give a farewell speech yet. Let's just get everybody healthy and on that tour."

"Okay," she said. "Thank you. You're the greatest."

CHAPTER 9

Feeling more capable of handling this new challenge, Elizabeth went to the bedroom to check on Jayson. She could see that he was awake when she entered the room. She sat on the edge of the bed, but kept her distance. "How are you?" she asked.

"I feel horrible," he said in a hoarse voice, and his eyes widened. "What was that?"

"What?"

"My voice. My voice worked fine the last time I opened my mouth to use it."

"I noticed that," she said and debated whether or not to tell him what she suspected. She decided that putting it off would only make it worse. He had to know what they might be dealing with. "According to what the nurse said, it's going to get worse before it gets better."

"What?" he asked as if he were being sentenced to death.

"If you have the infection going around that comes with the symptoms you have, it's going to get a *lot* worse before it gets better." She repeated what the nurse had said, leaving the final blow to the end. "And you're going to get laryngitis, and—"

"What?" he practically shrieked, except that it came out more as a croak. "I can't get laryngitis. I've got to—"

"Well, I'll see if I can find the form we need to fill out to declare you exempt from this virus due to your profession." He scowled at her. "It's a virus, Jayson. These things just . . . happen."

"Not to me, and not like this," he said. "I've hardly been sick a day in my life. And I've *never* had laryngitis. Why *this* virus? Why now?"

"I can't answer those questions. I've been crying to my father on the phone, and he can't answer them either."

Jayson groaned and pushed a hand through his hair. "Did I do something to offend God, or what?"

"You know that's ridiculous. Even *if* God retaliated offenses against Him in such a way, which He does *not*, you have not done anything to offend Him. It's just a virus."

"*Just* a virus?" he countered.

Elizabeth repeated the words of encouragement her father had said to her. He calmed down and agreed that he had to just accept the illness and deal with it. But he got emotional when he admitted to how horrible he felt physically, and how depressing it was to think of feeling that way for one to two weeks—and dealing with a cough and voice issues for some undetermined length of time after that. Elizabeth listened and acknowledged his feelings, reminding him that she shared them wholly.

"We just have to take it one day at a time, Jayson. You need to rest— your body *and* your voice." She made sure he had everything he needed and left his cell phone on the bedside table so he could call her if he needed something. She told him he didn't have to say anything. He just had to dial the number and she would come.

That evening Will and Marilyn came and brought dinner for the family, then they helped with the kids through the evening. After the kids were in bed, Roger came over at Elizabeth's request to help Will give Jayson a blessing. Roger spoke the blessing this time, but the promises were the same—Jayson would be able to meet his professional obligations; he needed to trust in the Lord and not weigh himself down with needless worry. God was in charge of the situation. "Just as the prophet Nephi declared," the blessing said, "the Lord would not ask something of you without providing the means for you to do it. Everything will go forward according to God's plan and His will."

Elizabeth found comfort in the blessing, and she knew that Jayson did too. But throughout the next few days he was so sick that it was almost frightening. She took him to the doctor when he *did* have trouble breathing and needed something to help him with that. He also needed something to ease the cough enough so that he could sleep. And he was tested for strep due to the horrific pain in his throat. The test was negative, which meant the virus just had to run its course. He lost his voice completely and could hardly get even a whisper out of his throat. Elizabeth got him a little whiteboard, about the size of a notebook, so that he could write down what he needed and not use his voice any more than absolutely necessary. She got him videos to watch and books to read, but his eyes hurt too badly to do either. She was glad that the cough medicine helped him sleep, and for days he didn't leave the bed except for short trips to the bathroom. He ate very little and slept as long as he had medication to calm the cough and keep the aches and fever under control.

A week after the symptoms had first appeared, no one else in the house was sick, but Jayson was still utterly miserable. He was stunned to realize how much damage a virus could do to a body, and grateful to live in a day when he could feel relatively certain that he wouldn't die from the illness—even if he felt like he might. The fever wasn't nearly so severe as it had been, and the aches had lessened. But the headache had actually worsened. His excessive coughing didn't help that any. His throat had been so sore for days that he'd hardly swallowed a thing beyond the bare minimum of food and drink necessary to keep his stomach from growling. Elizabeth had two humidifiers going in the room constantly, and she had babied Jayson and his throat in every possible way. But he still could hardly utter a sound. He longed to connect with his music, but traversing the distance from the bed to the piano felt like climbing Everest. Elizabeth had offered to bring his guitar, but he'd declined, knowing he didn't have the strength to even hold it. He assured her that he'd let her know if he wanted it. Right now, he felt like seeing it in the room would only make his separation from his music more painful. He thought of what Maren, his trusted shrink, had said about the way he relied on music to calm and soothe him. It kept his life balanced, and it fulfilled something in him that was an integral part of his soul. When he'd struggled with drug addiction it had been at a time when his injured hand had prevented him from playing music. He'd later learned that part of the reason he'd turned to the drugs was to replace the way music had medicated him. He recalled Maren telling him more recently, *"The pleasure and serenity that you get from your music is not a bad thing. Everybody needs something in their life for that purpose. If something occurred that prevented you from being able to play, I think you'd need to be very conscious of finding a healthy way to replace it."*

After spending what felt like endless hours just curled up in the bed wanting to die, or staring at the ceiling, Jayson asked himself what he could do *now* to replace his music. He reached for the scriptures on the bedside table. He'd attempted several times during his illness to read from them, but his eyes always hurt and he could rarely even hold them open. Even during the few times he'd had the television on, he'd been listening more than watching. Now, he prayed that he could have the strength, the lack of pain, and the presence of mind to read something that might help give him some perspective and hope, and that spending some time with the scriptures might help soothe his desire to have his fingers on the piano keys. He put on his glasses and almost laughed when the book fell open to Job. Then he had to ask himself, *Did it really just* fall *open to Job?* He'd thought of Job many times during his many weeks in bed—due to headaches and subsequent illness—but he'd never thought to actually read the story. In fact, he wasn't sure if he'd *ever* read the story. He'd grown up going to church on Sundays, and his mother had taught him much from the Bible. He *knew* the story of Job, but he couldn't recall ever actually reading it.

In little snatches over the next couple of days, he read all forty-two chapters. It was a pretty basic story. Job lost everything: his wealth, his family, his health. Then his wife turned against him, and his friends told him that all of this was a result of something he'd done wrong. Job defended himself to his friends, questioned God over the reasons for his suffering, but never lost his integrity or denied his testimony of the Savior. Then everything was given back to him—and more. But Jayson wasn't sure what exactly had preceded the ending of the trial. He could certainly see metaphorical lessons in the story, but he felt like it was supposed to apply to him in some way that was deeper than what he was getting. He prayed about it. He talked to Elizabeth as much as he dared with a voice that was barely starting to show signs of regaining some volume above a whisper. He continued to be miserable, and diverted his compulsions to play music by reading the story of Job *again.* Elizabeth found some related articles on the Internet and printed them off for him. He became utterly fascinated and kept wanting to dig deeper, as if he were being lured toward some profoundly personal message.

Twelve days after the symptoms first came on, Jayson ate the breakfast Elizabeth brought him, glad to note that his appetite was improving. And his throat didn't hurt when he swallowed. He'd not had any fever or aches for a few days, which meant that he was no longer contagious. He just had to get his strength back and get rid of the nagging cough and other associated symptoms. At times, Jayson would cough so hard it felt like his insides would be ripped out. But the doctor had assured them that there was nothing wrong that time wouldn't cure. *How much time?* Jayson wondered.

While Elizabeth was gone on some errands, having taken the children along, Jayson took a shower, then had to rest from the exertion. Nothing was stronger than his need to get out of this room—except for his need to get his hands on a piano. He walked gingerly up the hall, glad to be alone in the house if only so Elizabeth couldn't see how he had to lean against the wall and rest twice before he could get to the front room.

When he came around the corner and saw the piano, he took a deep, sustaining breath, then let out a little hoarse laugh. "Hello, my friend," he said and sat on the bench. For several minutes he just ran his fingers over the keys, letting them make whatever music seemed to come through them, with no apparent thought behind it. He played bits and pieces of his life that were represented in the songs he'd written over the years. Seeing a hymnbook open in front of him, he thumbed through it and found one of his favorites, "How Great Thou Art." He only had to glance at it to recall the rendition he'd come up with a long while back; he'd also played part of it in the medley he'd done in sacrament meeting. He played it through, hearing the words in his mind until he felt compelled to sing the chorus, even though it came out more as a rough whisper.

Hearing how pathetic his voice sounded, Jayson hung his head and sighed, trying not to feel afraid of what the coming weeks would bring. His throat felt like a war zone, and the doctor had told him that the effects of the illness on the vocal chords had taken many weeks to heal in other patients. He'd explained that in some cases the aggravation to the throat could last for months. Jayson had tried not to think about it. He'd prayed. He'd struggled for faith and hope. But he couldn't deny his concerns. He just didn't know what he was going to do. For now, he settled for just playing the piano and allowing the music to fill him. He was still sitting there when Elizabeth came home. Derek and Harmony came into the house first and saw him. They came running, and he lifted them up on the bench on either side of him, hugging them both tightly.

"How are my little snuggle muffins?" he asked.

"Daddy sound funny," Derek said.

"Yeah," Jayson said. "Very observant."

"Well, look at you," Elizabeth said. "Up and about."

"Up to the piano," he whispered and turned his attention to the children, letting them play gently with the piano keys until Elizabeth took them into the kitchen for lunch. Jayson went back to bed.

He fell asleep and woke up when he heard Trevin come in from school. Deciding he'd like to see his son without waiting for him to come to the bedroom, Jayson went carefully down the hall, then he stopped when he heard Trevin and Elizabeth talking.

"You will never believe," Trevin said to his mother, sounding angry, "what Clayton told me his mother said *this time.*"

"Do I want to know?"

"Probably not, but you *should* know. Maybe we shouldn't tell Dad 'til he's feeling better, though."

"What did she say?" Elizabeth asked with caution.

"She told Clayton that Dad was sick because God was punishing him."

"She didn't!" Elizabeth said, and she was so clearly angry that it was somewhat validating to Jayson. Still, he pressed his back against the wall for support then slid to the floor to sit there, stunned and overcome. It only took him a long moment to know that God was *not* punishing him, and Sister Freedman was wrong. Still, the words stung, and tears burned his eyes. How could someone be so utterly cruel? He just didn't understand. Hearing the conversation continue between Trevin and Elizabeth, he felt increasingly upset to realize how this was affecting his family. He swallowed his emotion and came carefully to his feet. He found that he was unusually calm, considering what he'd just heard, but perhaps the shock waves hadn't fully hit him yet. He came around the corner into the kitchen, and the conversation stopped abruptly.

"It's okay," Jayson said. "You can keep going. I already heard."

"You were eavesdropping?" Elizabeth asked, not entirely serious. He recognized her attempt to lighten the mood and he appreciated it, but he felt more inclined to address the problem.

"Since it was about me, I think I had a right to eavesdrop." Hearing himself talk brought home the stark evidence of his deepest concerns and the flickering thought that maybe Sister Freedman was right. He pushed the thought away and said what he needed to say. "Whatever Sister Freedman has to say obviously has nothing to do with what's really happening in my life. I don't know *why* this is happening to me, or whether or not God has anything to do with it. I *do* know that whatever it may or may not be, it is none of Sister Freedman's business."

"That's what I told Clayton," Trevin said.

"Kindly, I hope." Jayson leaned against the counter for support.

"Of course."

"Are you okay?" Elizabeth asked.

"Not really, no. Obviously I can get out of bed, but I can't believe how weak I am. And as you can hear, my voice is not cooperating with my forthcoming obligations."

"It'll be okay, Dad," Trevin said and surprised Jayson with a hug. They shared hugs frequently, but Jayson almost always initiated it.

"Thanks, Trev," Jayson said, and his son went downstairs to do homework.

"Are you ticked off with Sister Freedman again?" Elizabeth asked when they were alone.

"What good would it do me?" Jayson said, sitting down at the table. "Obviously I have bigger problems to contend with."

"Such as?" she asked, and he almost felt ticked off with *her* that she couldn't see the obvious. Or maybe she could and she was just testing him.

"I cannot sing, Elizabeth."

"Not right now, but . . ."

"You heard what the doctor said. This could go on for weeks; maybe longer. Remember when Trevin got bronchitis a couple of years ago? The kid coughed for *months.*"

"Yes, he did."

"And the more he used his voice, the more hoarse he got."

"I know," she said.

"Do you have any idea how much *voice* it takes to get through one concert?"

"Yes, Jayson. I know. I'm not disputing that your concern is valid, but we have no option beyond having faith and doing the best we can. It's just—"

"No one else can do what I do, Elizabeth." His tone didn't disguise how upset he was as he finally acknowledged the problem aloud, as opposed to just stewing silently about it. "No one can take my place. It's not like calling in sick to the office to have someone else go to a meeting or see a client on my behalf. It's not like my appointments can be cancelled or rescheduled. *Jayson Wolfe* has to get up on that stage and have energy and stamina—and a *voice*. I am indispensable in my profession, and at the moment, I *hate* that fact. How am I supposed to do this? Thousands of people have already purchased tickets for these shows. *Thousands.* I can't just cancel the tour because I can't stop coughing."

"You could, actually," she said with calm matter-of-factness. She was so calm, in fact, that it almost infuriated him further. "Tours have been cancelled before. Musicians *do* get sick. But *I* know, and I believe that *you* know you're not supposed to do that. This tour is important for reasons that you and I may never know about. We have been prayerful about our plans for this album and the tour every step of the way. If God wants you to do it—and He does—then He will provide a way. This is a matter of faith, Jayson. If we do everything we can do, then we have to trust in the Lord to make up the difference. You need to make your health your highest priority. You've got to eat well, get all of the rest you need, do what the doctor has told you to do, and then . . ." Tears crept into her eyes and cracked her voice. "Then we must stand still and allow God to prove that He won't let you down." She left the room saying, "Hold on." She came back with the scriptures, thumbing through them, and sat down across from him. "This is the verse," she said. "This is going to be our tour motto." She cleared her throat. "'*Therefore, dearly beloved brethren, let us cheerfully do all things that lie in our power; and then may we stand still, with the utmost assurance, to see the salvation of God, and for his arm to be revealed.*'"

"Where is that?" Jayson asked, feeling the words penetrate his heart with a sudden calm.

"The end of section 123 in the Doctrine and Covenants."

"Liberty Jail," Jayson said and took in a sustaining breath. "Okay, surely what I am facing is so minuscule and petty in comparison. If Joseph could express such feelings despite the circumstances he was in— and those of the Saints—then I can do this."

"Yes, you can. And what you are facing is not minuscule or petty. The scriptures are here to give us a point of reference and perspective, but they are not meant to diminish the severity of our trials. What you've been through is no small thing, and your concerns are valid. This *is* a big deal, and our Heavenly Father knows it."

He considered all of her words and had to admit for the millionth time in his life, "You always have the answers for me. I don't know how you do it."

She held up the scriptures and comically pointed to them. "They're not *my* answers. I'm just the messenger."

"Well, you always have the right message at the right time." He reached for her hand across the table. "And you love me."

"Yes, I do." She laughed softly. "And with any luck *I* won't get sick. If I start coughing too, that'll just add to the problem. However, *my* voice is not indispensable."

"Oh, yes it is!" he insisted.

"To you, maybe. But I don't think the audience would notice the absence of my backing vocals all that much."

"The song just wouldn't sound right; they'd notice that. Besides, if it weren't for you, the audience wouldn't get Jayson Wolfe at all. Not only did you stop me from committing suicide, you made me face up to doing another album. I need you onstage with me, even if our fans will never fully understand why."

Elizabeth kissed his hand. "I love you, Jayson. We're going to get through this."

"I believe you," he said, "but you might have to remind me . . . hourly."

"I'll do whatever it takes."

"Okay," Jayson said, hearing his voice diminishing due to the conversation. "I think I'm going back to bed now."

Once in bed, he felt too restless to sleep, and too awful to do anything. He was grateful for Elizabeth's perspective, but alone with his thoughts, it was difficult to hold on to that. His mind wandered through the miserable experiences of illness and pain he'd endured throughout the last several weeks. He wondered how people with chronic pain or illness could cope day after day. He thought of Layla and felt a deepening of empathy and compassion. She had a solution to her problem and she was making progress, but it was slow and she was still very weak.

As his thoughts tumbled through his mind, Jayson felt completely useless. He'd done nothing to contribute to his home and family throughout this illness, and very little in the previous weeks. He hadn't been to church much, and certainly hadn't gone to the temple. And his disconnection from his instruments paled in comparison to his inability to use his voice. His voice. Since his childhood, he'd had a clear, brilliant voice. His mother had praised and encouraged it. His voice had always been a part of his music for as long as he'd been able to make music.

He'd never even considered the possibility of losing his voice. When he'd lost the use of his hand, he'd been devastated, and he'd prayed many times that no such thing would ever happen again. But something like this had never crossed his mind. And the timing was simply horrid. If this had happened any time in the last two years, it wouldn't have been that big of a deal. But now? The musicians would be returning from Los Angeles in a week to begin intense rehearsals. How could he rehearse without his voice? But if he overused it and strained it—which he'd been told would only prolong the problem—how could he perform?

Sister Freedman's most recent attack assaulted his memory and crept into his spirit. He prayed for strength and understanding, then he pondered and stewed over it for another hour, and prayed some more. Was this meant to help solidify the experience of Job in his life? As he recalled the way Job's friends had told him that his problems were a result of his committing some sin, he found some inner comfort. Job had boldly countered their accusations, declaring in essence that he knew he was right with God. Jayson knew it, too. But under the circumstances, it was difficult to hold on to such feelings.

Jayson closed his eyes and prayed. He reminded God of the blessings he'd been promised through the power of the priesthood, and asked that he would be able to hold to those promises and claim them. He pondered faith and the need to trust in the Lord. He considered all the evidence he had that his music had been inspired, as was his decision to do this tour. If this was a test of faith, he prayed that he would pass it.

Jayson realized he'd dozed off when Elizabeth nudged him, saying, "The bishop is here. He stopped on his way home from work to see how you are. Do you want him to come in here, or—"

"No, I'll come to the front room, thank you," he said. "I'll be there in a minute."

He went into the bathroom, splashed water on his face, and ran a comb through his hair before he went to the front room to find the bishop there. He stood from the couch and greeted Jayson with a handshake, then hugged him before they sat across from each other.

"Elizabeth tells me you're doing better," the bishop said, "but your voice doesn't sound very good."

"No, it does not," Jayson said. "And since you brought it up, I guess I can tell you how worried I am about that."

They talked for a long while, as friends would, about his feelings and concerns, and the things that he and Elizabeth had discussed. The bishop added his vote to trusting in the Lord and carrying on, and he promised to keep Jayson in his prayers.

Near the end of the conversation, the bishop said, "You certainly have been hit hard the last couple of months. Opposition can be a real kicker, sometimes."

"Do you really think that's what this is? Opposition?"

"Well, it makes sense."

"Does it?" Jayson asked. "I mean . . . I'm not questioning your judgment, I'm just . . . trying to understand. I know that opposition is a part of the plan, and that God has to allow it in order for us to grow. But . . . I guess what I'm wondering is . . . well . . . does Satan actually have the power to cause pain and illness? Can he—or his angels—be literally responsible for what's happening to me?"

"That's pretty heavy doctrine, Jayson. I don't know that I can answer that question directly. I believe that sometimes things simply happen because it's just life. But I'd say there's a certain logic in it; knowing what we know, wouldn't it make sense that Satan could—and would—have his hand in such things?"

"I don't know what makes sense," Jayson said. "I just feel some days like he's trying to kill me. I still can't find any logic to all those headaches."

"They've been better?"

"Yes, actually. I've had headaches, but they feel entirely different. It's from the virus. And the coughing. Coughing my guts out tends to make my head hurt."

"That's understandable."

They chatted a few more minutes, and the bishop reminded Jayson to call him if he could do anything. On his way to the door, he said, "A thought just occurred to me. Something I learned in an institute class a long time ago. The principle is eluding me, but I remember the scripture. Why don't you look up what Paul said about the thorn in the side. It's in the New Testament; Corinthians, I believe."

"I'll do that," Jayson said and thanked him for his visit. And again he went back to bed. As he was laying there, his mind replayed all his recent thoughts, his inner questions, his need for answers, and the ongoing sense that he really was supposed to learn something from this. He recounted his conversations with Elizabeth and the bishop—and the latest jab from Sister Freedman. He turned his mind to prayer, and his prayer merged into thinking through the lyrics to the hymn he'd been playing on the piano. The chorus went over and over in his mind, and then he began to hum it. He sang it in a dry, husky whisper, then he started coughing violently. And then he started to cry. He could never explain the complete and utter humility he felt in that moment. His nothingness was blatantly clear. Most people would never understand why *this* was so devastating to *him*. But it was.

While he wept he continued to pray, and the story of Job trickled into his mind. And that's when he knew. One moment he didn't know, and the next moment he did. And he knew it with all of his soul. He knew the lesson of Job. He wasn't sure if this was the lesson that Job had learned before his trial was lifted, but he knew the lesson that God had wanted *him* to learn from Job's experience. Jayson knew—in spite of all he'd lost and struggled through in his life, and whatever ill might befall him in the future—he knew that his testimony of the Savior would not fail him. His testimony was stronger than any pain, or disappointment, or fear. Like Job, he knew that his Redeemer lived. And he also knew that God loved him. No matter how useless, how incapacitated, or how weak—in body or spirit—he might be, he knew that God loved him.

That's how Job had gotten through his trials with his integrity intact. He'd known that God loved him; he'd known that he was right with God in spite of anything that anyone might have felt or thought or told him. And it occurred to Jayson that even *if* his life were not in order, even *if* he'd committed sin or made mistakes, God would love him no less. The fact that he constantly strived to be a righteous man gave him the confidence to know that he was worthy of God's blessings, but it did not make him any more worthy of God's love.

As Jayson felt that love surge through him, he knew that everything was going to be okay. He didn't know *how* exactly, but he knew that it would. He just had to trust in the Lord. How had Elizabeth put it? He reached for his glasses and the scriptures and sat up to find section 123 in the Doctrine and Covenants. He read the whole section, then felt a reaffirming of spiritual peace as it concluded with the verse Elizabeth had read to him earlier. *Therefore, dearly beloved brethren, let us cheerfully do all things that lie in our power; and then may we stand still, with the utmost assurance, to see the salvation of God, and for his arm to be revealed.*

Jayson felt his hope increase, even if he was coughing while it did. He recalled the scripture reference the bishop had mentioned and turned to the topical guide, trying to find it according to key words. What had he said? *The thorn in the flesh.* He found it in Second Corinthians, chapter twelve. He read the verse that contained the phrase and felt intrigued, but he knew it was out of context, so he went back a few verses to read the entire concept, taking it in slowly, trying to apply it to his own feelings and situation.

For though I would desire to glory, I shall not be a fool; for I will say the truth: but now I forbear, lest any man should think of me above that which he seeth me to be, or that he heareth of me. Jayson's mind went to the countless times he'd encountered people who were in awe of his gift, and how some of them were not able to grasp what he knew: his gift was from God and he was just an ordinary man. He read on. *And lest I should be exalted above measure through the abundance of the revelations. . . .* He reread that phrase three times, thinking of the people he'd known that he could describe as being "exalted above measure" with their arrogance in regard to talents for which they gave no divine credit. He hoped that he would never fall into that category. He reread that phrase again, as well as the remainder of that verse. *And lest I should be exalted above measure through the abundance of the revelations, there was given to me a thorn in the flesh. . . .* There was that phrase. Jayson looked at the footnote to see that "thorn in the flesh" was synonymous with "pain." He took a sharp breath, recalling the horrific pain he'd endured with those never-ending headaches. So . . . did this verse mean that the pain was given to Paul to keep him from being "exalted above measure" because of the many miracles and wonders he'd had in his life? Jayson had certainly been given many miracles and wonders in his life. He didn't consider himself susceptible to becoming arrogant or forgetting the source of his blessings. It just wasn't in him. But then, it surely wouldn't have been in Paul, either.

Almost holding his breath, he went on, going back over that last phrase . . . *There was given to me a thorn in the flesh, the messenger of Satan to buffet me, lest I should be exalted above measure.* That was it! Jayson gasped. A warmth filled him, as if to confirm that this was the answer he'd been looking for. There it was in black and white. *The messenger of Satan to buffet me.* Of course. It *was* opposition. And it was allowed by God to serve His own purposes of humbling, teaching, and guiding His children. In essence, the story of Job had exactly the same message. Paul hadn't done anything wrong to bring his afflictions upon himself; they had purposes beyond his understanding. Jayson just knew. And it was evident that Paul *did* understand a great deal, and his words taught Jayson further as he read on. *For this thing I besought the Lord thrice, that it might depart from me.* Only three times? Jayson wondered. He'd nagged the Lord continually to free him from his pain and illness. *And he said unto me, My grace is sufficient for thee: for my strength is made perfect in weakness.* That's when Jayson began to cry. The witness of the Spirit crept through his entire being with the answer to this and every other malady in life. *Most gladly therefore will I rather glory in my infirmities, that the power of Christ may rest upon me. Therefore I take pleasure in infirmities, in reproaches, in necessities, in persecutions, in distresses for Christ's sake: for when I am weak, then am I strong.*

Jayson read it all through again, weeping as he did. Then he set the book aside and slid to his knees beside the bed, thanking his Heavenly Father for the power of personal revelation, for the scriptures, for an insightful bishop, and for a good wife. And most especially he thanked God for the sacrifice of His Son that made possible the perfect peace and hope Jayson felt. He didn't know how he was going to get through what was required of him. But he knew that he would. And he knew that he needed to remember each day—each hour—the lessons he had learned and apply them. The answers truly were rooted in the need to do all that was in his power, and then to trust in the Lord, and wait for His arm to be revealed.

That evening Jayson sat at the table and had supper with his family, then he stayed in the living room and interacted with the kids more than he had in nearly two weeks. After the children were down for the night, he snuggled with Elizabeth and shared with her the spiritual answers he'd been given, and the hope and perspective that he'd gained. She shared his joy along with his trepidation. They both knew that such answers didn't mean the path would be easy, and that surely their faith would be tested as opposing forces continued to battle around them through whatever might lie ahead. But they had each other, and they knew that God was with them in their endeavors.

CHAPTER 10

The following morning Jayson went again to the piano in the front room. He didn't try to sing, but he did sit there and play for a couple of hours. Elizabeth sat on the couch for a few minutes here and there in between taking care of the children and doing all that she needed to do. Between songs, while Jayson was flipping through the hymnbook, she said, "It's nice to hear you playing again."

"It's nice to *be* playing again."

"And it's nice to have you playing in the house. Before we built the studio, you always played in the house. I miss it. I love the way it fills our home."

Jayson had never really thought about it, but he said, "Point taken. I'll keep that in mind." He'd often heard Elizabeth playing the piano, since she rarely used the one in the studio. And Addie was taking lessons from her mother, so she played as well. But Jayson considered the fact that he should use his gift to bless his family. He often used the guitar for family home evenings or other impromptu family gatherings. But the piano was different. It was a magnificent instrument and close to his heart. He admired it now, running his fingers over the top of it with reverence. He recalled the devastation he'd felt as a youth when they'd had to move and sell the piano, and how those years without a piano in his home had been so difficult. He'd been blessed to be taken in by the Greer family, and the fact that they had allowed him to play their grand piano had been a slice of heaven for him. Now, he was blessed to have access to *two* beautiful pianos, and to regularly play the one at the church.

"What are you thinking about so intently?" Elizabeth asked.

"The piano," he said. "I was remembering how it felt when I first realized that my new friend Derek had one in his house. I nearly fainted."

Elizabeth smiled. "I remember how it felt to walk into my house and see you playing it. *I* nearly fainted."

"I remember you playing the piano for a number in the chorus concert when I had a crush on you and you didn't know I existed."

"I remember the first time I heard you play 'Funeral for a Friend' on the piano in our front room. I think that's when I fell in love with you."

"No, that's when you fell in love with my ability to play the piano. That's when you decided I wasn't *really* a rebel. I just looked like one."

She smiled. "Why don't you play 'Funeral for a Friend' anymore?"

"I don't know. I hadn't thought about it. I used to play it when I needed grounding. Maybe I haven't needed grounding for a long time."

"But that song connects you to your youth, your mother, your kinship with the piano. It's the song that really showed you what you could do."

"I know all of that."

"But maybe you need reminding. Maybe you should play it. The song doesn't require any singing. You played it at Derek's funeral, and you didn't sing."

"And my mother's; I know."

"So, play it. Play it for *me*. I'm making a request. Do you think the great Jayson Wolfe could play a song for his wife?"

"When you put it that way . . ."

"Do you feel manipulated?"

"Yes, but how can I refuse when you've taken such good care of me?"

"You can't," she said and laughed.

"It's been a long time," he said, situating himself in relation to the keys and the pedals. "I might make mistakes."

"I don't care. But it's like breathing to you. Just go for it."

Jayson closed his eyes, pulled the melody into his head, and started to play where his version of the song began, soft and slow. He smiled as he felt it coming back to him, like a faraway memory slipping from the darkened rooms of his mind directly through his fingers and into the open. As the song picked up speed and intensity, he surprised himself with the way he hardly missed a note. It was complicated and complex, but he knew it heart and soul. And the history he shared with the song coursed through him along with the music. Elizabeth was right. This song *did* ground him. He'd played it in times of celebration and times of grief for almost as long as he'd been playing. When he came to its triumphant finish, Elizabeth had tears in her eyes and a smile on her face. "See, I told you," she said. Harmony started to cry, and she left the room to take care of the problem.

As soon as Elizabeth had soothed Harmony from bumping her head, she heard Jayson start the song again, and she smiled to herself. She knew that playing it would be therapeutic for him; it always had been. And she would never grow tired of hearing him play that song!

As soon as Harmony was happy and playing again, the phone rang. Elizabeth smiled when she looked at the caller ID. It was Jayson's brother, Drew. Without saying hello, she said into the phone, "How did you know? ESP or something?"

"Know what?" Drew asked.

"Listen," Elizabeth said and moved closer to the piano in the other room. Since Jayson's back was to her, he had no idea.

"Wow!" Drew said into the phone and laughed. "He hasn't lost his touch."

"No, I don't think so."

"I take it he's feeling better."

Elizabeth moved back into the kitchen. "He's feeling well enough to sit at the piano for a while. He's pretty wiped out; really weak and tired. As you can hear, the song is almost over and you can talk to him."

After Jayson hit the last chord, Elizabeth said, "The phone's for you."

Jayson hadn't heard it ring. "Hello," he said as Elizabeth walked away.

"Hey, little brother," Drew said, "that sounded like old times. I should be there."

"You were listening."

"Well, yeah. Elizabeth said I must have ESP to have called right now. Maybe I do."

"Maybe you do." Jayson chuckled. "Or maybe it was Mom giving you a nudge."

"Maybe. You sound terrible," Drew said, and their friendly chitchat became immediately replaced by his overt concern. "How long did the doctor tell you this could last?"

"Weeks; maybe months."

"Rehearsals start in nine days. And we've got promotions in a few weeks; that means *you* singing on national television."

"You don't have to remind me of that," Jayson said.

"Maybe we should reconsider."

"Reconsider what?"

"Maybe we should . . . postpone the tour, or . . ."

"The tour is still several weeks away. I'll be fine," Jayson said.

"Is that optimism or denial?" Drew asked.

"It's faith," Jayson said and tried to give Drew a simple version of why he believed this was the right thing to do, and why he was going to press forward.

"Okay." Drew's voice held skepticism. "I admire your determination here, little brother, but . . . I just have to say that . . . I'm not sure you're being realistic. We can't do this without your voice. It's not an option."

"I know that, Drew. I've been killing myself over that for days now. But I know I'm supposed to do the show. God will not let me down. You're going to have to trust me on this."

The long stretch of silence let Jayson know that his brother was struggling to know what to say. He knew Drew well enough to know that his biggest concern was for Jayson. But faith was not something that Drew understood. He believed in God, and in life after death. He found comfort in believing that their mother lived on. But the rest was just irrelevant to him. They'd both grown up with the same mother who had taught them from the Bible, and had expected them to live basic Christian principles. But Jayson had always been more drawn to it than Drew. Jayson's decision to become a Mormon was something that Drew respected, and he'd never said anything negative to Jayson about it, even though Jayson suspected that Drew thought it was a little strange. In the same regard, Jayson had known it was best to respect Drew's desire to remain aloof from religion. Jayson's example would do far more in the long run than any attempt Jayson could make to share the gospel with his brother. Such an attempt would only dampen their relationship, and Jayson knew it. Drew and his wife and baby had spent a great deal of time in their home, but he'd never asked questions about Jayson's beliefs. Now, they had come to a place where Jayson's faith could not match up with Drew's lack of it. Drew could simply never understand where Jayson was coming from.

"Are you with me?" Jayson finally asked.

"Oh, I'm with you," Drew said. "You've never let me down yet."

"I don't know about that," Jayson said, "but I'd like to think I'm a little more mature than I was when I *did* let you down."

"You never let me down," he repeated. "You scared me a few times, but you never let me down."

Again there was silence. "You're not saying much," Jayson said.

"I don't know what to say."

"So . . . you're with me, but . . . you think I'm out of my mind?"

"I guess I'm just trying to figure out what's going on here."

"What do you mean, what's going on? I've already explained it."

"Okay, but . . . I know this religion stuff is important to you, but . . . can you really believe that God is somehow going to miraculously heal your voice . . . just because you want Him to?"

"No, I believe it will happen because I know that *He* wants me to do this tour."

"Well, I'd say you really do have a lot of faith."

"Was that sincere or sarcastic?"

"No sarcasm," Drew said. "If you can pull this off, I just might join this church of yours."

Jayson's heart quickened at the comment, then he had to tell himself that Drew was most likely teasing. When he didn't say anything, Drew mimicked him. "You're not saying much."

"No sarcasm," Jayson said, "but you're teasing me about something that I don't take lightly. And it's not *my* church. It's Christ's church."

"Okay, but . . . I'm not teasing," Drew said. "I mean it."

Jayson chuckled tensely. "Does that mean you're relatively certain I can't pull it off?"

"I didn't say that. I mean it. If you can pull this off, I'll do it."

Jayson chuckled again—with no humor. "Drew . . . this is not . . . the YMCA or something. You can't just . . . walk in and sign up."

"I know that."

"And you can't join because you've witnessed some miracle that convinces you God really exists. They call that sign-seeking in the Bible. If you don't do it for the right reasons, I don't want you doing it at all."

"And what do you consider to be the right reasons?"

"Because you know it's true; you have to know it beyond any doubt."

"And you knew that?"

"I did; I still do. Although . . . I *did* witness a miracle. It wasn't the reason I got baptized, but I have to admit that it made me stop and think about what was true and what wasn't. The answer I got was not the miracle. The miracle just made me pay attention."

"What miracle?" Drew asked.

Jayson realized he'd never shared the story with Drew. He hadn't even shared the nonspiritual side of it. At the time, they hadn't talked as frequently as they did now, and the drama had come and gone in between their conversations. He prayed for guidance in repeating the story appropriately, hoping it might leave an impression on his brother—the way it had on Jayson.

"It was before Elizabeth and I were married; Macy and I were living here with Elizabeth and her dad after rehab. Elizabeth started to hemorrhage, and I called 911. When we got to the hospital the doctor said she was going to bleed to death if they didn't take out her uterus immediately. Her bishop just *happened* to be at the hospital seeing someone else, and we'd called his wife before we left home, so she'd told him to find us. Elizabeth was begging me to tell the doctor not to do the operation because she knew she was supposed to have another baby."

"This was before you were married," Drew said for clarification.

"That's right. I argued with her; I told her I wasn't going to let her die. The bishop and one of his counselors showed up and gave her a priesthood blessing."

"A what?" Drew asked. "I think you've mentioned such a thing before, but . . ."

Jayson gave him a two-sentence explanation, then added, "So they gave her a blessing. She was told that the bleeding would stop, and she was promised that she would heal from the ailment and she would yet bring forth children into this world. A minute later they came in to take her to surgery. Elizabeth insisted they check her again. The bleeding had stopped. They did some tests and found a benign tumor in her uterus. They removed it, gave her some blood, and sent her home. As you know, she's had two babies since then."

Drew became silent again, but Jayson just waited until he said, "Wow. I never knew."

"Now you know."

"Well . . . I guess I can understand why you would have a lot of faith. You just tell me what you want me to do."

"I want you here on schedule to start rehearsals, and I want you to make sure that Brandon and Dalton are here, too."

"You got it," he said, and the conversation shifted to what their kids and wives were up to. When Jayson started coughing he had to sign off, but he could sense Drew's skepticism all over again with this reminder of

Jayson's ailment. Once his coughing had settled down, he found Elizabeth and told her about his conversation with Drew. She just smiled as if she knew a great secret and said, "The Lord works in mysterious ways."

* * * * *

Jayson was grateful to be in church on Sunday, and to feel well enough to help in the kitchen afterward and also go to choir practice. The following Saturday Drew and his family arrived. Jayson was feeling almost back to normal—except for his ailing throat. He was sucking on cough drops almost constantly, and occasionally had a coughing fit that would force him to get up and leave whatever activity might be taking place in order to get it under control in private. Most of the time when he talked, his voice sounded hoarse and gruff. But he was determined to press forward.

Throughout the first week of rehearsals, Jayson used the recorded tracks of his voice in order to spare his throat and let it keep healing. Drew suggested that they could just do the show the same way, but Jayson absolutely balked at the idea. It was too complicated, too vulnerable to problems that could be more embarrassing than a poor voice, and it wasn't what his fans were paying to come and hear.

While the band was in town, they had a couple of photo shoots for official promotional purposes. Jayson loved having Elizabeth in most of those photos. Every aspect of the business was better with her there by his side.

By the middle of the next week, he started singing, even though it sounded terrible most of the time. He prayed every day and did his best to follow his feelings. Now it felt right to sing, as if he needed to build up the strength in his voice and force those vocal chords to work through the strain. The band was patient, and everything was sounding great—except his voice. But he just kept going and tried not to worry about it. He was doing his best. The rest was in God's hands.

While the tour date crept closer, Jayson went to church every Sunday, faithfully fulfilled his calling, and had no trouble avoiding Sister Freedman, because she put so much effort into avoiding him. The Saturday before the album was to be officially launched and his promotional tour was to begin, Jayson knew he had scheduled television appearances the following week—where he would need to sing. The band went through the Mozart piece, and Jayson's voice came out clear and strong. Everyone cheered, especially Trevin, who was sitting in on the rehearsal. Jayson just tried to hide the fact that he was crying. They did "Good, Clean Fun" with the same results, then Jayson started to cough and they had to take a break.

The following day Jayson was sitting in testimony meeting, his mind wandering a bit, when his heart began to pound and he knew he was supposed to get up and bear his testimony. But he wanted to protest. The thought was immediately followed by a recollection of his own prayers, the repeated times he'd told God he would do whatever was asked of him. He stopped the internal arguing and went up to the pulpit at the next opportunity.

"I don't really know what to say." He was pleased to hear that his voice almost sounded normal. "I just know I'm supposed to be up here. I want to express how grateful I am to have the gospel in my life. It holds me together every day of my life. I can't imagine where I would be without it. I want to thank my wonderful wife for all that's entailed in standing by me through a very strange career. I guess it would be appropriate for me to express my appreciation for all of you, our neighbors and ward members who . . ." He became distracted to see Sister Freedman sitting in the back with her son. She hadn't left the chapel. He took a deep breath. "I want to thank those of you who have been so supportive of me and my family through some recent tough times. I wouldn't blame any of you for being embarrassed to live in the same ward with someone like me . . ." He tried to say it lightly, and he did hear a lot of chuckling, but he found it difficult to keep his composure. "I just want to thank you for doing it, and being kind about it. And I hope you don't believe everything you see or read in the grocery checkout lines." Another chuckle from the congregation. Was that a good sign? "Our family won't be attending church much in this ward through the coming months because we'll be on tour. I don't want you to think we've gone inactive. We'll be attending wherever we can, and we'll be working very hard to stand up for what we believe. And what I believe is . . . I believe . . . I *know* that . . ." His voice cracked. "I know that Jesus is the Christ. He carries my burdens; He lifts my pain; He guides my life. Nothing else matters."

He closed in the name of Jesus Christ and returned to his seat, where Elizabeth's hand was waiting to hold his. He'd only been sitting there a minute before he started to cough, and he had to get up and leave until he had it under control.

Jayson had to fly to New York the next day, along with Drew, Dalton, and Brandon, to appear on a national morning news program on the following day. They had four different appearances lined up through the week, all on reputable and popular shows. The interviews would be with Jayson, since it was technically his CD and his music. The rest of the group would be performing with him in relation to the interviews. Drew had always liked it that way. He never let Jayson forget that only one of them was born to be a front man.

Jayson was sitting on the plane, recalling his tender farewells with Elizabeth and the children, when it occurred to him that he had a marvelous opportunity before him. He knew that many people in the ward and neighborhood were aware that he was going to be on TV this week. Elizabeth had probably shared it in Relief Society in that good-news minute thing they did in there. And a lot of Americans who walked through grocery checkout lines, whether they actually bought the tabloids and read them or not, would be watching at least one of these shows. He had the chance to set the record straight, or at least to counter the evil a little bit. He prayed that he would be guided, that the interviewers would be guided, and that all would go well. He felt a quiet thrill to think of playing his songs on national television. And he felt sure his voice could handle doing just a couple of numbers. In most cases, they were only doing one, and it would be, "Good, Clean Fun." Even though "The Heart of Mozart" would be the first radio release, the record company wanted the great drum-guitar duet on television. Two of the shows, however, wanted a couple of songs to intersperse throughout their lengthy morning programs. And they were willing to provide the grand piano. So the band *would* be doing "The Heart of Mozart," but only the second part, and it wouldn't have the orchestra to give it the depth it should have. But it would hopefully inspire people to buy concert tickets. And concerts sold music. In some places, the tickets had been selling for weeks, but the promotion of the album would hopefully stimulate sellout crowds.

Other than eating a tolerable supper, Jayson did nothing that evening but lay on the bed in his hotel room and talk to his family on the phone. He talked to all the kids, then he and Elizabeth talked for more than an hour. He told her his feelings about the opportunity and she was pleased. By talking through with her the things he wanted to be able to express, he felt a little better prepared, and he actually hoped the tabloid issue would come up. Then Jayson set up the humidifier he'd brought in his luggage, took his cough medicine, and went to bed, praying that his voice would not fail him—that *God* would not fail his voice.

The following morning, Jayson wore the lightweight black coat Elizabeth had given him, along with black shoes and jeans and a white T-shirt. He felt relaxed and at ease as the cameras rolled and the interview began. In this case, since it was the first time he'd done this in a while, he was glad that they were not in front of a studio audience. The audience was outside where he would be playing his music.

After he was asked questions about the new album and the upcoming tour, the female interviewer asked, "So, what is it that people say to you that annoys you most?"

"Oh, that's easy." He chuckled. "I find it annoying when people say things that imply what I do is some kind of magic. Some people seem to think that I just sit down at the piano or pick up the guitar and am magically able to do what I do on stage. I can't deny that my abilities are a gift, and I'm grateful for that gift. But I think most people have no comprehension of the years of hard work and practice that have brought me to a point where I can do what I do."

"How many years?"

Jayson chuckled again. "My whole life. I've never done anything else. I was asking for a guitar when I was pretty little, and my mom put me in front of our old upright piano at a very young age. I was always lousy in school because I had music in my head. Music is all I've ever known. It's both a blessing and a curse, I guess. As I said, I'm grateful for it, but the obsessiveness can be a little daunting sometimes. It never goes away."

"So, you wouldn't ever consider a change in profession?"

"I don't know how to do anything else," he said lightly. "But I don't think I could let it go even if I wanted to. I'll probably be writing and playing until I die."

"For those of us who love your music, we certainly hope so. And speaking of annoying, I understand you've been pretty annoyed by the tabloids lately. Would you like to tell us about that?"

"I would *love* to tell you about that." He chuckled. "I'm always glad for a chance to set the record straight."

"We're all ears, Jayson," she said with a smile. "Tell us what's actually true."

"It is true that I found my ex-wife overdosed. Our daughter was trying to call her and had a bad feeling. I was in Los Angeles and my daughter asked me to check on Debbie. I did sit with her in the hospital for a while. Debbie is in rehab and doing well. She'll be staying with her parents when she comes out. That's it. The rest is just . . . garbage."

"The garbage makes you angry?" she asked.

"It sure does," he said. "If it only affected me, I'd still be upset, but I think I could handle it more easily. But it feels like an insult to my family, and the people I go to church with."

"It's true, then, that you're a church-going man?"

"Now *that* is true," he said with exuberance. "I play the piano for the choir, but that's not why I go."

"Why, then?"

"Because that's where God wants me to be on Sundays."

"How's your wife? She's not with you today."

"She's great," he said. "When we can't take the kids with us, we prefer to have one of us there to keep the home fires burning. She is an amazing woman. I love her more every day."

"Will she be on the stage with you this time around? She makes a lovely addition."

"She certainly does, and yes she will. We're taking the whole family on tour. We try to get some fun in between the shows."

She asked a couple more questions about the music, and they finished up by talking about how his brother was still his drummer. "I couldn't do it with anybody else," Jayson said. "We've been doing it together since we were kids."

"And you still get along," she said lightly.

Once the interview was over, Jayson went outside and played his music to hundreds of screaming fans. And he sang it with perfect clarity and strength. Getting a glimpse of the tour ahead, he actually felt excited. He thought of how resistant he'd been to take on this project, but now that he was here, he was glad that he'd been given the shove he needed. And he was glad he'd not allowed his illness to hold him back. He prayed that his voice would hold out and keep improving, but his faith was growing on that issue.

The rest of the week went well, some interviews coming off better than others. But Jayson still felt like he'd represented his family and his religion well, and he was glad to return home to both.

Now that the CD was actually out, Jayson had fun giving copies to friends and neighbors who had been supportive and interested. The cover was black and white, a simple abstract drawing of him playing the piano. Printed in a font that looked like handwritten script, it said *Jayson Wolfe* at the top, and *The Heart of Mozart* at the bottom. The family made a big fuss over it, and Macy insisted that Jayson and Elizabeth had to come and personally give Layla her copy. She was thrilled, and they had a good visit. She was looking better every time they saw her, but still discouraged over the realities of the disease. She said over and over that the CD would lift her spirits, just as all of Jayson's other music had.

Trevin reported that he couldn't go to school without being keenly aware that the CD had been released. Each of the students who had participated in the video shoot had received their T-shirts, CDs, and concert ticket vouchers. There was a buzz around the school about it, and wearing the shirts had become popular, because if you had one it meant you'd been there. Trevin was being asked a lot of questions by his peers, and he'd encountered a new surge of popularity, which he said was something like what he'd observed with a guy who'd done the lead in a school play. He took it all in stride, and told his parents that he hoped being noticed would make people notice that he lived the standards of the gospel. He also said that it wasn't hard to tell who his *real* friends were.

Elizabeth suddenly became overwhelmed when they had a wave of phone messages on the machine with requests for interviews from the local media. Jayson called Roger at the office and got right through to him. "Didn't you say work was slow?" Jayson asked.

"Yes, I did say that."

"How would you like a part-time job for a little while? All you need is a phone and a calendar, and the pay isn't bad."

"I'd love to!" Roger said. "And you don't even have to pay me."

"You don't even know what I want yet."

"If it will help you, I'd love to do it."

"Elizabeth usually handles scheduling things for me, and the record company does some of it. The tour coordinator is taking care of all of those arrangements. But at the moment, we have a long list of people to call back and things to arrange with the local press, and she's overwhelmed. So, what I need is a manager, I guess. I'll pass the messages on to you. We just have to coordinate my calendar, then I'll let you figure the rest out."

"I can do that," Roger said.

"Good." Jayson chuckled and crossed that concern off his list. He was glad to have someone he could communicate with easily to handle the problem, someone he could trust.

Two days later, Roger had lined up a number of things very efficiently. Coinciding with the official release of the CD, Jayson did a number of interviews on local television, on local radio stations, and for newspapers. But he was glad to do it when most of the press was good, and he kept getting one little opportunity after another to set the record straight. Now, he could rarely go anywhere without being recognized, but people were respectful and friendly for the most part, and he really didn't mind.

Ironically, the surge of good press seemed to incite Sister Freedman to wage a counter-attack. Elizabeth, the bishop, and members of the Relief Society presidency were getting frequent phone calls from ward members to report some matter of horrible gossip they'd heard. Some simply reported it, saying, "I just thought you should know what's being said." Others asked for assurance that it wasn't true, usually with the comment, "I didn't think it could be, but I just wanted to be sure." In almost every case, Jayson felt like the members of his ward were standing by him and had faith in him to do the right thing. He was unspeakably grateful, but the very presence of the situation was annoying and disheartening.

Now that the advertising for concert tickets had hit the press, another drama emerged. The good news was that the show in Salt Lake City sold out so quickly that they asked Jayson to consider doing a second night. He was glad to. He wasn't expecting sold-out audiences elsewhere, but this was his *hometown,* and he'd gotten a lot of local publicity. This was the crowd that mattered most to him in many respects. The bad news was that his performing locally didn't come without its trials. Bishop Bingham called Jayson in to discuss one of them.

After the usual small talk, the bishop said gently, "Roger really wants to take the young men to your opening night as a group." Jayson knew about this. It had been discussed and planned, but he wasn't sure about the verdict. Now he knew that was the purpose of this visit. "Since you're willing to donate the tickets, the cost is not an issue. Each of the parents has been asked to pray about the situation and make a decision as to whether or not they feel good about having their sons do this. We can't call it an official Church activity. It's more of a neighborhood thing. The leaders who are willing to take a group of boys there up are legitimate family friends of all those boys who want to go. Some of the parents have already eagerly volunteered to come along. It looks like everyone but Sister Freedman is fine with it, and Clayton really wants to go—if you ask him when his mother isn't around. I must admit that I'm worried about her believing that the activity *does* have Church endorsement, even if it's been made expressly clear to her that it doesn't. She's heard talk about it. She's made it clear her son won't be going, and she's disgusted that we're doing this. For the sake of clarification, I'm going to repeat myself. I have made it expressly clear to her and everyone else that it is *not* a Church activity, which means that whether or not anyone goes is not up to me. Still, considering the situation, I'm a little worried about the impact on certain people. We should make that a matter of prayer, of course."

"Of course," Jayson said and resisted the human urge to tell him how ridiculous this was. If it wasn't a Church activity, then the opinions of one member of the ward should have no bearing on the situation. He was glad to know most of the boys would be there, but he wished that Clayton could be among them. He *wanted* the boys to go, mostly because he wanted them to experience the reality that his show would be positive and inspiring. He wanted the negative things that had come to their ears to be proven wrong. He didn't want them to go through their lives wondering if whatever they chose to do with their lives might be wrong just because someone didn't like it. He wanted them to believe him when he'd told them that he knew his gift was from God, and that they could feel the Spirit in it if they'd only give it a chance. Truthfully, he'd like to have Sister Freedman *and* Clayton there, as well. But that was never going to happen.

Jayson felt a little better when the bishop said, "As for myself, I'll be there. I wouldn't miss it. I got tickets for the whole family for opening night."

Jayson smiled. "I'm glad to know you'll be there. I'll try not to disappoint you."

"I'm not worried about that."

"If you're close to the front, you might want earplugs. It's going to be loud; it has to be for a venue that size."

"I'll bring some just in case," the bishop said with a smile. "We *are* close to the front, actually." He chuckled. "I can't wait."

* * * * *

After checking her email, Elizabeth felt bored and did a Google search on Mozart, just for fun. Much of what she read was a review, things she'd learned about him when she was younger. Scrolling down, she laughed to see a black-and-white profile drawing of the great composer. She printed the picture and took it to the studio.

"Look what I figured out," she said with exaggerated excitement.

"Do tell," Jayson said.

"Check this out." She turned the picture around so he could see it. "You have hair like Mozart." Jayson grabbed the paper to look more closely, and he chuckled. "Maybe that's why you've been prone to wearing a ponytail most of your life," she said. "You probably had some deep instinctive desire to be like Mozart."

"That's exactly right," he said and laughed.

"Maybe you were just born in the wrong time . . . as far as hair fashion is concerned."

"Maybe." He chuckled. "But then, I don't think I could have handled living in a time without electric guitars."

"Kind of makes you feel sorry for Mozart, doesn't it."

"Yes," Jayson said as if it were a serious matter, "I do believe that Wolfgang Amadeus would have really liked electric guitars."

CHAPTER 11

They were only a few weeks away from the beginning of the tour when Jayson was in the studio and his phone vibrated on his belt. "I'm getting a phone call, kid," he said to Trevin, who was practicing the bass on the other side of the room. Jayson felt nervous for some reason before he even glanced at the caller ID to see that it was Dalton.

"You are never gonna believe what just happened to me," Dalton said without even a hello. He was obviously upset.

The principle of opposition and all of its personal examples in Jayson's life flooded into his mind. "Oh, I don't know. I'd probably believe it. Tell me so we can deal with it."

"I broke my arm," he said, and Jayson felt himself wilt. He couldn't even speak. "I don't know what happened. It was the strangest thing. You don't have to tell me the position this puts you in. I feel sick about it, Jayson, but there's no way around it. I just won't be playing anything for at least six weeks. The ironic thing is that my wife's telling me she's relieved. She's not doing well with the pregnancy, and she's glad I'm going to be home. I told her you wouldn't agree, but . . . what can I say?"

Jayson was surprised at how calm he felt as Dalton's explanation went on. He had no idea what he was going to do, but he knew that somehow the Lord would help him work it out. And that's exactly what he told Dalton. He expressed regret that they wouldn't be touring together, because he'd really enjoyed getting to know him. Dalton expressed appreciation for the experience, and for how kind he and his family had been. Jayson hoped that his family and the spirit in his home had left a lasting impression on Dalton. Jayson promised that he would call him in the future if he ever needed a bass player. They said good-bye with positive feelings between them. Jayson turned off the phone and stared at the floor, wondering what else might happen while getting this tour on the road.

"What's wrong?" Trevin asked, alerting Jayson to the fact that he was still in the room.

Jayson looked up to see him sitting on a stool, the bass guitar on his thigh. His impatience to start playing again wasn't as obvious as his concern over the phone call. Jayson was surprised to recall in that moment how he'd once been hired to play guitar on tour with another band when the guitarist had broken his arm at the last minute. At the time, Jayson's own band had fallen apart and he'd been depressed. The tour had been a huge blessing for him, and he remembered feeling guilty for being grateful that the guy had broken his arm. He felt that way now. In an instant, everything was perfectly clear. Before he could even answer Trevin's question, he chuckled to recall Elizabeth's sermon on opposition. *For every light there is darkness, for every darkness there is light.* And there was the light, sitting right in front of him. It had been there all along. Dalton *did* need to be home with his wife. This was the way it needed to be. He didn't need to find another bass player. He just needed to raise his allowance.

"Dad?" Trevin said. "Are you okay?"

"I'm great," he said, but he wondered if Trevin didn't know whether or not to believe him. Did he think Jayson was being sarcastic?

"What's wrong?"

"Nothing's wrong, Trev. All is well . . . thanks to you."

"I don't get it."

Jayson laughed. He was loving this moment. "That was Dalton. I should be very upset and completely freaked out by what he just called to tell me. But I'm not, because you're sitting right there—the answer to my prayers before I even knew what I needed to pray for."

"Why?" Trevin asked with a voice that sounded scared and eyes that showed a glimmer of suspicion.

"Dalton broke his arm, Trevin. I need to find another bass player. But I don't. Because here you are. You know it all. It's already in your head."

He saw Trevin lift a hand to cover his mouth. He wasn't one to get emotional very easily, much unlike Jayson. But he was emotional now, and Jayson knew it, even though he pretended not to notice.

"Well?" Jayson said. "Will you do it or not? If you don't want to, I need to—"

"Are you serious?" Trevin asked, composed now as excitement squelched any other emotion. "Are you seriously asking me what I think you're asking me?"

"If you think I'm asking you to be my official bass player for 'The Heart of Mozart Tour,' then yes, I'm serious. But you'd better ask your mother's permission. We have a deal. No big decisions without consulting each other." Trevin set his guitar aside and was off of his stool in one swift movement. Jayson chuckled and followed after him. This he had to see.

"Hey, hold up," Jayson said, and Trevin turned around. "First of all, let's clarify a couple of things. You've sat in on a lot of rehearsals and you know the music. You have the capability, and most of the bass isn't terribly complicated. But if you agree to do this, there's no backing out, no complaining, no missing any rehearsal or performance—ever. You're sick, you're tired, you're sick and tired of doing it, you still have to be there. Your life is over until this tour ends. You have catching up to do, because you're going to have to be able to play every song like breathing. You know what I mean because we've talked about it. You have to play a song hundreds of times to do that, and we've got more than twenty numbers. From this moment you're going to do whatever it takes to pull decent grades at school, and beyond that, you are mine six days a week, every waking minute. No drill sergeant was ever more demanding than I'm going to be. It takes stamina and commitment to do this. And your fingers are going to protest. I wouldn't have asked if I didn't think you could do it. You have always been responsible, and I'm not questioning that you would be any other way now. I just need to be clear. You and I have never had any grief between us, but if you let me down—even a little—on this, *we will.* This is as professional as professional music gets, and I expect you to be professional. Do you understand?"

"I do, Dad. I really do. I've seen how hard you work. I know it won't be easy. But it's weird, because . . . for a while now . . ." He got emotional again.

"It's okay, kid. If you can't cry in front of your father, who always cries . . ."

"I've felt like it should be me. I've watched Dalton play and kept thinking that I could do it. I guess that day on the football field got in my blood. And I've been telling myself to be patient. I'm just a kid, and I've got my whole life to do this, but then . . . I thought . . . I don't know if you'll tour again, and . . . I just really wanted to."

"Why didn't you say something?"

"You already had a bass player, and I'm just a kid."

"You're plenty mature enough to handle it," Jayson said. "Maybe this is the way it was meant to be."

"I'd like to think so." Trevin chuckled and wiped his tears.

"Okay, go talk to your mother. But make it good. You've got to pull her leg for at least a minute."

Trevin smiled. "I can do that."

They found Elizabeth in the kitchen with the entire pantry closet emptied. Cans, bags, and boxes of food were all over the kitchen floor.

"What *are* you doing?" Jayson asked.

"The pantry closet was disgusting. It's clean now, but I have to put all this stuff back."

"Okay," Jayson drawled, noting that Trevin looked amused.

"But . . . why the . . ." He motioned to the fact that everything was divided into three categories that didn't seem to have any rhyme or reason.

"Well, I was talking to Macy yesterday about the whole gluten thing with food labels, so I decided to give myself a lesson in empathy. My skills might come in handy someday." She pointed to the largest group of cans and boxes, which was much bigger than the other two combined. "This is food that absolutely contains gluten, and Layla could not eat it. Oh, and . . . speaking of . . . Macy told me that when you use wheat flour to bake something, it can remain in the air for as long as twenty-four hours, and if Layla breathes it in, it could go down her throat, and cause damage. So if they want to bake something for the rest of the family, they have to do some of the measuring and mixing outside. How's that for putting a cramp in family life?"

"That's insane!" Trevin said. "I don't know how they do it."

"I guess you do what you have to do," Jayson said, "but it *is* insane."

Elizabeth then pointed to the smallest group, which was *very* small. "This is the stuff that is gluten-free. It either says so on the label, or the ingredients are straightforward and simple and we can know for sure."

"And this stuff?" Jayson asked, pointing to the third group, which was somewhere between the other two in size.

"This stuff is a mystery," she said. "There are things listed like 'natural flavor' or 'modified food starch' or other mysterious things that no human being can pronounce, and we simply don't know if it contains gluten or not without contacting the manufacturer."

Jayson made a disgusted noise. "And the Food and Drug Administration of the United States of America can't fix this problem? How many Americans have this disease? Didn't Macy tell us?"

"More than two million. One in every 133 people. But there are many other people with gluten intolerance or allergies that also have this problem."

"Sounds like it's worth a change in the law. But what do I know? I'm just a guitar player." He glanced at Trevin and nodded to discreetly cue him. When Trevin didn't speak, as if he were nervous, Jayson said, "Our son has something he needs to discuss with you."

"Okay," Elizabeth said and stopped what she was doing to give him her full attention. "What is it?"

"I've been offered a job, Mom," he said, and Jayson had to put his head down so Elizabeth wouldn't see him biting his lip to keep from laughing. "It will mean putting in lots of hours, but I can do it."

"A job?" Elizabeth said. "But . . . it's not many weeks until school is out, and we're going on tour. Is this job going to fit in with those plans?"

"Yes, it will be good, Mom. I promise. Please tell me I can do it."

"I need to know more about it, Trevin. Do you know about this, Jayson?"

"I do," he said, taking a quick glance at her.

"Okay, what are you guys up to?" she demanded. They both chuckled, and she asked Jayson, "What did you ask him to do? Head roadie? Stage manager? What?"

"Actually," Jayson said, "head bass player." Elizabeth's eyes narrowed, and he added quickly, "Dalton just called. He broke his arm."

He gave her a moment to take that in, then she squealed with delight. Then she started to cry and threw her arms around her son. While she was hugging him, she said to Jayson, "I bet my brother had something to do with this."

"I wouldn't be surprised," Jayson said. "Maybe we need to get Trevin a silly hat."

"I don't think you could talk him into wearing it," Elizabeth said and took Trevin's shoulders into her hands. "Now, do you realize what this entails? Are you sure? Because your dad gets nasty when people don't play his music the way he wants to hear it."

"I do not!"

"Well, maybe not *nasty*. Testy, then."

"Okay, I can get testy," he admitted.

"We already talked about that, Mom," Trevin said. "I know I can do it."

They all moved to the other room to sit down, where Jayson reiterated everything he'd said to Trevin. Elizabeth suggested that she speak to Trevin's school counselor and see what could be arranged to cut back on his school schedule, so that he could attend enough to get the credits, but no more than absolutely necessary. Next fall everything would be back to normal.

* * * * *

Arrangements were made to shoot the music video for "The Heart of Mozart" in Salt Lake City. They would be using the Capitol Theater, which had a great classic look to it. The video included Jayson walking the streets of the city, as if going to the theater to do the show. Elizabeth was with him during the filming, watching as he walked and sang while the cameras moved with him. His voice ended up being horrible that day, but they were going to dub the recorded music in anyway. Bystanders gathered but were kept at a distance. It all felt a little surreal, in spite of how accustomed she'd become to most aspects of his career. There were also television cameras around, and she knew this would hit the news.

In the theater some costume and makeup experts were there to help Jayson do something he'd never done before. He was pretending to be somebody else. Elizabeth laughed when she saw him in the eighteenth-century clothes—not because he looked funny, but because it was so delightful. And she told him so. He actually looked really good dressed like Mozart. The ponytail was perfect! Jayson performed the song onstage multiple times, but it was only him and no one else in the band. This video would have more of an artistic composition to it, with Jayson being the focus, since it was in actuality a solo album. Jayson performed the song both in and out of costume, so that the modern Jayson Wolfe and his image as Mozart could be interspersed throughout the edited film. Footage of an audience in the theater would be cut into it later.

When the shooting was done and they were driving home, Elizabeth reached a hand behind Jayson's head to play with his ponytail. "That was awesome," she said and laughed. "Mr. Jayson Amadeus Wolfe!"

* * * * *

Jayson received a call from the bishop, and wondered if the conversation would be pleasant or difficult. Not because he didn't enjoy talking to the man or appreciate his support and friendship, but because he was often the bearer of whatever bad tidings might be occurring within the little flock that Jayson belonged to, and whom the bishop was in charge of. He reported that Sister Freedman's efforts at gossip had gotten way out of hand earlier that evening. She had come to the church looking for Clayton after the youth meeting. He was playing basketball at the church with some other boys. The bishop had been in the building but not present, but some youth leaders had been there. As the bishop understood it, she had struck up a conversation with another mother, who was also waiting for her son to finish the game. When Sister Freedman had said something critical to this sister about allowing her son to attend the Jayson Wolfe concert, this sister had hotly defended Jayson, saying that all of this gossip and judgment was ludicrous. Sister Freedman had become so angry that it had caused a scene, and the bishop had been called in to break it up.

"This is unbelievable," Jayson said. "What did I do to create this problem?"

"You keep asking questions like that," the bishop said, "and it's always the same answer. You didn't do anything beyond what the Lord wants you to do. In fact, I came across a couple of scriptures you might appreciate."

"Knock me over," Jayson said, knowing he sounded *testy.*

"The first is Nephi quoting Isaiah, in Second Nephi, chapter fifteen. He says, *'Wo unto them that call evil good, and good evil, that put darkness for light, and light for darkness, that put bitter for sweet, and sweet for bitter! Wo unto the wise in their own eyes and prudent in their own sight!'"*

"Okay," Jayson said, intrigued but wanting to hear the bishop's take on it.

"As I see it, he's saying that it's just as bad to call good evil as it is to call evil good. I think sometimes we're so caught up in trying to avoid the evil that is presented in the world as something good, that we forget it works the other way around, as well. In essence, that's it for you, I think. Your persecution will come in the form of people trying to call good evil. It's a prideful attitude that does such a thing. Let me clarify, however, that it's important in any situation not to counter-judge those who are judgmental. No matter how much grief this woman has caused, we cannot judge where she's coming from. I believe that underneath her pride there must be something else, but she hasn't let me in on that. Whatever we may learn about what's taking place here to help us understand and get through it, we have to be careful how we apply it to Sister Freedman's behavior."

"I understand, Bishop; I do. But I appreciate the perspective."

"With that in mind, I want to share another scripture. This one's found in section 121 of the Doctrine and Covenants, which of course is when Joseph Smith was in Liberty Jail. It says, *'Cursed are all those that shall lift up the heel against mine anointed, saith the Lord, and cry they have sinned when they have not sinned before me, saith the Lord, but have done that which was meet in mine eyes, and which I commanded them. But those who cry transgression do it because they are the servants of sin, and are the children of disobedience themselves.'*"

"Wow," Jayson said.

"The thing to understand here, Jayson, is that you haven't done anything but what you know the Lord has asked you to do in using the gifts He gave you. The wonderful thing is that the Lord understands Sister Freedman's heart as much as He understands yours, and He will make up the difference when all is said and done. I pray every day that she will be able to figure out why she's *really* so unhappy about this and get some help."

"I pray for that too," Jayson said. "Thank you . . . for your support, and your perspective. I really am grateful."

"We're in this together."

"I'm glad you feel that way. I'm not sure there are many bishops who would take me under their wing the way you have. I don't know how I would have made it without you."

"You would have made it somehow, because you've got the Lord on your side. Moving along, I need to tell you that after the little incident at the church, I invited Sister Freedman into my office, and we had a long visit. I told her that I had been very prayerful about the situation, and that I had no question as to your worthiness to serve in any capacity in the Church, or to attend the temple. And I made it clear that I meant it even with your continuing in your career exactly as you have been doing.

It's not the first time I've said it to her, but I felt like she needed to hear it again."

Jayson sighed so deeply that it came up from his toes and landed in his shoulders as they slumped with inexpressible relief. "I think I needed to hear it again too," he said.

Following a long moment of silence, the bishop added, "I also told her, as gently and appropriately as I could, that I could not tolerate gossip and criticism in this ward. I told her that she was entitled to her opinion, but that she should keep it to herself. We read some scriptures together about judgment, and I did my best to help her understand where you're coming from, but I don't know if I got through to her. I can tell you she didn't take it very well, but that's not your concern. I want to apologize to you if I said or did anything through all of this that's made it more difficult for you. Sometimes we have to live and learn. I just hope that my learning curve didn't give you too much grief."

"There's no need to apologize," Jayson said. "I've been learning myself, and you've been wonderful. I'm certain I haven't made this very easy on you. I think we've both been way out of our comfort zone."

"Yeah." The bishop chuckled wryly. "It's moments like this when I'm most grateful for the Atonement. If I had to believe that my best could be good enough, I'd lose my mind."

"I can agree with that," Jayson said. Then he said fervently, "Thank you, Bishop. Forgive me if I'm repeating myself, but I can never tell you what your acceptance, and your being my advocate, means to me. I will do my best to never let you down."

"It's not me you have to deal with, Jayson. Do your best not to let God down, and you'll do just fine—just the way you were doing long before I became your bishop."

With the air cleared and his own spirit vindicated, Jayson's thoughts turned naturally to Sister Freedmen. He asked gently, "Do you think she's going to be alright?"

"I don't know," he said, and Jayson felt the weight of the bishop's burden. "Right now I fear that if she could, she'd take her son and move away in a heartbeat. But financially she can't do it. My fear is that she will take this as some kind of amputation from the ward. I'm certain most people would reach out and give her love and acceptance if she would let them, but I'm not sure she will. She believes that she's right and everyone else is wrong, but as I've said, I believe there's a lot more beneath this than just pride. And I worry. I've already alerted the Relief Society president to the situation and she assured me that she will personally do everything she can to keep track of Sister Freedman, and have others do the same. We can only pray and do the best we can do. I prayed with her before she left, and I offered to give her a blessing, but she refused."

"I feel terrible," Jayson admitted.

"Why should you?"

"I don't know. It just feels like my fault."

"It's not, Jayson. I've been wondering if God sent her to this ward so that we could help her face whatever is going on, or if . . . I don't know. I honestly don't know." In a brighter tone the bishop added, "Thank you for the CD. We love it! I especially enjoy listening to the songs that I've heard you play in the studio."

"I'm glad you're enjoying it," Jayson said, wondering what he'd been thinking when he'd insisted that he didn't want to do another album. Everyone he talked to was enjoying it, and he was grateful for the opportunity to spread such joy.

"I'm looking forward to opening night," the bishop added.

"I'm looking forward to it as well," Jayson said and felt a weight lifting from him. If only he didn't feel so concerned about Sister Freedman, and how all of this was going to affect Clayton. When he pushed those worries out of his head, he had to wonder if he was going to be mortified by a voice that didn't work. He prayed that God's plan didn't include some form of public humiliation. Considering such a thought ridiculous, he focused on visualizing every song coming out of his throat with strength and clarity in front of sold-out audiences. And he prayed that the vision would become a reality.

* * * * *

During one of Jayson's usual visits with Macy, he brought up a point that he just felt had to be said. "You know that Trevin's officially in the band."

"Yes, that is so awesome!" Her enthusiasm was genuine. "He is amazing on that bass."

"Yes, he is. I was wondering if you wanted to be in the show as well."

Macy laughed. "What are we now? The Von Trapp family?"

Jayson laughed heartily. "I don't think 'Do Re Mi' is really my style. But hey . . . we *are* a musical family."

"I am *not* musical enough to go onstage. I know you're just trying to humor me because you don't want me to feel left out."

"You don't play much, but what you do, you do very well. If you would like to have the experience of being onstage for a number, we can do it."

Macy took his hand. "You're very sweet, Dad, but I don't need that experience. It's not something I crave, or you probably would have known about it long before now. My other family is completely supportive of me being the tour nanny, and I'm greatly looking forward to it. That's all I need."

"Are you sure?"

"About being the nanny, or being onstage?"

"Both."

"Absolutely. Of course I'll miss Aaron, and he'll miss me. But I think he will be able to fly out a couple of times to meet us during the times we talked about. The Relief Society is willing to help with meals for the family, but it's hard to have them know what Layla can eat safely. I'm already training a couple of Layla's friends to help her, and the kids will be out of school so they can help more, too. I'm training them as well. Now that we've come this far, I think it will be good for them to learn to do without me, and I could use a vacation."

Jayson chuckled. "If you think being tour nanny will be a vacation. . . ."

"Yes, it will. I don't have to watch the kids that many hours a day, and it'll be a lot of fun. It was last time."

"I'm glad you think so. We couldn't do it without you."

"I'm sure you could figure something out."

"Put it this way: there's no one we'd rather have looking after what's most precious while we're working."

"It's a pleasure and an honor. Oh, and by the way . . . I love the CD. Your work just keeps getting better. You know I've heard the songs along the way, but hearing it all put together that way is amazing. I really do love it."

"I'm glad. It means the most to me when people I love actually love my music."

"I'll always be one of your biggest fans."

He smiled. "So, how's Layla?"

"It's slow, but we're getting things figured out; the territory is getting a little more familiar. She's gone through a pretty rough emotional stage;

I think she's been grieving for the reality of how hard this is going to make her life, and all of the things she can't do anymore related to food. Food is such a big part of our culture and our socializing. Everything revolves around food. No more buffets or pot lucks—ever. The cross-contamination issue is too risky. There are very few places she can eat out; most fast food is completely out of the question. And the problem will be with her the rest of her life. If I was her, I don't think I'd handle it as well."

"I know I wouldn't," Jayson said.

They talked a while longer about Layla's situation, and Aaron's schooling and work. Macy still lit up when she talked about her husband. Jayson was glad to know they were happy in spite of being so busy.

While Macy had no interest in being musically involved with the family, Trevin took to it like a fish to water. Jayson was even more impressed than he'd expected to be with the way that Trevin rose to his assignment. He insisted that Jayson just let him practice with the recordings for some days before they started doing it together. They worked out a schedule of studio time so that Trevin could be in there alone for the hours when he didn't need to be doing his school work, and Jayson could be doing other things elsewhere. Jayson used the studio for his own ongoing rehearsing while Trevin worked on his education. When it was down to crunch time, Jayson told Trevin that they couldn't put off doing it together any longer, because Brandon and Drew were flying out in a couple of days to do the final stretch of rehearsals.

Trevin just said, "Whenever you're ready."

"Oh, I'm ready," Jayson said.

They went to the studio, took it from the top, and went through every single number as it would be for the concert, taking only one break where the intermission would be. Jayson had to stop a number of times to point out the need for a correction or to suggest a way to play it that would work better. Since Jayson had been the one to actually play the bass on the recordings, he knew exactly how it needed to sound. Trevin proved to be a quick study. He was open and receptive, and Jayson's criticism didn't cause any uneasy feelings between them. They took another break and went through the entire concert again and again. Along with getting the bass down, Trevin also had to do backing vocals in numerous places, but he'd learned them well from his practice with the recordings. At times Jayson's voice was tolerable; at others it sounded pathetic. After a fourteen-hour day, they both sat on the studio floor, drinking bottled water and sweating as if they'd just worked out at the gym.

"Can I say something that might sound kind of mushy?" Trevin asked.

"Mushy? You're worried about being mushy with me? I'm a blubbering songwriter, Trev."

"Yeah, I know, but . . . this is different. This is personal. I've been thinking about it a lot, and Mom says we should share thoughts that are important, and not keep them to ourselves."

"Your mother is a very wise woman."

"I've been thinking a lot about Derek—my uncle, not my brother. I love hearing you and Mom talk about him, and I love the pictures and stuff that make him seem real."

"Yeah, I love that, too," Jayson said.

"The thing is . . . when I think about what he was like, musically at least—I don't think he and I were much alike otherwise—but musically, we are, right?"

"You sure are."

"So, do you think that such gifts are genetic or spiritual?"

"Wow," Jayson said. "You're asking *me*? That's quite a question. You're the one who taught *me* the gospel, remember?"

"No, I just bore my testimony and gave you the book. You figured the rest out."

"Okay, but . . ." He thought about the question. "I think it's both, or maybe it's . . . the spiritual gifts are partly maneuvered through genetics, because God is in control of both. Your mom and her brother both have incredible musical talent, but neither of their parents did. Drew and I are connected that way, of course. But I didn't find out until I was an adult that my father had been gifted musically."

"Really?"

"Yeah. It was a strange moment for me. He was a horrible person. Always drunk and beating my mother. She divorced him and we moved away. I hated him. Then when I found his family and realized they were great people, I found out that he'd been very gifted on the piano. He could play by ear. I was stunned to realize that for all that I'd not wanted anything to do with him, it was from him I got this gift. So, that seems obviously genetic. But then, I know God gave me this gift. So in essence, genetic or not, gifts come from God."

"That makes sense," Trevin said.

"So, you're saying that because Derek is your mother's brother, you got the gift from him?"

"That's part of it."

"What's the other part?"

"This might sound strange, but . . ."

"But you're going to say it anyway."

"Yeah. When I was a kid, I always felt a little out of place with Bradley and my dad. You know he was a great dad."

"Yes, I know."

"But they were a lot alike. They were both really smart, into math and stuff. And they both liked sports. I wasn't really into either, so I felt a little odd. I'd go to the games and play with them and stuff, because we had fun together. But I was obsessed with music, and they just didn't get it."

"Okay, I can understand that."

"That's just it, Dad. You *do* understand it, but you're not my biological father. I know enough about your history with Mom to know that the two of you were meant to end up together. I really believe that. The thing is . . . and this is the mushy part . . . I believe I was meant to be *your* son."

Jayson's heart quickened, and his voice got stuck in his throat. It was simply something he'd never expected to hear, even though he'd had the same thoughts. He never would have wanted to say anything to Trevin that would have even hinted at putting Robert out of his proper place as Trevin's father. He was relieved when Trevin went on, because he couldn't speak.

"I was born long before you and Mom got married, but I think God sent me to her so that I could be your son. She's very talented, as you know more than anybody. But *you* are a genius, Dad. Your intensity and abilities are so incredible. And I think that we knew each other before we came here, and some of that ability just spilled over and I got a little bit of it."

"More than a little bit," Jayson said, his voice cracking.

"So, I guess that's the point," Trevin concluded. "I think I got some of it genetically, and some of it spiritually. I'm just glad that I have it, because I love this. And I'm grateful that I'm in this family. I've got the greatest parents on the planet, and not just because you're both famous and a lot of fun to work with. You're a great dad . . . and you're not too bad as my drill sergeant, either."

Jayson chuckled and hugged him. "You're doing great, kid. I knew you would. And for the record, the feeling is mutual." His voice broke again. "I've felt since before I married your mother that you were meant to be my son."

Trevin smiled. "So, can I change my name?"

Jayson was taken aback. "You're serious."

"I am. I want to hyphenate it. I know of a few kids at school that have hyphenated names. I want to be Trevin Aragon-Wolfe."

"It would be an honor to give you my name," Jayson said. "After all, we are sealed. We're going to be together forever."

"That is glorious!" Trevin said.

"Yes, it is. You'd better ask your mother about the name."

"Oh, she'll go for it," he said, and they hugged again.

CHAPTER 12

Elizabeth was pleased with the hyphenated name idea for Trevin. In fact, she thought the same should be done for Addie. As young as Addie was, they talked to her about it and she had no trouble understanding, even though she could barely remember her father. She wanted her name to be the same as Trevin's, and Elizabeth started the legal process to get it done. Addie had been going by the name Wolfe in school and with her friends ever since the marriage. She'd been younger, and it hadn't been the same issue as it had been for Trevin. But there had been some confusion on Church records. And now they figured it was time to make the change legally for both of the children.

Life got crazy when Drew and Brandon came from Los Angeles for a final stretch of rehearsals, which was more a matter of review and polishing. Trevin meshed with them so perfectly that Jayson was freshly amazed at the miracle of his gift, and the timing of his being in the right place with the right ability. They also did another photo shoot, since Dalton had been replaced by Trevin in the band, and the record company wanted up-to-date photos that would help promote the tour *and* the CD.

The day after Drew and Brandon left to go back home for a short break before the tour began, Trevin was at school taking a test, and Jayson was in the studio running through his numbers when Elizabeth came in, looking very subdued.

"What's wrong?" he asked and turned toward her as she sat down.

"Sister Mote just called. She's one of the counselors in the Relief Society."

"I know who she is," he said. "What's wrong?"

Elizabeth cleared her throat, and he knew she didn't want to tell him. "Um . . . Sister Freedman has been hospitalized; in the psych ward." He gasped. "Apparently she had a breakdown."

"What happened?" he asked, hating the fact that he felt somehow responsible.

"Clayton came home from school and found her completely despondent. He was scared and called the bishop's house. Sister Bingham went right over. The bishop was at work, of course. When she couldn't get any response from Sister Freedman at all, she called 911. Apparently this had nothing to do with drugs, or anything. She just . . . lost it."

Jayson sighed and hung his head. "And what about Clayton?"

"He's staying with the Binghams. Apparently they've taken in foster kids off and on in the past. I think I knew that, although they haven't had one for a while. But they're in the system, so it was easy to get temporary guardianship of Clayton, since there are no relatives to speak of, and there's no question about his mother not being capable of caring for him."

"Well, that's good, at least. How is he?"

"She said he seems okay, but they are concerned about him. I guess he'll be getting some counseling while his mother's getting treatments. That's all I know. She said the bishop had asked her to call and let us know what was going on."

Jayson sighed again. "At least they're both getting some help." He groaned.

"What?"

"I feel like it's my fault."

"How is that possible?"

"I had some pretty hefty arguments with her, Elizabeth."

"You were never cruel to her, and you didn't lose your temper. You were simply trying to defend your position. Obviously there's a big problem that was there long before she started taking it out on you."

"Yeah, well . . . I'm not so sure I handled it the way Jesus would have."

"You're not perfect, but—"

"No, I'm certainly not. And I was really angry."

"Understandably so. What's done is done. It's not your fault."

"It feels like it is. If not for my *questionable career,* maybe she would—"

"What? Still be drowning in her own self-righteousness? She's emotionally ill, Jayson. Maybe all of this was a good thing. Maybe something drastic needed to happen so she *could* get some help; so Clayton could get some help. He's a good kid in spite of some stupid mistakes. He loves his mom, but her attitudes have caused some serious confusion for him. Maybe you're the best thing that ever happened to both of them."

"Now, that's a stretch," Jayson muttered.

Elizabeth gave him a kiss and left him to his work. He practiced until he worked up a sweat, but he couldn't distract himself from his concern for Sister Freedman and her son. Trevin came in when he got home. They chatted as usual for a few minutes before they got to work. He didn't say anything about Clayton, and Jayson didn't want to bring it up. It wasn't his place to tell Clayton's peers what was going on. They went through every song once before Trevin went off to do homework, and a while later Addie came in. She was sitting on his lap, telling him about her day when Elizabeth came in and said, "There's someone at the door to see you."

"Me?" Addie said.

"No, it's for Daddy. Go put away your clean clothes, and then we'll go to Wal-Mart."

Addie ran off, and Jayson moved toward the door. "Who is it?" he asked, noting Elizabeth's cautious gaze.

"It's Clayton. He just asked if he could talk to you; he looks nervous."

"Oh, boy," Jayson said and took a deep breath.

"I'll be in the kitchen," she said to him. "If you need me, I'll come and save you."

"Thanks a lot," Jayson said and uttered a silent prayer on his way to the front room. He wondered if the boy would be angry with him, or just angry. Or if not angry, at least upset with Jayson for one reason or another. Other than the morning Jayson had lectured him on drugs, they'd had no personal interaction. He had no idea what to expect, or how to handle it. He could only ask for the Spirit's guidance and listen. But he'd done that with Clayton's mother, and it hadn't necessarily turned out the way he'd hoped.

"Hey, kid," Jayson said, and Clayton stood up. "You okay?"

"You heard about my mom?"

"Yeah, I heard," he said. "I'm sorry. Is there anything I can do?"

"No," Clayton said and became visibly nervous.

"Have a seat," Jayson said, and they sat together on the couch. "Now, why don't you say what you came here to say." Clayton didn't speak, and Jayson tried to guess. "Are you angry or upset with me?"

Clayton looked astonished. "No!" he insisted. "No. No. I just . . . I wanted to apologize for the way my mom has been. I know it's been hard for you; it's been hard for me, too."

"I'm sure it has."

Clayton chuckled tensely. "I guess that gives us something in common." He cleared his throat. "The bishop has been great. We've talked a lot. He's helped me understand some things. I just wanted you to know that . . . well . . . I've been embarrassed about what my mom has done, but . . . I understand why she's that way. I just hope she can get better."

"I hope so, too," Jayson said. "Whatever happens, you're going to be fine. You're a great kid."

"You think so?"

"I do. I really do."

"That's nice of you to say. You really are a nice guy. I don't know why my mom can't see it. I mean, I *do* know, but . . ." His words faded into nothing.

Jayson noted that was the second reference to something Clayton knew that explained his mother's behavior. He wanted desperately to ask, but didn't want to pry. Maybe it wasn't his place to know. He was wondering what else to say when Clayton seemed to have found the words to go on. "I mean . . . after what happened with my dad . . ."

"*What* happened with your dad?" Jayson asked, his heart quickening.

"I was too young to remember," Clayton said, as if he had no trouble talking about it. If anything, he sounded surprised that Jayson hadn't already known. "But Mom said that he was a pretty decent guy when she married him, or she thought he was. The only thing she didn't like was the kind of music he listened to." He listed some names of bands that Jayson knew well—or rather he knew *of* them. They'd never come close to being among his listening preferences. His mother never would have allowed him and Drew to listen to such music. It was commonly classified as acid rock—typically encouraging of drug use, and so frenzied and extreme that the spirit about it was most often truly evil. He already understood so much, even before Clayton added, "As Mom tells it, one thing led to another. He started spending more time with his weird friends than at home, he got into hard drugs, and he died of an overdose when I was three." Clayton let out a stilted chuckle. "From that lecture you gave me after my night on the town, I know you know about such things. I just could never convince my mom that your music wasn't like that. I've listened to the stuff Dad listened to. She doesn't know I did, but I had to know what it's like. I can tell the difference. There's a *big* difference. Night and day."

"Yeah," Jayson said, "night and day." *Light and dark,* he thought to himself.

"Are you okay?" Clayton asked.

"I . . . didn't know. I had no idea. I can understand why your mother is so afraid for you. I hope you won't let her down."

"I won't," he said. "You and Roger set me straight on that."

He stood up as if that was all he needed to say, and Jayson followed him to the door, thanking him for coming over, and for being so open with him. "If there's anything I can do, ever, please let me know."

"Thanks," Clayton said.

Jayson gave him a quick hug that turned into a longer one. He sensed that Clayton was feeling emotional, but he hurried out. A moment later Elizabeth appeared and said, "I confess I was eavesdropping."

"Wow."

"Yeah."

She said nothing more. She just put her arms around him and held him tightly. No words were needed to know that she understood. They would pray for Sister Freedman, and they were grateful they'd come this far without causing any damage from their own misunderstandings of the situation. Jayson felt especially grateful for that.

For a couple of days Jayson stewed over the situation with Bonnie Freedman. He wanted to be able to help, but knew that he was the last person she would want help from. He prayed about it, and he and Elizabeth did a twenty-four-hour fast on behalf of her and her son. Then an idea occurred to Jayson, and he called Maren, his counselor, who had connections in the psychiatric profession. She made a couple of calls for him, and while Elizabeth was at the temple with some ladies in the ward and the kids were with Will and Marilyn, he took his acoustic guitar with him to the hospital. He got right in when he told them his name, and Maren's connections paid off. He spoke with someone in charge to clarify a few things, then he was taken to a room where he knew that Bonnie Freedman was on the other side of the curtain, and he could sit in a chair next to an empty bed where another patient might stay if needed. He knew that Bonnie was barely this side of a catatonic state, coming around only enough here and there to be helped to the bathroom or to drink nutritional supplements and take her medications. He was assured that she could probably hear him, but she wasn't getting out of bed at all without help, and she couldn't possibly know that it was actually *him*. A nurse stayed in the room just in case, but he sensed that she was a fan, even if she wasn't admitting it, and she was a little in awe. He just ignored that and took out his guitar. He picked a quiet introduction, then sang softly his own version of one of his favorite hymns, "Be Still, My Soul." He did the whole song, a lengthy bridge with the guitar, then repeated the first verse again. The nurse wiped at her tears, which Jayson ignored, and he went on playing and singing hymns for more than an hour. His voice only went mildly hoarse a few times. Of course, this wasn't the intense singing he would need to do for a concert, but he still felt hopeful that when he needed his voice, the Lord would bless him to have it. His voice gave out sooner than he would have liked, but he felt like he'd at least made an effort.

When he couldn't sing any longer, he put his guitar back in the case, and handed a CD to the nurse. He had burned it in the studio just this morning, and on it he'd simply written with a marker, *Hymns.* They were recordings he'd worked on here and there for a few years. It was guitar and piano, mostly his voice, mixed with some backing vocals by Elizabeth on some tracks, and also some flute and violin. The hymns he'd chosen were those that specifically focused on the Savior and His love and sacrifice. Those were Jayson's favorites.

"It's just a little something I came up with," he said. "I talked to the head nurse about it. I'd like it played for her as much as possible. They said there's a CD player in the room?"

"There is. Thank you," she said. "It was beautiful."

"I hope it helps," Jayson said and left the hospital.

He said nothing to Elizabeth about where he'd been while she was at the temple. He figured it might come up eventually, but for now he wanted to hold his tiny efforts on Bonnie's behalf in his own heart. Funny how he'd started thinking of her on a first-name basis. The compassion he felt for her gave him a deep sense of connection that she would surely never feel for him. But that was okay. He'd given her his music, or specifically his testimony through music. As long as she never knew it was him on that CD, it might make a difference to her.

The following morning Jayson was startled to wake up and realize that tomorrow the official tour began. It wouldn't start for a few days after that for the fans, but the entire show would be set up and rehearsed the next couple of days in the arena in Salt Lake City where they would be performing on two consecutive nights. And then the five buses and three semis that comprised *The Heart of Mozart Tour* would begin their convoy across the country. There was a bus for the family, and one for the band. Trevin was actually going to be sleeping on the same bus with Brandon and Drew, which evened out the space a little. Since Macy was coming along as tour nanny, she would be on the same bus with Jayson, Elizabeth, and the kids. It was cozy, but it worked just fine. The fact that they could sleep or eat or play games while on the road was the only thing that made such an endeavor possible. Two of the buses were for the other musicians, one for the boys and one for the girls. It would be cozy for them too, but Jayson had told them if they couldn't get along they'd be grounded. They were all simply thrilled with the opportunity—and most of them were used to sleeping in college dorms. The fifth bus was for some of the crew, and there would also be security officers that had been hired from a private company to ensure that everyone remained free from harassment. The semis were loaded with lights, sound, and special-effects equipment, and all of the precious instruments—including an exquisite piano that Jayson had handpicked for the tour.

Jayson knew everything was as ready to go as it could be. Wardrobes had been carefully chosen for some measure of coordination, and multiple sets of every piece were ready to go. Jayson had five pairs of the same black lace-up shoes, black jeans, white T-shirts, and five elegant brocade vests in a black-and-white paisley, as well as other accessories. He had only one coat—the one Elizabeth had given him, which he would wear for only the first number each night; after that, it was just too hot. He felt a deep thrill of anticipation, and prayed that all would go well—that protection, health, and a great spirit of celebration would accompany their many weeks on the road.

It often took great willpower to keep his thoughts positive regarding his voice, when its condition varied from day to day, sometimes hour to hour. He was still babying it with humidifiers at night, cough medicine in regular doses, and throat lozenges almost constantly. But his throat felt like it had been through a war. It was rarely sore, but it felt immensely aggravated, and sometimes it just protested without warning.

He was managing to sing tolerably well when he rehearsed, but his voice lacked the strength and vibrancy that he was accustomed to hearing come out of his own mouth. And occasionally he'd get a tickle in his throat that would send him off on a coughing bout, or he would experience a sudden hoarseness, and nothing would come out but a sick kind of croaking. If he allowed himself, it was easy to become terrified of getting up onstage and humiliating himself in front of thousands of people. He'd imagined all kinds of comic relief he could use to soften the blow, and he'd determined that he might just have to resort to that. He'd come up with a few good lines that could get a laugh, but he prayed he'd never have to use them. He was well accustomed to talking a little between songs. He knew that part of being a good performer was having a good rapport with the audience, and for him that was getting personal or being funny between numbers. And he could do it. He just wanted his voice to be able to perform well so he would not have to be preoccupied with trying to make up for it by making stupid jokes. But all he could do was move forward with faith, and each time his worry came to mind, he would say a quick prayer and replace his anxiety with the image of himself at the microphone, singing clearly.

The day went smoothly as he and Elizabeth checked and rechecked every list, and she made some phone calls in order to be absolutely certain everything was covered. They paid a visit to Layla, which served a dual purpose in being able to check with Macy and Aaron and make certain everything was under control for Macy to start her official job as tour nanny the following day. She had also deemed herself the tour historian and was prepared with a digital camera and lots of memory cards, and she'd be taking her laptop along to download pictures along the way. Macy was excited, but she and Aaron both had mixed feelings about the amount of time they'd be separated. Layla was thrilled on Macy's behalf, and assured them all that everything was very much taken care of and they would all be fine. In fact, Layla would be attending the opening-night show, along with all of the children. She'd been looking forward to it and saving her strength, and she said she would be bringing along a friend that she had met during one of her hospital stays.

That evening Jayson and Elizabeth had a sendoff party at their house for family, friends, and some neighbors and ward members who had been especially supportive. It was a simple open house with refreshments, and the band doing a couple of off-the-cuff versions of a few songs in the living room. The bishop and his family were there, including Clayton, who was blending in with them very well. News was that there had been no change with his mother. Roger and his family were there, also. They all had a wonderful time, especially when Jayson and Drew started reminiscing by playing music from years back, much that they could barely remember enough to pull it off in any recognizable form whatsoever. But it did make for some good laughs.

After the party, Will and Marilyn and Macy and Aaron hung around, and every member of the family who would be going on tour was given a blessing. Jayson gave blessings to his wife and children, including Aaron, who would be without his wife. And Will gave a blessing to Jayson. He felt strengthened and comforted to hear the same promises given. Everything was going to be okay.

The following morning Jayson felt like he was seventeen again, doing his first gig with Derek, Drew, and Elizabeth. He shared his thoughts with Elizabeth and she agreed. "Who would have dreamed," she said, "that we would be doing this . . . without Derek . . . but with our son on the bass instead?"

"Who would have dreamed?" he repeated.

Jayson was especially mindful of the fact that he did *not* have a headache, and his voice was working. He expressed his gratitude to his Heavenly Father, and prayed that it would last.

Macy arrived to watch the kids and took one of the family SUVs, the one with two baby seats in it, so she could take them along on a few errands and then bring them back to the house for their naps.

When Jayson was ready to go but Elizabeth wasn't, he found himself in the living room, looking at the wall Macy had created with a framed history of his career. His eye was drawn to a copy of an old newspaper article. It was a large piece with a big picture of their first band. Their first review. Realizing he hadn't read it for years, he put on his glasses and leaned closer to take it in.

I've been reviewing hometown bands for years, you know. I'm certain many of you reading this have been following the trends right along with me. I know how these local dance halls work. If you get there at opening, it's practically empty and the crowds fill in slowly. So, naturally I wondered what might be going on when I arrived five minutes before the band was set to play and the place was packed. It soon became evident the regulars knew something I didn't know. The show was going to be good, and they didn't want to miss a minute. The curtain went up to a deafening roar, but when these four teenagers appeared on stage, I wondered what all the fuss was about. Then, as casually as breathing, they jumped into an impressive rendition of some of rock's hottest songs. And the crowds were psyched. The place cooled down a little with recorded music while the band took a half-hour break and we had a little chat in the lounge. I felt sufficiently impressed and ready to be on my way when, working my way through the crowd to the door, I was struck by a hot current in the air and couldn't resist holding out for just one more number. Pretty boy Jayson Wolfe stepped up to the— Jayson chuckled, recalling how offended he'd felt when he'd first heard Elizabeth read this out loud. He read on. *—stepped up to the microphone and greeted his fans with the announcement that it was Saturday. Their response alone threatened to bring the house down, then the mercury jumped to the top of the thermometer with a near-perfect clone of Elton John's classic, "Saturday Night's Alright for Fighting." By then I was so caught up in the feeding frenzy that I had to stay for the rest of the show. Lead singer, guitarist, pianist Jayson Wolfe is everything a front man should be. He seems to have taken a quantum leap from some unknown platinum musical cosmos where rare musicians are bred. It can be the only explanation to the questions on every tongue on the dance floor. Where did he come from, and where did he learn to woo these instruments with such finesse at such a tender age? One simply wouldn't guess that he's pulling a B-average at a local high school. Were these Wolfe boys weaned from Gerber to guitars? Jayson is kept on beat by his brother, Drew, who obviously eats and sleeps with perfect rhythm. Derek Greer, who expertly monopolizes the bass-line, is clearly as much at home with his instrument as the rest of his mates. Elizabeth Greer, the only female member of Wolves, improves the scenery onstage, although it's not difficult to imagine these good-looking lads gracing the covers of teen rock magazines. Beyond adding some feminine grace to the stage, Miss Greer adds texture to an already rich sound with a variety of unique additions to rock and roll. Appearing onstage with a flute or violin, one might expect something classical to roll off, but she blends the sound into a well-performed montage of rock classics and a few originals that bring the house down. The blended voice of Wolves is the icing on a cake that any rock fan should take a big, hearty bite of. Sit up, Portland, and pay attention. Better yet, get on the floor and dance. The opportunity isn't likely to last forever. I smell a record deal in the wind.'*

"Wow," Jayson said to the empty room, and he could almost hear Derek saying it right along with him. At the time, it had been easy to smell that potential record deal, but Derek had been killed, Elizabeth had left him, and the climb to fame had been much harder than he'd ever dreamed. He'd reached the top, then dropped to the bottom. Now here he was, reading words that almost seemed like some kind of prophecy. Trevin had gracefully stepped into Derek's shoes, and their dream had come true in ways more wonderful and grand than he ever could have imagined.

"Did you say something?" Elizabeth asked, coming into the room.

He pointed at the review. "I hadn't read it for a while. We've come far."

"Yes, we have," she said and kissed him. "Come on. We're late."

"They can't start without me."

"That's true," she said and took his hand. "You pretty-boy front man, you."

"You *have* read it recently!"

"No, actually. But I remember what it says. I was hopelessly in love with that pretty-boy front man at the time." She kissed him again. "I still am."

* * * * *

Jayson and Elizabeth walked into the arena from the back, wanting to see the stage. After a cell phone call to the stage manager to let him know they were there, he waved from the stage and they waved back before they sat down to watch the final preparations for the stage setup to unfold. The stage crew was also rehearsing the setup and takedown for the event. Even from the distance, they could see that the guys were all wearing matching shirts, and some of them had hats on—all part of the official *Heart of Mozart Tour,* done in black and red.

They watched in silence for a few minutes before Elizabeth said, "How many people does it take to properly display the musical genius of Jayson Wolfe?"

"Is this is a joke that has a clever answer?"

"No," she said. "It's a question. The answer is that I have no idea. I've lost count."

"I have too. But I'm sure you'll figure it out. You'll have a list by the end of the tour, so you can send them all thank-you notes and Christmas cards."

"How well you know me!"

"You'll probably send them Books of Mormon too," he said. "The ones that haven't already read it, anyway."

"I just might," she said.

Jayson's stomach flip-flopped when the stage manager did a mike check on Jayson's mike. He knew how tall Jayson was, and he could adjust its height perfectly.

"Okay," he said into the mike, "we're ready for you, Wolfe Man."

"Very funny," Jayson said to Elizabeth and they walked up the aisle to the stage. Jayson just wanted to stand in front of it for a minute and imagine the results. What he imagined made him smile. Trevin arrived a few minutes later with Drew and Brandon. Trevin had wanted them to see a local music store where he and Jayson liked to hang out sometimes.

The stage rehearsals started out with some ridiculous glitches in the sound equipment that began to get really annoying. It took nearly five hours to go through the show once. The situation was made more discouraging by the sorry state of Jayson's voice. They took a break and had a meal, then did it again, but the time was cut in half, and there were only a few minor challenges. Jayson's voice was a little better that time around. The third time through it went smoothly, but Jayson insisted on a fourth, even though it meant getting home very late. The last hour he sounded like a frog and was barely singing at all. But the show went smoothly and without a single problem otherwise.

Early the following morning they went through it once more, and Jayson's voice was tolerable; not at its peak, but not bad enough for anyone to really notice—he hoped. Once that was done, Jayson stepped boldly from preparation and rehearsal mode into performance frame of mind. Everything else that would be done in the coming months would be done in front of an audience. If glitches happened or mistakes were made, they would roll with the punches. He'd make jokes about it, and the show would go on. They drove back to the house to get a little rest before the big event.

Before leaving the house, Macy took a ridiculous number of pictures. The whole family—even the babies—had been equipped with matching polo shirts and jackets with the tour logo, the same that the stage crew and roadies would be wearing. Aaron had gotten the afternoon and evening off to be a part of the big event, and he too had the right wardrobe. Will and Marilyn were there and helped take pictures, so that the entire family could be in them.

The family and the band were all in the artist's lounge of the arena long before the doors were opened and concert-goers began filling the seats. Jayson took Elizabeth's hand and crept down the stairs and a long hall to the side of the stage, where they could hear the growing murmur of fans filling the arena.

"Do you hear it?" he asked, taking her in his arms.

"I hear it," she said.

"I first heard it in Portland when we were seventeen. The anticipation in the air."

"And you will exceed their every expectation."

"We. You mean *we.*"

"I admit it's a team effort," she said, "and I won't deny possessing a bit of talent, but—"

"A bit?" He laughed. "My dear Elizabeth. Do you remember that I fell in love with you while you were onstage?"

"That was *West Side Story.* This is different. I love every minute of working with you, Jayson Wolfe. I love every minute of living with you. And I have no problem with absolutely knowing that you are the genius of this operation. You were born to do this, and I love you for doing it so nobly. So, let's go change our clothes and get ready to make the stadium rock."

Jayson took a deep breath and laughed. A quick glance made it clear they were completely alone, so he kissed her, again and again. He finally took a sustaining breath and said, "Okay, now I'm ready."

A short while later they were all ready, and the anticipation was growing into a jittery sensation that every musician was sharing. Jayson had never had this many other people backstage with him, but with his mini orchestra *and* the band, there were a lot of nervously excited people.

"Wow!" Jayson said when he saw Trevin. They were dressed almost exactly the same, since Elizabeth had chosen the wardrobe. Trevin's vest was solid black, and Jayson's was paisley, with the coat over it for the first number. "You look great!" he said to his son.

"You too."

"Are you nervous?"

"Heck yes," he said and chuckled. "But I know the drill. Once we start playing, it's just us and the music, and it's like breathing."

"That's right. You're going to be great."

Elizabeth appeared, dressed much the same as Jayson, except her shirt was black and her vest was solid white. "You look like a rock star," Jayson said to her.

"*You* look like a rock star," she said. "I'm just filler."

"You're the missing ingredient," he said, and she smiled, reminded of the song he'd written with that title, which had come to him when he'd been trying to talk her into going onstage with him and she'd been reluctant. She'd prayerfully come to an absolute knowledge that she was supposed to be by his side—at home *and* on the stage. And she loved it! Most of it anyway. She loved the actual being onstage, at least. She knew from experience that the long bus rides with kids became challenging at times, but were still filled with the makings of great memories.

Jayson gathered his entire corps together in a discreet hallway and offered a prayer. There were only a few that weren't LDS, but they'd long ago learned that Jayson's religious values were a big part of everything he did, and they were used to it.

When they were down to about fifteen minutes to show time, Elizabeth said to Jayson, "Still no headache today?"

"Nope," he said, and with that one word he panicked. "What was that?" he asked and confirmed it. His voice was hoarse and croaky. "This can't be happening," he said, and it sounded worse. He used a throat rinse that the doctor had given him; something that was commonly used by professional singers in such situations, but he still sounded terrible.

Elizabeth said a silent prayer and wondered what she might do to help Jayson feel calm and confident about this. But it was difficult to know what to say when the problem was so obvious. The members of the orchestra were gathered elsewhere, but Trevin and Drew were both in the room with them and became alarmingly aware of the situation. Elizabeth could almost imagine Drew wanting to say that they should have postponed the tour, that he had seen this coming. But he was gracious and kept his mouth shut. She knew he would never be unkind to Jayson. But his concern was evident. Grasping onto the only idea that came to her, she told Jayson she'd be right back and went to talk to a member of their tour security before she found her cell phone in the dressing room.

Elizabeth called her father's cell phone, knowing he was in the audience only a few rows from the front. Hopefully he wouldn't have turned his phone off yet. When he answered, she said, "We need you and Roger back here for a few minutes."

In response to her panic, he asked, "Something wrong?"

"Jayson can't talk. A security guard is coming to the vestibule to your left. He'll bring you back here."

"We're on our way," Will said and hung up.

Jayson looked up to see Roger and Will standing beside him, and he started to cry, oblivious to the other members of the band seeing him reduced to tears. Brandon was the only one who hadn't seen it before. But he was practically family by now.

"I cannot believe this is happening," Jayson said, sounding terrible.

"It's going to be okay," Will said. "We're going to give you a blessing."

Drew and Brandon didn't leave the room, and Jayson wondered what they would think of all this. But right now his greatest concern was being able to do what he'd come here tonight to do. Thousands of people were out there in the audience. Surely God would not have brought him this far to have it not work. Would He? If this was a test of faith, he felt sure he was failing. He could feel himself crumbling as Roger and Will put their hands on his head.

"Jayson Amadeus Wolfe," Will began, then he hesitated. It was customary for every blessing to begin with the full name being stated. But Jayson felt something strange at the reminder that he and Mozart shared the same middle name. Following the standard protocol, Will said, "Your Heavenly Father is pleased with your performance, Jayson. He will not let you down." He hesitated again and closed in the name of Jesus Christ.

Jayson looked up at his father-in-law. "That's it?" he croaked.

"That's it," Will said and hugged him. "You're going to be great!"

Jayson received a hug from Roger as well, who said, "No worries, buddy."

They left to go back to their seats. Jayson turned and met the eyes of his wife, his son, his brother, and this good man he'd hired to round out the music he'd put so much heart and soul into. He didn't know what to say, was afraid to open his mouth. He rushed into the bathroom, turned on the fan, and dropped to his knees, crying like a baby and praying with everything inside of him that he could have the faith to step out onto that stage and truly believe that God would not let him down.

CHAPTER 13

Jayson heard a knock on the door, and the stage manager saying, "Five minutes, Jayse."

"Thank you," he called in a voice that croaked. He uttered one more prayer, came to his feet, and wiped his tears. He felt impressed to gargle one more time with that awful stuff the doctor had given him, then he went back to the lounge and found the others waiting, looking concerned. He could tell Elizabeth had been crying too, since she was touching up her makeup.

"You okay?" Drew asked.

Jayson just nodded, afraid to even make a sound.

"Let's do this," Elizabeth said with all the zeal and positive energy Jayson himself would have liked to portray. "It's going to be fine."

They moved in a group from the lounge to backstage. Once the stage manager saw them, he signaled, and the lights went down. The audience went wild. The roar was deafening and filled Jayson with a familiar adrenaline. But the fear was entirely unfamiliar. He prayed for the hundredth time in ten minutes that his fear would be replaced by faith. The orchestra moved into place with little flashlights and he heard Trevin say, "Oh, my gosh! I can't believe this is happening to me!"

"You'll get sick of it," Drew said and pushed him onto the stage. Drew and Brandon followed him.

"It's going to be okay," Elizabeth said and kissed him quickly before she followed the guys.

The four of them took their places with the help of tiny flashlights, while the rumble of the audience didn't relent. The decibel level increased when Drew started a steady drum sequence. After two bars the bass came in, then Brandon on the guitar. Jayson took a deep breath, focused on a positive image in his mind, and moved across the stage with a flashlight. He could tell by their response that the audience obviously knew it was him, even though it was completely dark. He sat at the piano, struck a clear chord, and in the next split second the tempo increased, colored beams of light filled the stage, and fireworks erupted from devices on the floor on either side of the stage. Jayson dove into playing the lengthy introduction of one of his big radio hits from years ago, a song that was familiar and well loved, with intricate, highly charged piano. He pretended that nothing in the world was wrong as he put his mouth to the microphone right on cue. He'd sung this song a thousand times, but it had never been hard, never caused him any stress. He tried to remember that feeling as he pushed the lyrics out of his mouth. He didn't know if he was entirely surprised, or not surprised at all, to hear his own voice sound more clear and strong than it had since before his illness. It took willpower to hold back the threat of tears in order to keep singing. He couldn't believe it! But he could! More accurately, he was in awe! Remarkably, humbly, and gratefully in awe! Within seconds he had relaxed into the reality that all *would* be well, and he had the crowd completely captured. They were his for the evening. He couldn't imagine any experience in the world that could be more exhilarating than this.

"Hello . . . Salt Lake City!" he said into the mike the moment the first song ended, speaking as clearly as he had sung. "*Still* my hometown!" He was met with great approval as he took up his guitar and the show moved on. He shared a quick glance and a smile with Elizabeth and Drew before he positioned himself at the mike at the front of the stage and began the next song.

After the first three numbers had gone off without a glitch, Jayson flipped the guitar onto his back and said into the mike, "Would you like to hear a story?" Cheers and applause. He chuckled. "You people must have been around the last time I toured. You *like* my stories." The response was even louder. "Okay, but this is a serious story . . . seriously." The audience laughed. "Seriously," he said again, then became serious. "If you go back and look at my first CD, specifically Gray Wolf, you'll see that it's dedicated to the memory of Derek Greer. Derek was my best friend in high school, and when it came to music we were like peanut butter and jelly." Laughter. "Seriously," Jayson said again, pretending to sound insulted. He chuckled and went on. "Derek was a genius on the bass, and we made great music together. His father treated me like his own son, and I fell in love with his sister, and I became a part of their family. I still am. But Derek was killed in a car accident not many days before we were all set to graduate from high school." A hush fell over the arena; now the audience clearly got what he'd meant by serious. "It was tough to get through that event for all of us who loved Derek, but I have felt his spirit in my music for many years. Derek's sister, Elizabeth, married a fine man named Robert Aragon. They had two sons, Bradley and Trevin, and a daughter named Addie. Robert and Bradley were both killed in a drowning accident." A hushed gasp from the audience. "No, I'm not making this up. It was after this that Elizabeth and her family took me and my daughter, Macy, into their lives, and eventually we all became one family." He chuckled. "You don't have to be serious anymore." Everyone chuckled. "We are a really great family!" More chuckling. "No, seriously!" he said, and the laughter was loud. Taking on an immediate tone of the ringmaster of a circus, marveling at the strength of his own voice, he said, "Ladies and Gentlemen, on the violin and flute, my lovely and talented wife, and the mother of my children, Elizabeth Wolfe."

Elizabeth stood from her stool and took an elaborate bow. While the audience applauded Jayson ran across the stage, kissed her, then ran back to the microphone. "So, back to my story," he said. "They say music runs in families. I think it runs in mine." Cheers and applause. "Ladies and gentlemen, on the drums, my older little brother, Drew Wolfe!" When the audience quieted down, he added, "So, back to Derek. I told you he was an incredible bass player, and you should have figured out that he was Elizabeth's brother. What you don't know . . . is that Derek's nephew seems to have inherited his talent." His voice boomed, "Ladies and gentlemen, on the bass, my son, Trevin Aragon-Wolfe."

After the applause settled once again, Jayson said, "We are a really great family. But you know what's great about family? We can adopt!" Laughter. "Ladies and gentlemen, on guitars and piano, Brandon Cook." Following the applause, Jayson said, "He deserves it, you know. You wouldn't believe what he's had to put up with rehearsing with this family. And now he's going on tour with us. But we are a really great family! Did I mention that?" Laughter. "Okay, story's almost over. I just need to intro-duce you to these great young people who sacrificed their summer, tearing themselves away from textbooks and calculators and college classrooms to go on tour with me. Ladies and gentlemen." He said their names quickly and clearly, "Lindsey, Jessica, Brittany, Rachel, Hannah, Chanelle, Angela, Corbin, Tyler, Spencer, Bryan, Sam, Joshua, and Jared!" While the audience cheered, Jayson ran in front of them, giving them each a well-practiced high-five. By the time he got back to the microphone, the next song had already started. After the song was finished and the audience had expressed their approval, Jayson made a sweeping motion with his arm to once again indicate everyone else onstage with him. "Aren't they great?" he said and was answered with more cheering. Then they moved into another song. As always, the concerts were like the CDs, a lot of vibrant, exhilarating music with a few tender love songs mixed in. The slower songs Jayson had written usually required more voice range and strength than the others, but he pulled them off without a problem.

When the first half of the show was done, they all left the stage for an intermission, and the house lights went up. Backstage Elizabeth hugged Jayson tightly and whispered, "I knew you could do it."

"Then you had more faith than I did," he said. "I was terrified."

"Hey," Drew said and put a hand on his shoulder, having overheard. "You're the one who opened your mouth to sing." He smiled. "That was incredible."

Jayson took a deep breath. "We're halfway there." He turned to Trevin. "How you doing?"

"I'm great," Trevin said. "And you sounded amazing out there."

Jayson shrugged and chuckled. Brandon walked by and gave him a pat on the shoulder. They all hurried to use the time to take turns in the bathrooms and refresh their appearance.

Following the intermission, the crowd started rumbling with anticipation when the orchestra musicians all filed onto the stage and took their places, but remained standing. The houselights went down, but the stage remained lit. Jayson and Elizabeth walked onto the stage while he held her hand poised in his as if they were royalty. Over the same clothes they'd been wearing earlier, they were both wearing matching tuxedo jackets, classic black with tails. Jayson had been waiting for this moment since this magnificent piece of music had first come into his head, with the vision of its performance very clear. "The Heart of Mozart" had been played on the radio enough for the audience to become familiar with it, and the album had sold enough that he knew anyone who had listened to the song on the CD would have heard the four-and-a-half-minute classical portion at the beginning of the song that was *not* being played on the radio. It was Jayson's hope that the tuxedo jackets combined with the manner in which they would begin the second half of the show would be enough to get the audience psyched. He wanted them to know which song he was about to play, and he wanted to hear their enthusiasm and approval. He had completely stopped worrying about his voice, even though this song would test its range and power more than any other he would perform tonight. He was practically holding his breath as he formally escorted Elizabeth to the center of the stage where they both took the kind of bow that would never be seen at a rock concert. And that's when it happened. The audience went wild. Jayson laughed and squeezed Elizabeth's hand as he escorted her to her place in front of the orchestra, where she took up the baton like any conductor would. The orchestra musicians took their seats and readied their instruments while Jayson walked to the piano and took another formal bow. The roar in the arena was deafening. This was the moment he'd been working for. He couldn't count the hours he'd spent writing, composing, teaching, recording, practicing. And now it was all coming together. This was his first audience for "The Heart of Mozart," and they were not disappointing him.

Jayson allowed the formality to slip into facetiousness as he dramatically flipped the tails of his coat behind him when he sat on the bench. He prolonged the adjustment of his feet at the pedals and the positioning of the bench. He stretched his hands, his shoulders, his neck, his hands again. The laughter of the audience didn't disappoint him, either. Then he put both hands into his hair and abruptly messed up the part that wasn't in the ponytail, just as he'd done the first time he'd played it for Elizabeth. The laughter rose several decibels, and before it faded he had shared the glance with Elizabeth that started the count, and they all dove into the song with perfect synchronization. The first part went off without a glitch, while Jayson wondered if he had ever enjoyed performing more than he did in that moment. Knowing there were people in this audience who knew and loved him didn't hurt. During the song Drew, Trevin, and Brandon had discreetly sneaked into position so they wouldn't be noticed. The first part of the song jumped into the second like the continued beating of Jayson's heart. The drums and guitars came in, along with a magnificent display of lights, and the entire arena shifted from classical to rock and roll in an instant. Jayson sang from the depths of his soul, realizing more deeply than he had since the song's first inception how much it spoke of his own feelings. Knowing how inspired it had been, how the lyrics had come in minutes, he could almost believe that the inspiration had been some kind of heavenly validation.

"*Hear the beat, beat, beat of my heart, heart, heart. Feel it stop, oh then feel it start. Who's that calling, who's that there? The sound is inside me, it's everywhere! The muse is amusing, it's magic and maze. The muse is confusing, it's blindness and craze. The muse is a monster, it eats me alive. It drives in high gear 'til there's nothing to drive.*"

He played a string of intricate piano passages while the orchestra and guitars became stronger, and then the chorus. "*But sanity comes at the edge of reason. The muse is a voice without limits or season. From the end of the world, right back to its start. It's been speaking and singing to the mind and the heart, Of madmen like me with the heart of Mozart.*"

He played an intricate bridge and went on to the second verse. "*Is this madness or magic? Am I lucid or lame? Will the noises inside me bring fury or fame? The muse is colossus, it gnaws from inside, 'Til there's nothing to spare, and nothing to hide. It haunts and it blesses, it curses then cries. It bleeds and it heals, it sings and it sighs. But how can I doubt it when I know life without it, Is colorless, noiseless, and turned out inside.*"

Starting the chorus again, the words seemed to ooze out of his soul. He'd lost the temptation to cry, and instead felt a bursting of joy that made it difficult not to laugh. "*But sanity comes at the edge of reason. The muse is a voice without limits or season. From the end of the world, right back to its start. It's been speaking and singing to the mind and the heart, Of madmen like me with the heart of Mozart.*"

The final bridge was a segment from the first part of the song, with that classical sound and the intense piano, but with guitars and drums adding texture to it. He finished by singing from the deepest part of his heart: "*Oh, bring on the madness! And help me to soar! Let the angels in heaven grant me more, more, and more. May the music inside me, let it always abide me. Let the muse ever guide me, the light never hide me. Oh, hear the beat, beat, beat of the heart, heart, heart . . . The heart of Mozart, yeah, the heart of Mozart.*"

When the song ended, Jayson erupted to his feet to take the formal bow of a classical pianist, knowing that all of the other musicians would be doing the same. The applause soothed and exhilarated him. What he hadn't expected was to see the entire audience come to their feet in unison—at least those who weren't already on their feet. The standing ovation went on for so long that Jayson had to either let the tears slide down his face or wipe them away with his hands, which would let everyone know that he was crying. Then it occurred to him that maybe they needed to know. He took another bow, wiped his hands over his cheeks, then lifted them high before he ran off the stage, pausing only long enough to take Elizabeth's hand. Then together they shared another elaborate bow.

Offstage he realized that she was crying too, but they had time only to share a quick kiss and an exuberant bout of laughter while they hurried to remove their jackets. They both dried their tears and shared another kiss. Jayson straightened his hair and ran back out holding his guitar, and Elizabeth came out more slowly with the flute.

"I have a story to tell you," he said into the mike, and the audience cheered. "I'll keep it short. We've got music waiting." Another cheer. "In high school I was dating this girl named Elizabeth." Another cheer. Jayson chuckled. "If you guys don't be quiet, we'll never get out of here." They went wild. "Be quiet and listen," he said, and there was laughter. "We'd known each other a long time before graduation. But that's when she saw that my middle initial was A." He motioned toward Elizabeth. "Am I getting it right, honey?"

"That's right," she said into her microphone. "It was on the graduation program. Jayson A. Wolfe."

"So, she started guessing what it stood for," Jayson said.

Elizabeth went comically through the list. "Alexander. Anthony. Antoine. Alfred. Albert. Adam. He told me I'd never guess. Then his mother told me that since they had the last name Wolfe, it reminded her of . . . Wolfgang."

He could hear some indication in the audience that some of them had gotten it. He said exuberantly, "Yes! My middle name really is . . . *Amadeus.*" Following a cheer he said, "For those of you who don't get it, go study your music history . . . or read that stuff in the CD case." He raised both his arms and sang more than said, "Thank you, Wolfgang Amadeus Mozart!"

Before the applause ended they had moved into another song. When it was finished and the applause had settled, Jayson said nonchalantly, "It's on my birth certificate, really; Amadeus."

"Your mother must have been psychic," Elizabeth said.

"My mother is an angel," Jayson said, and Drew did a drum roll that seemed to say *amen.*

For the next number the fourteen extras moved forward on the stage to microphones so they could do the choir backing vocals. The stage version of the song was much longer than that on the album, which had been recorded months ago with members of the ward choir. This choir sounded almost as beautiful as they sang with growing intensity through the song, *"How can we know? How can we know? Is this world the end or just the start? How can we know? Oh, how can we know? Search in your soul, oh, search in your heart. The heavens are open and peace is free. Search your soul and find your heart. Oh, that's how we know. That's how we know."* The number was filled with a building exuberance, and by the end Jayson had the entire audience clapping their hands above their heads and singing over and over, *"The heavens are open and peace is free. Search your soul and find your heart."* When the song ended he said into the mike, "It's true, you know. The heavens *are* open, and peace *is* free. Don't you ever forget it."

He comically feigned recalling something he'd forgotten. "Speaking of . . ." He turned to Drew. "Do you remember what our mama always used to say? That thing that always ended with . . ." He raised his voice to mimic a woman. "'Don't you ever forget it.' Remember that?"

Drew nodded and said into his mike, "I sure do." He also raised his voice to mimic their mother, 'Jayson doesn't have to do the dishes because he's practicing the guitar.'" This made the audience roar.

"That's not how I remember it," Jayson said. "It was more like, 'Drew doesn't have to take out the garbage because he's practicing the drums.' That's what I remember." The audience laughed. "But that's not what I'm talking about. She said . . ." He strummed the guitar and allowed a dramatic pause. "'This is what happens when mamas let their little boys play with drums and guitars.'" He went right into the strong guitar at the beginning of "Good, Clean Fun," and the finished production was every bit as amazing as he'd hoped. During the lengthy brass solo, Jayson and Trevin played guitars side by side, jumping in unison. And Trevin stayed at his side, as they'd rehearsed, while Jayson stood right next to the drums for the long brother duet in the middle. The memories and dreams of playing with Derek tempted Jayson toward tears again. In a way he missed Derek as much as he ever had, but in his heart he knew that Derek was still a part of the team. After he'd played the long, final note, he said into the mike, "And don't you forget it!"

One song merged flawlessly into another until the show came to its end. Jayson did a quick bow and ran off the stage, where he waited with the rest of them, just smiling and listening to the audience. Because the lights hadn't gone up, the fans knew the show wasn't *really* over. While they were waiting, an idea came to Jayson that filled him with a secret thrill. He quickly told everyone else who would be onstage with him, as well as the stage manager, so that he could radio the message to the sound and light technicians, that he just wanted a couple of minutes before they went into the next number. Everyone just needed to get into position and wait.

The band finally went back onto the stage in response to the audience begging for an encore, and their approval was touching. Jayson felt a little nervous, but thrilled at the same time, as he approached the microphone. With his guitar on his back, Jayson waited for the roaring to calm down before he said, "Thank you; you've been wonderful. Before we leave you tonight, I wish to take a moment for myself, and I ask for your patience. I have been richly blessed, and it doesn't seem right for me to end this show without taking just a minute to publicly express my gratitude to Him who gave me this gift and the opportunity to share it with you." Through the couple of seconds of silence between his sentences, he recalled with clarity the journey of pain and illness and his failing voice that had led to this moment. He found it difficult to keep his composure, and then instantly he had it and felt completely at ease. "It is my hope that whatever your beliefs may be, we can share a minute of mutual respect in that regard as we share this celebration of music." He closed his eyes and leaned closer to the microphone, singing in a clear, strong voice, a capella, the chorus of the song "How Great Thou Art." He drew out each note of the last phrase, and held the last one for as long as his breath would possibly allow.

Jayson figured one chorus was enough. They'd come for a rock concert; this moment was for him. He took a step back and was stunned by the applause, and then a standing ovation, as if every person on their feet was echoing what he'd just done. Of course, this was Salt Lake City, and he didn't know how it might fly in other places where the audience wasn't approximately half LDS, but he was going to do it anyway. He made the commitment there in that moment, between him and his Heavenly Father. For every show that he could perform, free of pain and illness, with a voice to express his God-given gift, he would publicly give praise to the source of all that he'd been blessed with.

Elizabeth was grateful to be standing in the shadows at the rear of the stage, near the drums. With the spotlight on Jayson, the rest of the stage was dark, which made it possible for her to wipe her tears privately. She had rarely, if ever, heard Jayson's voice sound so strong and pure. And the spirit of the message he'd just sung pierced her heart with such perfect joy that it had no choice but to overflow. She had been privileged enough to take every step of this journey with him, and no one knew what this moment meant more than she did. Noticing a small movement with her peripheral vision, she turned just slightly and saw that Drew was also wiping his eyes. She remained discreet so that he wouldn't catch her watching him. Drew didn't cry the way Jayson did. In fact, he hardly cried at all. It was a joke between the brothers. Had Jayson's performance tonight—and the obvious miracles behind it—touched Drew so deeply? She hoped so!

"Thank you," Jayson said, stepping back to the mike. "Now, before we all have to go home, let's have some Good! Clean! Fun!" The audience cheered, and the band jumped into one of the classics from Gray Wolf. Being a popular radio hit that had continued to get air time for many years, it was a huge crowd-pleaser. Through the applause Jayson gave up the guitar and sat at the piano to finish the show with a hit from his previous solo CD, "The Missing Ingredient." It had strong piano and was a great song to dance to. And the crowd *was* dancing! When he was done, Jayson jumped onto the piano bench, catapulted himself off of it with a leap that implied he was thirty years younger, then ran the length of the stage with his hand outstretched to touch all those on the front row who were reaching toward him. He came back to the center of the stage where everyone else was waiting in a long line, the orchestra musicians divided in half at each end, with Brandon, Drew, Elizabeth, and Trevin in the middle. He took his place between Elizabeth and Trevin, and they all bowed together while the applause never stopped. When they finally filed off the stage and the lights went up, there were many hugs and much laughter among those who had worked so hard together to get to this point.

"Thanks, Dad," Trevin said when Jayson hugged him.

"For what?"

"For letting me do it."

Jayson smiled. "You *earned* the right to do it. You worked very hard, and you did great. We're going to have a great summer."

"Yeah, we are," he said and hugged his mother.

When the others were all occupied elsewhere, Jayson and Elizabeth came face-to-face and shared a warm smile. "It was incredible, Jayson. It was perfect."

"I couldn't have done it without you," he said, and they shared a long, tight embrace.

"It was a miracle," she whispered near his ear.

"I know," he said and could feel himself trembling just before he realized that she was too.

"I love you," she whispered near his ear.

A rush of memories overcame him in an instant. How they'd met in high school and started making music together. They'd shared death and grief, heartache and despair. And they had shared much joy and many miracles. He thought of how she'd been at his side through every step that had led to this moment. He thought of her care and concern during his pain and illness. He thought of her faith and strength, her wisdom and insight. In that moment he felt as if they'd come full circle. This was the life he'd dreamed of when he'd first fallen for her, even though he never could have fully imagined the depth of his life that now existed beyond the stage and the public success. He'd had great moments with Elizabeth before, but something in his soul felt freer, deeper, more solid, more firm in his convictions, more capable of understanding and appreciating the most profound perspectives of life. This was that moment in the life of a human being when everything was perfect—it was all worth it, and the memory of it would carry into whatever lay ahead. It was a moment he etched into his memory, to hold there forever.

He tightened his arms more fully around his wife and felt her do the same in response. "I love you, too," he said and looked into her eyes. "Oh, how I love you!"

She smiled, and he barely had time to kiss her before the backstage party began. And oh, what a party! He couldn't recall how many backstage passes Elizabeth had given out to family, friends, and neighbors. The stage crew had been warned about this, and they were off to relax. But the equipment didn't need to be taken down tonight because they were doing a second show here tomorrow. Jayson and the rest of the band were quickly surrounded by people bursting with excitement, full of compliments and amazement, which Jayson and Elizabeth had both learned the art of accepting graciously. He noticed that Trevin looked a little stunned, but Jayson figured he would get used to it. He wasn't worried about it going to his head. It just wasn't in him. Brandon and Drew were being very gracious, even though they didn't know most of these people. Their wives and friends would be attending the show in Los Angeles in a couple of weeks.

Will and Marilyn were there with Addie. The other two children had been left with a sitter, surely too young to appreciate or enjoy the show. Macy and Aaron were there, along with Layla and all of her children. Layla looked tired but thrilled to be there, and it turned out that the friend she'd brought was a man. They appeared to be comfortable together and having a good time. However, Jayson's surprise that Layla was dating again didn't hold a candle to what he felt when he came face to face with Debbie. She looked so different that it took him a moment to realize it was her. This was the Debbie he remembered from their early years of marriage. She was dressed conservatively and modestly, with very little jewelry and makeup, and her eyes were clear and sparkling. She smiled and gave him a hug. "I hope it's okay to surprise you like this," she said. "Macy didn't want to tell you ahead of time. She thought you'd be happy to see me drug-free." She said it with a little chuckle, but he sensed her pleasure at being able to say it. He knew that feeling. "I really wanted to see the show, so I . . . came."

"It is really good to see you," he said, "especially drug-free. You look great, Debbie; better than you've looked in years, if you want my honest opinion."

"You've never been anything but honest," she said, then got a little teary. "I know you have many people who want to talk to you, but I need to thank you again. You saved my life, Jayson, both because you were there to call for an ambulance, and by what you said to me. So, thank you, and . . ." she laughed, "the show was great, Jayson. You were always great."

"I really am glad you came," he said and hugged her again before he took her arm and turned to seek out Elizabeth. "Look who's here," he said with pride to his wife, and he wasn't disappointed with the kindness and pleasant surprise that Elizabeth displayed toward the new Debbie. They even hugged.

Now that's weird, Jayson thought as he observed it; then he was drawn away by other admirers wanting to talk to him. All the young men he'd once worked with wanted his autograph on their backstage passes, and they were full of silliness and excitement. Roger gave him a big hug and a firm compliment that meant a great deal to Jayson. Jayson accepted handshakes and compliments from many neighbors and ward members; there were even more of them there than he'd expected. The bishop worked his way through the crowd to give Jayson a big hug and a friendly slap on the back. "It was more amazing than I could have ever imagined," he said. "I think you've changed my taste in music."

"Don't go getting weird on me," Jayson teased.

He greeted each member of the bishop's family, then he realized that Clayton was there with them. Jayson gave him a big hug and said, "I'm really glad to see you here."

"I'm *really* glad to be here," Clayton said. "It was way past incredible! I'm going to brag about knowing you for the rest of my life."

"It's the other way around," Jayson said, then he lowered his voice. "How's your mom?"

"The same," he said. "I go see her every day and just talk to her, but she doesn't respond." He shrugged. "I keep praying that she'll come around. Hey, was it you that left the CD of—"

"Shhh," Jayson said, glancing over his shoulder, "that's a secret."

Clayton smiled. "Well, one of the nurses says my mom likes it. I haven't been there when it's happened, but the nurse said the only words she's spoken have been asking for chocolate pudding and asking to hear the music."

Jayson felt warmed by hearing that. "We'll keep her in our prayers," he said. "And you, as well."

"Good luck with the tour. Hopefully things will be better when you get back."

"I hope so," Jayson said.

The crowd gradually left, including family. Jayson, Elizabeth, and Trevin left together, talking all the way home about the wonder of the experience. They slept that night in their own beds for the last time for many weeks. Tomorrow after the show they would go to bed on the buses, which would be leaving about midnight to start their winding trek all over the United States. Will and Marilyn would keep an eye on the house and take care of the dog while they were gone. Everything was set. Everything was perfect. Jayson had never felt so happy in all his life. He went to sleep with Elizabeth close beside him, basking in his happiness and the miracles of this day, and saying a prayer for Bonnie Freedman and her son.

CHAPTER 14

The following day was crazy with final packing and preparations to leave home, but once they all arrived at the arena in Salt Lake City, everything was calm and under control. Jayson's voice was a little hoarse, but he didn't feel concerned. Even if he did hit a croaky note here and there, he still had those jokes on hand to make up for it. After last night's miracle, being worried over his voice would simply demonstrate a lack of faith.

It was standard procedure for the band to be settled inside the venue long before the doors were opened for ticket holders. While everyone seemed to have something to do elsewhere in the building, Jayson found himself alone in the artists' lounge, reading a magazine that had been left there. He looked up to see Drew enter the room. "Hey, little brother," Jayson said, setting the magazine aside. "What are you up to?"

"Not much," Drew said and sat down.

"I hear Trevin's got a checkers tournament going on somewhere, and the girls are all painting their toenails, or something important."

"Both activities sound very tempting," Drew said facetiously, "but I think I'll just hang with my brother."

"I can live with that. Have you talked to Valerie today?"

"Three times."

"Everything okay at home?"

"Everything's fine. Why do you ask?"

"You have that look," Jayson said. "Concerned, intent; something. What's on your mind?"

"How are *you?*" Drew asked.

"I'm fine," Jayson said. Then he laughed. "In fact, I'm great. Last night was great, and we get to do it again. And again, and again," he finished with a little chuckle.

"You sound a little hoarse."

"Yeah, I sure do."

"You're not worried?"

"Should I be?" Jayson asked. "After what happened last night, do you think I should be worried?"

"I'm still trying to figure out what happened last night," Drew said, and Jayson understood the concerned and intent expression on his face.

"I should think it's obvious. You were there."

"But how do you explain something like that?" Drew asked.

"You can't . . . not in any terms that are comprehensible in a logical sense, that is. Which is why it falls under the category of miraculous."

"You believe it was a miracle."

Jayson chuckled and tried to conceal how delighted he was to be having this conversation. His brother was actually *talking* about spiritual matters. "What would you call it?" he asked.

Drew shook his head. "I don't know."

"So . . . you just don't believe in miracles, or . . . you can't believe that what happened to me last night on stage actually *was* a miracle?"

"I don't know what to think, Jayson; truly."

"So, stop trying to think about it with your brain and use your heart; use your spirit. You told me that if I could pull this off, you'd join the Church. You said you weren't teasing. I'm guessing you really didn't think I could pull it off. Or should I say . . . you really didn't think that God would show His hand so obviously in my life?"

"You're making me sound pretty callous."

"I'm just trying to understand what you're thinking, bro."

"Well, I would love to tell you if I knew."

"Okay," Jayson said and leaned forward, "I'll tell you what . . . I'd like to give you something to read. We've got lots of bus time, so I would think you can fit it in. You read it and we'll talk about it. Maybe what you're feeling will make more sense."

Drew thought about it and Jayson held his breath. If he didn't take this opportunity, it might be a long time—if ever—before Drew was receptive to such a conversation again. "I think I can live with that," he finally said, and Jayson smiled.

The show that night went every bit as well as the previous night. Afterward, as they were settling into the buses to begin their journey, Jayson gave Drew a Book of Mormon that had his own testimony handwritten inside the front. He also had a few passages marked and flagged, and he pointed them out to Drew with a brief explanation.

"Are you okay with this?" Jayson asked. "I mean . . . I did get through another show without croaking."

Drew chuckled. "Yes, you certainly did. And yes, I'm okay with it. You've never been pushy with this, and I appreciate it, but maybe it's time I started looking at things a little differently. I have to admit there are things about your life that have gotten my attention."

"May I ask what?"

Drew looked down. "I think we should save that for another time."

"Fair enough," Jayson said, and the conversation ended. He prayed that the journey Drew was on might end with them having the gospel in common.

The convoy embarked on their journey late that night, and the adventure began. About ten days in, Drew came to Jayson and asked if they could talk because he had some questions. Jayson spent a span of the journey on the bus with the guys so that he and Drew could have all the time they needed. Trevin sat in on the conversation, and Jayson was aware of Brandon being nearby. But whether or not he actually listened was anybody's guess. Drew summarized his own spiritual beliefs, then admitted that he'd felt more of a desire for some religious structure in his life. Seeing his daughter growing and starting to talk had brought home to him the importance of raising a child right. He talked of how their mother had raised them according to the teachings in the Bible and had taken them to church, but he didn't want to just start going to church for the sake of it. It was Valerie who had repeatedly mentioned to him the marvelous feelings she'd experienced in Jayson and Elizabeth's home, and that she couldn't help being curious over beliefs that could create such an atmosphere. They talked about eternal families, the plan of salvation, and the Book of Mormon. Drew admitted to having trouble with the Joseph Smith story, but he softened some when Jayson admitted that he'd had trouble with it, too. Trevin mostly listened, but when this came up, he said with quiet confidence, "I know it's true. If it was an easy story to swallow, there wouldn't be any test of faith. But I'm telling you that if you pray sincerely, just like it says in Moroni, chapter ten, you can know that it's true."

"You really believe it?" Drew asked his nephew.

"I know it. There's no way to explain how I know. I just know."

"I'll tell you an analogy Elizabeth once shared with me," Jayson added. "Say that I had discovered how wonderful a warm chocolate-chip cookie is, and you've never tasted one. I think it's heavenly and I would love to share the experience with you, but you adamantly declare that you don't want to taste it. I can't make you taste it. And if you taste it with a determination not to like it, you probably wouldn't like it anyway. And then we'd just end up arguing over whether or not a warm cookie is worth eating. But until you actually *taste* it, you'll never know. And there's no way to tell someone how it tastes. They just have to taste it for themselves."

"Okay, I can appreciate the theory," Drew said. He asked a few more questions and said he was intrigued with the book he was reading, and he would press forward with it. They talked a little more about prayer and the Holy Ghost, then the conversation shifted and they made some sandwiches while the buses rolled on. Later that day, Brandon took Jayson aside and said, "I couldn't help overhearing you earlier."

He seemed nervous, and Jayson said, "What is it? You can ask me anything you want."

"Really?" Brandon said. "I've spent a lot of time with you and your family. I knew you were Mormons, but I wondered if it was some kind of . . . secret or something . . . that you're not supposed to talk about."

Jayson chuckled. "Have we given you that impression?"

"I don't know. Not really, I guess."

"I've just felt that our example was better than trying to push religion on someone when they're not interested."

"Well, I'm interested," Brandon said, and Jayson felt the temptation to cry. "I was just wondering if . . . you have another one of those books. I think I'd like to read it."

"I do," Jayson said. "It's on the other bus, but—"

"Here you go," Trevin said, handing him one. He chuckled. "I always keep spares." Jayson tossed him a comical glance and he added, "Like I couldn't overhear *anything* on this bus." More to Brandon he said, "It's all yours. If you have questions, you know where I sleep."

The buses pulled into a rest stop for some fresh air and to give everyone a break, especially the drivers. When they started again, Jayson was on the bus with Elizabeth and the other kids, as he usually was. He shared with his wife and daughter the conversations that had taken place, and they both got a little teary.

"Now *that,*" Jayson concluded, "makes *everything* worth it. The album, the tour, the illness . . . everything. If . . ." he got teary himself, "if this experience will bring my brother to the gospel . . . I would gladly do it all again. I can think of little that would mean more to me than having Drew join the Church. And Brandon? That's just cool." He laughed softly. "Can't wait to see how all of this turns out."

As the tour pressed forward successfully, the "investigators" had a question here or there, but little was said about their ongoing studies. The shows were a huge success in every respect, in spite of some spurts of opposition. One of the semis was in a minor accident and got delayed, but it was still drivable and none of the equipment was damaged. They were just slow getting the stage set up because of the truck's delay, and the audience had to wait an extra forty-five minutes for the show to begin.

Little Derek fell while playing in the bus and hit his head on something. The cut required stitches in the next city they came to, which fortunately was less than an hour's drive from when it happened.

The worst problem that arose was a bout of food poisoning that hit the entire corps all at the same time—except for Harmony, who had gone to sleep in Jayson's arms during supper and hadn't eaten what everyone else had eaten. Fortunately, it was one of the nights when they were all staying in hotel rooms. The buses had arrived in the city in the late afternoon, and they had until the next evening before the show. They'd all gone out to eat and were back in their rooms for the night when it hit. There was a lot of misery throughout the night, and a lot praying. The vomiting and internal distress had stopped for everyone by early morning, and they were all able to sleep, except that they had two young children who *wouldn't* sleep, especially since one of them hadn't been sick. Macy insisted that she would watch out for them and rest later. She was the nanny, and everyone else needed their rest for the show. That evening as they went onstage, everyone was past the symptoms, but far from their best in energy and stamina. But the adrenaline kicked in and no one in the audience would have ever known what a nightmarish twenty-four hours everyone onstage had experienced. Still, they all agreed that it could have been much worse. It hadn't hit right before a show, and it hadn't hit when they'd been on the buses, all needing to share tiny lavatories.

Beyond that, everything went smoothly. They got some sightseeing in along the way, often going as a huge group of musicians, crew, and roadies to museums and national parks. Each and every show was fun and exciting, and the family just seemed to grow larger as all of the musicians and many members of the crew came to be on good terms and had a great deal of fun together.

Aaron flew out to meet them in Florida, where the tour had been scheduled with a few days off so that everyone could go to Disney World—musicians and crew included. They had a wonderful time, and Macy was glad to be with her husband. Drew's family came for the vacation as well. A few weeks later, Aaron flew out again and met them in Virginia, where a Wolfe family reunion was taking place. Jayson had worked it out with the tour coordinator so they could be in Virginia at this time with a couple of days off so the family could be part of a reunion that had been in the making for many months. He was thrilled to see aunts, uncles, and cousins that he hadn't known existed until not so many years ago. But now he'd gotten to know many of them well through prior family gatherings and by keeping in touch through email and phone calls. Attending the concert was on the agenda of the three-day reunion. Jayson provided the tickets, and nearly all of the adults and older children were there. He felt nostalgic to recall that the last time he'd done this, his elderly grandmother had been present. He'd barely gotten to know her before she'd passed away, but he was glad to have known her at all. His wife and children all had a great time, as did Drew and his family. Valerie and Leslie had flown out to meet them for the reunion as well.

During an opportunity to visit with his father's sisters, Jayson mentioned to them that he'd had his father's headstone on his grave changed. When Jayson and Drew had made the burial arrangements for their estranged father, they'd only known him as Jay Wolfe. Since he'd died homeless, they'd had nothing to let them know otherwise. After Jayson had found his father's family, he'd learned that Jay was a nickname, and his name was actually Lawrence J Wolfe. Wanting to cover both names, Jayson and Drew had made the decision for the headstone to read: Lawrence J "Jay" Wolfe. It had now been changed, and he'd brought pictures of it to give his aunts, who were all pleased. They each cried a little, but they'd actually lost their brother many, many years ago when he'd left home and never bothered to make contact with them again. Jayson was grateful for the divine intervention that had brought this family back together, and to be able to spend time with them this way.

When Aaron flew home after the reunion, Elizabeth and Jayson made the decision to have Addie go with him. She'd gotten terribly bored with the routine and missed playing with her friends. After Jayson and Elizabeth had discussed it with each other and with Will and Marilyn, they made the decision to let her spend the duration of the tour in the care of Grandma and Grandpa. They would certainly miss her, but they didn't want her to be unhappy and ornery, which made *everybody* unhappy and ornery. They knew she would be in good hands, and they would talk to her on the phone every day. Surprisingly, Derek and Harmony were both handling the experience fairly well. They'd quickly adjusted to sleeping and playing on the bus. And they had many opportunities for fresh air and new experiences. Many of the musicians and crew members started going out of their way to interact with the children and even help with them here and there, which gave Macy more of an opportunity to keep up her job as tour historian.

Some concern arose when Aaron called Macy to report that Layla had experienced a setback. She'd been hit with dramatic symptoms of her disease, much like she'd experienced when it had been at its worst before she'd changed her diet. She spent a couple of days in the hospital, and it was determined that somehow she'd gotten gluten. But they couldn't figure out how, because everyone had been so careful. They retraced each step of the food she'd eaten, going over it with the kids and the friends and Relief Society sisters who were helping prepare meals. They'd all been well trained, and they rechecked recipes and ingredients and cross-contamination issues, certain that everything had been done by the book. It was finally traced to some lip balm that had been given to her, which contained wheat germ oil. Because it was on her lips, it was getting into her mouth and making her sick. Everyone who got the step-by-step story through Macy was astonished that the disease was so sensitive, and that such a tiny amount from the strangest sources could cause such a problem. The conversations brought up a point that Macy had learned in her initial study of the disease.

"A person with Celiac Disease," she said, "cannot kiss someone who has been eating gluten until they've brushed and flossed. Serious."

"That's unbelievable," Elizabeth said. "So, has Layla's boyfriend been informed of this?" She was referring to the man Layla had brought to the concert. Aaron had mentioned that Henry was spending a great deal of time with the family, and that he'd taken Layla out a few times. "Or is he not a kissing boyfriend?"

"Oh, I think he might be," Macy said with a smirk. "She really likes him. I guess we'll see."

Regular family prayers throughout the tour included concern for Layla, and they were all pleased to hear that she'd recovered quickly from the setback and was showing steady improvement.

The tour went on, averaging four shows a week, with a lot of miles in between. On Sundays they usually managed to find an LDS meeting-house and attend sacrament meeting, and the rest of the day was gener-ally spent on the bus engaged in Sabbath-type activities as far as it was possible. The traveling just had to go on.

Trevin was thoroughly enjoying the experience until he cut his finger opening a can, which gave him some grief while playing for a week or so, but he still pulled it off and didn't complain. He was keeping in touch with his friends through text messaging, phone, and email. And even from a distance he was figuring out which friends were keeping in touch with him due to his present fame, and which ones genuinely liked him and cared about him.

While they were on the road, the tour coordinator got word that a big article on the band was running in a reputable entertainment maga-zine. In the next city, they acquired several copies and read them. The cover had an official promotional photo of the band, with the headline, *Amadeus and the Wolfe Gang.* "Catchy," Elizabeth said when she saw it. They all thought it was funny, if not a little silly. But Jayson was pleased with the positive review of the CD and the tour, and believed it was a good counteraction to what the tabloids had done. There were some great stage pictures, and a few candid shots of the family and the band clearly having a great time at Disney World,

Not many days later, pictures of Trevin hit the covers of three different teen magazines. He seemed a little embarrassed, but mostly thought it was funny. Following the release of the magazines, there was a definite increase in the appearance of young, frenzied girls chanting Trevin's name at concerts. They also gathered when the band would get on and off the bus, hoping to get Trevin's autograph. The family and band were skilled at avoiding problems with such things for the most part. They knew how to sneak in and out of hotels and venues, and their tour security was tight. It was more the emotional impact of the situa-tion that was a concern. Jayson and Elizabeth talked to Trevin about keeping perspective. They weren't necessarily worried, but they weren't going to leave anything up to chance, either. They wanted to be absolutely clear with Trevin about remaining grounded in the real world and to impress upon him the importance of keeping his values strong and firm—especially with being caught up in the music business. They felt sure he was doing fine and would continue to do so, but they were all grateful for the gospel in their lives, and for Jayson's clout that gave him the ability to keep his family in somewhat of a bubble as they went about their business.

During the course of the tour, Jayson often had days of talking like a frog, and occasionally he would almost completely lose his voice or have horrible coughing fits. But the band prayed together before going onstage each time, and he hadn't once hit a bad note or been unable to sing to his full potential when the time came. Drew was snagged for an interview in Minneapolis and was asked, "What's been the most unique aspect of this particular tour?"

Drew's answer hit the Associated Press and appeared in papers across the country. "Jayson was very ill before the tour, and it's been rough on his throat. During the days, he talks like a frog, but when the show hits the stage, he sings like an angel."

Jayson's personal addition to each show's encore—singing the chorus to his favorite hymn—had been expected by the crew and musicians, and so far it had been met with great applause. He joked about fearing that he might get booed off the stage somewhere along the way, but it never happened. In fact, mention of it also got picked up by Associated Press, along with a brief mention of his religion. He'd heard rumors of a little bit of negative flack from some concert-goers, but he'd heard much more positive response. Apparently the marketing feedback had shown that religious people were glad that he was doing something to remind the world of what was important. And the general view among nonreligious fans was simply a feeling that it was good for him to be able to freely express his views, and it didn't detract at all from the show.

About once a week Jayson would wake up with a migraine. There was only once when the medication didn't work quickly, but that was on a day when they were traveling and not performing. Following the migraines, his energy level was lower, and facing the shows was more of a challenge, but just as with his voice, his energy appeared when he needed it, and he never felt like his performance level was compromised by the problem.

Each and every day, Jayson was keenly mindful of how the Lord was keeping His promises. He performed every show to his full potential, and he was able to be with his family when they had opportunities for sightseeing and outings. Often in between, he spent more time in bed, either on the bus or in hotel rooms, than he would have liked. But Elizabeth reminded him frequently that he needed to know his limits and rest as much as possible, especially when he was still getting periodic migraines and the weakness that came with them. Still, he couldn't deny the blessings taking place, and he daily acknowledged God's hand in keeping him afloat. He began to see that the pain and illness had forced him to fully rely on the Lord to get through every hour of every day. He could never question the fact that God had been with him every step of the way, and for the rest of his life that lesson would be deeply ingrained because it had been so dramatic for him.

All in all, the results were good. In spite of the challenges, there was always evidence of equivalent miracles, and the show certainly did go on, with good reviews and huge crowds in every city. Of course, there were little stresses along the way. The kids were sometimes cranky and bored with the routine. Occasionally people got moody or testy, getting on each other's nerves. But such things were temporary and easily resolved in most cases.

When they performed near Jayson and Drew's hometown in Montana, there was huge publicity. And when they performed in Oregon, there was also a great deal of publicity regarding the roots of the music coming from a town near Portland where Jayson, Drew, and their mother had become good friends with Will Greer and his children, Derek and Elizabeth.

Beyond Macy talking to Aaron and members of his family on her cell phone multiple times a day, and Trevin doing the same with a few of his good friends, there was little to no communication with anyone at home, except for Addie, Will, and Marilyn. But they assured Jayson and Elizabeth during brief phone calls in between all the busyness that the house, the child, and the dog were fine, and the journey went on.

The final show was in Denver, with a day's drive from there to return home. The last performance always carried a great mixture of emotions. Everyone was tired and ready to go home. By this time, the show—or perhaps the routine surrounding the show—had started to take on some tedium, even if it was mostly remedied by the excitement of the actual performance. But to stand on the stage, realizing that it would never be this way again, was difficult for everyone—especially for Jayson. He didn't know whether or not he would ever produce another album and do such a project again. In some ways, he'd like to, and for other reasons he would not. But even if he did, it would never be exactly like this. He was grateful for the pictures Macy was always taking, and for the memories that would last him a lifetime.

Once that last show was over and the acceptance of its finality had settled in, everyone just wanted to go home. Will and Aaron drove two vehicles to Salt Lake City to meet the buses when they arrived, and the reunion was full of laughter—and exhaustion. Macy squealed and leapt into Aaron's arms. Addie did the same when she saw Jayson. She was thrilled to see her parents, but not as thrilled as they were to see her. And she certainly hadn't suffered for want of them through their weeks of separation.

The family exchanged farewells with the musicians and crew members they'd shared life with for months. It was hardest for Jayson to say good-bye to his brother.

"It's been amazing," Drew said, and they shared a tight hug.

"When are you going to come and see us?" Jayson asked, wondering if his study of the Book of Mormon had come to anything at all. But he didn't feel that it was the right time to ask.

"I'll call you soon and we'll get something on the calendar," Drew said, then he had to get back on the bus before it left him for its return to Los Angeles.

For the trip to Highland, Jayson drove one vehicle and Will the other. When Jayson turned the corner onto the street where they lived, he was stunned to see the trees in their yard full of hundreds of yellow ribbons, and a sign across the house that read *Welcome Home! We missed you!* Apparently Will had been communicating with some of their neighbors, because they had obviously known the minute of their arrival. There were about thirty cheering people on the front lawn when they pulled up. They offered hugs and pleasure at having the Wolfe family back. And they promised to clean up the ribbons the next day. Clayton was among the group, and Jayson was glad to see him looking very well. He hugged him and asked, "How's your mom?"

"She's doing better," was all Clayton said before Jayson was distracted by someone else wanting to talk to him.

Their welcoming committee was sensitive to the fact that they would all be exhausted, and quickly left them to settle in. The family worked together to do minimal unpacking. They ordered pizza for supper, and they all went to bed early, grateful to be in their own beds. The following day was slow and lazy, and Jayson told Elizabeth they were going to need many such days before any of them might come out of this wet-blanket stage enough to have any energy. Unfortunately, Derek and Harmony were full of energy. The silver lining came in the form of Addie, who *also* had energy and was happy to help watch them—even more than usual because she had missed being with them. Jayson, Elizabeth, and Trevin barely managed to work together to do some laundry, fix sandwiches and canned soup, and lay around watching videos.

Three days after their return, Jayson and Elizabeth were in the kitchen cleaning up after a supper of grilled cheese sandwiches and canned fruit while the kids were downstairs watching a movie. The doorbell rang, and Jayson went to answer it while Elizabeth stepped into the entry hall to see who it might be.

Jayson pulled open the door and held his breath. It took him a moment to recognize the woman standing on the porch. She looked dramatically changed, but it was definitely Bonnie Freedman. Her hair was different, cut short but stylish. Her countenance was soft and relaxed. She looked ten years younger, and she was *not* holding a purse.

"Hello," she said, looking nervous. "I know I'm probably the last person on earth you want to see, but there's something I have to say."

"Okay," Jayson said. "Would you like to come in?"

"Let me just say it first, and then we'll see if the invitation still stands."

"Okay," Jayson said, aware of Elizabeth appearing at his shoulder.

Bonnie smiled faintly and nodded toward Elizabeth to acknowledge her.

"Hello," Elizabeth said. "You're looking well."

"I am, thank you," Bonnie said, then looked directly at Jayson. "I just want to say . . . that I would like to start over." She held out a trembling hand, appearing downright terrified. Did she fear that Jayson would yell at her and tell her to leave his home? "Hello, Brother Wolfe, I'm Bonnie Freedman, and . . ." her voice quivered slightly, "I understand that you've . . . had a profoundly positive influence on my son. I want to thank you for that."

Jayson could hardly breathe. He eagerly took her hand then threw his other arm around her, unable to keep from hugging her. She returned the hug and started to cry. Jayson looked at Elizabeth over the top of Bonnie's head, and they shared a gaze of absolute amazement, both getting a little teary.

"Forgive me," Bonnie said, easing away from him to pull a tissue from her pocket. "I was hoping to get through this without crying, but . . ."

Elizabeth urged her further into the hall and closed the door. "Come and sit down," Jayson said. He took a seat on one of the couches, and Elizabeth sat close to Bonnie on the other one, taking her hand.

"I don't mean to keep you," Bonnie said and sniffled. "I just hope that you can forgive me for all of the grief that I caused you."

"That was done a long time ago," Jayson said, and she looked more than surprised. She looked completely dumbfounded.

"But . . . how could that be possible, when . . ." Her chin quivered, and he suspected she was too emotional to finish her sentence.

"Clayton told me what happened to your husband. Your fears on behalf of your son were understandable."

"Perhaps," she said, her voice trembling. "But I had no right to take it out on you, when I really didn't know anything about you. I was prejudiced and full of pride. I was wrong, and I apologize from the bottom of my heart."

"Your apology is accepted from the bottom of *my* heart," Jayson said, "but it's important for you to know that all was forgiven long before we knew the circumstances . . . long before you showed up just now to apologize. We've been concerned for you."

"But . . ." Bonnie fumbled again for words. "I was so . . ."

"It's in the past," Elizabeth said.

"You're very kind," Bonnie said and stood up, as if she were so overcome she needed to be alone. Jayson and Elizabeth stood as well. "Thank you for your time, and your kindness."

"Thank you for coming by," Jayson said.

"You're welcome anytime," Elizabeth added.

"Thank you," Bonnie said and hurried away. She turned back only long enough to say to Jayson, "And thank you for the music. The CD was beautiful. It helped me get through my illness."

After the door was closed, Jayson chuckled. "My eyes have beheld the parting of the Red Sea," he said.

Elizabeth laughed softly and hugged him. "An excellent description," she said, and then gave him a comical scowl. "What CD? If she's been listening to Gray Wolf I'd say the parting of the Red Sea is not an adequate description."

"Didn't I tell you about that?" he asked with feigned innocence. "Sorry. With the tour and all, I must have forgotten."

Jayson took his wife by the hand and sat in the front room, near the piano and beneath the picture of the Savior, to tell her about the day he'd visited Bonnie Freedman in the hospital without her knowing, and about the CD of hymns he'd left behind.

"You're an amazing man," she said.

"I'm married to an amazing woman who keeps me on track."

"I do my best," she said and kissed him. "You're not bad on the piano either. Have you ever considered a career in music?" She kissed him again.

"Nah," he said. "I think I'll retire."

CHAPTER 15

Jayson got his hair cut on Saturday, and just like the last time he'd had his ponytail cut off, Elizabeth wanted to save it. Trevin suggested that she could sell it on eBay and make a lot of money, but she wasn't interested. Returning to church in their home ward on Sunday was a delight, and that afternoon Jayson attended choir practice. His substitute was glad to have him back, since she'd been pulling double duty with the Primary *and* the choir. Seeing Sister Freedman and Clayton together at church warmed Jayson, but not as much as when she passed by him and smiled, saying simply, "Hello, Brother Wolfe. It's good to have you back."

"It's good to be back," he replied. "And how are you?"

"I'm well, thank you," she said and moved on. Jayson silently thanked God for the miracle.

That evening they went to visit Macy and Aaron at their home and to see how Layla was doing. She looked so much better that it seemed miraculous. The man she'd been dating was also there, and they took the opportunity of the family gathering to announce their engagement. It was obvious the children really liked Henry, and Layla looked healthy and happy.

The following day, Jayson received a call from his record company, telling him that one of the reputable news programs he'd been on last spring wanted to do a followup, hour-long feature on him. They'd had a lot of positive feedback over his comments about his wife and family, and they were well aware that the concert tour had been a huge success. They were hoping that he'd be willing to let them come to his home and see the reality of Jayson Wolfe's life, as opposed to the tabloids' version. Jayson felt as if he'd just been handed vindication on a silver platter. He readily agreed once he'd consulted Elizabeth, and a date was arranged.

Before the day arrived, Jayson was also informed that marketing research had indicated the sales of classical CDs by Mozart had shown a marked increase through American distributors in the last few months. He joked with Elizabeth about what it might be like to meet Mozart when he got to the other side of the veil. Mozart had inspired Jayson Wolfe from his childhood, and Jayson Wolfe had revived an interest in Mozart. And they shared the same middle name.

The day before cameras and news people were scheduled to spend several hours in their home, Elizabeth had everyone cleaning. Macy came over to help, and Jayson had insisted that she and Aaron be around during the event. They were part of the family.

While Jayson was taking a break, Macy approached him and asked, "Can I talk to you, Dad?"

"Of course," he said and patted the couch next to where he was sitting.

She sat beside him and said, "I want to ask for your help. Aaron and I have discussed it and prayed about it. We both feel good about it, depending on how *you* feel about it, of course. The first thing is, we *do* feel like it's time to move out of Layla's house. Since she's getting married and she's doing so much better, it's obvious the time is right. But we're having trouble finding an apartment that isn't either a fortune, or a dump. We were hoping the offer was still open to use your basement apartment and stay here for a while."

"Of course," he said and laughed. "We would love to have you stay."

"Don't you need to talk to Mom?"

"No, she'll be thrilled."

"Oh, I'm so glad," she said. "I wasn't worried, but . . . I'm so glad. The thing is, when I can start working, I can help pay rent—or maybe we could work toward buying a house, but right now I want to go to school. And that's where I'm going to ask another favor. You always said that you would pay for any education I wanted to get. Did you mean it?"

"Of course," he said.

"You're the best!"

"It's not hard to throw money at you when I have too much," he said. "But I know you don't love me for my money, so it's okay. I'm glad to be able to do it. What kind of school?"

"I want to be a massage therapist, Dad."

"That's great!" he said and laughed. "It's perfect."

"Yeah, it is. If I go full-time during the days, I can get through school in seven months, which is perfect, Dad, because . . . I can be finished before the baby comes."

Jayson couldn't help but feel choked up. "You're pregnant?" he asked, knowing it was a stupid question. She nodded and hugged him. "That's wonderful news, Macy. Little else could make me happier."

"Well," she said leaning back, "we just have to hope and pray I make it full term this time. If not, I guess we'll deal with it. But we're going to plan that way. And like I said, I can be done with school before the baby comes, and then I can contribute to our income and work at home."

"It sounds great, baby," Jayson said, hoping they would actually be living here when the baby came. The very idea was joyous.

* * * * *

The presence of network television in the house for a day proved to be a unique experience, but it went well. Jayson and Elizabeth had decided they were not going to stress over the children being normal. Other than making certain the house was in relatively decent order, they were determined to appear as normal as possible. If nothing else, they didn't want their children to see them behaving any differently with cameras in the house than they did any other day. The interviewer had a long conversation alone with Jayson, and another with Elizabeth, then she talked to them together while they sat on the couch in the living room. They talked about their history, their marriage, their religion, their children, and the challenges they'd conquered in their lives. They discussed Jayson's work schedule, and he loved being able to talk about how he never worked on Sundays, and how he usually stopped to share evenings with his family.

Elizabeth insisted on feeding their guests a simple lunch, but she hadn't expected the typical activity in the kitchen while they were all eating together to get caught on camera. Only when the cameraman was eating did they not feel conspicuous.

Cameramen then followed Jayson and the interviewer through parts of the house. They took a long look at the career wall, and asked Jayson many questions. Jayson couldn't help thinking of how the cameras also went past pictures of the temple and the Savior. He hoped some of that footage would end up in the final cut. They took a tour of the studio, joking about the commute he had to take to get to work. For a long while they sat in the studio and talked some more, then Jayson was asked to play some samples of music for his fans. He did a little on both piano and guitar, and he made the interviewer laugh by making up words as he went along.

Trevin came in from school and was caught on film. He was interviewed on camera for quite a while, since his own musical talents and involvement with the band were of interest. Then Addie came in, and she was adorable with these people. They finished up with the entire family together, including Macy and Aaron, and they were encouraged to just talk like a family about some of their tour experiences, and memories of living in the midst of the music industry.

The next day everything was back to normal. Jayson went running with Roger early in the morning, and he enjoyed catching up with his friend. With the exception of their dramatically different careers, they had a great deal in common, and Jayson suspected this would be a friendship that lasted a lifetime.

A couple of weeks later when the program on Jayson Wolfe was set to air, the entire family, including Will and Marilyn, gathered to see the end result. Some of it was funny, some very serious, and much of it amazing. Jayson got teary a couple of times: once when his religious beliefs were expressed so clearly and with such sincerity on national television, and the other when he once again had that feeling of being so thoroughly vindicated after the tabloid nightmare. He also knew that most of the ward was watching the show—because Elizabeth had announced it in Relief Society during the good-news minute. Overall he was pleased with the results, and felt that the opportunity had been a great blessing.

Jayson faced a bit of a dilemma when his record company wanted the band to do a brief European tour during the fall. He and Elizabeth fasted and prayed over the matter and both came to the firm conclusion that they should remain at home. Jayson believed the album would sell whether he did the tour or not, and being home together as a normal family was more important, especially after such an extraordinary summer.

As life began to return to normal, Jayson smoothed over some of the rough edges on the collection of hymns he'd recorded. He worked out a deal with an LDS distributor and released his CD of hymns about the Savior. It came out for Christmas and sold very well. Jayson donated all of the proceeds to the missionary program.

Christmas gave Elizabeth the opportunity to send out Christmas cards with personal notes to every single person who had worked with them on the tour, as well as some people at the record company. In them she included pass-along cards from the Church, offering a free video about the Savior.

The holidays were a wonderful celebration with family and friends, and halfway between Christmas and New Year's, Drew and his family came to stay, as they always did. The first evening they were there, after the children had all gone to bed—except for Trevin, who was out with friends, the adults sat down to visit without the noise and interruptions of little ones. Jayson was surprised to hear Drew say, "We've decided to leave Los Angeles. We're really getting to hate it there." Drew and Valerie both talked about growing problems in the neighborhood, and of how they really didn't have friends there anymore that they ever saw or did anything with. For many years Drew had been involved with a number of different projects in the music business, but those had all been wrapped up or had faded away. There was nothing keeping them in Los Angeles anymore.

"Where do you think you'll go?" Jayson asked, wondering if he could talk his brother into moving nearby. Prior to Jayson coming to Utah, they'd always lived close to each other, if not under the same roof. He wanted to mention that it would be great to see their children grow up together and be close as cousins, to say nothing of all the things they could share as families. He hoped that if Drew lived in a Mormon neighborhood for a while, he'd come to see the gospel truly in action and it might soften his heart. But he kept all of these thoughts to himself and just waited for an answer.

"How about down the street?" Drew asked, and Jayson laughed.

"Are you serious?" he asked.

"We noticed a couple of For Sale signs on our way in," Drew chuckled. "We *were* paying attention, because we've been talking about this for a while. We wanted to spring it on you, face to face. Do you think you could handle having us live in your neighborhood?"

"Are you kidding?" Jayson asked.

"Am I serious? Am I kidding?" Drew chuckled again. "Make up your mind."

"It would be so great!" Jayson said. "If we can live with you under the same roof for weeks at a time, I think we could handle it."

"Well, it feels right," Drew said. "We've been around here enough to realize that this is a great area, a great place to raise a family . . . which brings us to our other news."

"Yes?" Jayson drawled and felt Elizabeth reach for his hand. He knew her thoughts were the same as his. He was aching to hear some evidence that Drew had taken a serious interest in the Church.

"We're going to have a baby," Drew said, and Jayson wasn't disappointed at all by such news. It was wonderful, and he told them so. And he could find great hope in knowing that Drew *was* moving to the area. If they were able to spend more time together, surely it was only a matter of time before his heart was softened.

They joked about how Drew and Valerie were too old to be having children, even though Valerie was younger than Drew. And they all found it ironic that Jayson would be having a grandchild around the same time that Drew would be having a child. Of course, Jayson's children were spread out in age considerably, but since Jayson was younger than Drew, the irony of him becoming a grandfather while Drew's children were toddlers was worth noting.

Once the holidays were over, Drew and Valerie were able to find a home they really liked less than a mile away. Jayson flew to Los Angeles to help the family move, and Elizabeth arranged for members of two elders quorums to be there to unload the truck when it arrived. And neighbors were bringing food to the new occupants of the neighborhood without any nudging from Elizabeth. For Jayson, having his brother nearby seemed to be the final meshing of the good from his old life to the magnificence of his new one.

The same week that Layla and Henry got married, Will and Marilyn left to fulfill a mission call to Australia. It was hard to see them go, but they all knew it was a great thing and looked forward to the adventures they might have and share with their family. Their home was rented to a fine family for the duration of the mission, and everything fell into place for them to do this great work.

Jayson and Elizabeth did a fireside in their own ward, and the response was very good. Jayson felt acceptance and support from the ward members who attended, and it seemed to have a rippling effect afterward. He felt completely accepted among these good people, and it felt good. And best of all, Bonnie and Clayton Freedman were in attendance.

Jayson and Elizabeth loved having Macy and Aaron in their home. Even though they had their little private apartment, they spent a great deal of time in the house interacting with the family. It was nice to get to know Aaron on a deeper level, and to be all together as a family in a way they never had been before. Macy was enjoying school, and no one was surprised that she was very good at it. Jayson and Elizabeth both enjoyed being her guinea pigs, and they took turns going to the school to get a massage.

Drew and Valerie had barely settled into their home when the brothers and their wives—and Trevin—flew to Los Angeles to attend the Grammy Awards. This year Jayson and Drew would be presenting an award as they had the year before, but Jayson had also been nominated for two awards for "The Heart of Mozart." On top of that, the band had been asked to perform a number on the show, which meant that Brandon would be attending with them, as well.

During the performance, Jayson felt a strange sense of déjà vu. Of course he would. He'd performed on the Grammys before. But it had been a different world then, a different life. The only common element was Drew, who had always been on the drums behind him while he'd been the front man. Beyond that, there was little similarity between then and now. He remembered the thrill of achieving the goal of being asked to perform before such a prestigious audience. He remembered being thrilled with the awards. But at the time he'd had no comprehension of the ugliness and horror that awaited him in the pitfalls of life. And he never could have comprehended the blessings that would come into his life through the gospel and the woman who had always been there for him. Now, with Elizabeth and Trevin onstage with him, he was so grateful to be where he was now—more metaphorically than literally. He had everything a man could ever want.

Later in the evening, Jayson was given one of the awards he'd been nominated for, and even though it was for him, he took Elizabeth, Drew, Trevin, and Brandon to the stage with him. At the microphone he started out by saying that even though "The Heart of Mozart" was a solo album, he couldn't have done it without his team. He thanked his wife and family, his brother, his band, and his friends. And lastly he said,

"And I thank God for this blessing and privilege."

Returning to Utah was doubly pleasurable in having Drew and Valerie return, as well. A few days later they were submerged in a beautiful snowstorm. Jayson stood at the window of the front room, looking out on the quiet gentleness with which the tiny white flakes covered the ground and had a great equalizing effect on everything they touched. It felt to him like a profound metaphor of the blessings of God and the workings of the Spirit. He felt as calm and at peace as the falling snow, a stark contrast to the storms of life he'd endured in the past. A lyrical line popped into his mind, and he muttered it into the empty room. *I'm connected to heaven with the silence of snow.* Nothing more followed, so he didn't figure it would actually end up in a song, but it made him smile. Then he went to tell Elizabeth his thoughts.

* * * * *

Life quickly settled around them as if it had never been any other way, and Jayson loved having his brother live nearby. At least once a week they just spent a day in the studio, jamming and having a good time. As the brothers started reminiscing about their early years and the music that had made them musicians, they began to resurrect some old material. Some of it was their own originals from way back, and some of it was music they had listened to on their mother's records and had learned to play because she loved it. Trevin often joined them after school, and having him play bass so much like Derek made it easy to do a lot of their old stuff and make it sound great. Members of the family often came into the studio to listen, and a lot of fun and laughter often surrounded the music there.

When the brothers discovered a great song that had been on their mother's favorite album and that was predominantly piano and drums, they wondered why they had never bothered to learn it before. The two of them got so excited about learning it now that they started joking with the family about the great Elton John number they were working on, and that if they were lucky they'd be invited to its unveiling. They wouldn't let anyone in the studio when they were working on it, and the secrecy added to the joke.

"Just like old times?" Elizabeth asked.

"*A lot* like old times," Jayson said.

"I can't wait," she said and kissed him. "It's nice to see you so happy."

"No happier than you."

"That's true," she said. "But I guess after all those years of the people we loved dropping dead all around us, we've earned some happiness, don't you think?"

"Absolutely," he said.

The following week in the middle of one of their jam sessions, Drew asked Jayson out of the blue, "Would it be okay if we come to church with you this Sunday?" While Jayson was trying to get his voice past the knot in his throat, Drew added, "I know we technically live in a different ward, and we've had lots of neighbors invite us to attend there, but I think I'd like to go with you to start out and get my feet wet."

"Start out?" Jayson asked, then chuckled when he saw Drew smile. "If you're getting your feet wet, does that mean you have plans to get dunked completely?"

Drew's smile broadened. "Let's just say we're sure considering it. We had missionaries at our house last night."

Jayson couldn't hold back tears. But Drew didn't seem surprised. He'd known Jayson longer than anyone still living. He knew how easily Jayson cried. What surprised Jayson was to see Drew crying, as well. "I can't say that I absolutely know it's true, Jayson. But I know it's good, and I'm working on it. Valerie and I both agree there couldn't be a better way to raise a family. And we really want to be together forever; we want what you and Elizabeth have. I think that summarizes what we've always wanted; we just couldn't quite put a finger on it. So, be patient with me, Jayse."

Jayson couldn't find words. He just stood up to embrace his brother, wondering what other blessing could be poured into his life that he might not have room to hold.

Later that day, while Jayson was floating on the anticipation of having his brother go to church with him, he got a call from the bishop's executive secretary, asking him and Elizabeth to meet with him. It was impossible to tell if this appointment was for Elizabeth's benefit or his own. But he didn't feel nervous. He just wondered what new adventure they might have before them.

Once in the bishop's office, their friendly catching-up went on for so long that Jayson wondered if there was any other purpose to this visit. He appreciated the friendship that had developed between him and the bishop, and was glad to be reminded of that. But he was beginning to feel a little nervous. He was entirely unprepared to hear Bishop Bingham move from talk of how well Trevin was doing in the Young Men program, to asking Jayson if he would serve in the organization.

"With the young men?" Jayson asked, certain he'd misunderstood.

"Yes," the bishop drawled, then chuckled. More seriously he said, "I want you to know, Jayson, that this comes from the Lord. This is not an attempt for anyone here, especially myself, to try to make up for challenges of the past. I have absolutely no doubt that the Lord wants you in this position, and no one else."

"Which position, exactly?" Jayson asked, his heart beating quickly.

"Roger is being released," the bishop said. "He's been in there a long time. He's being called to something else. So the entire organization is being restructured. Some of the men will be staying where they are, but it's time for some changes. You are being called to take Roger's place as president of the Young Men."

It took Jayson a minute to regain his composure, and during that minute, he recalled in excruciating detail his joy when he'd first been called to serve with the Young Men, his devastation when he'd been released, and all of the torment that had followed. He thought of Job, of how he was given back far more than he had lost. And he knew that God was merciful. In that moment he knew that his release had been as inspired as this call was now. He knew that God's hand had been in both. He'd needed the growth and humility that had been spurred by that event. Its challenges had been difficult to understand at the time. But looking back, he could see that it had been far more important for Clayton to remain a part of the Young Men program than it had been for Jayson to be a leader. In spite of how horrific it had seemed at the time, Jayson wouldn't have wanted it any other way, now that he'd come this far. Miracles had occurred with Clayton and his mother. And a miracle was occurring right here and now. The bishop filled in the silence by asking if Jayson would like some time to think and pray about it.

"I don't need any time," Jayson said as his voice cracked. "It would be an honor. I know it's right; I can feel it."

"I suspected you might," the bishop said with a smile. He turned to Elizabeth. "Are you okay with Jayson taking on this calling? Do you have any concerns?"

"None at all," Elizabeth said. "I'm certain my husband can do a great deal of good with these boys, and I am more than happy to do everything I can to support him."

"Good," the bishop said, and they started talking about some of the young men specifically, and concerns the bishop had. The conversation went on as if they had all the time in the world. Either the bishop had no other appointments, or he'd scheduled a long visit. Whatever the case, Jayson was enjoying his time with this man who had stood by him through some tough things. He'd become Jayson's friend, as well as his ecclesiastical leader, and Jayson respected him as much as he liked him.

Jayson was surprised once again when the bishop said, "It's occurred to me recently, since the two of you are converts, that neither of you may have had a patriarchal blessing. Trevin's getting to the age that he should have one, and I noticed that he hasn't. Then I realized that the two of you probably haven't, either."

"No, we haven't," Elizabeth said. "Should we?"

"It's up to you, but it's a wonderful opportunity." He went on to explain more about the purpose of such blessings. Some of it they had heard before, but he answered some questions and went ahead with the paperwork they would need in order to meet with the stake patriarch.

On Sunday, with Drew and his family sitting on one side of him, and Elizabeth and his own family on the other, Jayson stood in sacrament meeting to be sustained as the president of the Young Men organization. As he sat back down, Trevin caught his eye with a grin. Jayson smiled back, taking the moment into himself. With Macy and Aaron attending church in the same ward, and Drew's family there as well, they filled up an entire center bench. He thought of the first time he'd come to church with Elizabeth and her father; Trevin and Addie had been so young. He never could have comprehended such a moment.

During the meeting, Jayson couldn't help thinking of how far he'd come, and how much he'd learned since he'd been called to serve with the young men about a year and a half earlier. He thought of the blessing he'd been given when he was set apart, and was surprised at how clearly it came to his memory. It was as if the Spirit wanted him to remember and understand its meaning, now that the lesson he'd been meant to learn had apparently come full circle. In the blessing he'd been told of the great influence for good that he could have on the young men in his stewardship, and how his unique gifts would have a positive impact on some in particular. He was admonished to be patient with himself and with others, not to judge, and to trust in the Lord. He was also told to remember that God loved all of His children. Then the blessing had become more personal as he was told that the path he was taking in his career was pleasing to his Father in Heaven and that he would be richly blessed as he diligently pursued that course. He was told that God was pleased with the way Jayson had used his gifts, and that he would continue to receive guidance so long as he sought for it and kept his covenants. Jayson marveled at the prophecy included in the blessing, and felt grateful to be reminded of it now.

When sacrament meeting was over, everyone scattered to get the kids to Primary and get to their separate classes. Drew and Valerie started out of the chapel with Jayson coming behind them when Sister Freedman approached him and shook his hand. "Congratulations on your calling," she said with quiet sincerity. "You'll be wonderful. Clayton's thrilled to have you back in there."

"I'm thrilled too," Jayson said. "Thank you."

"I'm truly sorry for the way I—"

"Hah." He put up a finger to stop her. "That's all in the past. We've come far."

"Yes," she said. "And you've been so kind; everyone has been so kind . . . and forgiving."

"That's the way Mormons are supposed to be."

"And you exemplify that well," she said.

Jayson still had trouble believing that such things could come out of Bonnie Freedman's mouth—in reference to him. But he just smiled and said, "That means more coming from you than anyone else."

She smiled back. He impulsively gave her a quick hug, and they went their separate ways.

In the Gospel Doctrine class, Jayson was thrilled to be able to introduce his brother and sister-in-law, and when he mentioned that they had recently moved here from Los Angeles, many people expressed pleasure. By the end of the meetings, Jayson wondered if he should avoid asking Drew any questions, but he felt near to bursting as they stood in the hall, waiting for their families to meet them. "So, what do you think, little brother?"

"I think we should save that conversation for later," Drew said, and Jayson honestly couldn't read him enough to know if that was good or bad. He felt slightly on edge about it as they all returned to Jayson's home and shared Sunday dinner. Drew and Valerie both appeared to be in good moods, and they made some positive comments about the meetings during the meal, but Jayson still wondered what might constitute a conversation *later*. After dinner was cleaned up and the little ones were all down for naps, Elizabeth took Valerie in the other room to show her some genealogy she'd been working on, and Drew and Jayson ended up in the living room alone.

"It's later," Jayson said without any preamble.

He thought Drew might question what he meant since it had been hours, but it was evident he knew *exactly* what Jayson was talking about. But his approach was not what Jayson had been expecting.

"I never felt older than you. I mean . . . I'm not much older, and once we were out of school, our age difference didn't mean a thing. But . . . I always knew I was supposed to be the big brother, but I think God made you taller for a reason. You always led the way . . . with everything. You always knew what you wanted and did it. I think it's fitting that you're the front man on the stage, because you're the front man in life, too."

"I'm afraid I really don't know what you mean," Jayson said, wondering what this had to do with Drew's impressions of attending church.

"As much as I love drumming, and I can admit that I'm good at it, I never would have pushed for a career the way that you did. I never could have—or would have—done it without you. If not for you, I wouldn't have the financial security I have today. I probably would have ended up managing a movie theater, or something. You've always been amazing, Jayson; always been my hero."

Jayson sensed a "but" coming at the end of this oratory. *But* I can't share your religion. Or *but* I don't agree with your beliefs. When Drew said nothing for several seconds, Jayson felt the need to remind him, "I've done some pretty stupid things, Drew. Remember when I smashed the piano with a fire poker?"

"Yeah," Drew chuckled, "I remember."

"You bought me a new one."

"Yes, I did . . . with money I never would have made if you hadn't needed my drumming skills."

"And you can't be forgetting that I became a drug addict and almost took my own life."

Drew was very serious as he said, "No, I will never forget that. In fact . . . I regularly thank God that you are still here. I don't take your being with us, or being my brother, for granted. But all that drug stuff . . . that was just . . . circumstantial. I've always wondered what I could have done through those years to make things easier for you. I don't think I was a very good brother. I had a way of avoiding the things that made me uncomfortable, things that I didn't know how to fix."

"You never could have fixed me."

"No, but I could have been there more. I was hanging out with friends, working with other bands. And you needed a brother."

"That's all in the past, Drew. We talked about this in counseling years ago. We were all just . . . trying to figure life out. You *were* there for me. I was lying to you when you asked me if I was alright. I was too proud to admit I had a problem and ask for help. I don't understand why this is coming up . . . now."

"I just wanted you to know that I've always admired and respected you. Even your mistakes never made you lose hero status with me. I think *you* are the big brother. You just have the personality and the determination to make things happen. I'm a follower. Now I've followed you to Utah."

"I am more glad for that than I could ever tell you."

"Me too," Drew said. "I wish I'd done it years ago. I have no desire to be involved in the music industry any further, except for whatever we might do together. Los Angeles doesn't have a lot of appeal for me when that connection is no longer an issue."

"Yeah, I know what you mean," Jayson said, still waiting for the "but." This all just felt like a need to remind Jayson of all that was good between them so that Jayson wouldn't be hurt or offended by Drew's opinions on religion.

"And today I realized," Drew said, "that once again you have it all figured out way ahead of me, and I'm just following behind you, wondering what I was thinking all these years while you knew that all this stuff was true."

Jayson's heart quickened. "What stuff?" he countered.

"All of it," Drew said and chuckled. Then he became sober and met Jayson's gaze firmly. Jayson saw moisture gather in his brother's eyes, and he held his breath. "It's all true," Drew said, his voice breaking. "I got my answer today, Jayson. I was beginning to think that it wouldn't come—

not so much because it wasn't true, but maybe because I wasn't worthy of such an answer. But it came today. And it didn't just come once. It came over and over. The music. The talks. The lessons. I felt it over and over. Everything I heard today, and everything I know about this church . . . it's true."

Jayson managed to croak out a response despite his own overwhelming emotion. "Does Valerie know how you feel?"

"I told her in the car on our way here after church. She's thrilled. She told me she knew it was true days ago, but she wanted me to get my own answer." He glanced down and cleared his throat. "So . . . I guess what I'm saying is that . . . I'm glad you had the good sense to figure it out, and to be such a great example, and to not be pushy when I would have resented it, but to know when I was ready." He met Jayson's eyes again. "I'm ready now . . . to follow in your footsteps." He looked again at Jayson. "I want you to be the one to baptize me."

Jayson couldn't speak; he could barely breathe. Instead he just hugged his brother tightly, and they both cried for a good minute.

"Wow," Jayson finally said and chuckled, wiping at his face. "I've been hoping and praying . . . but you still blew me away."

"I feel a little blown away myself," Drew said, and they talked for a long while about aspects of the gospel that intrigued Drew the most. He asked Jayson some questions, and he answered them with his joy deepening by the minute. He'd always loved and admired his brother, always felt that their brotherly kinship was rare and precious and one of the most valuable things in his life. But when Jayson had stepped into the gospel, it had created a chasm between them. There had never been contention or lack of respect over it. But for Jayson it had just never felt quite right to not have this most wonderful aspect of his life in common with his brother. Now that chasm would be bridged, and he truly could find no words to express what this meant to him.

"Who baptized you?" Drew asked.

"Will," he said. "Aaron baptized Macy, and Will baptized me. It was an incredible day. Now we will have another incredible day."

"Yes, we will," Drew said. "I wish Mom could have found this. I think she would have latched onto it very quickly."

Jayson took the opportunity to tell Drew something that never would have mattered or made sense before. "All of Mom's temple work has been done; Dad's, too."

Drew got fresh tears in his eyes. "Wow," he said and seemed to be taking it in. "That is really cool."

"Yes, it is," Jayson said. "Maybe she's been pushing you along."

"Maybe," Drew chuckled. "I wouldn't be surprised. I think she'll be happy about this. I think she's happy about our living in the same neighborhood again."

"Yes, I think she is," Jayson said and hugged his brother again, certain that every member of the family on both sides of the veil had to be feeling pretty happy right now.

CHAPTER 16

A date was set for Drew and Valerie's baptisms, but Jayson still felt like pinching himself to be certain this was really happening. Through emails exchanged with Will, Jayson knew that he was as thrilled as the rest of the family for this great event. Will would have liked to be present, but he and Marilyn were doing great things on the other end of the world.

Just a few days before the baptism, Jayson, Elizabeth, and Trevin all went together to visit the stake patriarch to receive their patriarchal blessings. The experience was so amazing that it felt almost surreal. Jayson listened to the words being spoken about his wife and son by a man who knew nothing about them, and in fact had never met them. There was no doubt about the true source of the blessings. Trevin was told, among many things, that he would serve a mission in a faraway land, and through the course of his life he would bless the people of the world in ways he'd never anticipated. Elizabeth was told that her special talents would continue to bless others throughout the remainder of her life. The blessing stated that her tender charitable nature in being a wife and mother would radiate out to others and change lives, and that her musical abilities were a gift from her Father in Heaven, and He was pleased with the way she had used those talents.

Jayson felt decidedly nervous when it was his turn. He found it ironic that he wasn't at all surprised by what he heard, only deeply validated. In essence, he was told the very same thing he'd learned many months earlier when he had been miraculously shown by the Spirit the purpose and meaning of his gift. It had been given to him long before he was born, and he had brought it here with a specific mission attached to it. He was told that the Lord was pleased with the way he had used his gift for good, and that opportunities to use his gifts would continue to present themselves throughout the course of his life, and that he should never deny those opportunities. He was also told that that many of God's children would be led into the fold by his example. He was told of his value as a husband and father, and also that his posterity would call him blessed. Of course he cried through the whole thing. But Elizabeth was there with tissues handy. She was used to it, and he was grateful as always to have her by his side.

* * * * *

Jayson had a mental list of the greatest moments in his life, and stepping into the baptismal font with his brother was high on it. Following the simple ceremony, they hugged tightly while standing in the water, and Jayson *knew* his parents were present. And he knew that Derek was, too. It stood to reason that the veil would be thin for such an event. He was just grateful to be able to feel the evidence of their presence.

Life settled more deeply into contentment and fulfillment for Jayson as he observed Drew and Valerie becoming actively involved in the gospel they had embraced. While he and Drew worked here and there on some musical projects, their families thrived and blossomed together. They helped each other through the challenges and had a great deal of fun together.

Jayson loved working with the young men and found great fulfillment in it. He became attached to each and every one of them, and considered it a great privilege to be involved in their lives.

Macy's pregnancy went well, and she finished school just after her eighth month. Three weeks after graduating, she gave birth to a healthy and beautiful baby girl. For Jayson, holding that baby in his arms only an hour after she was born moved high on that list of great moments in his life. How could he not think of the baby that Macy had given to another family because she'd not been ready to take on motherhood? And how could he not remember the day she had miscarried and the grief they had all felt? As he held his granddaughter against his chest, taking in the newborn smell of her, a deep healing filled his being, and he silently thanked God for yet another miracle in his life.

Because Macy and Aaron were still living with them and attending their ward, the baby was blessed there, and Jayson counted it as one of the greatest moments of his life to stand in the circle when his precious granddaughter was blessed and given her name. Leslie after his mother, and Ruth after his grandmother. She would go by Ruth, or Ruthie as they'd started calling her, to distinguish her from Drew's daughter.

Later that day, the family was all gathered in the living room following Sunday dinner. Drew and Valerie were there as well. Valerie was getting near the end of her pregnancy and was feeling fairly uncomfortable; they knew the baby was a boy, and they were all anxiously looking forward to his arrival. Jayson and Trevin both had their acoustic guitars, picking out some Primary songs while they all sang them together. The doorbell rang, and Aaron went to answer it while the rest of the group finished singing, "A Child's Prayer." On the final note Jayson looked up to see that Aaron had brought Bonnie and Clayton into the room. She was holding a package wrapped in pink and silver paper.

"Come in," Jayson said, setting the guitar aside as he came to his feet.

"Oh, we don't want to intrude," Bonnie said. "We just . . . brought a little something for the baby."

"You're not intruding," Elizabeth said, standing also. She insisted they both sit down, and told them that the brownies would be out of the oven in a few minutes, and they must stay and have some. Clayton looked pleased. Bonnie looked a little nervous, but didn't protest.

"Here," she said, handing the gift to Macy, who was sitting close by on the floor. "It's for the baby. It's nothing really; just something I do in my spare time." Jayson reached for Elizabeth's hand and shared a discreet glance of amazement with her. Macy pulled away the paper to reveal an intricately crocheted blanket that was exquisite. It was white, with pink satin ribbon woven around the edges and tied in bows at the corners.

"Oh, it's so beautiful!" Macy said.

"It is!" Elizabeth added, and Addie moved closer to touch it with fascination.

"Thank you so much!" Macy said and stood up, leaning over Bonnie to hug her.

"That's really very sweet," Elizabeth said.

"It's nothing, really," Bonnie said. Then her eyes widened as they were drawn to the career wall. "Oh, my," she said and came to her feet as if she felt compelled to look closer. But there was no criticism or anger in her eyes; only intrigue and curiosity. "How old were you here?"

she asked Jayson, and he stood up to look closer while everyone else in the room became unusually quiet, as if they sensed the irony in the moment.

"Seventeen," he said. "And that's Elizabeth in the picture with me."

"Oh, it is. You've known each other a very long time."

"We have," Jayson said.

Then Bonnie Freedman turned and looked into his eyes. They shared a long, silent moment of perfect healing and acceptance before she said, "Tell me about your music, Jayson. May I call you Jayson?"

"You may," he said.

"I've been listening to your CDs," she said, and Jayson resisted the urge to allow his mouth to fall open. "Clayton insisted. It was part of an agreement we made in counseling. I must admit it's an agreement that I'm glad I made . . . even though I confess that I was reluctant at first." She looked again at the pictures on the wall. "I'm very interested to know more . . . if you don't mind. Apparently I'm not leaving until the brownies are done."

Jayson put a hand on her shoulder. "You're welcome to stay as long as you'd like, and to come back often. What do you want to know?"

"Oh, everything!" she said. "Start at the beginning."

Macy said, "I never get tired of hearing this stuff."

"It's been a long time, actually," Trevin said.

"The beginning," Jayson said, "would be that my mother loved music, and she believed in me and my brother." He turned and pointed to Drew. "That's my brother, by the way, and his sweet wife." He made official introductions, then went on. "Let me tell you about my mother. She was an amazing woman who had survived some pretty horrible things. I think the two of you would have liked each other."

"She's passed away?"

"Yes. We lost her to cancer years ago."

"I'm so sorry," Bonnie said, and they sat back down. "Tell me about her. Tell me one of your best memories of your mother."

"Oh, that's easy," Jayson said. "It was the day she told me we were going to have to sell the piano so we could make the move to Oregon in order to get away from my drunken father. I was devastated. Her mother's old upright piano was the most precious thing in the world to me, and she knew it. But we couldn't afford to keep it, and we couldn't possibly move it. I went outside after she told me, because I didn't want her to see me crying. She came out to find me, and she said something to me that I never forgot."

"I don't think you've *ever* told me this before," Macy said.

"I've never heard it," Trevin added.

"Well, you're going to hear it now." Jayson laughed softly. "Funny how I remember it verbatim after all these years. She took hold of my shoulders and looked into my eyes, and she said, 'Great people rise out of the dust of adversity, Jayson. You have a gift and the drive inside of you to bring that gift to its fruition. Don't you ever forget that. Don't you ever let go of it. God sent you to this earth to make magic with the instruments you play. Your guitars will go with you. They will keep you connected to that gift. And I promise you . . . *I promise you* . . . that God knows the sacrifice you're making to help keep this family safe, and He will bring a piano into your life. I don't know when, or how, but He will. You just have to believe in Him, and in yourself, and it will happen.'"

"That's glorious," Trevin said.

"It's like she summed up everything you are right then and there," Drew said.

"She did," Jayson said, "even if I didn't know it at the time."

"Did He bring a piano into your life?" Bonnie asked, then she chuckled. "Obviously . . . you have a piano now, but . . . back then?"

"He did," Jayson said, amazed at how perfectly comfortable he felt talking to this woman, while her son looked on, thoroughly pleased with the situation. "In Oregon I made a wonderful friend who was also a musician. His family took me in like their own. They had a beautiful grand piano, much like the one we have in the front room." He pointed at his wife. "It was Elizabeth's family."

"That is so sweet," Macy said.

"Yeah," Jayson said, looking at Elizabeth. "I fell in love with her the first time I saw her. It was like I just knew my soul was supposed to be linked with hers." He impulsively sang lyrics that he'd written for her all those years ago, lyrics that were impossible to forget, lyrics that he could sing a capella with no effort. *"You stand tall while I stand in awe, yearning from a distance. My awakened senses yearn to sense you . . . close to me. Our two hearts are only one, divided by time and air and space. In another time and place . . . our two hearts were one . . . and they will be again."*

"Oh, that's lovely," Bonnie said when he finished and gave Elizabeth a quick kiss.

"Amen," Elizabeth said, and the timer in the kitchen started to buzz.

"Brownies!" Addie and the three younger children squealed and ran in that direction, with Macy following to take the goodies out of the oven.

"I think the brownies are done," Jayson said through everyone's laughter.

"You think?" Elizabeth said. Their visitors just smiled and looked as if they could bask indefinitely in the love they could feel in the Wolfe household. Jayson knew the feeling well.

While everyone was eating warm brownies with vanilla ice cream and chocolate syrup, Trevin said with intense astonishment, "Hey, I just thought of something." He pointed his fork at his father. "You guys have cheated us!" He then pointed the fork at Drew.

"What?" the brothers asked at the same time.

"That Elton John number you were making such a big deal of. That was *months* ago. You promised an unveiling. We never got it."

"That's true!" Macy said, facetiously sounding as if she were *very* angry.

"What are you going to do about it?" Elizabeth asked Jayson.

"It's really not that big of a deal," Jayson said. "Everybody was busy at the time, and then we were just working on other stuff."

"Okay, well . . ." Valerie said, "I don't think you guys are going to get out of this. We want our song."

"Fine, fine," Drew said lightly. "You don't have to get all huffy about it."

"If it weren't Sunday," Trevin said, "we could go unveil it right now."

"Good thing it's Sunday," Jayson said, particularly aware that Bonnie was here. He couldn't quite imagine unveiling an Elton John classic with her in the studio. But he only said, "It's been a while. We will need a *little* practice."

"Okay," Elizabeth said, as if this were a serious matter of business, "we will all reconvene tomorrow evening at seven. You have until then to get it ready."

"Yes, ma'am," Jayson said with a laugh.

"How about if we make it six and we can all have dinner together first," Macy said. "I'm cooking."

"Works for me," Drew said. "I'll drum for food."

"And that includes you," Macy said directly to Bonnie, who looked stunned.

"Oh," she said, sounding flustered, "you don't need to—"

"I insist," Macy said. "It's my night to cook, and I can invite whoever I want."

"I'm down," Clayton said. "I'm all for dinner, but I would never turn down a chance for a live performance."

"Nor would I," Bonnie said with genuine enthusiasm.

Since everyone in the room knew the history between Bonnie and Jayson, there was no way to avoid the stark silence that followed her comment. Jayson felt compelled to ease the tension, but also to make a clarification and not leave any room for misunderstanding. "Okay, Bonnie," he said. "May I call you Bonnie?"

"Of course," she said.

"Okay, Bonnie, you're scaring me." His tone was light enough to keep the comment from sounding objectionable. "Are you really saying that you want to be in the same room with me and my music . . . live?"

"If it's a problem, then . . ."

"Oh, it's not a problem," Jayson said. "It's just . . . well . . . it'll be . . . loud. And it's so . . . rock and roll."

"I told you I'd been listening to the CDs," she said, not sounding concerned or awkward—even with the entire family present. It was almost as if she'd been expecting—or perhaps hoping—for this conversation. "Clayton's told me so much about the concert, and I really wish I could have been there. Of course, I was in the hospital having a nervous breakdown, so that would have been impossible, and if I hadn't had a nervous breakdown, I never would have gone. But . . . if you believe the changes in me are sincere, I would love the opportunity to hear you play. To be truthful, I . . ." She got emotional but Elizabeth handed her a tissue. "I've been praying that such an opportunity might occur, but . . . I didn't really know if it would ever be possible." She sniffled, and Elizabeth put her arm around Bonnie's shoulders. "I've heard others in the ward talk about being in the studio with you, and . . ." She laughed softly. "I'm really making a fool of myself."

"Not at all," Jayson said. "It wouldn't be the first time prayers had been answered around here. It seems that you're invited to the unveiling tomorrow evening. And dinner, too. I have only one condition."

"Anything," Bonnie said with such determination that he wondered if she believed she needed this opportunity in order to feel as if she had fully made restitution. Maybe not, but the idea stuck in his mind, and he couldn't fully discredit it. Whatever her reasons, he was more than happy to bridge any remaining chasms between them. For all the healing that had taken place between them, he'd never imagined it coming to this. But God had a way of working things out in ways that mortals could never imagine.

"If you *don't* like the music," Jayson said, "don't tell me, and don't let it come between us."

Bonnie just smiled. "I don't think either of us has anything to be worried about."

"Glad that's settled," Macy said.

"Almost," Elizabeth stated firmly. "I don't think unveiling one song is going to be enough. I think Bonnie and Clayton deserve more than that. Besides, you're unveiling a performance of someone else's song. I think we need to hear at least a few Jayson Wolfe originals. We'll just . . . make an evening of it. So, you guys had better do some *serious* practicing tomorrow."

"Did you have a list of requests, Mrs. Wolfe?" Jayson asked.

Before she could answer, Macy said, "Mozart," at the same time that Trevin said, "Good, Clean Fun."

"Oh, I like both of those!" Bonnie said with enthusiasm, and Jayson exchanged a subtle glance with Elizabeth.

She smiled at him and said, "You know what *I* want to hear."

Jayson turned to Drew. "I guess we've been given our orders."

"I guess we have," Drew said.

"What new song by Elton John *have* the two of you been working on?" Elizabeth asked. "You've never told us."

Jayson was going to say that was part of the secret, but Drew said, "B-B-B-Bennie and the Jetsssss." He said it the way Elton sang it in the very popular hit from the seventies.

"Oh, I *love* that song," Macy said. "Grandma and I used to listen to that song and dance."

"Serious?" Jayson asked.

"Yes! We had so much fun."

"I would have liked to see that," Drew said.

"Me too," Jayson added. "I never knew."

"Bennie and the Jets?" Trevin said. "That is glorious. I can't wait."

"Me neither," Elizabeth said.

"Oh," Drew said with a chuckle, "you are not gonna believe how great Jayse sings this song. The way he stutters the Bs and hisses the Ss. It's incredible."

"Oh, will you shut up!" Jayson said with mock anger.

"And the falsetto!" Drew added as if he were Jayson's biggest fan. "The way he hits those falsetto notes then drops back down. It's incredible."

"Shut *up!*" Jayson repeated and laughed as if they were teenagers again.

"Not to mention," Drew added, purposely talking louder. "The way he plays the piano . . . wow!"

"And you've been holding out on us all this time?" Valerie asked.

"Well, Drew does the drums pretty well, too," Jayson said. "It was all just kind of a joke. I didn't think anybody was going to get all huffy."

"It's not a joke," Aaron said. "It's our greatest entertainment."

"Amen," Macy said. Bonnie Freedman and her son just listened to the conversation with apparent fascination. Jayson took in her fascination and couldn't keep from laughing for reasons he didn't bother sharing.

* * * * *

That night, Jayson climbed into bed and put his head on Elizabeth's shoulder. They both laid there for a minute, then started laughing at the same time. "Are you thinking what I'm thinking?" she asked.

"Are you thinking that it is insanely unbelievable that Bonnie Freedman spent the evening in our home, and she's coming back tomorrow for a mini concert?"

"That's what I was thinking," she said, and they laughed again.

"Who would have dreamed?"

"Indeed!" Elizabeth said, and once more they both laughed.

The following day, Jayson and Drew were in the studio right after breakfast to go through several numbers. It didn't take much to review what they would play that evening, and when Trevin came in after school they reviewed some songs that needed the bass.

"This is so weird," Trevin said.

"What?"

"Clayton's mom. It's just . . . weird . . . in a good way."

"Yeah," Jayson said. "In a good way."

"You nervous?" Trevin asked.

"No, should I be?"

"You don't think she's going to freak out and yell at you, or something?"

Jayson smiled. "I think her change of heart is deep and genuine. I think she is a walking testament of the healing power of the Atonement. And with any luck she'll actually like what she hears. But even if she's just being diplomatic, her efforts at healing our relationship are touching and should be appreciated."

"Oh, I get that," Trevin said. "I think it's more like she's gonna become one of your best friends. Or at least your biggest fan."

"Maybe," Jayson said and chuckled, really liking that idea. Since Bonnie and Clayton didn't have any family to speak of, the thought of having them more involved with *his* family was a good thought, indeed. She really did remind him of his mother; a single mom with no family connections, struggling to overcome some awful things in her life.

Seeing the time, they had to wrap it up and get into the house for dinner. Bonnie and Clayton were the last to arrive, but they both seemed thrilled to be there. Macy had made tacos and a great Mexican dip that was one of her specialties. She'd learned a great deal about cooking during her time in Layla's home. Now her own family was reaping the benefits. Elizabeth and Jayson both hugged Bonnie and Clayton when they arrived, and they made certain their guests felt comfortable. Jayson observed them judiciously during the meal and felt some evidence to back up his theory on their need to become part of a family. The whole thing was just so incredibly ironic—in a good way.

Once dinner was cleaned up, the family all moved into the studio. Elizabeth and Bonnie were the last to come, since they were chatting comfortably while putting the kitchen in order.

"I think we're missing the party," Elizabeth said to her as she hung up the dish towel and realized they were alone. She marveled over the comfort level she felt with this woman, and how open she was being about her distorted attitudes in the past and the reasons for them. Elizabeth was enjoying their conversation and genuinely liked her. It was remarkable! She just hoped the evening would go well, and that this wouldn't be too much overload for a woman who had loathed rock and roll not so many months ago.

Elizabeth watched Bonnie closely as they stepped into the studio where everyone was chatting and laughing, with Clayton in the midst of the group. The children had come with some quiet toys to play with on the floor to keep them occupied. Little Ruthie was in her baby seat, her eyes open and taking in her surroundings. She'd been in the studio before, and she'd never been alarmed by the loud music. In fact, Macy joked that she'd heard it so much from the womb that it was like a lullaby to her.

Bonnie took in the room, the piano, the other instruments, the sound booth, and the recording equipment, and she smiled. "Oh, it feels magical in here," she commented.

"Yes, it does," Elizabeth agreed and took her arm to guide her. "Let's get a front-row seat." They took a couple of chairs near the piano, next to Valerie, who was already seated. Everyone else got comfortable on the floor while Jayson was making adjustments to the microphone and Drew was getting settled onto his stool.

"Are you ready for this?" Elizabeth asked Bonnie.

"Oh, I am!" she said excitedly. "I went to some concerts when I was young, and I remember enjoying them, but that all got lost and distorted in . . . well, you know. We don't need to go there again."

Elizabeth put a hand on Bonnie's arm and asked, "You want some earplugs? It's going to be a little on the loud side."

"Oh, no; I want to hear it all. I think I can handle it."

"What are you playing first, Daddy?" Addie asked from where she was playing with Harmony.

"This is a concert, baby girl," he said. "You'll just have to wait and see." He then said to Trevin, "You're on with the first number, kid. You just gonna sit there?"

"Sorry," Trevin said and jumped up to get his guitar ready.

Jayson turned to Bonnie and said, "Here's the test. If we can still be friends after this, then you'll practically be family."

She smiled and mimicked what he'd said to Trevin, "You just gonna sit there?"

Jayson chuckled, turned to Drew, and nodded. Drew picked up the cue, hit the sticks together for a one-two-three, and they dove into the song, "The Missing Ingredient." Elizabeth watched Bonnie and smiled to see her countenance brighten eagerly.

Jayson focused on the song, but he could see from his peripheral vision that Bonnie seemed pleased. He immersed himself completely in the music. At such moments, he felt a sense of surrealism surrounding him. He was well accustomed to being able to sing and play these instruments to express the music that came without compulsory means to his mind. And he'd become used to the amazed response of people who were exposed to his music. But there were moments when the reality of what he was capable of doing would hit him in a way that was almost detached, as if he could stand on the outside of himself and see what others might see; hear what others might hear. And he had to concede that he too was overwhelmed. Not in a way that was arrogant or prideful, but quite the opposite. In his mind there was no explanation for such abilities beyond divine intervention. His surreal assessment had only one firm conclusion. Why had he been privileged enough to be the recipient of this gift? And it deepened his sense of wanting to always live his life worthy of such a remarkable blessing. With that theory deeply rooted in his soul, he just let his fingers move with ease over the piano keys, and he put his mouth to the microphone, finding joy in the electric current that charged through the room. He'd felt it in arenas filled with thousands of people, and he felt it now in his own little studio with people he loved as his audience.

When he finished the song, Bonnie was the first to start the applause, then everyone cheered and applauded sufficiently to make up for three times that many people. Jayson stood up and put his guitar strap over his head. Once he was adjusted and ready, he went right into the guitar version of "Good, Clean Fun," then the bass and drums came in. It sounded a little hollow without the brass, but he didn't really want to mess with playing the track. This was as much a jam session as a show, and he just wanted to have fun.

Elizabeth kept a discreet eye on their guest. When Jayson first started in with the guitar, she looked a little stunned, and it was difficult to tell whether she just didn't like it, or if she was simply amazed. As the song progressed, it was evident that she *did* like it. She was moving to the music and completely focused on Jayson playing that guitar. The drum/guitar solo went off with extra finesse, enhanced by the way that Drew and Jayson focused on each other while they played, laughing occasionally as if they were having the time of their lives. At the completion of the solo, as Jayson moved back to the mike, everyone cheered, including Bonnie.

Following a few more numbers, they did "The Heart of Mozart," and Jayson *did* use the recorded track of the orchestra. It just wasn't right without it. This was where Bonnie leaned over to Elizabeth and said, "He is incredible! I've heard this song on the CD, but . . . to see it. My goodness!"

"Yeah, I know what you mean."

When that was done, Jayson stood as if he were truly doing a concert. Trevin took off his guitar and sat down. It was now time for the brothers to do their thing. "Thank you. Thank you," Jayson said. "You've been a great audience. Now we come to the moment you've all been waiting for, but in order for you to fully appreciate it, you have to know a little history. So, you want to hear a story?" They all cheered. "You guys have been to too many of my shows," he said and laughed. "Okay, well . . . you probably all know that my mother listened to Elton John when Drew and I were kids. We grew up on it, and while there were some songs she wouldn't let us listen to, the good ones had an immense impact on us. Most of you know that some of those songs have been very important to us through the years, and have become a part of our history. Most of what we play are originals, but once in a while, just for the fun of it—or for the sake of nostalgia—we have to go back to the things that connect us to our roots. The song we want to do for you now is something our mother *loved!* When we were very young, just learning to play, this was a song we messed around with and tried to learn. We never learned it very well, and then it just faded into other things. When Drew mentioned the song a while back, we knew it was the perfect song for us to help bridge the present to the past. We have a little more skill now. Ladies and gentlemen . . . 'B-B-B-Bennie and the Jetsssssss'—Wolfe Brothers style. Just for fun."

Huge applause accompanied Jayson to the piano, where he adjusted the microphone there. Elizabeth saw him meet Drew's eyes, and she knew they were doing a silent count that preceded beginning together at exactly the same moment. Elizabeth immediately got chills. The piano was crisp and sharp and intricate. The beat was semi-slow and steady and in perfect synchronization with the piano. It was one of those moments when it felt like the Wolfe brothers had the same heartbeat. When Jayson started to sing, she got chills again. His voice rang clear and strong, and she marveled anew at how he could play such complex piano pieces and sing at the same time without a glitch.

Bonnie leaned over and said to Elizabeth, "It's like he plays the piano blind; he hardly even glances at the keys. How does he do that?" The volume of the music made it possible for Elizabeth to hear Bonnie speaking close to her ear without anyone else being disturbed by it.

"That piano is like an extra appendage," Elizabeth said. "He feels it; he plays a song over and over until it becomes like breathing, and he doesn't even have to think about it."

"Amazing," Bonnie said.

As the song went on, Drew's description from the previous evening became evident. Jayson stuttered the Bs and hissed the Ss and hit the falsetto with perfection. He smiled the first time he did it, and everyone cheered. She could tell he was having fun; they were all having fun. He had a way of just spreading simple joy with his abilities. Macy got the guys to start waving their arms back and forth in unison, as if they were really at a concert. Valerie and Elizabeth starting doing it as well, then Bonnie joined in. The little ones got in on it, and their comical off-rhythm way made everyone laugh. During a lengthy bridge with no lyrics, Jayson turned his head to take in their antics. He chuckled and said, "You guys are weird." Of course he didn't miss a beat, and the song went on. The falsetto increased in the final sequence, and Elizabeth loved hearing her husband's incredible voice range, an ability that neither of them took for granted.

When the song was done, the audience response was ridiculously exuberant, making Drew and Jayson laugh as they both stood and did a high-five that took Elizabeth back to their high school days.

Jayson tried to say they were finished, but everyone protested, and Elizabeth knew full well he was just getting them to beg for an encore that he had every intention of playing. It was the same tactic he used with public performances, and he was very good at it. He and Drew then played their version of "Harmony," also by Elton John, and he dedicated it to their wives. When he was finished, he turned to Elizabeth and said, "What now, Lady?"

"You know very well what," she said. "You're just teasing me."

"Or testing you."

"You know that I know, and I know that you know."

"So, tell us," he said.

"You could not end such a performance without doing *the* song."

"Tell them about it the way you told me that day when I'd been sick and I was so discouraged. Do you remember?"

"I remember," she said. "This is the song that connects you to your youth, your mother, your kinship with the piano. It connects you to Derek; you did it at his funeral. It's the song that really showed you what you could do. And it's the first song you played for me. It showed *me* what you could do."

Jayson smiled at his wife, then turned to look at Bonnie. "Drew and I learned how to play this song so we could give it to our mother for her birthday. We were sixteen and seventeen at the time. As Elizabeth said, it has a lot of history for us. It's called 'Funeral for a Friend.'"

Jayson turned to face the piano, and immediately started into the first slow, methodical chords of the song. As it progressed with speed and complexity, building intensity along with the drums, Elizabeth realized she was crying. She was taken back so completely to that day in the front room of her home in Oregon when she had first realized the musical genius of Jayson Wolfe, and she'd come to understand the deep affinity she'd felt for him. If she had known then what she knew now, what would she have thought? She looked around the room at the family and friends surrounding them, and a lifetime of experiences rushed through her memory like a hot wind. Every joy and heartache, every bit of suffering and triumph. It all came together in that moment. Hearing Jayson and Drew do this song together now left her feeling that they had come full circle. And yet they had their whole lives ahead of them, raising their family and celebrating the glorious gift of music that had brought them together and had made their lives such a unique adventure.

Bonnie apparently noticed that she was crying and passed her a tissue. Elizabeth smiled and took it, wiping at her eyes. "He really is remarkable," Bonnie said.

"Yes," Elizabeth said as she put a hand on Bonnie's arm, "he really is."

Author's Note

When I first realized that I needed Macy's mother-in-law to have a health issue in order for the plot to go as it should, I had no intention of using this particular ailment. But it just kind of fell into the book as if it were meant to be. I was reluctant to write about Celiac Disease, since it hits very close to home. I was diagnosed with it in January 2008, after more than eight years of unexplained health issues. My symptoms were much different from those I gave to Layla, but hers are more typical. I'm grateful to know what's wrong with me, but the reality of living with it is a daily challenge. I've come to know many people of all ages who struggle with the same challenges, and my heart goes out to them because I've come to understand it. My mother had Celiac Disease, but they didn't understand it back then as they do now. We now know that it was the cause of the cancer that took her life ten years prior to my diagnosis. Because there are more than two million Americans with CD, and many more with gluten intolerance, it is my hope that this story might add another drop in the bucket of raising awareness regarding the difficulties of this disease. I would ask that if you or someone you love has unexplained health problems, that you request testing to be done for this. I would also hope that as more people become aware of the problem and understand it, that those of us who struggle with it—or other food sensitivities—will be able to safely get our prescriptions and be able to eat with less stress and concern. For more information, visit www.celiac.com.

ABOUT THE AUTHOR

Anita Stansfield began writing at the age of sixteen, and her first novel was published sixteen years later. Her novels range from historical to contemporary and cover a wide gamut of social and emotional issues that explore the human experience through memorable characters and unpredictable plots. She has received many awards, including a special award for pioneering new ground in LDS fiction, and the Lifetime Achievement Award from the Whitney Academy for LDS Literature. Anita is the mother of five, and has one adorable grandson. Her husband, Vince, is her greatest hero.

To receive regular updates from Anita, go to anitastansfield.com and subscribe.